ANGELA DU MAURIER

Treveryan

Truran

Published by Truran 2003
Truran is an imprint of Truran Books Ltd.
Croft Prince, Mount Hawke, Truro, Cornwall TR4 8EE
www.truranbooks.co.uk

ISBN 1 85022 179 0
First published June 1942 by Michael Joseph Ltd

Cover photograph © Christian Browning
Cover designed by Peter Bennett, St Ives

Printed and bound by Short Run Press,
Bittern Road, Sowton Industrial Estate, Exeter EX2 7LW

Dedicated
with much Love to
DAPHNE
my Sister

TREVERYAN

' But that I am forbid
To tell the secrets of my prison-house,
I could a tale unfold whose lightest word
Would harrow up thy soul . . . '

UNLIKE THE GHOST of Hamlet there is no prison-house to forbid me. A tale. Queer, old-fashioned, unsatisfactory little word for what may be bleak tragedy.

I must admit my heart misgives me for I know that I am not competent enough to give clearly to the world the truth and tragedy of Treveryan. I have tried and am trying to resurrect occurrences and conversations that took place before I was born; that it has been possible for me to do so is due entirely to the long conversations I had with my godfather, Oswald Martineau, before he died, and to the fact that he allowed me to read all his papers and gave me access too to Lerryn's diaries which she kept so strictly.

Even as a child I remember thinking that my godfather led some secret existence. I was about ten when I noticed for the first time that sad, far-off look in his eyes, and became aware that frequently when one asked him some question or other, he would not answer. I remember taxing my mother with the subject. She made some evasive reply, and told me not to be silly and imaginative, which, of course, only whetted my curiosity further. I thought, when I grew to be a little older, that the mystery with which he continued to be enshrouded in my eyes, was probably due to something that had happened to him when he lived in India. But I soon realized this was not the case.

I was an only child living in the depths of the country, with few companions of my own age. Therefore very early in life books became my friends, and perhaps for that reason led me to weave romances where none existed, and visualize drama into often enough drab lives. Probably most children have some character, culled from legend, fiction, or real life, whom they admire or, at any rate, in whom they are interested above others. Oswald Martineau, my godfather, was such to me.

When he talked to me it was to some purpose, and I never remember his ' talking down ' or treating me in conversation as inferior to my parents.   When he was silent I would notice with smug satisfaction that the rest of the company were as included in his silences as myself.   He seemed to change very little in appearance as the years went by; I picture him now as I did all the years I knew him, an oldish man with great dignity; one of those people whom it is almost impossible to imagine as a young man.   He must have been seventy when I saw him for the first time; I am twenty-five and he died last year in his eighty-sixth year.   I have said he was an old man, and so he was in years, as I fear all men seem to the very young after their first youth has passed them by.   He was not old in appearance or in spirit; his tall, erect carriage could easily have shamed many men his junior; to me he was perhaps ageless rather than aged, his snow-white hair and piercing blue eyes bore a resemblance to the pictures of God that had hung in my nursery from childhood days.   As I grew older we began to form that rare attachment that grows out of perfect companion-ship and understanding.   My holidays would find me more and more in the flat of his charming Regency house in the Hove end of Brighton, as I was sent to school only a few miles away; for it was during my school days, half holidays and such, that I began to know him and he to know me.

   " You are as my own child, and better.   For I can spoil you if I wish without compunction, and my responsibilities towards you are nil," he would say with one of his all too rare smiles. It was due to him that I was allowed to go to London Uni-versity; through him that I was able to lead my own life independently of my family.   I have said we were friends and gave each other companionship.   And it was so; yet for a long while much of his life was a closed book to me.   Much I did know of—the years in India, the years of which he enjoyed talking most.   It was my life, my future, my interests, that moved him most.   It was abstract philosophy and world affairs about which he could, and did, hold forth with all-absorbing knowledge.   And then I would catch him off-guard as it were, and suddenly see the expression of infinite sadness on his face, and at once I was a small child again weaving some tale of mystery round him; and the grown-up me would, for the following day, be curious and yet too shy to ask him what lay behind that mask. I never guessed he had been famous. It was not until I was asked by someone at school if my god-father was *the* Sir Oswald Martineau, that I realized he was someone of importance. Even so, I felt I could not ask him for what he was famous, and stored the question up to ask my parents. I was about sixteen then, and when I was told that he had been one of the youngest Judges in India, had come back to England and had been somehow or other involved in a big trial, and had given everything up afterwards, I was not really interested.

The flat in Brunswick Terrace was a charming one, full of nice things : elegant if rather solid furniture, a great many books, some valuable water-colours, few if any ornaments beyond one or two oriental bronzes; a man's flat for a man living alone, with only a devoted man-servant in attendance, and his faithful Mrs. Leigh coming in daily to cook. Yet sometimes when I visited him, and we played chess, my eyes would wander about the room in which we played, and it would strike me that the place, however comfortable it was, lacked personal warmth and that *gemüthlich* atmosphere that fills a really well-loved home. Some houses are full of the presence of their owner, whether he be there or not. When one visited Oswald Martineau one basked, as it were, in the sunlight of his personality—at least, I did. But if one should arrive and he was away, the rooms would seem singularly dull and bereft of character.

It never struck me that one day Oswald Martineau might die. I had never known him to be sick or sorry. So that when, two years ago, he told me he was going to have a major operation, I could hardly believe him. He had persuaded the specialist, a great personal friend, to allow him to be operated on at the flat.

" I have a horror of dying in some beastly home—one's body being hustled into the nearest mortuary," he grumbled.

" You're not going to die, O.M.," I said; " I can't grow up properly without you."

He liked that, for I remember he made some joke or other and said that he would try to ' hang on ' for a bit longer if only to please me.

The operation was fairly successful, but the doctors told me that he would not live much longer, a few months, perhaps a year.

" His heart is amazing for his age, he has a great constitution. But, after all, he is an old man."

He did not look any older when I went to see him for the first time after the operation. His eyes seemed bluer and clearer if anything. But his face was pale like old parchment. And his hands, lying calm upon the sheet, were much thinner. He smiled and I wanted to cry, so pushed the grapes I had brought him on to the bed, and laughed with forced gaiety. I wanted to say so much, and found I could say so little. All the things I was grateful for tumbled pell-mell into my mind, and yet I stood staring and mute, whilst a bright young woman in striped starch moved about the room, eyeing me with suspicion, deftly arranging things unnecessarily; I knew we both wanted her to depart.

When we were alone I found I was still shy and stupid. Shy, because the man I'd looked up to all my young life for strength, now lay helpless as a baby at the mercy of any fool. Stupid, because I myself was without knowledge of nursing or medicine and knew therefore I was useless. I held his hand then, and smiled, and he smiled, too, and I realized that words were not really necessary.

" You are going to be all right, aren't you? " I said presently.

He nodded. And once again I was reassured and felt that the doctors had been alarmists.

I looked about the room. It was queer, but it dawned on me then that I had never been in O.M.'s bedroom before. I began to look about me with new interest. It was more personal than the other rooms. For once his own presence seemed to cling to the lares and penates that lay around. The late sunlight shone into the room and lit the walls, and the yellow dahlias and Michaelmas daisies which I had sent, took colour from the sun. There was a coal fire, too, which perhaps added to the human touch about the place. I looked across the room and saw for the first time his pictures. Over the fireplace was the coloured engraving of a very beautiful house. I gazed at it a long time. Presently I turned, and saw he was

watching me. I noticed the far-away, sad expression, and I
knew then that the picture of this house had something to do
with it.

" Where is this ? " I heard myself asking.

" That's Treveryan," he said.

" What a lovely name," I answered.

I longed to know more and to ask further questions. I went
back to the chair beside the bed. It was then I noticed her
picture for the first time. It was old-fashioned and must have
been taken a great many years ago, I thought. I felt I had to
stare at her, and all the time I knew I was gazing at O.M.'s
secret heart, but I could not stop. It was a face that held one's
eyes, no great beauty in it, and the clothes of the day were, to
me, ugly and cumbersome, but there was something in her face
that I knew I should never forget.

" Who is that ? " I stammered.

" That was Bethel Treveryan," he said slowly.

**PART
ONE**

I

THERE WAS NEVER a time when the family did not
think Treveryan the loveliest and stateliest home
in Powder, in all Cornwall for that matter, nay,
the whole of England.

Proud and loving they were about the house;
proud, too, at the knowledge that none but Treveryans had
lived there from the time it had been seized by old William
Treveryan, after the dissolution of the monasteries in the early
days of the Reformation, to the present day.

For generations and centuries their own people had breathed
the air they now breathed, walked through the grounds,
climbed the giant oaks in the park, fed deer, watched the wild
swans yearly come, nest beside the shores of the lake, and
depart. Their ancestors had been born, had lived and had
died in the rooms which they had known completely and
intimately since their own births. Sometimes as children, they
would play Veryan's favourite game, which was to walk
through the vast picture gallery, pick out a portrait of one of
their ancestors, and become the Treveryan in question; the
girls—Bethel, four years Veryan's senior, and little Lerryn, a

mere toddler still—would play up to him and be the Ladies of the house. Sometimes, if the character had been involved in any historical occasion, such as the time when St. Just Treveryan had entertained Charles in the Civil War; or when their grandfather, Luke, had returned, armless and blind, from Waterloo, then Bethel would refuse to be the lady of the day, and insist on being Charles or Luke, and Veryan would be Luke's aged father, who died of a stroke at the shock he received by his son's appearance. Bethel's favourite game, one which they all enjoyed, was pretending to be a stranger, paying sixpence, and being shown over the estate by Veryan— little Lerryn panting behind her brother and sister, lisping and echoing their questions and replies. The children were left very much to themselves when small; their mother always a strange yet lovely shadow in the background, coming and going as Bethel once remarked, like the wild swans.

" Mama is very like a swan, I think," Veryan had answered.

" And what about Papa?   What do you think he is? "

A cloud crept over the sun as she spoke, and they shivered. Just then Lerryn began to cry.

" Don't be silly, baby," Veryan scolded.

" Papa, papa," the small child whimpered.

Bethel picked her up.

" Don't cry.   Papa is gone away."

There was a strange silence, and after Lerryn had scrambled away to play, the elder child turned to her brother and said, as though with difficulty :

" She's terrified of Papa.   Didn't you know?   It was stupid of me to mention him."

Veryan did not answer. There was something very odd about their father, and what was odder still, he now began to think, was that baby Lerryn was the first to have drawn their attention to the fact.

The Squire scarcely saw his children. He lived in a secluded part of the house, far from them. For years now he had lived the life of a recluse; it was as though he shunned all and any society beyond that of his wife.

As the years crept by, the Treveryan children were forced to lean upon each other more and more for company. Their father withdrew further into his hermit-like solitude as time passed, and their mother's visits to her own family became more frequent and of longer duration.

" Does it strike you we're rather like dogs?   Kennel dogs? " Veryan said one day to his sister.   She looked surprised and faintly alarmed.

" I'm sure other children don't lead the same lives as we do."

" But we're happy.   How do you mean?   You don't want to live anywhere else, surely? "   Her voice shook with scandalized indignation.

" No, of course not, silly.   What I mean is that Papa and Mama are so different from other people's fathers and mothers. They hardly ever see us.   Honestly, we might be Tabb's spaniels, for all Papa sees of us.   In fact, I should say he knows their habits a good deal more than he does ours, for all that he doesn't go out much.   And Mama. . . .   Why doesn't she take us with her to Hereford when she visits Grandmama? "

" I expect travelling with children would be very tiresome. I'm glad she doesn't.   I should hate to leave Treveryan.   So would you."   She spoke with heat.

" I shouldn't mind seeing another house.   Just for a visit. Don't you realize how different we are from other families?"

" I'm glad," Bethel said.

Veryan laughed.   She asked the reason.

" You're funny, Beth.   Sometimes I think you're two people.   Nobody enjoys a dance at the New Year more than you do, and you cried last winter when the Tremaynes put us off because the twins had scarlet fever.   Yet you now say you don't want to go out of this house.   At least, that's what it sounds like to me."

Bethel was sixteen then.   That night in bed she thought over her brother's words.   Up till now she had not been a girl given to introspective self-questioning or analysis.   Hers were not the days when young women busied their minds with either their own psychology or anyone else's.   But Veryan's words took root, and she began looking at herself, and then her family, as though with the eyes of a stranger. Perhaps he was right and, young as he was, had realized before she did herself that conflicting emotions would some day war against each other in her soul; and that possibly there might come into being two Bethel Treveryans, the Bethel she knew so well and understood, for whom Life and Treveryan House were one and the same thing, whose vision hitherto saw little beyond the lodge gates and her own immediate Family; and another as yet unborn Bethel, who would stand tip-toe at life's threshold searching through keyholes, as it were, hoping and longing for excitement, taking with pleasure and gratitude joys as yet unknown. She felt suddenly troubled and restless. Why had Veryan spoken as he had? She did not want to be different. She began to think of her parents, and was startled and dismayed at realizing the truth of Veryan's remarks. Mama was lovely, and she was proud of her, she knew that; but how aloof in her behaviour to them she was compared to Mrs. Tremayne and her children, and comfortable Lady Rogers with Nicolas and Mary. Even the Vicar's wife, Mrs. Penrose, read to Little Brigit every evening; and although the Polcasters were very strictly brought up, and both her and Veryan's hearts sank if they were asked to tea, she knew that Mrs. Polcaster and the General saw a great deal more of Fred and Dorothy in a week than her own parents saw of herself and Veryan in a month. She supposed that her brother was right and that she did enjoy going to parties at other people's houses, but he must know, surely, that half the pleasure was the subsequent return to beloved Treveryan, with the full knowledge that none of the houses visited could hold a candle to it, and that it was their home for ever. That she might one day marry and leave the place had never entered Bethel's head, nor did it now, as she lay in bed unable to sleep. Veryan's remarks still preying on her mind. She was devoted to her brother; thrown together as they were, taught by the same tutor (for the Squire had strange theories on education and disapproved of schools), it was not surprising that the difference of years between them appeared to vanish, and that from an early date their companionship grew in strength and loyalty. Veryan resembled their little-known father as far as appearance went. He was dark, rather stocky in build, though possibly he might grow to a better figure as he grew older. Little Lerryn, as yet so much the baby of the family, was like their mother. Pale, with fair, soft hair and the same ethereal personality, she looked as though she should be nursed in one of the hot-houses in the gardens, instead of running wild in the woods and down by the lake at the other children's heels. Bethel looked like neither parent. There was a certain likeness to Veryan about the dark eyes and low, attractive forehead; their colouring, too, was very much the same. Both had the complexions of magnolias as children, but there the resemblance ended, for Bethel was tall as a young larch, and her nose straight and exquisitely shaped; whereas Veryan, like his father, had an almost Semitic look, as many Cornishmen have.   .

It was shortly after this conversation had taken place that the lives of the three children were upset for the first time that any of them could remember.   One afternoon in the autumn of 1878, as they returned to the house after nutting down by the lake shore, they saw a brougham standing by the pillars and steps of the front door.

"It looks like Dr. Pearce," Veryan said.   "What has happened do you suppose?"

At that moment, as though she had been watching for them, Mrs. Mitchell, the housekeeper, ran down the steps and bustled them indoors and across the large stone hall and through the baize door which separated the schoolroom from the rest of the house, but not before Veryan had caught a glimpse of the doctor and his mother coming down the wide staircase.

"What's happened?" he whispered excitedly, guessing as children will that something untoward had occurred which it was evidently hoped to be able to hide from their eyes.

"H'sh, now!   Don't start asking questions," was the old woman's exasperating answer.   He shrugged his shoulders helplessly and looked at Bethel.

"I feel something has happened to Papa," she whispered, and then felt uncomfortable as she became aware of the housekeeper's eyes upon her.

"What's that you're saying, Miss Bethel?"

She suddenly felt frightened, as though she were seven instead of nearly seventeen. Mrs. Mitchell had been at Treveryan for years and years, way back in her grandfather's day, and had known Papa when he was a boy. She looked now like an old witch, Bethel thought, as she vainly tried to regain composure.

" I said I thought Papa must be ill," she began.

" How do you know? What have you heard? " demanded the old woman.

" Why, nothing," the girl replied. And then gaining courage, continued :. " I'm sure Mama was seeing Dr. Pearce into his brougham just then. So if nothing is the matter with her, it must be Papa who's ill."

The old woman grunted, gave them all a cursory glance and left the room. Lerryn sat on the edge of a chair and looked as though she wanted to cry. An eerie silence seemed to hang about the place, and none of the children spoke. Suddenly Lerryn began to cry.

" Oh, shut up! " Veryan said crossly.

" Want Tooder," she sobbed. Tudor was the children's old nurse.

" Go and call for her, Veryan," Bethel urged.

" You go," he answered unwillingly.

" You're younger than me," she began.

At that moment the door opened and Netta, the nursery-maid, peered into the room.

" For goodness' sake take Lerryn upstairs, she is being an awful nuisance," Veryan said.

The girl picked up the child and, after glancing queerly at the other children, hurried from the room.

" Everyone seems to have gone mad," the boy grumbled. " Not a sign of tea, the fire's gone out, and they all look at us as if someone's dead."

Bethel paled.

" Perhaps that's what's happened. Perhaps Papa is dead."

Veryan looked at her sceptically.

" He's not been ill even. Why should he die? " he answered.

" I don't know, but I wish someone would come and explain. This is horrid, like being imprisoned suddenly for no reason."

It began to get dark, and still nobody came. The lamps had not been lit, and the children were always expressly forbidden to light them.

" Let's go upstairs," said Veryan presently, when the room was in total darkness. " I'm frightfully hungry; we might at least find biscuits in Lerryn's nursery."

" Suppose we run into Mama ? "

" I hope we do.   At least we may learn what's happened."

Outside in the hall the servants had behaved with usual normality it seemed, for the curtains were drawn, the lamps burning brightly, and the log fire blazing away in the large open fireplace.   Suddenly the drawing-room door opened and the children saw their mother come out into the hall.

" Mama . . ." they began.

Anna Treveryan looked at her son and daughter.   Her face was paler than usual, her hair slightly awry, and there was an almost distraught expression about her eyes.   She stood still, and yet both the children knew that she did not see them. Presently she shivered violently, and, like one coming out of a trance, looked about her in a dazed fashion, and then went back into the drawing-room, the door banging noisily behind her.

Veryan took Bethel's arm and slowly they went upstairs, neither speaking a word, humouring each other's fear and respecting the reticence that forbade speech which might conceivably have been overheard.

· Neither during that evening nor the following morning was their curiosity to be satisfied.   The servants went about the house with expressions ' like walls,' as Veryan described them to his sister;   old Mrs. Mitchell was nowhere to be found, and even Tudor refused to be questioned.   Their mother remained closeted in her apartments, to which in any case the children never went unless sent for.   It was after lunch that the door of the schoolroom opened and old Dr. Pearce came in.

" Well, my boy !   Well, Bethel, my dear ! "   He took out a pinch of snuff and looked at both their young faces as if wondering what to say next.

" Do tell us what's happened," Bethel began.   " We know someone must be ill, and we think it's Papa, but no one will tell us.   In fact, no one will even speak to us."

" Papa is dead, isn't he ? "   Veryan tried to look upset, but could not keep the excited importance he was feeling from his voice.

The doctor looked surprised.

" No one been near you ?   Ridiculous !   Absurd !   No, Veryan, my boy, your father isn't dead.   But he's ill.   Very ill.

And it may be necessary—in fact, it will be necessary—to send you all away for a while."

" Where to? " Veryan asked with interest.

"Away? For long? " Bethel spoke at the same time, dismay creeping into her voice, and then, as if to seem polite, added, " Is it catching? My father's illness, I mean."

" Yes, what's he got? " Veryan asked.

Dr. Pearce walked over to the window.

" You are going to your grandmother's at Hereford. I can't tell you, my dears, for how long. Possibly a few months—maybe longer, maybe you'll be back sooner. It'll be a pleasant change for you, I hope you'll enjoy yourselves. Make new friends."

"Are Mama and Lerryn coming, too? " Bethel asked.

" Lerryn, yes, of course. I don't know about your mother. She may join you, she has not made up her mind yet."

" Then it is something catching? "

The doctor looked at his watch and patted Veryan on the head.

" Well, I must be going. Don't worry. You try and enjoy yourselves while you still can," and he walked quickly from the room.

The two children remained in silence for a few minutes, then—

" He was very peculiar, I must say," Veryan said. " Enjoy ourselves while we still *can*. What did he mean? "

" Probably means while Papa is still alive," Bethel answered.

" Sounds rather callous. I mean—well—we're not really fond of Papa, are we? But children must feel something about their fathers and mothers, even ones like ours."

Bethel shivered.

" Suppose it's something too awful; like small-pox, for instance? " she said.

The next day, after what had seemed hours of packing, the long journey to Hereford began.

After they had been there four months their grandmother broke to them the news that their father had been dead for several weeks.

FOR MANY YEARS to come the people of the West Country would speak in bated breath of the gales which wrought widespread havoc and destruction in the early part of 1880.

One afternoon in late February, Bethel Treveryan could have been seen scanning the channel from the windswept Dodman headland. The rains had abated, but the howling gale still raged, and the few trees which had survived the January storms now lay strewn upon the ground like victims of some savage battle. Indeed, the girl could not help thinking a battle had raged for days now within the elements, and there seemed little enough likelihood that it would finish yet awhile, though the first terrifying intensity had died down somewhat.

Never could Bethel remember such a winter, and the villagers for miles around had gone about with their faces drawn with anxiety, as they recounted the daily losses that had taken toll on farms, homesteads and on the sea. Even in inland Tregony roofs had been torn off the cottages, thatch lay about the streets in queer shapeless tufts, slates and windows were broken and fallen in; and the bodies of sheep and cattle lay on the shore, below the headland, whither the poor beasts had been blown defencelessly and battered to death on the cruel rocks below.

The afternoon was already drawing to a close, and Bethel, wearing a fur cape and bonnet, started to retrace her steps, holding with one hand her bonnet, with the other her skirt, both of which the high wind was doing its best to tear from her. She laughed and called to the two figures ahead of her.

" How exciting it is! Must we really turn back? Searle has the horses safe in the barn at the bottom of the lane, and we shan't take long getting home."

The boy turned as he heard his sister calling.

" Can't hear you," he yelled, and put one arm round the body of the younger girl. " Hurry up, Beth, Lerryn's ear is hurting her. You can't really like this frightful wind."

They stopped and waited for her. Veryan watched his elder sister with admiration and some amusement. He thought then, as he often did, what a pity is was that she had not also been born a boy. How those frightful clothes must irk her, as she strode across wet clumps of ankle-deep heather, he was thinking, with strides that would more befit him than the young lady she was shortly to become. At that moment a gust of wind blew off her bonnet, and her dark hair blew in untidy abandon about her face.

" I could remain up here all night," she panted as she reached them. " How wild and beautiful it is. Only the small oak trees have been able to stand, and even they look bent and tired as if they can bear it no longer. Oh, how I adore the wind in my hair ! " And she shook her head as if to free herself, and her curls fell about her shoulders.

Lerryn tugged at her hand.

" We shouldn't have brought you, baby, should we ? " she smiled down at her little sister. " I know what : let Searle take her home and you and I can walk. I want to go down to the shore somewhere and get closer to the sea itself."

" But dusk will be on us in half an hour," the boy objected, " and who knows if the storm won't get worse again. The tide is still rising, and last night, you remember, the gale was at its height then. It's quite a few miles, you know."

" By road, but not across the fields," Bethel answered.

" My dear girl, you can't walk across fields in the dark with your skirts falling over your feet and dragging in the mud. You'd soon wish you hadn't."

" I could take them off ! "

Even Veryan looked scandalized, and Lerryn's eyes opened wide.

" Whatever would people say ? " she sighed.

" Oh, I suppose I mustn't. How I wish I was a boy ! "

The next day the gale was still blowing hard, three more trees had fallen in the night in the park, and two of the Scotch firs in the avenue lay across the road, barring all access to the house.

In the morning Bethel drove down to the tiny village of Port Holland to see of what use she could be. Two of the fishing boats had been lost, and the girl's heart was wrung with pity as she noticed the little groups of people gathered together, grief on their faces, as they waited and watched for news. She had brought old Tudor, the nurse, with her, and together they enquired at the stricken cottages, leaving what comforts they

could. Presently there was a shout, and all pointed to the sea
where a speck was discernible. Broken wreckage had for
hours past been washed ashore, but now this looked like a
rafter coming in with something clinging to it.. The men
waded out when it was safe enough to do so and brought in
the body of a young boy whom Bethel recognized. He was
still breathing.

" Come home now," she whispered to the nurse, " we
brought things which will help. They won't want us any
more."

That afternoon Bethel went down to the shores of the lake.
It seemed deserted, the birds had flown inland, the wild swans
had not yet returned. The wind played wild music in the
rushes, and Bethel sat down on the broken trunk of a fallen
tree. Over the lake and across the park she looked lovingly
and longingly at Treveryan, standing nobly and, as she felt,
for all time.

This week their mother would return to Cornwall after one
of her prolonged absences. It was two years now since the
Squire had died, and neither Bethel nor Veryan had heard the
details of his illness and death. If anything, Mrs. Treveryan
appeared more withdrawn from her children than ever, it
almost seemed as if she was hostile to them, although she
petted Lerryn occasionally.

" I see Mama staring at me," Veryan said one day. " It
gives me a beastly creepy feeling. I wish she wouldn't. And
did you notice how peculiar she was when Lady Rogers said
how like Papa I was getting? Honestly, Beth, she shuddered! "

Bethel thought of these words as she sat on the tree trunk
ruminating on her mother's return. How she wished her
mother would make more of a friend of her. She would be
eighteen very soon now, and this year she would ' come out.'
There were to be great festivities all over the county, and if it
were not for Mama's odd behaviour she would be looking
forward tremendously to the business. She considered herself
lucky to be coming out this year, for in May the Prince and
Princess of Wales were coming to Cornwall to be present at
the laying of the foundation stone of the new Cathedral at
Truro. It was the first time a Duke of Cornwall, as of course
he was, had visited his Duchy since Charles II had raised his

father's standard in the ill-fated days of the Civil War. If she were lucky, Bethel was thinking, she might be able to make her curtsey to the beautiful Princess of Wales, which would be far more thrilling, she thought, than travelling to Windsor or London to attend a drawing-room and be presented to the old Queen. She supposed that, too, would be exciting; but something in her withdrew at the idea of going away from home. She knew no one in London, and she would be considered a gauche country mouse, and Mama would be queer and tiresome, and the whole business would fall flat. In the country things would be different, she hoped and believed. Even if Mama was her usual aloof self she could be relied on to bring her daughter out into Society with the correct conventional flourish, and that should mean a ball and perhaps even a garden party at Treveryan. And, as everyone who was anyone knew everybody else—at least, slightly—Bethel looked forward to a sunny future.

A few evenings later mother and daughter were sitting in the drawing-room after dinner. Mrs. Treveryan was reading a novel by Thackeray, Bethel was engaged with a piece of needlework. The violent storms had died down, and all was quiet outside save for the occasional cry of a screech-owl. A peat fire filled the room with its scent and warmth, and from time to time the girl would glance up at the shadows on the pictures of her ancestors cast by the flickering light of the candles and lamp. How peaceful it was. She liked to think of her forbears sitting exactly as she sat now; generations of Treveryans had passed, more, please God, would come. She began to wonder what her home had been like in those far-off days before the Reformation when monks had lived there. It had been they who first made the lake and filled it with carp. A great deal of the mansion had, alas! been destroyed by fire at the end of the seventeenth century; there was now no trace of the refectory hall, and the chapel was in complete ruins. The picture gallery had been added by the first Veryan Treveryan in the reign of James I, and, much later, the brothers Adam had been the architects of the larger part of the house as it was now.

Bethel folded her work and, face cupped in hands, watched the fire. Not yet had Mama said anything about the future, and the girl ached to know what she proposed to do with the summer.

"Mama," she said presently.

Mrs. Treveryan looked up from her book.

"I shall be eighteen in a month's time. Do you . . . have you forgotten . . .?"

"I suppose you really want to know if you're to come out this summer? I expect I shall have to see about it. Lady Rogers's girl will, of course; and I believe Clara Polcaster is taking Dorothy to London. Well, Bethel, I can't promise you that, but I'll try and give a ball for you. I know the county will expect it, and this year, with the Prince and Princess coming, I daresay we should start soon to make plans. Why, child, you've gone quite pale!" she exclaimed, and, indeed, Bethel did look paler than usual. She laughed.

"It's the excitement, Mama! Oh, I am grateful! I never really dreamed I would have a ball of my own," which was true in a sense, for she had been afraid lest Mama would not ʾ come up to scratch' as Mary Rogers would have said vulgarly.

For the next few weeks Bethel could think of nothing else. Even the events of the country itself faded into oblivion when the girl dreamed, thought, and planned for the great day which was to be her own.

The month of May came fast enough, and with it such a round of gaiety as Cornwall had rarely witnessed before. The great day came at last for the old market town of Truro when the foundation stone of the new Cathedral was laid, and the Treveryans with other distinguished families watched the ceremony at which the royal couple were present. Bethel's eyes riveted on the beauty of the Princess of Wales, Veryan equally enthralled by the gallant appearance of 'the Duke,' as his people in the Duchy were thinking of him.

Balls and garden-parties were given all over the county. Never had Cornwall looked more beautiful. The rhododendrons and azaleas were a blaze of colour for miles around, and the early summer weather was for once behaving in exemplary fashion.

At a garden-party given by Dr. Benson, the Bishop, Mrs. Treveryan was presented to the Prince and Princess, and Bethel's happiness was complete when she also was noticed by the Loveliest Lady in the Land, and in her turn was bidden to make her curtsey.

The evening for the ball came at last, in early June. Even her mother seemed to have altered with the season's excitement, and entered into the spirit of Bethel's own thrilled pleasure, it seemed.

Treveryan looked like any romantic girl's dream of fairyland. Delphiniums, irises and peonies filled the rooms in great profusion; fairy lights hung in festoons from the house to the lake; and in their light the wild swans slowly swam across the water like beings enchanted.

People came from far and wide, and the house itself was filled with guests whose carriages could not take them back long distances the same night. The only stranger in the house-party was a cousin of Mrs. Treveryan's, Gwyllim Llewelyn, a stranger to the children, whose presence they were at a loss to understand.

" Why suddenly hurl a complete stranger in our midst? We never even met him when we were at Hereford that time," said Veryan.

" He seems quite nice enough," Bethel answered, " and he and Mama seem to know each other well. But it's funny, as you say."

" H'mmm, he's given you a jolly decent present," Veryan continued.

For the strange cousin had brought the young girl an exquisite pendant for the occasion of her coming-out dance.

" I thought Mama looked rather flustered when he gave it to you."

Veryan himself was present at the ball at Bethel's insistence, wearing a new Eton suit, and Little Lerryn was allowed by Tudor to peep through the banisters at the awe-inspiring gathering below, in their billowy satins and brocades and jewels. There was a string band and a marquee on the terrace; and in the orangery, sipping lemonade, Bethel sat with Mr. Oswald Martineau, to whom she had been introduced earlier in the evening.

"so you don't think you will pay us a visit to London during the season, Miss Bethel? How disappointing for your many friends up there." The young man gazed at his companion with frank admiration.

"But you see I haven't any friends up there. That's one of the reasons I do not really want to go. There's some talk of our going up later in the year, to one of the winter drawing-rooms. That might be more pleasant, for I shouldn't feel so shy; you see, I should have got used to this sort of thing."

He smiled at her naive simplicity.

"And do you never wish to leave Cornwall?" he asked rather daringly.

"Oh, *no*!" the girl exclaimed with horror.

"Tell me," Oswald Martineau asked, as he led her back presently to the ballroom, "the history of your attractive names. Bethel is surely very unusual? And your brother has also a name I never heard before."

She smiled.

"It seems to have been a tradition in our family for genera-tions to call the children by Cornish place names. Bethel and Veryan are such; my little sister is Lerryn, that is a little village also, but some way from here. One of my grandmothers, my father's grandmother it was, was called Tregony—I often wish that was my name. I don't care for Bethel; it's hard, don't you think?"

"I think it has character," he answered, "it sounds as if much might be expected of anyone bearing the name."

"Oh, dear!" she laughed, "I'm afraid I shall let the name down then. I expect you connect it with the Bible. Our Bethel is away up in the mining district. No, I wish it was Tregony, though it does not go very well with Treveryan."

"That may not be your name always," he replied, glancing at her.

"It was my great-grandmother's. She married her cousin."

At that moment another partner claimed her as a polka started up, and Bethel forgot the young man.

She met him again two days later at a garden-party at Tregothnan.

" Miss Treveryan ! " and she turned and saw her late dancing partner beside her.

" Still in Cornwall ! " she smiled up at him. " I shall begin to think you are as reluctant to leave it as I am myself."

" You would be right. I am fast falling in love with your Duchy. I have never seen more beautiful country in England, and I could dearly wish to remain. Alas ! I return to my dismal London lodgings to-morrow, but one day I hope to get rooms in the Temple, and that will be nearly as pleasant as living in one of your wonderful old mansions."

" The Temple ? " Bethel's voice was tinged with surprise. "Are you a clergyman ? And do they live in churches in the City ? "

Martineau threw back his head and roared with laughter.

At that moment the Bishop stopped beside the young couple, and Bethel dutifully turned from her young escort to speak to that important personage. Martineau had vanished when she next looked round for him, and she saw Nicolas and Mary Rogers bearing down on her.

" Lost your swain ? " Mary giggled; " he is giving mother an ice. My dear, I think you have made a hit; but don't lose your heart I beseech you. He has absolutely no money, at least, not what we should call money. He's a friend of Nico's really."

Bethel blushed.

" How absurd you are ! " she said, and longed to add, " and how vulgar."

" Do let me give you some iced coffee or something, Bethel." Nicolas Rogers spoke to her now. He was an attractive young man and had just come down from Cambridge. Bethel walked off happily with him, dismissing the penniless barrister from her thoughts, and everyone turned to watch the handsome couple they made, the tall girl swinging gracefully her parasol, looking for all the world like a du Maurier drawing.

" How the Treveryan girl has come on," remarked the old Duchess of Penzance, she who had been the daughter of a

Williams of Trewinnen, and a bosom friend of Bethel's grandmother, now dead.

" Everyone was so surprised when Anna Treveryan gave the ball for her," Lady Rogers answered.   She and the Duchess were seated together in front of a bank of prize rhododendrons. " I only hope Anna doesn't leave it at that.   She must want the girl to make a good match, but she's such an odd woman. One never sees her really, and with her looks one would imagine she'd be the belle of the county."

" I never see them."   The Duchess spoke thoughtfully. " Haven't been to Treveryan since dear Adelaide's death. Simon never asked one.   Curious creature.   I wonder what he really died of.   It was very much hushed up."

Millicent Rogers shook her head.

" I agree, most extraordinary.   They say he was perfectly well one moment, and then there were odd rumours, and the next thing one heard was that he was dead."

" Can't you ask the girl ?   Bethel, isn't her name ? " enquired the Duchess with curiosity.   " I shall.   After all, her grandmother was my greatest friend, and I dandled her father on my knee."

" You know there always has been a mystery about the place.   And about the family.   Something rather horrible I believe.   I should have thought you would have known more about it than anyone else, as you were such a friend of Lady Adelaide.   Did she never let you into the Treveryan secret ? "

The Duchess shook her head.

" The persons concerned are often the last to know about such things, and the women of such families least of all."

Just then some heavy drops of rain fell, and the many guests with one accord fled towards the house, and the Treveryans, as a subject of gossip, were forgotten.

.   .   .   .

And there, just as Lady Rogers had shrewdly guessed, the matter of Bethel Treveryan's entry into society rested.   True, she was asked to some parties, and in the following winter stayed with friends for the hunt ball, and in a small way she entertained as far as was possible in her own house.   But it was Bethel herself who had to make such tentative suggestions

to her mother, who sometimes would acquiesce with a certain
amount of grace, and at others would assume such boredom
or even impatience at the prospect of a dinner party or a small
dance, that her daughter would only too thankfully let the
matter drop.

There was plenty for her to do at home and in the village
she soon realized, as the months went by. There were old
people to whom she could minister during the bleak winter
months, occasional parochial matters of which she could
relieve Mrs. Penrose, whose bouts of rheumatism often made
' visiting ' out of the question. She found a new interest also
in the stillroom, when Alice, the stillroom maid, was suddenly
sent packing in disgrace, and a new girl could not be found
at a moment's notice to take her place. Old Mrs. Mitchell
' graciously allowed '—as Bethel reported to Veryan—Rose,
the cook, to give her lessons in the making and baking of
bread, cakes and scones; and on many a wet afternoon the
girl would emerge from the back regions of the house clad in
an apron, her face flushed and powdered with flour, to the
tolerant amusement of Mrs. Treveryan, who seemed less averse
to her pretty daughter spending hours in menial household
tasks, than joining her friends at dances and games at neigh-
bouring houses.

Both Bethel and her brother had horses and, although they
were far from the nearest hunt, they thoroughly enjoyed
hacking through the pretty lanes, and the park which sur-
rounded Treveryan was large enough for them to enjoy
many a good gallop.

The days became months and the months years, and world
affairs left the family untouched and even uninterested. They
were far less rocked by the horror of the Czar's assassination
than they were by the great fire at Lanhydrock, Lord Robartes'
stately home a few miles away, and both Bethel and her mother
seemed a great deal more perturbed lest a similar fate might
overtake Treveryan than that a war might break out on the
Continent.

When Lord Beaconsfield died they did not turn a hair, for
they supposed that, like most Cornish, they were Liberals, and
' anyway politics are men's business.' Anna Treveryan continued her strange, aloof existence, giving nothing of herself

to any of her children except perhaps Lerryn, who was growing in appearance to be a miniature likeness of herself, and shutting herself up for hours in her own sitting-room, writing.

" Whom does she write to? " they asked themselves, but without any great interest.

There was, of course, great excitement when the Bishop was given the Primacy in 1882, and even Veryan, who had always shown himself bored by Church matters, said with youthful swagger, " It's rather fun to know the Archbishop of Canterbury."

Veryan continued his tutoring at home until he was eighteen, when Mrs. Treveryan suddenly informed her children, to their surprise, that he was to go to Oxford.

" It was always your father's wish," she answered to their many questions.

And so in the autumn of '83, Veryan departed for Christchurch, where he was to conduct himself as a gentleman, and without any great distinction, for the next three years.

Bethel missed her brother more than she would allow herself to realize. They had never been a day apart, and although he was four years younger than herself, the fact that they had learnt under the same tutor and had shared the same interests, seemed to have mitigated the disparity of years.

They wrote continually to each other, and their letters seemed to draw the bond of union between them even closer. There were times when the girl felt a sudden dread, a tinge of jealousy, that some new friend might estrange her brother from her, and she was often afraid lest he should wish to spend weeks of the vacations away from Treveryan. She hoped that with his departure her mother might unbend; surely she must realize a little the loneliness she felt without Veryan about the place? But the strange woman still remained in a state of spiritual isolation as it were, a stranger to her daughter. There were times when the girl thought she detected a puzzled frown on her mother's face, and once, when caught unawares, there was a look of fear in her eyes as Bethel unexpectedly walked into her room, to find Lerryn playing in a corner of the room and her mother watching her.

" I wish I could make Mama out," Veryan said one evening during the Christmas vacation following his first term at the

House.   " Sometimes I believe she frankly dislikes me."

Bethel was silent, and then spoke suddenly and thoughtfully.

" I often wonder if she disliked Papa.   Even perhaps hated him.   You are getting very like him to look at, Veryan. Perhaps if that were so, it would account for her coldness to you.   For I've noticed it myself."

" I call it all damn unnatural.   I'm sorry ! "   He walked moodily across the room and kicked back a log that had fallen from the fire.   " Have you noticed, for instance, Beth, when we say good night to her, how, although she seems to tolerate a peck from you, she visibly shrinks when I kiss her?   God knows I've no wish to, but I supposed it my duty," the young man began to work himself into a temper.

" Oh, surely you exaggerate," Bethel said.   " She's always been cold and undemonstrative.   Queer, anyone as beautiful as she is."

" Seems a waste, doesn't it ? " he spoke.   " She has as much temperament as a statue.   Lerryn seems to be the only one who understands her.   What a miserable soul she must have, poor thing.   She knows plenty of people, but has no friends, and her own children repel her ! "

Bethel was shocked, but loving Veryan as she did felt powerless to rebuke him.   Moreover, there was a good deal of truth in what he said.

That winter there were more bad gales, and rather to Bethel's surprise, her mother evinced a sudden anxiety and solicitude for the sufferers in the nearby villages and harbours.   She even began to unbend a little towards Bethel, asking her advice on what to take with her when she ordered the carriage on a mission of pity, and usually wished her company as well.

" Perhaps she's really dreadfully shy," Bethel thought once, when she realized her mother was struggling with the effort of trying to appear natural and sympathetic to the family of a young fisherman who had been drowned in the recent storms.

In the spring and early summer of '87 politics once again began to play a great part in the neighbourhood, for the by-election which was to take place at St. Austell; and Bethel, very much to her surprise and rather to her consternation, was asked to help with the distribution of pamphlets in the nearby villages, for the Liberal candidate.   It was during the week

preceding polling-day, when one evening she was dining with
some supporters of McArthur, that a young man whom she
had not noticed at dinner came up to her later in the drawing-
room.

"Miss Treveryan, I fear you don't remember me," he said.
For a moment she hesitated, and then—

"Did you not come to my ball? Aren't you the barrister
that hoped to live in a Temple?" she smiled, and Oswald
Martineau noticed two dimples and fell in love with her.

"Who do you say the young man is?" Anna Treveryan
enquired a few days later when she and Bethel returned from a
call on the Penroses to find Martineau's card in the hall.

"He's a great friend of the Rogers'," Bethel hastened to say,
and was disturbed to feel herself blushing. "He came to my
dance, and we met him at a garden-party at Tregothnan, too.
He's a barrister. Quite an important one, I believe." She
spoke a little breathlessly and realized that for all she knew she
was guilty of exaggeration, for he certainly had not spoken of
himself as being important; but anyway he had achieved his
ambition as far as living in the Temple went, so he must be ' a
good barrister,' she told herself.

"But why on earth call? And without the Rogers', I notice.
Most extraordinary!"

' To see me again ' the girl's heart cried, and longed to be
able to so confide in her mother. She remained silent and
looked out of the window.

"Rather late to be paying a formal call after your dance,
Bethel, upon my soul," Anna Treveryan remarked. "I don't
know what we can do about it. Veryan is away, we can't
have him over."

"Could we not perhaps invite the Rogers' to dinner, and
him, too?" Bethel enquired rather timidly. Her mother looked
surprised.

"How extraordinary you are! What a thing to think of
suddenly."

"But Mama . . . there is so much entertainment going on at
the moment, what with the election, and one thing and
another." Why, she asked herself, did she want to see Mr.
Martineau so much?

" But the Rogers'? They're about the one family who aren't interested. Neither am I for that matter—I have never been able to understand how you have become so embroiled, Bethel. Politics are not a woman's job; so unfeminine and unnatural. And anyway, I don't particularly want to ask Millicent Rogers over, she was distinctly ill-mannered the last time we met."

Bethel saw it was useless to remonstrate, and went to her room in dejected spirits. She missed Veryan badly she realized at this moment. She began to think of Oswald Martineau, and was angry and dismayed when she found she could not picture his appearance. She shut her eyes, but only a shadow was visible, a shadowy stranger it seemed, who could neither speak to her nor leave her vision free. A few days later, in Truro, she ran into Mary Rogers, who mentioned in the course of conversation that Martineau had returned to London. It was the first and greatest disappointment Bethel had known. She was simple and innocent and ignorant, and only knew that the sun had stopped shining; that she did not care whether her new dress would become her or not; and that the Jubilee festivities, to which she had been looking forward with some excitement, could be cancelled forthwith for all she cared.

PART ONE 4

AS IF FATE was determined to take a hand in all their affairs, a letter came from Veryan to Anna Treveryan telling her that he had secured seats in a window near the Abbey for the Queen's Jubilee procession, and that both she and Bethel must make the effort to come to town.

' It's a chance in a million,' he wrote, ' that I got the seats. A friend of mine, whose father is rather a swell, had the window, and something has happened by which he can't possibly use it. You and Beth will regret it all your lives if you don't come, and I shall be hurt and disappointed, too.'

For once Mrs. Treveryan seemed anxious to fall in with the plan, and Bethel found herself once more taking an interest in the hurried choosing of new frocks, and the promise of gaiety with Veryan.

It was decided they should go up to London a week before the great day, so that they might participate in some of the preceding festivities and galas of which London would be in the throes. They would stay in a quiet hotel that Anna Treveryan knew to be both good and reputable, yet well in the centre of things.

Both Bethel and Veryan were surprised at the change that came over their mother in London. She seemed a different person. It was almost as if, they agreed, she had escaped bondage, and now, free of fetters, was the very ringleader of the three of them in enjoyment of anything the gods were ready to provide as entertainment.

She knew so much also, which came as a surprise. For one living in the depths of the country and leading the isolated life they knew her to lead, they were amazed at her knowledge of pictures and galleries, plays, artistes.

"Poor Mama! We have horribly misjudged her," said Bethel one evening, after a morning spent at the Royal Academy, where they had greatly admired the works of Millais and Fildes and Leighton, and an afternoon at a matinée of the thrilling new play, "The Red Lamp," in which Mr. Beerbohm Tree held his audience spellbound through a play about Russian nihilism. Another morning they went to the summer exhibition at the Grosvenor Galleries and saw the pictures of Watts and Alma-Tadema and Burne-Jones.

The operas of Sir Arthur Sullivan and Mr. Gilbert were greatly in vogue still, and although the new "Ruddigore" disappointed for the most part, the Treveryans thoroughly enjoyed it, and Veryan made amusing remarks *sotto voce* during the scene in which the ancestors appear from their portraits to declaim to Ruddigore.

"Let us write a burlesque and call it Treveryan," he whispered at the end of the evening.

They met several people they knew from Cornwall, and one day Anna Treveryan suggested the two 'children' should amuse themselves, as she was lunching with her cousin Llewelyn, 'and you don't want to waste your time with us old fogeys,' she added, to the greatly astonished and rather bewildered brother and sister.

"I'd forgotten all about him," Bethel said.

"I should have thought he'd have liked to see if you still wear his pendant," Veryan teased.

Brother and sister sallied forth, and for once Veryan did not object to Bethel's entreaties that they should 'go slowly' up Bond Street. They stopped in front of all the most amusing windows, and it was when they were peering with admiration at some Chinese jade that Bethel heard a startled voice behind her exclaim, "Miss Treveryan! By all that's wonderful!"

She turned and found herself face to face with Oswald Martineau.

"I don't suppose your brother remembers me," he smiled, as Bethel made the introductions.

After that it seemed natural that he should join brother and sister, and the three of them began to wander back towards Piccadilly. Bethel was vastly relieved to see the two men take to each other immediately, and was quite content to walk silently between the two, knowing that Martineau's eyes seldom left her in spite of the fact that he addressed himself almost entirely to her brother.

"Why shouldn't we all lunch together?" he exclaimed, on hearing the two had not to return to Mrs. Treveryan. "Unfortunately I cannot ask you to my rooms to-day, for I know there would be nothing to eat. But it would give me great pleasure if you and Miss Bethel would lunch with me in town?"

This suggestion was, of course, accepted with alacrity. As they stopped to hail a cab, a carriage went by and Bethel saw that many heads were turned towards the occupant.

"That is Madam Patti," he exclaimed. "I suppose you have been to the opera?"

When they mentioned their visit to 'Ruddigore,' he said:

"Ah, you must hear some real music now that you're here. The de Reszkes and Nordica are singing during the season at Drury Lane, and you should go to Covent Garden, I think, for Albani is still over here. Perhaps you will come as my guests to 'Lohengrin.' I have not met Mrs. Treveryan since the night of your ball, but I have a friend who lets me have his box at the opera from time to time, and if you will all come with me I should indeed be happy."

Bethel was delighted at the prospect. She knew so little about music, and felt her education had been sadly neglected, but even the few hours spent listening to ' Ruddigore ' had made her realize that a world of beauty lay ahead for her, if only she could discover and learn more. She dimly remembered her mother playing the harp when she had been a very little girl. Why had she given it up, she wondered?

"As a matter of fact," Martineau said during lunch, " there is a wonderful concert this afternoon. Richter is conducting Bruckner's seventh symphony. If I can get tickets, will you both come? "

Veryan looked uncertain, but one glance at Bethel's expression settled the matter. ·

When for a moment Martineau later on found himself alone with her, he said without further ado:

" I called on Mrs. Treveryan when I was in Cornwall. I was dreadfully disappointed not to find either your mother or—you," and he paused.

" I know," Bethel replied, " it was sickening." And then, fearing she had said too much, she quickly asked, " Have you seen Mary or Nicolas? I fancy they're up."

" They're dining with me to-morrow at my rooms. I saw Mary yesterday at her grandmother's house in Portman Square," and Bethel for a moment felt a pang of absurd jealousy rush through her.

" You know she's just about to announce her engagement to young St. Hilary? " he continued.

" No, indeed! This *is* a surprise. Dear Mary, she's one of my dearest friends at home," Bethel replied, her heart suddenly full of warm affection for the girl.

" I like your brother," Martineau spoke again.

" I love him more than anyone in the world. I'm glad you like him. He's much younger than you, of course, but he's grown up a lot since he went to Oxford."

The music held her spellbound, she had never in her life imagined anything like it. Oswald Martineau watched the young face beside him with ever-growing tenderness. He saw how moved she was by the grandeur of the symphony, and he saw that something lay asleep in the girl which, if awakened, would plunge the awakener into very heaven.

" Promise you'll come to ' Lohengrin ' ? " he said as he bade them good-bye at the end of the afternoon.

Mrs. Treveryan was in great high spirits when they returned to the hotel. They found her in the drawing-room taking tea with her cousin.

" Wonder what she sees in him," Veryan said later on to Bethel.

" I'm sure they'd been having a high old time," said Bethel, " and then he completely dried up when we appeared. Didn't you notice? I heard them both laughing like anything before we reached the room. Still, he's awfully handsome."

That night they dined quietly at the hotel.

" Why doesn't our cousin ever visit us at Treveryan, Mama ? " Veryan asked innocently as they were taking dessert.

" He's not often in England," Anna Treveryan answered after a slight pause.

" What is he ? " Bethel asked.

" Something in South America. I never quite know what."

" Were you children together? " Veryan persisted.

" Yes. We grew up more or less together."

" How odd we've heard and seen so little of him, Mama," Bethel now spoke.

" Do you like him? " Both brother and sister were startled by their mother's voice. Bethel looked and felt uncomfortable, seeing her mother's eyes upon her, the voice had held entreaty one might almost have said.

" Yes, of course," the girl answered.

" There was a family row about him years ago," Anna Treveryan continued. Still her voice sounded unnatural to her children; this time a tone of apology seemed to creep in. " That's why you would not have heard him mentioned at Hereford."

" Bad luck ! " said Veryan, trying to sound sympathetic.

" Before you were married? " Bethel asked.

" Why, yes." Again they thought their mother seemed strange.

" What was it about? "

" You're too young to understand," she said, and started to rise from the table. "And it was all very long ago, and is now forgotten and over, thank God ! " And this time she spoke with defiance. " Come, let's have coffee in the drawing-room, and you tell me more about this young Mr. Martineau."

That night Veryan went into Bethel's room to borrow some nail scissors.

" I suppose he's in love with you, Beth," he began without mentioning any name. Bethel wheeled round from the dressing-table where she sat plaiting her hair.

" Oh, Veryan! Do you think so? " She spoke with so much intensity that Veryan threw her a piercing glance.

" Well, I gather you are with him. Who is he, anyway? "

There was not much to tell Veryan when all was said and done, she began to think.

" What *do* you feel about him, Beth," her brother asked inquisitively, later.

" I don't know. Not really. I only know I like him more than anyone I've ever met."

" More than Nico Rogers? "

" Good gracious, yes." She spoke impatiently.

" Funny . . ."

Three nights later Bethel's heart beat as it had never done before, as she stepped out of the cab behind her mother and brother and walked across the courtyard that led to Oswald Martineau's rooms. She tried to take in the settings about her, but could think of nothing but the agony she was feeling, sweet agony she felt it to be, a mixture of absurd shyness and eager pleasure.

Martineau's rooms were charming. Panelled, and hung with old prints. One side of the room was entirely lined with books, ' much too heavy and boring for you to bother about,' he said smilingly to her as she wandered over to the shelves; there were carnations on the dining table and on the mantelpiece.

" You look very young to know so much," Anna Treveryan said at the close of dinner, as he finished telling them about an absorbing trial which had lately horrified the country.

" I'm thirty-four. Not so young. But the law has always interested me beyond all else. Since I was quite a small boy I was determined to study it. I'm very ambitious! " he laughed, as he poured out more liqueurs.

" Would you rather defend or prosecute? " Veryan asked.

" Oh, I suppose defend. Surely it is only the man who is a little—shall we say sadistic?—who wants to prosecute. However, I daresay—and hope—if I'm lucky enough, I'll get plenty of both before I'm through."

" It must be frightful to have to be in a murder trial," Bethel said quietly.

" Depends which party you are," Veryan laughed.

" I couldn't bear to prosecute a man for murder," she said.

" What about the victim? " Martineau asked her.

" I should never feel I was doing right. Persuading men to send another man to his death." She shuddered.

Martineau looked at the clock.

" I think we must stop this rather lugubrious conversation and take ourselves off," he remarked.

The performance of ' Lohengrin ' was to be one of only two during the whole season, and the theatre was filled with all the *élite* of fashionable and musical Jubilee London. Bethel, and indeed Mrs. Treveryan and Veryan, too, sat entranced. Veryan, who was not stirred by music in the same way as the two women, said, ' By Jove ' and ' great stuff ' as the evening drew on.

Anna Treveryan was chiefly interested in the opera from a technical point of view, and showed surprising perspicacity in her criticisms of both music and singers.

There were two people who sat in the box, however, caring for nothing but what the music did to their own souls. Bethel became almost frightened by the emotion she felt, and Oswald Martineau who watched her knew that beside him sat the only girl he had ever loved or would ever love, and that without her his future would be utterly pointless.

" How did you like Oswald Martineau, Mama? " asked Veryan as he bade his mother good night.

" I thought he seemed a nice young man," she answered, a trifle evasively, he thought.

· " Very decent of him to have taken us to-night, anyway," he continued.

" Yes, it was most enjoyable, I must admit. Has he "—and she seemed to hesitate—" made any further plans to see you? "

" It's Bethel he wants to see, I imagine."

As he spoke Veryan immediately noticed a change come over his mother. Gone in a trice it seemed was that look of charm and gay interest that she had worn since their arrival in London, and once again the well-known ' Cornish expression,' as he termed it mentally, took its place.

" Bethel? I'm not going to have any nonsense of that sort starting."

Veryan looked at his mother and spoke quickly, indignation ringing in his voice.

" What do you mean—nonsense? Sometimes I fancy you forget Beth is twenty-five. Most girls are married with children of their own by that age."

" That will do, Veryan. When I think it's time to look for a husband for Bethel I'm quite capable of finding one for her myself."

" Hang it all, Mama, I wouldn't ever say this to Beth, but she's getting on. Most mothers are only too anxious to get their daughters off."

" What do you know about such matters, pray? "

Veryan remained silent. It maddened him to think that Bethel's happiness was likely to be sacrificed for no reason that he could think of, and it annoyed him that the evening should be brought to such an unpleasant end.

" Have you any reason to imagine this Mr. Martineau is more than politely taken with your sister? "

' Your sister,' thought Veryan angrily, ' why not call her by her name? '

" No," he answered sulkily.

" Well, then, I particularly ask you not to put ideas into Bethel's head. I do remember he called on us a few months ago. I never did anything about it. He is a friend of Nicolas Rogers, I know, and he talks as if he's well received by Millicent. That, however, doesn't mean that I wish to listen to any such nonsense as you seem to imagine. And now, Veryan, good night. I have a nasty head coming on."

Next morning brother and sister breakfasted quietly together. Bethel's head was full of the music from the night before, and she found it difficult to refrain from seeing the image of Martineau in Lohengrin's armour, which kept rising to her eyes. She was blissfully unaware of Veryan's silence.

When she went in to see her mother, Anna Treveryan said
good morning coldly, and told her that she wished her to go
shopping with her. Bethel, however, noticed nothing odd in
her mother's behaviour. The storm burst on their return to
the hotel, when in the sitting-room the two women found a
box of very beautiful roses addressed to Bethel, with a card
from Oswald Martineau attached.

Bethel's face became suffused with blushes, and she could
only stammer her pleasure and surprise. Anna Treveryan read
the card and threw it aside with a sniff.

" How long has this been going on, Miss? " she asked
coldly.

" What do you mean? " the girl asked.

" This absurd—business? "

" I don't understand, Mama. You know Veryan and I met
Mr. Martineau that day he took us to lunch and to the concert.
And then there was last night." She faltered. How long ago
last night seemed. " And now these flowers have come.
That's all." Slowly the colour began to leave her face.

" All? What do you mean by all? "

Bethel was frightened. Her mother was adopting such a
very menacing attitude. Surely the sending and acceptance
of flowers was nothing very dreadful? " I mean . . . that's
all," she ended lamely.

" It's got to stop."

" What? "

" This—friendship. I don't wish you to see Mr. Martineau
again."

" Mama ! "

" You must have encouraged him exceedingly as it is, for
him to be paying you such attentions."

Bethel bit her lip. Was Mama off her head that she should
make such a fuss about a bunch of flowers?

At that moment Veryan came into the room. One look at
his mother and sister told him enough.

" You might look after your sister with more care, although
I might have expected you are not to be trusted. But the lax
life you lead at Oxford does not entitle you to let Bethel take
up with any Tom, Dick or Harry whose fancy she takes."

The boy looked in bewilderment at Bethel who by this time

was in tears. She pointed to the flowers and he then noticed Martineau's card.

"You must be mad to make such a scene over such a little matter, Mama," he said angrily, walking over to Bethel and putting his arm through hers.

"*How dare you speak to me so!*"

Anna Treveryan's children started at their mother's voice. They were used to cold tones in her voice, at home she generally spoke in little else. Since their visit to London they had been surprised but grateful for the change in her, for a human being of ordinary flesh and blood had seemed to take the place of the statue they knew and to whom they were so used. This was another and equally new Anna Treveryan that looked at them both now, her eyes alight with fury, almost fear, Veryan thought. And her voice shook with suppressed rage. Both remained silent, as if rooted under a spell. Then Mrs. Treveryan swept from the room.

Bethel collapsed into a chair and Veryan held her in his arms.

"Don't cry, darling. It's ridiculous to make all this fuss, something must have unhinged Mama. I'm sure it'll come all right."

"Oh, Veryan, I'm frightened. I know I shan't see him again. Oh, I hate her!" and she burst into a flood of tears. Veryan continued to stroke her.

"You love him then?" he asked.

"Yes. I know I hardly know him, but I do. I think I've known it since we met a few months ago and he called and Mama wouldn't do anything about it. I didn't know I loved him, but I wanted to see him again most dreadfully. When I heard he'd left Cornwall I felt so miserable, Veryan. And now . . . oh, I'm sure I love him. I'm twenty-five, Veryan, surely I'm old enough to know."

"I wonder." Veryan suddenly felt very old himself, and Bethel seemed little more than a child. Yes, she was twenty-five, and although he would not be twenty-one till Christmas, she might have been Lerryn he knew, for all the experience she had had. What could she know of love, locked up at Treveryan leading the life of a nun in a convent, he thought angrily, suddenly realizing in full the sheltered existence their mother insisted upon. All these years she could have gone about leading as gay a life as any of her contemporaries in Cornwall, but he knew that, with few exceptions, Bethel remained at Treveryan, seldom going far afield and meeting no one but their immediate neighbours. What lay behind it all? Surely there must be some reason for their mother's extraordinary behaviour. If it were not for the fact that she herself led such a secluded life, her son would have been tempted to believe that jealousy prompted Anna Treveryan in keeping her children in the background. But this was surely not so. Never mind, he thought; in December he would come of age and then Bethel should have his consent to marry Martineau if the business was as serious as all that.

Luncheon was eaten in gloomy silence, Bethel scarcely touching a morsel of food. At the end of the meal Mrs. Treveryan said icily :

" We're returning to Cornwall."

Her children looked at her aghast.

" When ? "

" To-morrow."

" But Mama ! " Was she indeed crazy, Veryan wondered ? Had she forgotten what the day after to-morrow was ?

" Have you forgotten the Jubilee, in heaven's name ? " he asked in exasperated tones.

" No, I've not. But I've decided to take Bethel back. I don't care what you choose to do, but I've made up my mind as to your sister. It's her own fault. I consider she's behaved slyly and made herself horribly cheap into the bargain."

" You speak as if I were a child, Mama ! " Bethel for once flared at her mother.

" That will do ! "

" Do you want to miss the procession ? You realize it's something that may never occur in history again ? All because a young man sends Bethel flowers. My God ! "

" You forget yourself, Veryan. Don't use language like that to me."

" Mama, please." Bethel laid a beseeching hand on her mother's arm. " What have you against Mr. Martineau ? I'm sure he treated us all with the same politeness last night."

" I've nothing against him personally," was the surprising reply.

"Then why, in heaven's name? Surely there's nothing wrong in Bethel having an admirer? I expect his intentions are all that they should be——"

"Quite likely. And Bethel looks like ceding to them. I have reasons why I wish to stop the whole business."

"I think we have a right to know them; Bethel most certainly has."

"I'm the best judge of that, thank you. And Bethel and I are returning to Treveryan."

It was not surprising, therefore, that even members of the household noticed the marked restraint in the relations of mother and daughter on their return. Only Lerryn greeted them both in unseeing innocence, kissing her mother and throwing her arms round Bethel. She was now a pretty child, but in spite of a certain seriousness, still seemed very much the baby of the family.

"How sweet she is," thought Bethel as the child, flushing with youthful excitement, told of the giant beacon that, like others round the coasts of the United Kingdom, would set ablaze the Queen's glory the following evening, from the top of the hill beyond the lake.

"It will be as thrilling as the procession itself, Beth," Lerryn exclaimed, "and much more frightening. Just think! From the north of Scotland to Land's End the beacons stand. Aren't you glad you've come back?"

"I mustn't let my own unhappiness damp her joy," Bethel thought.

"Yes, pet. I daresay it will be just as much fun. And possibly the crowds would have prevented us seeing the Queen herself." She tried hard to believe the excuse. Anyway, what fun would there have been in remaining in town knowing that any sight of Oswald Martineau would have been out of the question?

The day of the Jubilee dawned. There were to be services of thanksgiving in churches throughout the country, and Bethel, with Lerryn hanging on to her arm, went in search of Anna, as the carriage was waiting to drive them all to church. To the girls' astonishment they found their mother still in bed.

"Aren't you well, Mama?" Bethel asked politely.

The woman shook her head.

" I feel so ill. I think I must have eaten something which has disagreed with me. I'll have to stay in bed. Ask Dr. Pearce to call in some time if you see him in church."

" Oh, poor Mama ! " exclaimed Lerryn sympathetically. " It will be sad if you cannot see the beacon to-night."

Anna Treveryan closed her eyes. " I don't expect I shall," she murmured.

The country service in the old Norman church was very beautiful thought Bethel, as with the rest of the congregation she stood to sing ' Now Thank we All our God ' and tried to keep her thoughts on the lonely widow who was at that moment herself giving thanks to Almighty God in Westminster Abbey, and not on a young barrister whose face would appear instead of that of the dignified, white-capped old lady. Imagine having to rule for fifty years, her thoughts ran, without any loved husband any more beside one, on whom to lean for advice or support. A little old lady with an empire at her feet. A tear trickled down her face, and she was glad when Mr. Penrose's voice called them to kneel in prayer, so that she might wipe her eyes without being noticed.

Dr. Pearce showed great surprise at seeing her when they left the service. Hurriedly and without thinking, Bethel gave her mother's sudden illness as the excuse for their return. He promised to ' look in ' during the afternoon.

Anna Treveryan showed no signs of recovery when the girls arrived home, and the doctor, after he had seen her, shook his head and said he could not say anything for a day or so, but that he didn't ' like the look of it.'

Bethel tried to feel sorry for her mother, but her heart was still bitter, and she was glad that the excellent Prudence was fully capable of ministering to her mother.

" Come on, Beth. It's time." The child tugged at her sister's arm.

" Look, the moon is showing, and I can see at least three stars, in spite of the sky being so light still. Oh, come on, don't be late."

Bethel opened the door which led out into the garden from the library, and flung a shawl over her head as protection against bats, of which she admitted a ridiculous fear. The two girl's walked across the lawn, passing the lake on which the swans were still visible, and climbed the hill. Quite a crowd of villagers were there when they approached, and there were greetings of ' Evenin', Miss Bethel; evenin', Miss Lerryn,' from all sides.

With strange suddenness the evening seemed to darken, and in the distance an owl screeched.

' Mind out ! ' cried a voice, and then there old Will Searle ran forward brandishing the flare, and suddenly the beacon was alight. There was a crackling and a hissing, and a great noise that seemed almost impossible could emanate from the faggots on the hillside, and for a moment, as a gasp of admiration tinged with fear rose from the crowd, Bethel thought that a great fire would be the disastrous result. But no, the men kept the beacon in good order, and soon she looked around and saw in the distance other crimson patches which told of like beacons elsewhere. As the flames grew and kindled in intensity the faces of the onlookers became visible, and the sisters amused themselves by playing a game, a race of recognition. Suddenly Bethel's heart seemed to stop beating. Was she dreaming, were her fancies playing such havoc that she had to see his face even through this Cornish beacon fire ? Her hand went to her throat, as if to stop the feeling of suffocating joy that was fast taking hold of her. This was no dream, no vision, but truly Oswald Martineau in the flesh. Quickly he came to where she stood, and in silence took her hand. Neither of them spoke. They watched, as the rest of the little crowd watched, the beacon's flames die gradually down, and only great glowing embers remain. Quietly people dispersed, and Bethel never noticed Lerryn depart with old Tudor to the house. Presently they were alone.

" I love you. But you knew that, didn't you? I couldn't let you go as you did." He took her hands and kissed them, looking up to her face.

" Why did you come? " she whispered.

" Veryan told me everything. I don't know what your mother has against me, but I'm going to find out. I love you, dear Bethel, sweet Bethel. Tell me I may call you by that name? Tell me you care—a little? "

Bethel's shawl fell to the ground, and her dark hair tumbled about her shoulders.

"How lovely you are," he whispered.

"I can't believe you are here," she said.

"Say you don't mind," he begged.

"Mind!" her voice betrayed the love she felt.

"Bethel!" he whispered.

"I love you! Oh, I love you! I shall always love you, whatever Mama's orders!" Her voice trembled passionately.

Then Oswald Martineau stood up and drew her to his side. Gently he kissed her eyes, her cheeks, her lips.

"You will marry me, my Bethel? Whatever your mother's opposition."

"Nothing shall keep us apart."

Slowly they traced their way from the hill to the lake.

"When did you first love me?" Bethel asked a little shyly as they stood by the rushes, and she felt his arm once more encircle her waist.

"I think always. I think I fell in love with you at your own ball, seven years ago."

"Why have you spent all these years without me, then?" He kissed her hand.

"What had I to offer you in those days? Nothing."

"I hardly remember you at my dance. Oh, how faithless of me!"

Here Oswald must needs kiss his love again, and assure her she had no reason to have remembered the struggling young barrister. They walked on in silence.

"It's growing dark and late," said Bethel, "and Mama is ill." And she told him of Anna Treveryan's sudden and strange malady.

"I will not come as far as the house, sweet. But send word to me somehow or other when I can see you. I've got a room at 'The Crown' for the time being."

At the foot of the terrace they parted. As Bethel turned again from his arms a moth brushed her hair, and a cloud passed across the moon.

PART ONE

5

TWO DAYS LATER Dr. Pearce confirmed his fears, and told Bethel that her mother was suffering from typhoid fever. They supposed that this might be easily accounted for, as Anna Treveryan admitted to having drunk water during her visit to London without enquiring the source, also to have eaten watercress. Veryan was sent for, but before he arrived Anna had lost consciousness. A nurse was installed, and with the help of Prudence, the maid, Bethel was spared the task of nursing her mother and coming into risk of contagion.

Veryan found his sister at her wits' end, and it was not long before the whole story was poured into his sympathetic ears. He learnt that Oswald Martineau was still at ' The Crown Inn,' but that Bethel had hardly dared leave Treveryan since the sudden grave turn her mother's illness had taken, for fear she might be needed, and realizing only too well what food for gossip her meetings with a comparative stranger might call forth. And now a note had come to the house from Oswald telling her that he must return to London to-morrow.

" That's all right," Veryan said. " I myself will send word to him and ask him up. No one is to know that he's not a friend of mine."

"Ask him up after dinner, then," Bethel answered, after a moment's hurried thought. " The servants won't think that so queer. They might wonder at your asking someone to dine with Mama as ill as she is."

So at nine o'clock Oswald Martineau found himself walking quickly up the long beech avenue at Treveryan. On any other occasion he would have stopped to admire the natural beauties of the place, the more so as he knew from their conversation in the spring how Bethel adored her home, and what the place meant to her. But now all he could think of was seeing her again and quickly, and enlisting young Veryan's sympathy and help. It hardly made sense, he told himself, that a woman to whom he had shown every respect and politeness, as he had to Mrs. Treveryan, should so suddenly and without reason show herself the arch-enemy of his suit to her daughter. Moreover, he was doing very well, and was in a position to keep Bethel in the way to which she had been used, as the Rogers could easily vouch for. Such obstinate antipathy both frightened and angered him, and to crown all the wretched woman must needs get ill enough to prevent Bethel leaving the house during the few brief days he had been able to be near her.

Typhoid was a bad and dangerous illness—he hoped to God Bethel was not having to busy herself too much in the sick room. Dangerous. . . . He remembered hearing that the death rate was pretty high. Perhaps . . .?

Veryan himself was standing in the doorway and, after welcoming the other warmly, immediately led him to the library where Bethel sat, half anxious, half excited. She rose to greet him and he kissed her fingers.

" You have understood—Oswald . . ." she hesitated and blushed slightly, realizing it was the first time she had spoken his name aloud, " how impossible it has been—trying to meet you, I mean? As I wrote you, Mama is very ill indeed, and I couldn't leave. Thank God Veryan has come."

" Thank God, indeed," Martineau replied, " for he will be able to take the burden off your shoulders. I for my part shall be eternally grateful, for his appearance has enabled me to see you before I leave."

" Do you really have to go, Martineau? " Veryan enquired.

" Indeed, yes. If it hadn't been that I had to see your sister again I should never have left London at this moment. I have a big case coming on—that is to say, one for which I'm briefed as Junior Counsel, and I must definitely return to-morrow."

" What sort of a case? " asked Bethel, trying to sound interested, though longing for her brother to leave the room so that Oswald should take her in his arms.

" Embezzlement." He did not vouchsafe further details, and who shall say whether he was not echoing Bethel's wishes in his own heart.

He turned towards the younger man.

" Veryan—I hope I may call you by your first name? I have asked your sister to marry me. Of course I realize that your mother's grave illness makes her consent out of the question for the time being. But if I thought I had your support, I should leave here with greater ease."

" My dear fellow," said Veryan gravely and with all the dignity his twenty years could muster, " Bethel's happiness is the most important thing in the world as far as I'm concerned. Of course you have my blessing, both of you."

"Darling Veryan, how sweet you are!" the girl cried, and ran and kissed him.

"You realize, don't you," he continued a little guiltily, "that I'm not of age until the end of the year? Also that I should ask you a lot of embarrassing questions, I believe, none of which I know how to!" He turned to Martineau with a disarming smile, which the other returned.

"I think I can satisfy you, young sir, that your beloved sister will be safe in my hands! But, of course, we will meet and discuss matters in the correct way whenever it is convenient."

"Am I now properly engaged to you, Oswald?" Bethel asked joyously.

"You are, my dearest. As far as I am concerned, at any rate."

Veryan poured out three glasses of Madeira, saying :

"I wish I had something more worthy in which to toast you both! However, here's to wishing my Beth all joy and eternal happiness, and you, Oswald! Well, all I can say is that you've won a prize and are the luckiest man in the world."

Bethel's eyes filled with happy tears, and Oswald Martineau, as he raised his glass to his lips, answered :

"God bless you, Veryan! May you one day be as happy as I am."

At that moment there was a knock at the door, and old Hockin, the man-servant, beckoned to Veryan.

Oswald Martineau led the girl across the room to the tapestried stool in front of the fireplace.

"My Bethel!" he said, and his eyes held hers for a minute before he bent and kissed her lips.

He sat beside her, and for a few minutes neither of them spoke.

"And are you really willing to leave Treveryan, leave all this——" and he turned and gazed with growing awe and appreciation at the splendour of the room in which they were, "for one whom you know so little?" he asked. Bethel gazed into the embers of the dying fire and spoke thoughtfully and slowly.

"Before I met you I never thought of marriage," she began.

"Perhaps I'm different from other girls. All this—as you say—has been my life and been enough. Until now. I don't think any girl can have loved her home more than I have. I've worshipped Treveryan. I feel I am it, and it is me. But now that has changed, and you, my darling, have changed it for me. I know now that there are other things, fuller things —a fuller life—than the stone walls which a very beloved house can offer. As your wife, with your arms about me, pray God I shall find them. I think, perhaps, I never grew up till now, Oswald. I feel happy—so happy! And yet a little afraid, too."

"Afraid, my sweet!"

"Afraid I may fail you in lots of ways. I'm so silly, so ignorant. You ought to have a smart, fashionable wife who would be useful to you in the kind of life you lead. I know nothing. I'm a foolish country——"

He kissed her mouth.

"Darling dear!" he whispered, "I don't know what to say to you. I'm so wretchedly unworthy of you. You make me feel a thief."

"A thief?"

"I feel a plunderer, a pirate. I'm robbing Treveryan of its most precious possession."

"Foolish one!" Bethel whispered.

"No, I'm serious. What if I don't make you happy? What if you find my arms and my love empty of the happiness Treveryan has always given you? It's I who have need of fear, my dear one, not you."

Bethel stood up.

"Kiss me," she said simply.

Oswald took her again in his arms and kissed her with reverent passion.

"These are now my walls," she said when she unclasped his arms from about her. "Walls of flesh and blood. My Treveryan lacked warmth and human love. I never realized that. How can my life be empty when I have your kisses and your love?"

She slowly crossed the room.

"I wonder why Veryan was called away? Look! He never drank our health, his glass is untouched. What a shame!"

Then she walked back again to join him by the french window where he was standing.

" Let's go out for a little while," she said, " these summer evenings are very lovely when dusk has fallen."

They strolled across the sloping lawns to the shores of the lake and stood silently gazing at the moon's reflection in the water. The air was soft and warm, and all was quiet save for the strange hum of an occasional night-beetle, or when a tiny puff of wind rustled amongst the reeds and bullrushes. How beautiful Treveryan looked silhouetted against the Irish yew and ilex trees, Bethel thought. Was she indeed planning to leave it all for ever . . .?

" Bethel Treveryan of Treveryan, in the county of Cornwall." Oswald Martineau pronounced the words slowly and distinctly, as if he were giving sentence.

" What do you want of her? " Bethel asked.

" So much. Everything." And then, after a long pause— " or nothing." And sensing her enquiry continued, " Nothing—if I cannot make her life so full of happiness that she shall never regret the step she takes when she becomes Bethel Martineau."

She took his hand and held it against her heart.

" Feel how it beats for you," she said. " It is yours for ever, whatever my name should be," and suddenly she shivered.

" You are cold, and it's getting late. Come back to the house, and then I must leave you."

" How ghost-like Treveryan looks now in the moonlight," Oswald Martineau remarked as they approached the terrace, " is it haunted? "

" No," she replied, " I don't really think so. It used to be said that a monk walked amongst the ruins of the chapel, but I think that was just a tale. I've never seen a ghost. There are various superstitions about Treveryan however. One is that if ever that old yew over there falls or dies," and she pointed to where an ancient and isolated tree was just discernible, " the end of Treveryan is in sight. But whether the saying means the house or the family or both I can't say. The tree is hundreds of years old, so we don't worry! And they say, too, that when there are no more Treveryans there will no longer be any wild swans here."

" Queer how these superstitions begin. I wonder what the reasons for them are," Martineau said.

" I suppose curses in mediæval days were responsible for a good many."

When they reached the library they found Veryan there.

" Forgive me, I had to send for Dr. Pearce. Mama seems worse."

He looked worried and pale.

" I'm so sorry," Martineau said, with as much feeling as he was able to put into his voice. A few minutes later he told them he must be getting back to the Inn.

" You will write to me, Oswald? " Bethel pleaded. Veryan left the room tactfully, saying he was going to find a lantern, aware as he was of the brightness of the moon and stars.

" Poor Oswald ! " she continued, " what a wretched week this has been for you. First you find you love a girl whose mother disapproves of you for some unknown reason, and then the girl is spirited away from under your very eyes. Then you follow her, thereby missing one of the greatest historical occasions we shall ever have the chance in our life-times to watch. And then when you track her down you can scarcely see her. It would have been better to have stayed and seen your queen perhaps."

He took both her hands and raised them to his lips.

" I have seen my queen," he answered.

A discreet cough in the passage outside told them that Veryan was about to enter the room.

" Farewell for a short while, my Bethel," Oswald said, releasing her from his arms.

" I love you, Oswald. For always."

PART
ONE

6

ANNA TREVERYAN DIED at the end of the second week of her illness. She never regained full consciousness. Her mind wandered, and her garbled ravings made no sense to the women who were looking after her, and Dr. Pearce was strangely unforthcoming, the nurse thought, when she told him with obvious curiosity some of the things her patient had cried out in her delirium.

In common with so many people who die comparatively young, Mrs. Treveryan had made no will, nor had she left any personal papers that anyone could find.

After the funeral, which had taken place in the village church and had been largely attended by the county, Bethel and Veryan had returned to the house, accompanied by various old friends who had come from afar; but the atmosphere was naturally strained, and both brother and sister were relieved when the last carriage drove away and they were alone.

Now that everything was over they were both aware that neither had discussed ' Mama,' and each guessed the secret and horrified relief in the other's heart. Only Lerryn seemed really upset, and this Bethel felt to be due more to the child's fear of death than to any real personal loss.

Things went on, they found, just as they always had. Bethel discovered that her mother had been a mere cipher in the hands of Mrs. Mitchell, who showed at once that she had no intention of allowing the girl to take over the housekeeping, any more than she had allowed her mother before her.

Old Hockin let Veryan imagine he was giving orders, but they quickly discovered that suggestions as to wines and other matters always came from the old man. Prudence said she would remain, as she was keeping company with one of the under-gardeners, and Bethel soon realized that if she was expecting to learn more about the business of keeping house she was likely to be disappointed. It was, of course, expected that the girls should wear deep mourning and go out even less than before, and the summer and autumn would indeed have passed with grim slowness for Bethel if Veryan had not been at home the greater part of the time.

Although there was now no further obstacle to their marriage, Martineau himself advised a postponement of any announcement whilst the family were in the first few months of mourning, and Veryan's suggestion that in the circumstances a small party at Christmas, to celebrate jointly his coming-of-age and Bethel's engagement, should be held, was welcomed warmly by the other two.

' Gradually, however, by word of mouth, the rumour of her

romance spread. Oswald Martineau came down for short visits twice before Veryan went up to Oxford for his last term, and the servants were quick to notice the attentions paid to Miss Bethel, and the girl's expression of adoration gave her away. There were soon whispers in the village, and nudges when Bethel, accompanied by both Veryan and Oswald, appeared at church during the occasion of Martineau's second visit. Mrs. Penrose, the vicar's wife, was the first person to tackle Bethel on the subject, and was all sympathy and understanding when told of their secret engagement which could not be announced 'just yet, because of Mama's death.'

Lerryn, of course, was highly delighted, begging to be a bridesmaid at the wedding, and astonishing Bethel further by demanding Confirmation as soon as possible.

"But why? You can be my bridesmaid without being confirmed," she laughed.

"But I couldn't be a godmother. And darling Bethel, when you have a baby I simply *must* be its godmother." And the child wondered why Bethel's face and neck should become suddenly suffused, and her head bend over the work-basket.

It was shortly after this that Bethel noticed a curious difference in old Dr. Pearce's attitude to them.

Whenever they ran across him in the village or at church, it seemed to her that he was trying to avoid them. She wondered if the rumour of her engagement had reached his ears, and that he was shocked at the idea of her sudden happiness coming so quickly upon her mother's death. Or was he offended because Mrs. Penrose had wormed the whole story from her whilst he, who had brought her into the world, had been kept in ignorance of her impending marriage?

However, there were other and more important things to think about that autumn than an old man's touchiness. Once again Cornwall was being brought into the limelight, and in November Truro's new cathedral was consecrated, which brought an even greater galaxy of famous folk to the service than the laying of the foundation stone had done. The Prince of Wales was present once more, and the Primate himself conducted the service, supported by the Bishop and other notable pillars of the church. For such an occasion Bethel thought that she and Lerryn could and should appear, and in deep mourning they took their place beside other representative families of the Duchy. It was the first time that the girls had been seen since Anna Treveryan's death, and the various people whom they saw in Truro that day seemed uncertain whether to hail Bethel with delight or give both girls wintry sympathetic smiles and quickly turn away. Suddenly Bethel felt someone touch her on the elbow as they were making their way out of the cathedral. It was Mary Rogers, whose engagement had been announced a few weeks before and who was to be married in the New Year. She showed none of the diffidence so apparent in most of Bethel's friends and acquaintances, and with a bright gleam of mischief in her eyes squeezed Bethel's arm and whispered :

" I know all about it. I'm positively thrilled ! "

Bethel looked startled and made as if to hush the other.

" It's all right. No one knows what I'm whispering about. He told Nico and he, of course, told me. My dear, what faithfulness—he must have loved you all these years ! Aren't you in a swoon of excitement ? I know I am. You know I'm marrying my Jack in January ? We're going to have a simply enormous wedding. And where do you think ? *Here !* " She babbled on, her voice now far above the whisper with which she had started. Bethel tried in vain to silence her.

" My poor dear ! I forgot ! Of course you cannot enjoy the same fun that I can, can you ? Well, rely on me, I won't utter a sound. But I am so glad you're going to be married, too. We shall have so much to tell each other," she giggled self-consciously, and then waved good-bye.

Bethel was silent as they drove away from the town.

" I don't think I like Mary Rogers very much, Beth," Lerryn suddenly remarked. Her sister looked at her with startled surprise. She had imagined her young sister to be in deep thought, remembering the great service, and was a trifle amazed to find that both of them had been thinking of Mary.

" Oh, she's all right," Bethel said with reserve.

" She's noisy and talks too much," answered the little girl.

" My ! Miss ; how you study your elders ! " Beth could not help laughing.

" Yes, I do," was the rather strange reply, uttered in most sage tones for one so young. " I write about everyone and everything I know. In my diary. Only it's a secret, and you mustn't tell anyone ever. Not even Veryan and Oswald."

" Good gracious ! But why have you told me ? "

" I don't know. Except that I love you best in the world and it's more fun to share a secret," and Lerryn slipped her arm through her sister's.

As Christmas drew near, Bethel found herself beginning to make plans for the dinner which was to be the joint celebration of Veryan's coming-of-age and her own engagement to Oswald Martineau.

" Oh, Lerryn, pet, do you imagine we could drop our black ? " she said at lunch one day, as both girls were busy making plans.

" Surely we can," said the younger in tones of rapture, and—

" Oh, Beth, you will let me stay up, won't you ? "

" Of course you shall, precious. And you shall have a new white frock, and you'll look just like a fairy queen on top of a Christmas tree, and no one will notice poor me or Veryan at all ! "

" Oh, Beth ! " And once more they fell to their task, which was the compiling of a list of names.

" The difficulty is," said Bethel, " getting the right number. We mustn't have too many as it's only to be a dinner party, and yet I know lots of people will be offended if they're not asked. And there are several of Veryan's own friends whom he wants to ask, from Oxford." She sat sucking the tip of a pencil, looking worried.

" What will you wear ? " Lerryn asked.

" I don't know. I wonder what I ought ? Not a colour."

" White—like me ? "

" No, I don't want a white frock until I have my wedding dress. Oh, Lerryn," and suddenly the puzzled frown left her face and she looked as young as Lerryn.

" What will happen to me when you're married and have gone away ? " the child asked rather plaintively.

Bethel was silent for a moment; she felt suddenly guilty. So engrossed had she been with her own happiness and thoughts of her future with Oswald, that she had not realized the little girl would miss her.

" Veryan will be here. You will have to keep house for him," she answered.

" Could I really? And stop lessons? "

It sounded a wonderful plan, Lerryn thought, and worth the departure of her sister.

" Well, I don't know about that," Bethel answered tolerantly.

" I should never have time for them, you see," Lerryn said importantly.

" Well, we'll see. We'll see what Veryan has to say when he comes home. After he's twenty-one you'll have to do everything he tells you, you know," Bethel teased.

" Oh, goodness ! Anyway I'd rather do what he tells me than old Tudor. I'm much too old for her now. Surely I needn't go on having a nurse when you are married? I know, you must have a baby at once, and then you can have Tudor, too."

At that moment Hockin came back into the dining-room and Bethel hurriedly changed the conversation.

" I shall go and ask Mrs. Penrose's advice about what colour I can wear," she said, and a few hours later the girl was sitting in close confabulation with the vicar's wife, who, sworn to secrecy, gave her full attention to the all-important matter of whether lilac or dove-grey were suitable yet girlish enough colours for a girl on such an important occasion.

PART
ONE

7

DECEMBER THE TWENTY-SECOND was the great day. A convenient date, everyone agreed, for it meant that those who had far to come (and several of Veryan's 'Varsity friends came from distant parts of England) could return to their own homes in time for Christmas, after enjoying the full extent of the Treveryan festivities—' such as they are,' Veryan added, for of course things could not be done on the scale they would have been had the family not been still in half-mourning.

The house was as full of guests as was thought fitting in the circumstances, including of course Oswald Martineau.

" How sad you have no family, darling," said Bethel, as

they sat playing picquet together after tea. " I should dearly like to have known your father and mother. And, of course, I do understand that the journey is far too long a one for your grandfather to have made. But it seems all wrong that you should have no one of your own here."

" You're all I want," he answered.

Bethel tried to look shocked.

" It's no use your trying to scold me, sweet one ! As I told you, my parents died when I was a baby. I can't even remember them, so how can I pretend to be sorry they're not with me? "

Bethel knew she had never looked better, as she glanced at herself in the long cheval mirror in her bedroom before going downstairs to receive the guests. The pale lilac taffetas suited her colouring and tall, graceful figure, down to the ground. The dress had the largest bustle she had ever worn, and the frills, she thought, trimmed with real Valenciennes lace, set the whole creation off as the best work of art that Madame Denise had ever produced.

Round her neck she wore a necklace of amethysts which had belonged to her mother, and some more lovely lace —found in one of Mama's cupboards—adorned her shoulders. She hoped that Oswald would approve of her looks, as un-known to anyone she had had her photograph taken for him in Truro, wearing the very dress. It was to be one of her Christmas presents to him. She need not have worried, for all the men gave cries of admiration as she came slowly down-stairs. She smiled at them all, but her eyes held Oswald's alone.

"Am I right in thinking we shall have other toasts to drink to-night? " asked one of Veryan's Oxford friends of him.

The young man put a finger to his lips and nodded.

" Lucky feller ! " the other ejaculated with admiration. " I wondered if that was how the wind blew when he didn't come out shooting."

Twenty-four sat round the table, which looked resplendent with all the Treveryan silver and glass, the table lit with candles and decorated with white camellias and smilax. Only young people had been asked ultimately ; it had seemed the best way, and there was less likelihood of offending ' old family friends,' the contemporaries of their parents. Bethel had been a little sad at not having the Penroses, but ' we simply cannot start making exceptions,' Veryan had said, and, of course, although she admitted this to no one, it was a relief not to have had to ask Dr. Pearce, whose strange reticence of late had not abated. However, on second thoughts, she had realized he would not have been able to come anyway, as he had been away taking the cure at Bath for some time now, and was not expected back until Christmas Eve.

The dinner was a gay and joyous affair, rather to the disapproval of Mrs. Mitchell, who hovered nearby in the background. She had never cared particularly for Anna Treveryan; but mourning was mourning and decency was decency, and for the life of her she could not understand why Mr. Veryan could not have postponed such hilarity till the summer. However, things being as they were, she had her reputation as housekeeper to keep, and she certainly saw to it that the dinner seemed a veritable banquet.

Veryan's health was drunk and speeches were made to which he fittingly replied. It was then that he broke the news of Bethel's engagement. The announcement created a considerable stir. The girl realized at once that in spite of the fact that Mary Rogers had known the secret, and one or two people in the village, the story had not spread, and had come as a great surprise to all. Congratulations were showered upon her, and many of the guests who had met Martineau at different times, warmly felicitated him.

" My word ! It's a brave man who takes it upon himself to snatch Bethel from Treveryan," said Ned Tremayne, as he shook the prospective bridegroom by the hand.

" We shall often come back here," Bethel answered, slipping her arm through Oswald's.

" How thrilling, Bethel ! I suppose you will live in London. How I envy you."

It was Mary Rogers who was speaking now. "As far as I can see, *I* shall be wedded to Cornwall for *life*," and she sighed in an affected manner. " Jack cannot *abide* town, and simply *dotes* on St. Hilary."

" We shall have to come to London in a bunch if we hear

you're likely to defend a murder trial," young Mrs. Fred Polcaster gushed.

Martineau laughed.

" That's hardly likely to be for some years yet," he said.

At that moment Veryan broke into the group surrounding the happy couple.

" I'm being neglected, this is my birthday, too ! " he cried in mock depression. " Who's for charades in the drawing-room ? "

At once there were screams of delight from the women, and groans, albeit good-hearted ones, from the men.

And so the merry evening proceeded to its end, and long after the last guests had departed the men of the house party remained cracking jokes and telling stories downstairs, and Bethel alone in her small bed upstairs sighed softly, and with happiness in her heart, went to sleep.

Only Oswald Martineau remained at Treveryan for Christmas, and it was while they were all looking at presents and cards before leaving for church that a note was brought in to Veryan.

It was from Dr. Pearce, and it had come by hand.

" Extraordinary ! " he muttered, frowning a little as he read it.

" What is the matter, Veryan," asked Bethel without paying much attention. Oswald had just given her his engagement ring, a beautiful thing of pearls and opals.

" It was my mother's," he said, as he slipped it on her finger, kissing it as he did so, " the only bit of jewellery she had."

" It's lovely ! " she answered quietly, and indeed it was the prettiest ring she had ever seen.

" I know your birthday isn't in October, sweetheart, but I'm not superstitious. Are you? " and he looked half anxiously at her.

"Anything as lovely as this could never bring ill-luck," she answered. " How you spoil me," she said a few moments later as he pinned the charming cameo brooch into the fichu she was wearing.

" That's my Christmas present," he said, " the girl's profile reminded me of you.   Only, of course, she's not as attractive."

" Flatterer ! " laughed Bethel, and gave him her presents, the photograph and an elegant tie-pin.

It was then that she had noticed Veryan's pre-occupied air.

" Some daft note from old Pearce.   The old fellow must be potty.   Says he must see me within the next couple of days. Will I look in to-morrow without fail."

He tossed the note on to the table.   Bethel could not have said whether it was a premonition of fear that took hold of her at that moment, but she turned deathly pale.   None of the others noticed it, and she was relieved when Lerryn remarked on the lateness of the hour and the importance of being punctual for church.   The Christmas hymns and the holly decorations that she and Lerryn had helped with, and the feeling of peace and goodwill in the lovely old twelfth century church soon banished the uneasiness Bethel had felt, and by the time they arrived home for a good luncheon of roast turkey and plum pudding, Dr. Pearce and his letter had been forgotten.

It was a glorious day; the slight frost which had lain on the ground during the early part of the morning had vanished, the sun shone, and there was not a cloud in the sky.

" What shall we do ? " Veryan asked after lunch.   " Why don't you take Oswald for a ride ?   He can have Vicki."

" What about you ? " his sister asked.

" Oh, I'm all right.   I've eaten too much lunch, anyway," and he yawned.

" Lazy great thing ! " Lerryn joined in.

" Hi !   Where are your manners ?   And what do you think you're going to do anyway ? "   Veryan started to pull the younger girl to him, " You won't be wanted by *them*, I warn you ! "

Lerryn wriggled herself free.

" I have my own arrangements."

" Have we indeed !   And might one enquire as to their nature ? "   He winked at Bethel and Martineau.

" Certainly you can.   I'm going for a walk with Brigit Penrose and going back to tea at the Vicarage.   So there ! "

" Don't be pert ! "   Veryan pretended to sound annoyed. At once the child flushed.

"It's all right, pet," said Bethel hurriedly. "He's only teasing."

"'Course I am. Anyway, I'm highly delighted to get rid of the pack of you and have my mansion to myself."

A little later the horses were brought round and Veryan saw them off.

"Look where you go," he said as he helped Bethel to mount. "Incidentally, where are you taking him? Show him some of the high spots, that is if he can take his attention off your noble self for a few minutes."

"How absurd you are, Veryan," Bethel said with a laugh. "Actually I have every intention of showing him the sea. I thought we'd ride out towards Nare Head."

"Lovely. Well, have a good time. I shall have a 'shut-eye' and then probably take the dogs for a walk." He waved them good-bye and saw them move off down the avenue.

⁂

PART
ONE

8

THE HORSES HAD been safely tethered to one of the stunted oak trees nearby, and Bethel and Oswald Martineau stood with the sea-wind in their faces on the headland. The gulls wheeled in the air, shrilly calling to each other, and the lovers held hands and watched a schooner in the distance making for Falmouth.

"When I realize all I am taking you away from, I wonder at my temerity," Oswald said presently.

"Darling Oswald! I wish you wouldn't worry so much. Surely by now I've managed to convince you of how much I love you."

"You have, dearest—it isn't that . . ."

"I'm not a child any longer. I know my own mind."

"Yes, I think you do. But I'm beset with fears that you will be homesick, Treveryan-sick."

"Even if I were—and I shan't be—your love is strong enough to fight it. I couldn't lose you now."

"My Bethel, my dear love," he murmured, and they walked on a little further to where there stood a gate.

"Where does that lead?" he asked.

" To the ruins of a little cell. They say it belonged to a hermit; there's a well, too. Saint Perri, he was called."

" Never heard of him."

" There were lots of Cornish saints. I don't suppose you have heard of many of them. Come, I'll show it to you." They scrambled down the footpath which was cut in the face of the cliff, and presently, in a hollow, came across the disused well and the ruins of the ancient sanctuary. Ivy had grown over the stone walls which crumbled at the merest touch, but a cross hewn in stone was still visible, as well as what might have been the remains of a carved figure. A robin sang lustily from the naked branches of the dwarf oak tree close to the entrance, and seemed in no way disturbed by the strange appearance of two human beings. Oswald and Bethel remained in silence for several minutes, and then he said :

" I don't think I've ever been in a more enchanted place. Your old saint has left his holiness here."

" He's buried here, but his grave is so grown over that you couldn't find it. Dear old man."

" I'm glad they haven't tried to restore it. It's so peaceful."

" There will soon be nothing at all left, I fear," remarked Bethel.

" Forgotten . . ." Oswald seemed suddenly distrait, and for quite a long time remained in silence.

" It's getting cold," Bethel said presently, " and the sun has gone down. We must get back or we shall be late. It will take us every bit of half an hour to get home, and there's a lovely Christmas cake for tea."

Oswald sighed, as if loath to go.

" I'm glad we came. I'm glad you showed it to me. I shall always remember this place. Saint Perri . . ." he murmured the name softly. " I wish there was something to take away; I should like something by which to remember Saint Perri's resting-place."

But there was nothing they could take it seemed, so——

" Kiss me instead," he said.

" Do you think one ought ? " Bethel was not at all sure such an act in such a place might not amount to sacrilege.

" Of course we ought. In fact, I should like our marriage to take place in this little cell," and he drew her close to his heart.

" Oh, my darling, how romantic that would be. And how surprised, and probably shocked, everyone would be. Imagine it, after Mary's grand wedding in the cathedral ! "

" Give me this," said Oswald, looking round once more. " Yes, I think I shall abduct you and get an old friar to wed us in the middle of the night, as Friar Laurence married Romeo to Juliet."

" You forget they were unable to be married anywhere else," objected Bethel. Oswald smiled.

" I suppose all women want a big fuss, and a lot of billowy satin and bridesmaids, and the whole shoot."

Bethel squeezed his hand.

" Perhaps," she laughed softly. " But come on, we must go."

" One more kiss then," he said, and when he had released her he took her hand and kissed the ring he had placed on her finger in the morning, and said :

" With this ring I thee love, and with my body I thee worship," but Bethel suddenly withdrew her hand and ran from the cell. He followed her, calling :

" What's the matter ? Why do you run away ? I didn't scare you, did I ? "

" I wish you hadn't done that. I wish you hadn't spoken those words," she said.

" But why ? " he said, amazed.

" I don't know. But I'm sure it's unlucky," her face had gone pale and she spoke with a troubled air.

" How could they be unlucky ? I do love you, and my body worships yours. What's unlucky in that ? "

At that moment the sun dipped behind the clouds in distant Roseland, and a bird flew across their path. A feather dropped from it and Oswald bent to pick it up.

" Here is a keepsake after all," he cried. Bethel turned and recoiled in horror.

" It's a magpie's feather ! " she said.

" Well ? I think it's lovely ! "

" Was it alone ? "

" Yes, surely you saw it ? "

" No, I never noticed it. I realized a large bird flew out of the trees, that was all. But one magpie is terribly unlucky, surely you know the old saying, ' one for sorrow, two for joy '? ''

" You *are* superstitious, darling! '' laughed Oswald. " I suppose that's the Cornish in you.''

" I am Cornish," Bethel replied.

They walked on in silence.

" If you love me you'll throw the horrid thing away," she said as they reached the gate at the top of the hill.

" No, Bethel, I'm hanged if I'll do anything so ridiculous. You really mustn't be so childish."

Bethel led the way back to where the horses were standing. She was near to tears. It was unbearable that Oswald should think a very real fear was nothing but a childish fancy. Coming on top of his words in the hermit's cell as it did, she was sure it meant no good.

The delight of the afternoon was spoilt now, or certainly would be if he kept the ill-omened thing, she told herself.

They reached the horses, and Oswald went forward to help her mount. He noticed the unshed tears glistening in her eyes.

" Baby! " he whispered.

" *Please*—Oswald." She looked at him beseechingly. " Please throw away the magpie's feather."

" Very well." As they rode slowly down the lane he took it from his pocket.

" There! " He blew it from his hands and it sailed away on the wind for a few seconds and then fell into a ditch.

" Happy now? " he asked.

She nodded and laughed.

" Forgiven? " she asked.

A little while later they sat in front of a big log fire in the library of Treveryan eating saffron buns and Christmas plum cake, and the magpie was forgotten.

" Where's Veryan I wonder? " Oswald asked presently, as Bethel poured out a second cup of tea for him.

" He doesn't always put in an appearance at this hour," she said. " Didn't he say he was going to exercise the dogs? He'll probably shut himself into his study and write. He must have a good many birthday letters to answer."

After Hockin had cleared away the tea she brought a cushion and sat down near his feet, resting her arm upon his knee.

Only the crackling of the logs broke the stillness in the room. Presently Bethel sighed deeply and happily.

" I was thinking," she said. " I was wondering if we could look into the future what should we see? Christmas twenty years hence. Shall we be together like this, I at your feet, utterly content, or will you be a terribly important person, and I be busy over the final preparations for an enormous dinner party. Which picture do you like best? " and she stared into the fire.

" The first," he answered, stroking her hair, " but I am ambitious, too. I should like to be famous so that I could give you everything in the world you want."

" I remember your telling me you were ambitious. It was ages before you fell in love with me, so don't pretend, and make an excuse of me ! "

He smiled.

" All men should be ambitious," he said.

" I don't think Veryan is," she said.

" He's different. He has all this. In a way that's ambition fulfilled. He'll have his hands full looking after it. He tells me he intends to be his own agent."

" That's so. But he knows every inch of the place and adores it. He'll do well."

Oswald thought he detected a tiny sigh. Once more he was haunted by the spectre of failure.

" Do you know what I should have done if you'd said you would not marry me ? " he said a little later.

" No, what ? "

" I should have gone to India. I had a wonderful opportunity to go out there."

" When ? "

" Recently."

" And you refused it? Because of me? " She knelt upright, looking into his eyes. He nodded.

" I couldn't have taken you," he said, " or rather, I wouldn't have. Most of my duties would have taken me to the plains and worst climate of the country. It would have been rank cruelty to take you from here to a place from which you couldn't get away."

" India . . ." She said the word slowly, and then repeated it.

" You're right, Oswald," she continued a minute or two later, " I should hate to leave England.   I don't think I could bear it . . . yet.   Perhaps one day . . . Oh, Oswald, dear heart, I pray I shan't be a selfish wife.   Promise me you won't let me get in the way of your work.   I should hate myself for ever if you sacrificed yourself in anything, just in order to suit me.   Did you want to go to India?   Are you disappointed? "

He shook his head.

" Not I," he answered with a smile.   " With you beside me I have every intention of remaining in my native land and ending up as the Lord Chief Justice ! "

Bethel sprang to her feet.

" May heaven forbid ! " she laughed.   " And now I will take you on at chess and beat you before we have to change for dinner.

Bethel looked at the clock.   It was after half-past seven.

" I wonder where my naughty young brother is ? " she said, as she started putting away the chessmen.   " He generally comes in to see us before this."

At that moment there was a bang from the outer door.

" That must be he.   Veryan ! " she called.

But, although they could hear his footsteps as he crossed the stone flags of the hall, he did not answer.

As Bethel was changing for dinner there came presently a knock on the door.

" Come in," she called, knowing it was Lerryn come to bid her good night.

" Well, my sweet?   Did you have a nice afternoon? " she asked.

" Yes, very nice," Lerryn answered, seeming preoccupied. As she turned to go she looked at Bethel and asked timidly :

" What's the matter with Veryan? "

" The matter?   Is anything the matter?   I've not seen him for hours."

" He's only just come in," Lerryn said, " and he's in an awful way over something."

" What do you mean? "

" He's all wet for one thing," Lerryn answered.

" Wet?   How can he be? "

" It's pouring with rain."

" Raining? But it's been a heavenly afternoon. I don't believe it."

" I can't help that, it's been raining for the last two hours."

" Well, I suppose he's been out in it," Bethel said, " nothing very awful in that. He may have gone out without a coat and got chilled, silly boy. I expect that's all," she rose and patted the frock she had put on, arranging it in front of the mirror.

" I don't think so. He looks *awful*. As if he had seen a ghost or something."

" Come Lerryn, don't be such a goose! I think you and Brigit have been telling ghost stories, isn't that it? I don't know what Oswald would say to you. He was so cross with me when I was frightened by one magpie this afternoon."

" I hope Veryan isn't ill. Why should he have gone to Dr. Pearce? "

Bethel turned sharply.

" Dr. Pearce? How do you know he went to see Dr. Pearce? "

" Brigit saw him."

Bethel suddenly felt frightened. There was really no reason to be alarmed, she told herself, but Dr. Pearce's behaviour of late had been odd to say the least of it. And then she remembered the note, sent by hand this morning. Why should he want to see Veryan so urgently?

" I don't suppose it's anything very much," she told Lerryn, and opened the door. " Probably someone in the village has had an accident or something. We forget now that Veryan is of age he starts to take new responsibilities on his shoulders."

Yes, that was it, she tried to reason to herself, as she made her way downstairs.

Oswald was in the library alone.

" I think Veryan got caught in the rain," Bethel began apologetically, " Lerryn tells me the weather has suddenly changed. I don't suppose he will be very late though."

Just then Hockin entered the room.

" Mr. Veryan says will you please start dinner without him. He will be down as quickly as he can."

Bethel shrugged her shoulders. " Come on then," she

called to Oswald, and they followed old Hockin into the dining-room.

They had finished soup when Veryan appeared. Even Oswald could see that something was amiss, but deemed it prudent to say nothing. One look at his haggard face and distraught expression was enough for Bethel. Something appalling must have happened, she told herself. All colour left her face, and her hand trembled as she raised a glass of claret to her lips. Veryan asked them how they had enjoyed the afternoon, but it was obvious he was paying little, if any, attention to Martineau, and deathly silences ensued throughout the meal. Bethel noticed that he left practically everything on his plate untouched, yet his glass was filled again and again. Suddenly an idea struck her. Was he in trouble? Had he got some girl in the village into trouble? She had only a hazy idea as to what that meant, but it could account for Dr. Pearce's urgent summons, and for his behaviour now. Poor, darling Veryan, she was sure, would never harm anyone. Words of which she knew not the meaning flashed through her mind. Blackmail? What was blackmail? Mechanically she turned from the dessert which Hockin handed her.

In silence they rose from the table and Bethel crossed the room.

" Don't be too long," she said, as Veryan opened the door for her.

Veryan closed the door and made his way back to the table, pouring himself out another glass of port before sitting down. Oswald looked at the young man with curiosity.

" I should go slowly with that, old fellow," he said kindly. " I don't know what's up, but I can see you're upset about something. Too much of that won't really help, you know."

Veryan glanced up at him. He looked distrait and as if he had not heard Oswald's words.

" Can I help you? " Oswald asked. "After all," he continued, for Veryan still remained in silence, " you know you can look on me as an elder brother from now on."

To his dismay Veryan shuddered and buried his face in his hands.

" I can't. That's it. You must get that out of your head once and for all."

" What on earth are you talking about ? "

" You and Bethel. You cannot marry. You must not."

" For God's sake pull yourself together and don't act like a madman," Oswald Martineau said, and shook Veryan roughly by the shoulders. That seemed to sober the boy. He looked at Martineau and there was horror in his voice as he spoke.

" I heard to-day . . ." his speech came slowly and was little more than a whisper, " that my father died insane. But hopelessly and incurably insane. It's in our family . . ." His voice began to rise with anguish as he seemed to take in himself the dreadful words.

Oswald Martineau remained speechless, dumbfounded.

" My mother knew," he continued, " but would not allow us to be told. I was to know when I came of age. That was what the old doctor wanted to see me about so urgently."

" Go on," said Martineau tonelessly.

" When you both went off this afternoon I never intended going to see him. Then later I thought I'd take the dogs for a stroll. Without really thinking where I was going, I found myself a hundred yards from old Pearce's house. Then I remembered his letter, and I thought I might as well go in as I was so close. They were just sitting down to their tea —there was a huge Christmas cake for their grandchildren. Christmas Day! Oh, God ! "

" Yes. Go on, Veryan," Martineau urged, and poured himself out another drink.

" The old man looked pretty surprised to see me. He seemed upset, too, and said he hadn't meant me to bother about coming to-day, he'd said to-morrow. Then he wanted to know if it was true about Beth—and you. I said yes, and wasn't it great, and the rest of it. I thought it damn odd he didn't seem to see it like that, nor send Beth congratulations. However, we couldn't talk much, the children were making a row and pulling crackers and one thing and another, and then he took me to his consulting room and told me. My great-grandfather married his cousin, the bad streak came from her side of the family. There's a picture of her in the library, Tregony Treveryan. She was lovely and she was all right, but one of her children was frightful—a monster; luckily it was all kept very quiet, hardly anyone knew about that. It died before it grew up. My grandfather was healthy enough until he was wounded and blinded at Waterloo, but mentally nothing was wrong with him. But he had a sister—Blanche —apparently she was queer, too; had bouts of it, had to be locked up from time to time. She wasn't dangerous, but beastly, poor thing. But only sometimes. My father was an only child. He seemed absolutely all right, Pearce told me, until a few years before he died, when he became frightfully morose and insisted upon shutting himself up and seeing no one. He never knew about the madness until after he had married it seems. He married Mama very suddenly; met her and fell in love with her before he told my grandmother anything about it."

" Do you suppose she knew? "

" My grandmother? I don't know. I didn't ask. Probably not—after all, my grandfather was all right."

" That was why your mother was so unaccountably strange about Bethel and myself," said Martineau.

" Poor Mama! Can't you see how frightful the whole thing must have been for her? Oswald, he tried to kill her! "

The other man started back in horror.

"Apparently he was shut up in his room writing as usual, and Mama went in and disturbed him. So he said. But she always went in there and took him his tea. He adored her. He never took any notice of any of us; but he worshipped Mama in a strange, cold sort of way. But, anyway, apparently he just went across the room and started to strangle her. She fought herself free and started to scream. Old Mrs. Mitchell was in a room across the passage, luckily, and heard her, otherwise he'd have killed her. Then they sent for Pearce. God! I remember the day. We always wondered why Papa's illness and death were kept so secret from us. Bethel said she wondered if it was small-pox. I remember her voice quite distinctly—small-pox! Would that it had been! We were sent away to Mama's mother, we hardly knew her. She had never cared for Mama's marriage, nor taken to Papa. We were only there a few months."

" Did your mother remain with him? "

" Yes, incredibly, she did. He had two male nurses, and of course he was unable to make any further attempts on her life. Old Pearce wouldn't tell me much more. He said it could only be painful and would serve no purpose. I gather it all got pretty frightful. It was God's mercy he died."

" How did the doctor know so much about your antecedents ? "

" Oh, the practice has been in his family for generations. Father to son sort of thing—you know."

Veryan stopped talking and laid his head wearily on the table.

" What are we going to tell Bethel ? " he mumbled. " She'll have to know. Apparently the reason Pearce wanted to see me so urgently was that I should know before a public announcement is made in the papers of your engagement. Oh, God . . . ! "

Oswald began to think rapidly.

" Shall we tell her you have consumption in the family ? Oh, it's monstrous, it's devilish. I love your sister. I don't believe . . ." he began incoherently.

" Do you still love her ? " Veryan asked slowly. " In spite of what you've heard ? "

" Good God, yes ! " the other replied impatiently.

" Marry her. Now. At once. Before anyone can do anything to stop it ! " Veryan spoke urgently.

Oswald started to pace the room. Every conceivable emotion fought together in his heart. Horror was mingled with pity, love with wisdom; above all, he was not even certain that he knew what he wanted. Veryan's words hammered his brain.

" Is that what you would do if you were in my place ? " he suddenly asked.

" Yes. No. I don't know . . . I've never been in love. I can't tell."

" We should never be able to have children," Oswald Martineau said slowly.

" Bethel would hate that," her brother said.

" She's twenty-five. We must tell her the truth. She can choose." Martineau spoke slowly. He knew that for once he was afraid. Let the decision rest with Bethel.

" I thought you two were never coming," she said, when they reached the library.

They said nothing.

"Please tell me what's the matter?" she asked. "I can bear anything. It's just this horrible suspense, knowing something is worrying Veryan, that I cannot bear."

"You will have to be very brave, sweetheart," Oswald began. "Veryan heard some very bad news to-day. It concerns you all, as a matter of fact; but you—I will say us—more immediately."

"What sort of news?" she asked, and felt an icy, unknown fear clutch at her heart.

"You tell her," Oswald said.

There was a moment's pause and then Veryan spoke.

"It was about Papa."

"*Papa?*" What news about their father learnt now could be so very frightful?

"Bethel . . ." Veryan spoke with difficulty, "Papa died of —of an inherited disease."

"Oh! But what of it? I don't quite understand."

"It's something that we have in our family."

"But lots of people have things in their family. What's all the bother about? Look at the Coombes in the village, they've had consumption for generations. Nobody really cares. Don't look so serious, darling! Poor Papa! Did he die of that? I don't think one should pay much attention to these sort of things when one is young and healthy. Good gracious, how morbid we should all become if we sat around wondering what family ailment was likely to carry us off in old age. As long as madness isn't in one's family I don't think we should worry. That indeed . . ." her voice trailed off, and in the ensuing silence, broken only by the ticking of the grandfather clock, Bethel stood as if frozen and rooted to the ground on which she stood. Gradually her voice came back to her, and she turned facing both men.

"Is that it?" she whispered in terror.

Veryan nodded slowly, and Oswald caught her as she fell.

When Bethel came round she found she was in her own room. Someone must have carried her upstairs, for she was on her bed, the quilt over her. For a moment she could not think what had happened, and then the full horror of Veryan's revelation burst upon her afresh and she started from the bed with a little cry.

"I'm here," it was Veryan's voice, and he came quietly to the side of the bed.

"Tell me it's not true. Tell me I've been dreaming," she begged.

"Would to God I could!" he said brokenly.

For a little while she lay back on her pillow, as if stunned. And then as the realization of all it meant pierced her mind she flung herself into Veryan's arms in a paroxysm of tears. Veryan held her gently, soothing her as best he could. The shock had been appalling to him, but he knew that it must come worse to Bethel now.

In about half an hour her sobs subsided and she lay back exhausted.

"Insanity . . . madness . . ." the words tumbled from her lips. "Veryan, it can't be true. Who told you? Who can know?" And so, once more, Veryan poured the long story forth. It was nearly three o'clock when he had finished talking.

Bethel got up from the bed and walked over to the fire, where some embers still showed a dim light. She felt desperately cold.

"What does one do?" She spoke at random.

"There's nothing we can do," Veryan answered in a tired voice.

"What shall we tell Lerryn?"

"Lerryn?" He had forgotten all about her. How like Bethel to remember Lerryn in the midst of this hideous misery to herself.

"We must keep it from her. She must never know. It would probably prey on her mind and drive her crazy,"

As the full portent of her own words struck her she shuddered. She had spoken naturally, without thinking.

"Never mind about her now. What about you? And Oswald?" He swallowed as he forced himself to speak such words to her.

"That's over. That's all about me. I must forget it, forget Oswald." As if she could ever forget him. . . . "And he must forget me. He must take that job in India.

He must leave me, he must leave England. I could not bear
it if I thought he was in England and I couldn't see him. We
must say good-bye to each other. For ever." Good-bye.
Dear God . . .

She wondered how she was managing to speak to Veryan as
she was. Perhaps none of it was true. Perhaps it was really
all a hideous nightmare. She clasped and unclasped her hands.
She felt the ring upon her finger. The ring he had given her
only this morning. She looked at it. Opal—yes, that had
brought her bad luck. She started to remember other things
then; the magpie, the queer, unreasonable fear she had felt as
Oswald had murmured those words from the marriage service
to her in the hermit's cell. It was true then. And people
were right to be superstitious. She would never laugh at such
things again, she had always known in her heart that some
truth must be attached to the old sayings. She was right, she
had always been right. Cornish people knew. It was Oswald
who had laughed at her who was wrong after all. Oswald.
Oswald . . .

"I'm so tired," she said suddenly, and groped her way back
to the bed.

"Let me help you undress," Veryan said. Without waiting
for her to answer he started to unhook her dress. He pulled
her clothes off one by one. She seemed helpless, like a little
child.

"Would you like me to sleep with you," he asked.

"No, I'm all right." He helped her get into the bed, and
covered the clothes about her. She looked as if she were
already asleep when he tiptoed from the room.

They made her stay in bed next day. During the morning
Veryan told Oswald Martineau of his talk with Bethel.

"Does she want me to go?" he asked, bewildered.

"I don't think she really knows what she wants," Veryan
replied. "Poor darling, how can she?" And then, after a
pause, "I wonder if Dr. Pearce ought to have a look at her."

But when Veryan mentioned this idea later to her, Bethel
shrank from the suggestion.

"I'm all right," she said. "I'll get up after lunch and come
downstairs. We don't want to have the servants talking; I've
never been ill in my life. Besides, there's Lerryn to think about."

Veryan shrugged his shoulders. He felt that she must know best what to do for herself.

The rest of the day passed like a nightmare. Conversation was embarrassingly and horribly strained. Already Oswald felt an estrangement between himself and Bethel, they were both on edge, yet dare not pull down the barriers that had sprung up between them. They were not helped by Lerryn who, knowing nothing, and having forgotten Veryan's anguished appearance of the evening before, kept putting questions to Bethel and Oswald about their future, and plans for the wedding.

Just before tea the clang of the front door bell announced the arrival of visitors, and Veryan only just managed to stop Hockin from admitting the callers.

" I expect it was someone coming to congratulate you, Beth," remarked the younger girl. " Why don't you want to see anyone? It's Boxing Day, and there's plenty to eat. I saw such a quantity of cakes down in the stillroom."

" Oswald goes to-morrow," Bethel found herself saying, " I want him to myself," for the last time, a voice cried in her heart.

Lerryn looked surprised.

" But I thought you weren't going till the end of the week," she said.

" It's bad luck, Lerryn. I find I have to go much sooner than I expected."

Bethel got up and left the room. She felt that in another moment she would have screamed. Talk, talk, talk . . . Oh, would it ever come to an end? The way in which they were all calmly discussing plans and everyday matters . . . she could not bear it. The sooner the end came for her the better. Better for Oswald, too, she was sure. Life would be over for her when he departed from Treveryan, but anything would be preferable to these hours of torture.

That night after dinner Veryan excused himself on the ground that he had important letters to write. Both Bethel and Oswald were grateful for what they knew to be merely an excuse to leave them together.

" Do you really want me to go? " he asked, as they stood together by the fireplace. Above hung the portrait of

Tregony Treveryan. Bethel nodded. Suddenly her eyes
rested on the picture.

"Your fault," she said slowly, bitterly. "I've always loved
you, thought you so pretty, longed to have been called Tregony
instead of Bethel. Oh, how I hate you now!"

Oswald caught hold of her, pressing her passionately, and
kissed her forehead.

"Darling, my darling! I shan't give you up. We'll not
think of it. You don't realize what you said when you told
Veryan you wanted me to go. Marry me Bethel beloved,
soon, now. Good heavens! I don't care with what blood
your family has been tainted in the past. Forget it, sweet . . ."

She broke away from him in horror.

"How can you ask such a thing?" she cried. "It would
be wicked, criminal, insane——" once more the full meaning
of the word struck her as she sank on to the sofa.

"How could we bring more children into the world diseased
and fouled as they would be? How can any of us dream of
marrying? No, this must be the end. Treveryan must finish
with us. As long as the three of us are alive, Veryan and
Lerryn and I must dedicate ourselves to each other, and to—
Treveryan alone." Her voice sank in a whisper. "Don't
you realize," she continued, "that any of us may become like
my father? That even I . . . Oh, Oswald . . ." A look of
such fear came into her face that he hastened to her side and
once more gathered her into his arms.

"Calm yourself, dear love, I beseech you," he begged.

"I'm better now," she said quickly a little later. "And
now I want you to say good night to me. And . . . good-bye.
I cannot bear this. The thought of losing you for ever is
worse than death to me. Far, far worse. If only I could
die . . ."

"Don't talk like that," Oswald said hoarsely.

"Why not? What have I to live for? *What have I?*
Remember us, my darling, as you know us now, young and—
gay," here she laughed bitterly, "remember us—but no,
forget us. Forget us quickly. Forget me. Forget the mad
woman you so nearly married but from whom Fate mercifully
saved you——"

"I shall never forget you. Always, always in my heart I

shall hold you, keep you, worship you. Till death us do part. Bethel, my beloved——"

He caught hold of her as if he would never let her go.

" I, too," she whispered, " I love you, now and for always."

They clung together for a while, and then——

" Go. Go to Veryan——"

She never saw him leave the room, nor did she know how she ever reached her own.

He had gone when she came downstairs the following day. Lerryn, who was in the library, looked at her and said nothing. She was frightened by the pallor of Bethel's face and the hollow, darkened rings below her eyes, but Veryan had warned her that she must not talk about Oswald, and she sensed something was more amiss than that he had merely gone back as usual.

" I'm going to lie down," Bethel said after lunch. It was a stormy day, rain pattered against the panes in the windows, and Veryan pressed his sister to rest.

It was late in the evening when they noticed her disappearance. They had not been surprised when she had not come downstairs to tea, and it was when Lerryn had gone to her sister's room and found the bed unslept in that he ran to Veryan in consternation.

At once a search party was formed. The grounds were hunted and scoured, but it was not until ten o'clock in the evening that Veryan himself found her, lying in the reeds down by the lake. She was alive, but completely unconscious. She wore no hat and her cape was torn, her body soaked from the storm and lake water. It seemed a miracle to Veryan that she was not drowned.

They carried her back to the house and Dr. Pearce was immediately sent for.

For several days neither Veryan nor the doctor was far from her side.

" Will she pull through? " he kept asking in agony.

" I think so, I think so," the old man would murmur.

When the congestion of the lungs finally eased, it was her brain that appeared affected. Veryan looked at the doctor with terror.

" No, no," he said in reassurance to the boy's unasked question.

" Your sister is very ill. She's suffering from brain fever. Don't alarm yourself unduly. I'm not surprised when I think of all she has gone through. It's a wonder she's alive after her ordeal in the storm."

" I'm sure she meant to kill herself," said Veryan brokenly.

" We don't know, we mustn't assume that. It's more likely she was beside herself with grief, and just did not know what she was doing. She slipped and fell. Her ankle was badly sprained, you know. One must be thankful she lay by the lake and not by the seashore."

Through weeks of delirium Bethel lay, calling on Oswald or Veryan, or her father.

" Why does she keep calling for Tregony," asked the nurse, " it's the village, isn't it ? "

No one seemed to know the answer.

PART TWO

I

ON A WET afternoon during the summer of 1900, a group of women were sitting round the table of the big, disused dining-room of Castle St. Hilary. On the large table were spread bundles of bandages of every size, and garments of different kinds in the making. Desultory conversation started from time to time, but for the most part the women stuck busily to their work, and seemed too preoccupied to talk much.

At the head of the table Lady St. Hilary presided. A vast change could be noticed in her since the days when, as Mary Rogers, she had danced and hunted her way through the early 'eighties, till finally, falling in love with Jack St. Hilary, she had married him in the Cathedral, at what was long afterwards discussed as the biggest and most glittering wedding the county had witnessed for half a century. Her white apron almost hid her mourning; but there was no hiding the sadness in her face. Jack St. Hilary had been killed last December with Buller's forces on the Tugela river, and Nicolas, her brother, at Mafeking. The war had lasted many months now, and there seemed no hope of an early peace. For seven months Mary

St. Hilary had presided at the weekly work-parties held at the Castle since their inauguration, and every third week a handsome consignment of comforts for the wounded were dispatched by herself and other ladies to the Guild which undertook their safe delivery.

At half-past four the party ceased, and the workers began to put away their things, fold up the remaining garments, and collect their clothes.

Most of the women left, and only one or two of Mary St. Hilary's 'specials' remained behind for tea.

"Come and tell me how London was looking," she asked Mrs. Trehearne, a newcomer to the neighbourhood, whose husband was also fighting.

"London was great fun," she replied, "no one would think there was a war on."

"How dreadful!" said Mary.

"I suppose if one hadn't relations or friends in the midst of it all one wouldn't think of it a great deal," one of the other women remarked, "after all, one must remember that South Africa is a long way off."

"Of course, everyone talks of the war," continued Mabel Trehearne, "what I mean is that life goes on the same. The theatres are crowded, shops full of the loveliest clothes. By the way," she said, taking another bun, "I travelled from Exeter on with such a charming girl. She comes from Cornwall, we got talking somehow, I wish I'd asked her who she was. I'm sure you'd know her. Very pretty. She kept her gloves on, so I don't know if she was married."

"I wonder who she was? Young?"

"In her twenties, I should say. Very fair."

"Did she get out with you?"

"No, I think she got out at Grampound Road."

"My dear, could it be?" another woman, Mrs. Gendall-Jones looked at Mary knowingly.

"*I wonder.*" Lady St. Hilary suddenly lost her air of sadness and became alert and interested.

"You're both very mysterious," Mabel Trehearne said.

"We're intrigued. Try and remember more," they answered.

"Did she mention her family?" it was Norah Tonkin, the secretary of the work party who spoke now.

"You know who we mean?" Mary asked.

"I imagine you think it might have been Lerryn Treveryan."

"Lerryn Treveryan? What a marvellously romantic name! Do tell me about her, who is she?" Mrs. Trehearne asked with curiosity.

She was a little surprised by the air of silence which greeted her innocent question.

"What *has* happened to them, Mary? You knew them better than anyone else," Gladys Gendall-Jones said.

Mary shrugged her shoulders.

"I don't know more than anyone else does. The whole business was just one of these inexplicable mysteries of which one remains in complete ignorance."

"I heard *he* had gone to South Africa with the Imperial Yeomanry," said Miss Tonkin with slight relish. It was always gratifying to be able to tell someone like Lady St. Hilary something she did not know herself.

"He?" both women exclaimed.

"The brother. Veryan Treveryan," she answered.

"Who told you? How do you know?"

"I don't remember, but I heard it some time ago. He went out in the spring I think."

"How extraordinary!" There was a long pause.

"Oh, *do* tell me what you're all talking about!" begged Mabel Trehearne, "I'm intrigued to death and, after all, I did tell you about her."

"Her?"

"Miss Lerryn What's-her-name."

"Oh, Lerryn? Yes—Lerryn." Lady St. Hilary's voice tailed off. For a minute or two she seemed miles away.

"Did she seem happy? Well?" she then asked.

"I think so. She had nice clothes. I particularly admired her dress. I should have looked a fright in it, but it looked lovely on her. Liberty's, I'm sure."

"Lerryn can't be very old, can she? Time does fly . . ."

"How old was she when . . .?"

Once again Mrs. Trehearne felt she was on the fringe of

some strange scandal about which they wished to keep her in ignorance.

"I suppose you didn't see who met her at the station?" someone asked.

"No, I didn't."

"Wasn't your brother a friend of—the man?" Gladys Gendall-Jones asked Mary St. Hilary.

"Yes, indeed. You know he went to India? Oh, yes, almost immediately. Nico saw him once or twice out there. He's done frightfully well."

"Really? Perhaps it was all for the best."

"I suppose one will never know the truth . . ."

Just then the door opened and Mary St. Hilary's children came into the room. Silently and politely they shook hands with their mother's friends, and then went over and settled themselves with toys in a corner of the room. Mabel Trehearne rose.

"Well, I must go," she said, "it's been very nice chatting over this mysterious train lady, I don't seem to have learnt much, however! Good-bye, my dear, and thank you for my nice tea. See you next week."

As she ran down the castle steps she heard the front door shut again, and found Miss Tonkin on her heels.

"I thought we might as well walk back together," she said. "Extraordinary business all that was!"

Mabel Trehearne knew instinctively to whom Norah Tonkin was alluding.

"Yes?" she encouraged.

"That girl you met. It must have been the younger Treveryan."

"And who are the Treveryans?"

"Do you mean you have not heard of the Treveryans? Or Treveryan?" The woman seemed vastly surprised, and then added, "But of course it's all so long ago. Long before you came to Cornwall. They're forgotten. As I imagine they wish to be."

"But who are they?"

"Treveryan used to be one of the show places of Cornwall. It really was—is, still, no doubt—a very remarkable house. Very beautiful indeed." She paused as if to let her words sink into her hearer's ears. It was not often Norah Tonkin had an audience to anything she wished to say, and she was going to make the most of it.

"The family has lived there for centuries," she continued. "The present lot consists of the girl you probably saw, the brother Veryan, who is the present owner, and the elder Miss Treveryan; Bethel Treveryan." She said the name slowly and with relish.

"Yes? Do go on."

"The late Mr. and Mrs. Treveryan died when their children were comparatively young. No one ever knew what *he* really died of, in spite of queer rumours. They were a strange couple. She was very stuck-up, I believe, though beautiful—she died of typhoid. Anyway, at a party given a few months later, for young Treveryan's coming-of-age, Bethel's engagement to a friend of the Rogers' was announced. His name was Martineau, Oswald Martineau, you've probably heard of him. *But*—and this is where the mystery begins and really ends—no further announcement was made; Bethel Treveryan became desperately ill, the man went off, nothing further happened, and the entire family *have shut themselves up ever since.*"

"Shut themselves up?"

"That all happened over the Christmas of '87 and early part of '88, thirteen years ago. And not a soul is supposed to have seen Bethel Treveryan since, I give you my word for it."

"What an extraordinary story! Didn't it all give rise to a great deal of gossip?"

"Gossip! I should say it did," Miss Tonkin was thoroughly enjoying the conversation; "of course everyone was very sorry for Miss Treveryan to begin with, being so ill and that, but when as months passed and she refused to see any of her old friends or anyone, naturally a good deal of talk started."

"What sort of—talk?" Mabel Trehearne wondered why the strange story interested her so much. She supposed it was because of running into one of the family in the train.

"Oh, well . . ." the other woman hesitated, "I've really rather forgotten. It all happened so long ago. There were various ideas and opinions about the whole thing I do remember. The man going off to India, for one thing.

Some people said that, of course, he had chucked her, and there were others who said that Bethel Treveryan had given him up because of his appointment out there. Quite a number of people thought that, I fancy. She was always a very odd creature. Morbidly fond of her home and her brother, I've heard it said."

" But what about the brother and the girl I met in the train? Have they never married? She was so very pretty, I thought," Mabel Trehearne said.

" I can only tell you, Mrs. Trehearne, that practically no one sees any of them. They go nowhere, and not a soul is ever invited to Treveryan. I'm told that Miss Treveryan gives up a good deal of time to good works. Now, of course, Veryan Treveryan is at the war. And a very good thing, too."

By this time the two women had reached the cross roads where their paths diverged, and each bade the other a good evening.

And not so very far away, a few miles at the most, the two Treveryan women were at that moment busily putting away jam in the store-cupboard which led from the stillroom of Treveryan House. Bethel stood mounted on a pair of steps, while the younger sister handed up the jars to her.

" That's the last half dozen plum," said Lerryn, " do you feel up to starting on the apple jelly? "

" Now that we're here and I have the key, we may as well go on," Bethel Treveryan replied, " there's not such a very great deal either, is there? " She looked down to where her sister was perched on the side of a table.

" I shouldn't sit on the edge if I were you, that table's not too strong."

Obediently the other moved away.

" Two dozen pots. Come on then," and once again she handed the large two-pound jars, one by one, to her sister.

" It's a lovely evening," she said, " it seems a waste to be indoors."

" S'sh. Don't talk. I'm counting." Bethel's preoccupation seemed very unnecessary to her younger sister and she sighed with relief when the last pot had been put away, the cupboard closed and locked, and Bethel had descended the steps.

"There!" said the latter, "nobody should want this year. I do hope dear Mrs. Penrose won't be as silly as she was last year and forget to tell me if the wretched Ticketts are in want again. I fear that new wife of Hugo Tickett is an unfortunate creature and not much of a stepmother to poor Bella's children."

As they made their way upstairs Lerryn Treveryan could not help wishing that she could share her sister's obvious interest in the people of the village. It was no good, she simply could not absorb herself in the new arrival of a small Libby or Toms, any more than she could listen for hours to dear old Mrs. Puckey with her long stories of the latter's rheumatics. And as to being able to copy Bethel in the manner in which she would frequently sit up all night in someone's cottage when a death was expected—no! That was quite beyond her.

They reached the hall where the afternoon's post was still lying unread and untouched.

A large box lay on the table.

"Another new dress?" Bethel's eyebrows lifted. Lerryn blushed.

"I couldn't resist just sending for it on approval, Beth. It's one out of Liberty's catalogue, and I do love their things so much." She spoke apologetically. Bethel shrugged her shoulders.

"My dear, if you like wasting your money on clothes no one ever sees . . ."

Lerryn bit her lip. How maddening darling Beth could be. Yet only when she was tired. The hateful jam business had done it, two hours they had been in that dreary little room. She resisted the temptation to argue with her sister, much as it was on the tip of her tongue to say that it was no fault of hers that no one saw her in her pretty clothes.

That evening, feeling a little guilty, Lerryn came down to dinner in her new amber velvet gown. She looked quite lovely as she came into the room, her very guilt prompting a look of defiance in her expression.

Bethel had on the usual old green silk she had worn nightly throughout the summer. Lerryn was startled and ashamed when she saw tears in her sister's eyes.

"Forgive me, pet," Bethel was saying. "You mustn't

mind sometimes when I am cross and stupid. You look adorable. I love to see you in pretty things when I know you love wearing them."

"Darling!" Lerryn went over to where Bethel sat, "I know you get tired. You're only a cross-patch then. You do too much. Why do you bother?" She walked to the window, and did not notice the look of hopelessness on the other's face. Presently she wandered back.

"You ought to get new frocks, too," she said," you've no idea the difference it makes. I feel years younger this evening. I daresay it's very vain, but I don't believe it's wrong."

"What would be the point?" Bethel asked slowly.

Dinner was announced at that moment and the two women left the library for their solitary meal.

"Beth!"

The elder woman looked up from the book she was reading. She saw her sister's needlework lying idle, and the girl's fingers fidgeting.

"M'm? What?" she asked.

"I want to ask you a great favour. But first promise you won't be cross."

"I won't be cross. There! Now what do you want?"

Lerryn hesitated. She felt a little nervous.

"Beth, couldn't I—couldn't I possibly go over to the St. Hilary work party?"

She was quite unprepared for the sharp "No" that shot from her sister's lips, and the curt refusal without any explanation made for further obstinacy on her part.

"Why not?" she began to argue, "surely we ought to make some sort of effort to help. I should have thought with Veryan in the thick of it you'd have been only too pleased to be making dressings and bandages and whatever else they do there. At any rate, you might let me go, even if it doesn't appeal to you."

"Who's been telling you about the party?" Bethel asked sharply.

"It's common knowledge in the village. Clara Libby is engaged to one of the footmen in the castle."

"Listening to servants' talk!"

"For goodness' sake be reasonable, Beth." Lerryn flared, "Clara told Prudence, and Prudence was telling me all about it when she was in my room this morning. I should think the village thinks we're pretty idle, if you ask me."

Bethel was touched on the raw here.

"Idle! No one in the village can say that about me. I'm sure I work my fingers to the bone."

"But I don't."

"Oh, be quiet. I've said no to this request, and I mean no."

There was a pause, and then:

"How like Mama you're becoming," Lerryn said quietly. Bethel got up and left the room.

Lerryn strolled over to the piano. She felt thoroughly annoyed with her sister, and was determined to let her know it. She sat down and started to strum. She knew that Bethel disliked music for some reason, had, in fact, taken a most inexplicable dislike to it ever since her illness. After she had been playing for about half an hour there came a knock at the door and Prudence came into the room.

"Miss Lerryn," she whispered, "Miss Bethel says will you please stop that. She has an awful head, she says, and can't sleep. My! But you do play pretty, Miss Lerryn, it's a pity you don't play more often, that it is."

Lerryn got up wearily.

"Miss Bethel would always have a headache. Now you know." She threw herself into an armchair.

"Oh, what a shame! Poor Miss Lerryn, I do call it a shame."

"She's as cross as two sticks to-night, Prue. All because I suggested going to St. Hilary. You know, to that work party."

The maid looked worried.

"Did you go and tell her I told you?"

"Yes, why not? We do simply nothing for the war."

"Come, Miss, you oughtn't to say that, with Mr. Veryan out there and all——"

"Oh, Prue! If only I could go out to the war. As a nurse."

The servant looked horrified.

"Don't look so shocked. Lots of ladies have gone. Oh, I know I often say I hate illness and horrid things, but a war . . . Besides, soldiers would be different."

" That they would ! "

" I'd see new people. New faces, new places . . . but what's the use of talking? I know she'd never allow me to go. Prue, why do I let myself be ruled by her as if I were a child still? It's absurd."

" Poor Miss Bethel, one has to think of her side, too, Miss. You and Mr. Veryan are all she's got, and with him away . . ."

" She's become a real typical old maid. I know it's beastly of me to talk like this to you . . . but you're different, Prue, you've been with us for such years and years now. You can remember what she was like." Lerryn sighed. She knew she ought not by rights to discuss her family with Prue, but with Tudor dead these five years now, the housemaid had done everything for the girl, and Lerryn knew the servant adored her into the bargain.

" Well, I must get along, Miss Lerryn. It'll never do for someone to see me here gossiping away like this. You do look lovely in that dress, Miss ! That colour suits you a treat. It does seem a shame——" she stopped abruptly.

" What? Go on, Prue."

" Nothing, Miss Lerryn."

" Nonsense, you stopped in the middle of a sentence. What were you going to say? What's a shame? "

" I only meant, Miss Lerryn, excuse the liberty, it does seem a shame you have no young gentleman."

Lerryn laughed.

" I agree," she replied.

That night in bed Prudence's words came back to Lerryn. A young gentleman . . . Why was it that both Veryan and Bethel alike seemed determined to keep her from meeting people of her own age, of either sex? Or if it came to that, people of any age of their own class? Just because of Bethel's shattered romance of thirteen years ago she, too, was expected to live the incarcerated life of a nun, it seemed. For years she had put up with it; while Veryan was at home life was more fun anyway, and Bethel herself was different with him about the place. How she had wished she had never made that childish promise to her brother all those years ago, that she would never mention Oswald to Bethel, nor her illness, nor this strange, isolated way of living. Her only friend, now

that Brigit Penrose was married and living in London, seemed
to be Prue, unless one counted the twins at the Lodge, for
whom she indulged a strange and rather patronizing affection.
Sally and Ted Truscott were the children of the Treveryan
lodge-keeper. They were slightly younger than she was, and
both worshipped Lerryn, thinking her the loveliest creature
on the face of the earth, but they held Miss Bethel in awe.
Old Truscott had been found dead in the drive some years ago,
and his widow had been allowed by Veryan and Bethel to
remain on at the Lodge. Ted had a job at the inn in the
village, but Sally, his twin sister, a pretty dark-eyed typically
Cornish little creature, helped her mother, and did odd work
up at the big house, wore all Lerryn's cast-off clothes, and
took in the young ladies' laundry. She copied everything
that Miss Lerryn did, and tried to copy her speech, too, with
quite a bit of success. They were certainly different from the
rest of ' the village,' and, perhaps for that reason, none too
popular. It was thought that Sally ' curried favour,' for she
was frequently seen with Lerryn blackberrying, nutting, and
even on occasions bathing.

How she missed Brigit, she thought, as she lay in bed, and
now that she was married to her curate in Kensington and
already the mother of two children and expecting another, she
did not have much time to write these days. Dear Brigit, if it
had not been for her and kind dear old Mrs. Penrose's abetting
her, Bethel would have remained adamant three years ago,
and the invitation to spend that week in London with Brigit
and Kenneth to see the Diamond Jubilee would have been
flatly refused. Queer, she reflected, how Mrs. Penrose was
the only person able to hold her own with Bethel. She never
seemed to mind what the vicar's wife said to her, and it wasn't
as if, the girl thought, her sister was very religious. She was
pretty sure that Bethel really only went to church because of
the ' example ' she was supposed to be setting. What fun that
week in London had been.

Trips, excursions, excitements of any sort were few and far
between. What a blessing Bethel seemed to tolerate an
occasional visit to dear Miss Garth, her old music mistress, at
Exeter. ' I suppose she knows there's nothing much to get
thrilled about there,' and Lerryn wondered why it was really

that she looked forward so eagerly to these visits.   As she fell
asleep her thoughts drifted to memories of the great cathedral.

PART
TWO

2

WHEN THE NEWS came that Veryan had been
wounded and was to be invalided home, both
Bethel and Lerry were beside themselves with joy.
For weeks before his arrival they started to make
preparations, and when his telegram arrived
saying that he had reached England, Bethel for once behaved
as any other normal woman in such circumstances would have
done, and announced her intention of travelling to London to
meet him.

Lerryn was astonished; but too glad at the change in her
sister to say anything about it beyond remarking that it would
be pleasant if they could both go.

" No, I think you'd far best remain at home and see that
everything is ready for dear Veryan," Bethel answered kindly
but firmly.   " Besides, we don't want him to get too excited,"
she continued.

Lerryn sighed.

" Excited at being met by his sisters ? "

" Of course."   Bethel spoke quite sharply.   " He adores
his sisters.   You know what we are to each other.   All of us.
And anyway, we don't yet know how seedy he may still be."

So in a great hurry and flurry Bethel went up to town, at the
last moment taking Prudence with her.   Lerryn felt oddly
lonely left suddenly by herself, and in spite of the knowledge
that this state of things would only last for a day or two, and
that she should be feeling enormously excited by Veryan's
return, she did, in fact, feel nothing but a blank depression.
Even arranging the flowers, a task which as a rule took all her
attention, failed to arouse the usual enthusiasm.   Everything
had really been done by Bethel days beforehand, and the
younger girl was definitely at a loss.   She wandered about the
house and the grounds disconsolately, and even found herself
regretting Prue's absence.

As dusk was beginning to fall she came indoors—it was
getting chilly out in the garden—and going over to the piano

she sat down and began to play.   Here, certainly, was a chance
to give rein to her enjoyment of music, but the very fact that
her freedom was complete seemed to diminish the joy of it.
She played some Liszt, some Chopin; but neither suited her
frame of mind.   Suddenly she saw an album of Brahms pieces
which had fallen to the floor.   She picked it up and idly
started one of the waltzes.   Looking through the pages of the
book she found an intermezzo which she remembered loving
when Miss Garth played it.   She never heard the footsteps on
the gravel outside the drawing-room, and not until she had
finished did she look up, seeing a shadow fall across the ground.

" Who's there ? " she called sharply.

To her surprise it was Ted Truscott who stepped into the
room.

" Good gracious, Ted !   What on earth are you doing up
here at this hour of the evening?   You startled me ! " she
smiled at him.

" Sally's not feelin' too good, Miss Ler'yn, so I thought
maybe I'd best bring up the things she washes for you, like.
I just took 'un around the back and was goin' home, and I
stopped to listen to your piano-playing.   It was beautiful."

" Are you fond of music, Ted?   Come in and I'll play some
more."

He looked slightly embarrassed.

" I'm not properly dressed for coming into the house, Miss.
Me boots are a bit muddy, I guess."

" Never mind.   I don't."

She could not say that he looked a hundred times more
attractive in his old clothes—corduroy trousers and open-
necked shirt—than he would have done had he come by
invitation, when he would have shone like a new pin and worn
his Sunday blacks.

" What shall I play you? " she asked.

" I don't rightly know the names of the tunes you play."

" D'you like this ? " and she struck up one of the little
Brahms waltzes again.

" Yes, that's fine," he said, " makes you feel you'd like to
dance."

She then played a few Sullivan airs and ended with the
Cornish Furry Dance.

"I often wished we kept that old custom in our village," she said, "it must be so amusing dancing in and out of people's houses."

He smiled.

"You'd not be one to join in, would you?" he asked.

"Why not? I should."

"I didn't think you cared for things like that," he said slowly.

"Just because I never go to dances, nor have a dance here, I suppose?" she sighed. "'There are more things in heaven and earth than are dreamt of in thy philosophy.'"

"What's that?"

"That? Oh, it's only a line from a play called 'Hamlet'." She spoke quietly.

"Oh, Shakespeare." He nodded his head gravely.

"D'you know Shakespeare? How surprising of you, Ted," and as she said this could have kicked herself for the patronage the words suggested. Of course he'd know Shakespeare, the schools made boys like Ted learn Shakespeare nowadays.

Ted Truscott did not seem to be aware of the tone she had unwittingly used, however, or at any rate seemed not to resent her words.

"I like Shakespeare. I like 'Julius Cæsar'. And 'Romeo and Juliet,' too."

"What's the matter with Sally?" she asked.

"I can't make out, but she just isn't well," he said. "She's been poorly these last few days."

"Has she seen the nurse?"

"No. Snapped my head off when I told her she'd better. Cried, she did, and told me to leave her alone."

"How very unlike Sally," Lerryn replied, "I'll come down to-morrow and see her. Tell her I'm all alone, and want cheering up, too."

"Is that true, Miss?"

She nodded.

"Beth has gone to meet my brother, she wouldn't take me!"

"I guess you'll be proper glad to have Mr. Veryan home. It'll be like old times," he said.

"Yes, I suppose it will," Lerryn replied without great conviction. There was a pause and for the first time she felt slightly embarrassed. How peculiar it was, that the two of them should be sitting talking together like this in the drawing-room of all places, and at such a late hour. Of course they were old friends—Sally she was particularly fond of . . .

"You're not like Sally, are you? I mean, considering you're twins," she said inconsequently.

"Sally takes after Mother," he answered, "I'm more like me Dad."

"Yes." She wondered how much like his Dad, as some of Prue's stories crossed her mind. Stories not meant for the ears of well brought-up young ladies, but there were times when Prue liked a good gossip and Lerryn, if in the right mood, was nothing loth to draw the woman out and listen. Yes, if Prue's stories were true, 'Dad' Truscott had been somewhat of a dog in his day. The ladies and the bottle . . . so Prue had informed her. She looked at young Ted, and for the first time realized the gentian blue of his eyes, the red gold of his hair, his giant physique.

"Do you still enjoy working at 'The Crown,' Ted ? " she said.

"Oh, it's not so bad. I get plenty of tips." He blushed furiously at this piece of news which he had not meant to impart, "it all goes to help mother, you know."

"Where's it going to lead you?"

She had a sudden vision of the taproom at 'The Crown,' smoky and full of drunks, and Ted going the same way as his father.

"I might go into the hotel business," he said, rather grandly.

"Oh, Ted!" She looked horrified.

"Doesn't that sound good to you, Miss? It does to me. Why, I might one day have a pub of me own."

"Oh, Ted . . . no. At least, I've no business to say what I think or what I don't think."

"You see, one sees life in places like that."

"Life?"

"You'd be surprised. Why, all sorts of people turn up at hotels, even inns like 'The Crown,' here. You hear things. Tips, racing tips——"

"Ted, you don't *bet?* "

Young Truscott looked surprised by the horror in her voice.

" I have a tanner on, sometimes a shillin'. You don't think it's wrong, do you Miss? *You?* "

" Why are you surprised if I am shocked? " she tried to prevaricate.

" If it were Miss Bethel I'd know she'd think it bad. But you, you're different. Sally and me always say you're, well . . ." he stopped in the middle of the sentence, and went crimson.

" How would you like a job here, at Treveryan, Ted? With us? " she asked.

" What sort of a job? "

" I don't know quite. But I'm sure we could make one. On the farm, or in the garden."

" I don't know, Miss. You see—I kind o' think that if I stick at this it will lead to other things. I . . . but it's getting late, Miss Lerryn, I guess I ought to be getting back."

Suddenly he became stiff and formal. Lerryn felt cross with both him and herself.

" Yes, you'd better go," she said rather coldly, " Good night."

" Good night, Miss Lerryn." She went over to the piano and began to put away music, and did not see him watching her as she did so.

It was pouring with rain when Lerryn woke next morning, and she forgot all about her promise to go and see Sally Truscott. Veryan and Bethel were catching the first train down and she was determined, if it cleared, to go in the landau and meet them at the station.

She was happily surprised at Veryan's appearance. She had not known quite what to expect, but to have him home with all limbs intact seemed too good to be true. A nasty wound in the shoulder and a bad go of enteric had, apparently, been sufficient cause to send him back to England.

" God! It's good to be home," he said, as they strolled through the garden before dinner. " You girls don't know what Treveryan is till you've left it."

" I don't need to leave it," Bethel answered, " but oh! Veryan darling, if you knew what it's been like without you ! "

"You should have come, too," he answered unthinkingly, and immediately felt her hand slacken on his arm. "It's looking more beautiful than ever," he said hurriedly changing the subject. "I don't believe my going has mattered a jot."

"I've done my best to look after things while you've been away, dear," she said, "but it needs you back badly. All sorts of things at the farm need seeing to, a new roof is wanted for instance for the big barn before the winter. I've been leaving that for you to see about, and there are lots of things we shall have to go into. Oh, Veryan! I have enjoyed it in a way, looking after it, but only because I hoped I was doing it for you."

"For us. Bless you, Beth." He squeezed her arm. "And what about our Lerryn? What has our youngest been up to?"

He still adopted the same playful attitude towards her, Lerryn noticed.

"Up to? Up to nothing." Did that sound ungracious? She had not meant it to.

"Oh, the child has been all right." Bethel smiled indulgently. "You'll have to curb her of her extravagant whims now you're back, V. She spends all her time and money making herself look beautiful."

"That's not fair," began Lerryn.

"I'm only teasing, pet. Put on that pretty new frock to-night for Veryan to see."

But Lerryn felt annoyed with Bethel and, when she saw that Prudence had laid out the golden Liberty gown, she threw it into a chair and put on an old grey muslin that she had not worn for ages and had put by for Sally Truscott.

She went downstairs feeling sulky, and was completely taken aback with astonishment to see Bethel herself in a brand new London creation.

"Beth——" she stammered   The elder sister laughed a little self-consciously.

"I wanted to celebrate Veryan's return. D'you like this?"

'This' was a soft black velvet, very severely cut, and she wore nothing with it but her mother's pearls.

"She looks stunning, I say," said Veryan, "it's worth going to the war to come back to Treveryan and you, Beth."

"It's lovely," said Lerryn quietly, but the other two did not seem to hear her, and later, when Bethel raised a glass of champagne to her brother, Lerryn could only choke back something very akin to tears.

It seemed to the younger girl as the weeks sped by that she had never known such loneliness as she now felt since Veryan's return. It was not that either her brother or her sister meant to hurt her, or snub her; she knew that. They seemed to want no other company but each other's, in a way that seemed new to the younger girl. There had been the three of them for so long now, so she felt doubly resentful of the possessive manner in which Bethel appeared to look on Veryan, as though he was utterly hers, relegating the younger girl to an almost 'schoolroom' background. Yes, that was it she thought, one afternoon in the late autumn, riding home alone; Bethel was possessive. She supposed she had been becoming so for years, but it had never struck her with such force until now. All these months, moreover, when Veryan was away in South Africa, she had been possessive with her also. Ordering her to do this, bossing her about that—owning her; as she now tried to own and possess Veryan. As, indeed, she tried to own and possess Treveryan itself. And yet Lerryn loved Bethel. She knew that the true Bethel had been so stunned by the past that this woman, rising Phœnix-like from the ashes of the girl as it were, was an unreal creation, as unreal and sham as the false limbs which were being given to the maimed and wounded. It was queer, she thought, that it had not struck her until lately, when in actual fact Bethel obviously appeared happier and more radiant than she had for years. Often enough Beth had irritated her, antagonized her; yet now, when on the face of everything she was altogether more genial, she herself must needs realize the more fundamental difficulties of her sister's nature. It was not as if she felt jealous of Veryan and Bethel, she knew that was not really so. It was, she told herself, this infuriating habit they both had of still looking upon her as a child.

She arrived home to find them, as usual, closeted in Veryan's study. That was another thing about them which she found ridiculous. Why must they disappear into that little room of

Veryan's to discuss estate matters when there was the library, the drawing-room, even the dining-room—for old Hockin was far too deaf these days to listen to anything they might want to keep private. It was almost as if they wished to keep Treveryan matters from her. She went upstairs in a thoroughly disgruntled frame of mind.

Meanwhile neither Veryan nor Bethel had the faintest idea that their young sister was unhappy or depressed in any way. Bethel continued as before, busying herself with household and village matters, with the difference that those with whom she came into contact remarked on the change of her appearance and expression.

" She must certainly ha' missed Mr. Veryan. She's mighty fond of that there brother," and " our Miss Bethel's happy again."

And Veryan? Not even to himself would he admit that, much as he worshipped Treveryan and adored Bethel, a strange restlessness was already beginning to gnaw at him by the New Year.

In January the Queen died, and the country was plunged into grief, the nation as a whole adopting national mourning.

" I shall go up to the funeral, of course," Veryan remarked. Bethel looked surprised.

" Will you? " she said.

" Oh, let me come with you, Veryan," begged Lerryn.

" Of course not. Women don't go to funerals," said Bethel hurriedly.

It was Veryan's turn to look surprised.

" There'll be thousands watching the Queen's passing," he answered. " Come if you want to. Why don't you both? It'll be something you'll never forget."

For the first time since he could remember he noticed the stubborn look about Bethel's mouth, and he was reminded of Anna Treveryan.

" Thank you, no. I detest funerals. And you know how I loathe London."

" You went up to meet Veryan," Lerryn said.

" I've told you both, I don't wish to go. However, don't let me interfere with your pleasure," she answered coldly.

" Hardly pleasure," Veryan remonstrated gently, " if I go I

intend it as a mark of respect to a wonderful old lady."

" You're different, V. You fought for her, you've been a soldier, I daresay you ought to go. I merely think it's ridiculous of Lerryn to want to go up. It'll only mean hanging about in a crowd and probably catching her own death."

" Oh, well, we'll talk it over later." Veryan shrugged his shoulders and left the room.

" Why don't you want me to go," Lerryn asked. Bethel was silent. She could not explain her feelings even to herself.

" Oh, go if you want to," she said wearily

The next day Lerryn heard from Miss Garth.

" I've had another sort of invitation from Exeter," she said, reading through her letter. " Miss Garth is going to a retreat at some convent near Exeter, something special because of the Queen, I think. Anyway, she wonders if I'd like to join her."

" I don't see you with a lot of nuns, my dear," Bethel said with a laugh.

" What on earth would you talk about? " said Veryan.

" You don't. You're silent," Lerryn said.

" Will you go? What about your London jaunt? " Bethel could not help the ironic tone creeping into her voice.

" I could go on. I daresay it would not matter being a day or so late." Lerryn was determined to assert herself at last, and made up her mind that she was going to London and to Devonshire.

Veryan stayed up in London for two weeks, much to Bethel's secret misgiving, and the few days alone with him which she had promised herself during Lerryn's absence never materialized, as her sister returned first.

" Well, how were the nuns? Was it interesting? " she asked. It was typical, thought Lerryn, that she made no mention of the funeral, ignoring all reference to the true and original reason of her going away.

" It was very interesting. Very strange. I've never felt such peace," she said.

" Oh." Bethel remained silent. Religion, like the facts of life, was one of those strangely personal topics about which she was shy and even rather ignorant. She could not have discussed either subject with her sister.

" M'm——" the younger girl murmured, "I was happier there than I've ever been anywhere, I think."

" I hope you're not thinking of becoming too religious? " Bethel said then, in sudden alarm.

" Could one? '

" Don't be silly. You know what I mean. You're not going to become a Roman Catholic or anything, are you? No Treveryan ever has."

How odd Bethel was, Lerryn thought.

" No, I don't suppose so."

" I think it would be rather a lovely life," Lerryn said to Veryan later when he was asking her about the retreat.

" I don't see our little Lerryn cut out for a nun, V., do you? She'd have to cut off her pretty hair. And good-bye to her Liberty frocks which she loves so much," Bethel teased.

" Those are only temporal vanities," she replied.

Both brother and sister laughed.

" Hark at her! Quite the little mother superior," Veryan pulled her down to his side, " you're too pretty to be a nun, sweet," he said, not giving much thought to his words.

" I'm getting on. It doesn't look as if I were going to be married, does it? We don't seem to be a marrying family." Lerryn's voice was hard. Dead silence greeted her words and Bethel left the room. Lerryn looked up at her brother guiltily.

" Now look what's happened," she said, and was dismayed and annoyed when Veryan only sighed, and left the room as if to follow her, saying quietly, " My poor Beth! "

It was soon after this outburst that Lerryn realized that it had been some weeks since she had heard or seen anything of Sally Truscott. On her way back from Tregony, where some business for Bethel had taken her, she told the coachman to stop the dog-cart at the lodge gates.

" I'll walk back," she said, and knocked at the door of the Truscott's cottage. Sally herself opened the door.

" Miss Lerryn! " she exclaimed and immediately went a dull crimson.

" I've not seen you for weeks, Sally. What have you been up to, hiding away from me? I declare you've neglected me of late! Dear old Prue cannot make my things look nearly as pretty as you do."

To her consternation the girl burst into tears.

"I thought you'd heard something. I thought that was why I never saw you these days," she cried.

"Sally! Dear Sally, what's the matter? I was only teasing you." She went into the cottage, shutting the door behind her. The girl led her into the one and only sitting-room.

"Sit down, Miss. Mother's out, it's all right. Oh, Miss Lerryn!" Once again she started to cry.

"But tell me what's happened, I can't help if I don't know."

"I'm in trouble. Oh, Miss Lerryn . . ."

"Yes—but what sort of trouble?"

"I thought he loved me," Sally Truscott sobbed, "I thought everything would be all right, he said it would. Else I'd never o' let him . . ."

Dimly Lerryn began to see light.

"Oh, Sally, darling! What's . . . happened?"

"I don't know what to do. Mother won't speak to me, and even Ted says I oughta have seen more sense."

Hardly daring to ask the question and in a voice she barely recognized as her own, Lerryn said:

"Are you going to have a baby?"

The girl looked at her in surprise.

"Of course. That' what I was telling you."

"What . . . Who . . .?" she began awkwardly.

"He was so wonderful, Miss; he was ever such a gentleman. Talked the same as you and Mr. Veryan. He stayed at 'The Crown.' I washed his shirts for him." The very memory of such an intimate task set the poor girl to weeping again.

"I see," said Lerryn, and tried to conjure up the type of man most likely to frequent the inn. Some sort of 'traveller,' she supposed, showing off London airs and graces and seducing—she was proud she recollected the word from Prue's vocabulary—poor Sally into the bargain.

"He was an artist," Sally said, as if in answer to Lerryn's thoughts. "He painted ever such pretty pictures."

"Oh?" Lerryn was more interested. "Did he paint you?"

Sally shook her head.

" He said he'd like to, but he didn't.   He painted the church
and the street, and some lovely pictures of the sea.   He said
as how lots of his pictures were bought."

Such an idea seemed even at this late hour to inspire the girl
with awe.

" He must have been good, then," said Lerryn naively.

" Oh, he was good," replied Sally with almost reverent pride.

"And did you love him—very much? " asked Lerryn
wistfully.

Sally's eyes lit pathetically.

" I never thought anything like that *could* happen to me with
a real gentleman.   Oh, Miss Lerryn, he was so good, so
kind," and then, after a pause, and lapsing into the Cornish
idiom, she whispered as though to herself, " Oh, he were
'andsome."

Lerryn felt singularly ill-equipped to deal with the situation.

" I suppose he won't marry you, Sally? " she asked
apologetically.

" He's gone," the girl answered, " and he doesn't know
about it."

" Does Ted know the whole story? " Lerryn asked.

" I never told him it was him.   I was afraid he might do
him an injury.   You know Ted's strength, like a young bull
he is, isn't he?   Nigel—" and she paused shyly and a pink
flush covered her face—" that's his name, Nigel."   Her voice
seemed to cherish the name as though it were a jewel of great
value.   " Nigel could never stand up to Ted, he's so—beautiful, Miss Lerryn.   Like that stain-glass window of St. John
in the church—you know."

" Poor Sally!   I wish I knew what I could do to help."

" I guess it's m'own fault.   I knew it was wrong, but I did
love him.   And I thought, maybe, Nigel would make me a
lady.   Like you, Miss Lerryn."

" Oh, Sally! "   Lerryn went over to where Sally Truscott
was sitting huddled in the chair.   She put her arm round her
and kissed her.

" My poor Sally! "   She felt like crying and laughing at the
same time.   Wretched as the girl's pitiful story was, there was
something pathetically comic in the idea of seduction turning
one into a lady.

" You'll stick by me, Miss ?" the girl cried, clinging to Lerryn.

" Of course I shall. You can call it Lerryn if it's a girl, and I'll be its godmother," she replied, feeling extremely daring. Sally Truscott's eyes shone.

" Oh, Miss Lerryn, I think I'm glad it's happened ! "

Lerryn was puzzled by Prue's behaviour that evening. She noticed that the servant, as a rule so voluble, was strangely silent as she brushed her hair. She wondered if kitchen gossip already knew and talked about Sally, and whether the older woman disapproved of Lerryn's visit to the cottage. It was quite feasible that Toms, the coachman, had told them he had put her down there. She was right.

" I shouldn't 'ave thought it of you, Miss ! "

Prudence evidently could not keep the matter to herself. She sniffed ominously.

" What ? "

" That Sally going and getting herself in the family way. Disgraceful, I calls it. And now you go aiding and abetting her." Lerryn immediately noted the tone of jealousy creeping into the housemaid's voice. She had always resented the notice taken of the girl by Lerryn.

" Don't speak like that," said Lerryn with as much hauteur as she found possible.

" What can you wonder at though? " Prudence continued, in no way disconcerted, " bad blood in that girl's family. 'Aven't I often told you what 'er father was like? Blood always outs and tells."

She pulled the girl's hair.

" Do be careful, Prudence ! What's it got to do with you, anyway ? "

This was too much for the old servant.

" Nothing, I'm glad to say," she glared, " but I'm sorry any young lady of mine should get herself talked of by befriending anyone like Sally Truscott, as is no better than she should be, *and* everyone in the village knows it by now."

" Really, you forget yourself, Prue ! Look at Miss Bethel. She always helps people in the village."

" Miss Bethel wouldn't go getting herself talked about with a girl like Sally Truscott. She helps respectable people that are——"

"All right and don't need helping. No, I oughtn't to say that. I don't believe Miss Bethel would be hard about Sally. And I'm surprised you are, Prue. When I think of the stories you've told me . . ."

" That's different, Miss. Stories are stories. When things happen in your own place to girls you've seen grow up under your eyes—well, it makes you feel different."

" He was a gentleman, Sally said."

" Then I call her downright bad; she oughta have known no gentleman would mean to do right by her." Prue spoke indignantly.

That night after dinner Veryan asked her what was on her mind, as she was so silent. She told them of Sally's trouble, and of the hard manner in which Prue had spoken. Rather to her surprise, Bethel seemed the more upset by the story. Veryan merely shrugging his shoulders, saying :

" Doubtless she led him on and only gets what she deserves, silly girl."

" But she's very young, V.," said Bethel. " Poor little thing, of course we must do what we can for her."

" I was shocked by what Prue said," Lerryn said slowly, " about gentlemen not meaning anything."

" Prue has no right to speak to you as she does," said Bethel brusquely. " Oh, I've heard her often enough. A young innocent girl like you."

Her sister tried not to look amused.

"And what about you? " she asked.

" Prue wouldn't dream of talking to me the way she does to you. And if she did, I'm a great deal older than you, in any case."

" Veryan," Lerryn began later, " would it be so impossible for Sally's Nigel to marry her, if he could be found? "

" I shouldn't think he'd marry her for a moment. Why should he? A village—trollop ! "

" You can't call Sally Truscott that," said Bethel, " she's been a perfectly good girl till this business. She's more refined than any of the other girls by a long way. I agree with Lerryn, the man ought to be found. After all, possibly he does care for her, was really in love with her . . ."

Veryan smiled.

" How incorrigibly romantic all women are," he said.
" What about his people? And how d'you know he hasn't a
wife already? What would you all say if I brought back a
common, pretty little wife? "

"As that's out of the question . . ." Bethel started.

" I shouldn't mind having Sally in the family," Lerryn said.
" She's a pet, and she's so terribly pretty."

" One doesn't marry into the lower classes, my dear child,
because one's attracted physically for a short spell."

" How snobbish! " said Lerryn indignantly. " If one can
fall in love enough to do what Nigel has done to Sally, one
ought to marry."

" It's all very difficult," said Bethel.

" Personally, I can't imagine becoming involved in such a
situation," Veryan remarked. " Can you, for the sake of
argument, consider yourself falling in love—as you put it
—with a yokel? That girl's brother, for instance? The idea
is revolting. Forgive me. I should not be talking to you
two like this." Bethel did not appear to be listening any
longer, she was busy searching for something in her work-
basket. Lerryn was silent. She was remembering Ted
Truscott as she had seen him here in the drawing-room, that
night when she had played to him.

" What on earth could one talk about to an uneducated
person? " Veryan was murmuring, as he went to open the
door to one of the dogs who was scratching to be let in.

Ted had loved her music, Ted knew quite a lot about
Shakespeare, thought Lerryn. Of course, people like the
Treveryans never considered the local village folk as being
attractive or not. Lerryn realized that. But she realized, too,
that the girls in other families like hers had scores of friends of
their own age, and were for the most part married by the time
they were twenty-four or five. Sally Truscott's Nigel was an
artist; artists were different from other men, she believed,
They were casual, forgetful perhaps, but not snobs. The
more Lerryn thought of Sally's young man the more certain
she was that he had loved her. She went to bed that night
troubled over many things. Sally's face kept coming before
her eyes, but the expression it wore was not that of shame and
despair, but one that lit suddenly with worship and glory.

She heard again the village girl's voice saying, ' Oh, he was so good, so kind,' and again the tone of almost smothered adoration when she had half whispered, ' he were 'andsome.' And Lerryn felt envy in her heart for Sally Truscott.

PART
TWO

3

IT WAS IN the early spring that Veryan startled his family by telling them that he was thinking of going abroad again.

" Not to the war? " Bethel said in anxious tones.

" No," he said.   "Actually it is an appointment which I have been offered: one which I cannot very well refuse.   You know the Duke is going on a world tour during the summer to represent the King?   Well, I have been asked to go as a member of his staff.   He's going as Duke of Cornwall and York, as you know, and I suppose they want some representative sort of a bloke from here.   Alas! most of the old lot are dead—Nick, for instance, and Jack St. Hilary.   It's a great honour, Beth, you should be proud of your little brother!   Don't look so glum."

" I shall miss you so terribly," Beth said tonelessly.

" Well, I think it's wonderful," Lerryn cried.

" Oh, darling, it is, of course it is! "   Bethel looked up as she spoke again.   " It's only that I'm horribly, beastly selfish," she said.

" Will it be for long?   And how was it all arranged? " asked Lerryn.

" The tour will only last for a few months, so I don't suppose I shall be away for more than the summer."

" Where will you go? "

"Australia to begin with.   H.R.H. is to open the new Parliament there."

" What I want to know is, how long you've been toying with the idea? " Lerryn asked.

" Since our trip to London, Miss Inquisitive.   When you were making merry with your nuns I was seeing influential folk in London, my dear! "   He spoke with mock pomposity.

" I think you might have told me, Veryan," Bethel said.

"Frankly, I was asked not to mention it to a soul," he replied.

"But to your own family—me?"

About a week before Veryan sailed Bethel caught a bad cold and was forced to stay in bed. Thus it was that Lerryn found herself accompanying her brother alone out riding. The conversation naturally turned to Veryan's coming journey.

"It seems funny, in a way," Lerryn was speaking, "that after so many years of Treveryan, never going away for a single visit, you should want to be off again so soon after your return from Africa."

Veryan remained silent.

"Is it that you feel—restless?" she said. He looked at her with surprise.

"What do you know of restlessness?" he asked.

"I'm not a fool," she answered, "nor the baby sister you seem to think I am. Even I can see how Beth absorbs you, so to speak. Saps you . . ."

"I won't have a word against Bethel!"

"Oh, I know you're wrapped up in each other," she said impatiently, "but admit that you long for other society than ours sometimes. I know I do." She sighed.

"Poor sweet," he said. Lerryn looked at him curiously. Had he meant herself or Bethel, she wondered.

"I don't mind telling you I envy you," she said; "moreover, you don't know how difficult Beth can be when we've only got each other."

"Nonsense, you exaggerate. Beth is a very wonderful woman, you ought to be ashamed to speak unkindly of her."

"Oh, I know she can do no wrong in your eyes," she said rather wearily.

"You've not had your life shattered as she has," he said shortly.

"*And* none of us is allowed to forget it," Lerryn answered quickly, "in spite of the fact that one mustn't talk of the past! Shattered lives forsooth! Mine has all the appearance of being shattered before it's begun to be a life!"

"You don't know what you're saying, my dear. Bethel's love for Oswald Martineau was something . . ."

"And am I never to have the chance of an Oswald of my

own?" she interrupted. "Good heavens, Veryan! Surely even you can see the selfishness of it. Here we are, you, Beth and I—the three of us—and Treveryan. Above all, Treveryan. Am I never to see beyond the four walls of the house in which I was born? Do you think that sometimes I don't want to scream for very boredom?"

"You never were like this," was Veryan's reply.

"Perhaps I'm older. Perhaps I realize things more. After all, things are different. We've got a new King, we've begun a new century. We've been at war for eighteen months nearly. I should like to be nursing the wounded, but can you imagine Bethel's feelings if I so much as suggested going, especially when I tell you she wouldn't even let me go to the St. Hilary work party.

"Bethel has her reasons," he said.

"I love Treveryan. Please don't think I don't. But oh! to see other people sometimes. What I should do without Brigit and Miss Garth I don't know, and heaven knows I see them little enough. It's all very well for you, you're a man, you can go off if you want to. And you do."

"Try to understand Bethel, dear," he said.

"I wouldn't mind if only she'd let me go to places or have people here. This great place, indeed, and never a soul to entertain! I think it's so morbid. Why, when I think of all the fun we had when you were twenty-one! Even with Mama we did a certain amount. One would almost think she had some very real reason for not wanting me to meet people."

Veryan remained silent.

"I can look after myself. I shouldn't get hurt by someone in the way she was hurt by Oswald. You never told me the story but I imagine they had a quarrel and he jilted her."

So that was what Lerryn had imagined all these years. He longed to tell the girl the truth, but it had been Bethel herself who had been adamant about shielding her sister from the full and horrible reality ; wrongly, he had always thought, and now he was more convinced than ever that they both owed the truth to Lerryn. But he felt powerless to speak to her without Bethel's consent, for he had given her his promise.

As his departure abroad grew nearer Bethel seemed to cling to her brother with greater force than ever. Long before she had properly recovered from her cold she insisted on coming downstairs to lie on the big chesterfield in the library. Her meals were carried in to her on a tray, and as often as not Veryan would join her after the first course on some little pretext or other.

"I wish you hadn't come downstairs," he said, "you know how treacherous this March weather can be, and how important it is that you don't get bronchial or anything."

"I must see as much of you as I can," she answered.

"Dearest," and he kissed her on the brow. "There's one thing I know, and that is no man could leave any place in better or more competent hands than yours. You're a marvel."

She smiled.

"There's nothing very wonderful in looking after a place which one adores as much as I adore Treveryan. It's my life after all. It and you. And Lerryn, of course."

There was a pause.

"I wish Lerryn felt the same love for the place as—we do," he said.

"Why? Why d'you say that? Lerryn is perfectly happy." She spoke quickly.

"I'm worried about her, Beth. I hate to talk about this, for God knows I loathe bringing up the subject, but I honestly believe in all fairness that—Lerryn—should—*know*."

Bethel closed her eyes.

"No," she answered, "no. I beg you, my darling, I do know what I'm talking about. She's a child and . . ."

"That's where you're wrong, where we're both wrong, Beth. We'd forgotten. Because we've been making time stand still for us, we've not realized that Lerryn is now a grown-up woman, wondering at the restrictions we . . ."

"Has she been complaining?"

"Not exactly," he answered, "but I can see she longs to get out and see people. Which is natural."

"Not for us." Bethel said in a tone of despair.

"Well," he sighed and stood up, "as ever, I leave it in your hands. You're the eldest and, I suppose, the wisest."

She took his hand.

"Darling. I know I'm right. And now let's change the distasteful and horrible subject. Tell me once again where

you expect to stop first, so that I may send you a cable.   I'm
sorry if I was beastly about this trip to begin with.   I know
it's going to be wonderful and I'm dreadfully proud in my
heart that you've been chosen to go.   Really I am.   The only
thing that sometimes worries me is the thought that you may
become so fascinated with some place that you won't want to
come back."

" That won't happen."

" I hope it won't."

" I was glad enough to leave the Cape, God knows."

" That was war," she answered.

" True.   All the same, my Beth, I can't conceive of a place
that could seduce me from Treveryan."

" And yet I sometimes think that the war and Africa made
you restless.   The seed of travel was started by your going
out there, V.   You've never really settled down since you
came back, you know.   Oh, I've watched you and realized,
my dear, and seen you doing things, little things, that are
foreign to you."

" As, for instance? "

" Oh, just silly little things.   You never used to bite your
nails, for instance.   Now, why, you're like a child, always
gnawing away at a thumb!   You wander off, too, in a way you
used not to.   Half the things you start you don't finish.   I'm
thinking of business letters now.   Half of your correspondence
you forget about, if it were not that I go over your letters I
don't know where Treveryan would be."   She laughed softly
and patted his hand.   " I only say I do see a difference.   Don't
think I mind or blame you.   Good heavens!   You've a
right to be restless after all you went through in
Africa."

" Funny . . ."   He dropped her hand and walked over to
the window, speaking so quietly that Bethel only just caught
his words.   " Lerryn said it was restlessness."

" Lerryn?   Did you discuss yourself with Lerryn? "

Immediately it seemed as if she was filled with jealousy.
Veryan turned slowly and looked at her.

" Beth," he said, " how fond of me are you? "

" I—why, you know I love you better than anyone," she
answered.

"Then I want you not to resent the question I am going to ask you."

She looked at him expectantly.

"Are you jealous of Lerryn?"

She looked at him aghast.

"Jealous? Of Lerryn? What do you mean? How could I be? Haven't I loved her almost as if she were my own child?"

He could see that she was hurt, outraged, at the very suggestion. He sighed.

"Forgive me. I'm a clumsy idiot. Men don't understand women."

"No," she said slowly.

He noticed her eyes began to fill with tears which presently ran down her cheeks. He quickly strode to the sofa and knelt down beside her.

"We're not like other people. Not like other families. We're cursed. And you and I are the only ones that know it. We must keep close together, we three, we must not let ourselves become out of tune with each other. Promise me, my dear, that while I'm away you'll try and be more tolerant with Lerryn."

"Tolerant!"

"Understanding, then. You see she does not understand. And that is what makes you irritable with each other; you're neither of you in complete tune——"

"Yes, I see," she whispered.

"Perhaps I am restless. Probably it is due to the war. You know, as nobody else knows, what you and Treveryan mean, so you needn't worry. I shall come back quite soon . . . I shall be all right."

The night before he left Bethel surprised both Veryan and Lerryn by ordering an almost banquet-like dinner and champagne to drink.

"It isn't everyone who's asked to go on a royal tour," she said gaily. No one could have guessed the misery she was feeling, nor could they have known how each morsel of food seemed to choke her.

They drank the health of the royal couple, and Bethel insisted on toasting her brother as well.

" And another to your safe and speedy return! " she said smiling.

" By the way," Veryan said later, " I heard a piece of news to-day which will certainly please you, Lerryn. I'd forgotten it until this minute. Your protégée is going to be made an honest girl of, as the saying goes."

" What! " both sisters exclaimed.

" Yes, the Truscott girl. The young man has just turned up out of the blue and is going to marry her."

" Oh! " For a moment Lerryn felt speechless.

" I am glad," said Bethel. " She was always a nice little thing, she'll probably make him a very good wife."

" Who told you, Veryan? " Lerryn asked.

" I forget who told me in the first place—one of the men down at the farm, I believe. But I ran into the brother this afternoon. He wanted a job, as a matter of fact."

" Ted does? Are you going to give it to him? " she asked anxiously.

" I told him I couldn't possibly do anything at this late hour. However, I said he could speak to you, Beth. I don't somehow fancy him about the place."

" Why not? Ted's all right." Lerryn spoke quickly.

" Also a protégé? Have a care, little sister! He may be all right, but I don't fancy a lad who's been kicked out of ' The Crown ' for getting drunk."

" Is that the truth? " Bethel asked.

" It isn't, of course it isn't." Lerryn spoke at random.

" What do you know, Lerryn? " Veryan asked with impatience.

" I only know Ted would never do anything bad. If he got drunk, I'll swear it was the first time, and probably someone made him on purpose. Horrible people go to public houses, I always begged him to leave it, and if he's asked for a job, Veryan, it's my fault, as I said ages ago you would give him one."

" Well, well, well! " Veryan looked slightly taken aback.

" She's very impulsive," Bethel murmured. " I'll see Ted Truscott anyway, and perhaps something can be found for him."

" Just as you like, dear," Veryan answered.

When they went to bed, only Lerryn's thoughts were centred not upon the coming royal tour, but on Sally Truscott and her brother.

PART
TWO

4

BY MIDSUMMER Ted Truscott was firmly ensconced on the Treveryan home-farm; and by midsummer it was known that the royal tour had been protracted to further dominions, and that the Duke and Duchess would not return until the autumn. Bethel read the news in the papers before getting a long letter from Veryan written on departure for New Zealand.

" Of course he cannot come home until the whole business is over," she said in a voice by which Lerryn knew she was excusing the circumstances for her own benefit. When letters began to arrive more regularly and showed by their tone how much Veryan was enjoying the cruise, Bethel's heart misgave her. There was no attempt in any of them to make plans upon his return, and more than once the lines, 'I leave so-and-so to you,' or ' you decide what to do,' filled her with forboding. Lerryn felt sorry for her sister and would say :

" You worry needlessly, you know. He must come back with the *Ophir*, he wouldn't be able to stay anywhere, even if he wanted."

And Bethel with almost pathetic gratitude eagerly accepted such crumbs of comfort as the younger girl could give her.

It seemed that Veryan's talk with both sisters had borne fruit; for the first time for many years Lerryn noticed a marked change in Bethel's attitude towards her. She seemed altogether more like the Bethel of her childhood days. Gentler, sweeter, more understanding. Lerryn thought of the trouble Bethel had taken over finding a suitable job for Ted Truscott, and how generous she had been in the matter of a wedding present to Sally. The girl had gone away with her artist lover to London and they had been married at a registrar's office, much to Lerryn's disappointment, who kept saying that she would have been the prettiest bride the village had seen for many a day. Bethel, however, took the view that the business was a difficult one, anyway, and that Sally was better out of the way for the time being. She sent her ten pounds, some lace and a coral brooch, and Lerryn felt ashamed that she should have ever looked upon her sister as cold, hard and unromantic.

There was plenty to do at Treveryan in the summer of 1901. Two of the under gardeners developed scarlet fever which made help short in the garden, and Bethel and Lerryn themselves frequently worked until bed-time, helping old Pucky. Once again there was jam-making with which to contend, and the usual amount of social work in the village and countryside, with which Bethel never failed to help Mrs. Penrose. Then there was the haymaking which Lerryn always enjoyed, and it was then that she suddenly expressed a wish to Mrs. Mutton, the farmer's wife, to learn to milk.

" What's come over you, Lerryn," laughed her sister, " that after all these years you should suddenly want to blossom into a dairymaid? You know you've always been rather nervous of cows ! "

She failed to notice the colour rise in Lerryn's cheeks, and was quite surprised when a few days later she came across her sister flushed, and hair awry, in the cowshed. Ted Truscott looked in while she was standing by.

" Mrs. Mutton says you'd be a brave milker if you'd get over your distrust for the cows, my 'andsome," he said with a laugh. " Your fingers are fine, she said to me. You just need confidence."

He smiled at her and went on his way. Bethel remained thoughtful for a few minutes and then said :

" I don't think young Truscott should speak with quite such familiarity to you, darling."

" Oh ! " Came a slight pause, then, " I don't expect he means anything. We've known each other all our lives, after all."

" I know. And you're Miss Treveryan and not the milk-maid. And you're too old to allow liberties."

At this moment they were joined by Mrs. Mutton, and the conversation was dropped.

In August the Penrose's daughter Brigit came to the vicarage on a visit, with her husband and young family, and Lerryn found her time fully occupied with her work in the garden and being at the beck and call of her friend.

It was delightful to talk about London and the world beyond the Tamar, and the curate from Kensington's young wife was most gratified on realizing she was to appear as the embodiment of the metropolis to Miss Treveryan.

"How do you think Bethel looks?" Lerryn asked her one afternoon. They had taken the jingle to Veryan Bay and were enjoying a picnic tea.

"Candidly, she gave me rather a shock," the other girl replied. "It's a long time since I've seen her, you know. Of course, she's very striking to look at. But—I don't know—she seems so hard."

"I know what you mean," Lerryn said, "and yet she isn't really." And she told her friend of the Sally Truscott affair.

"M'm! I'm surprised. She seems such a regular—*spinster*, doesn't she? I'd have imagined a scandal of that sort would have shocked her."

"It didn't. I think poor Beth is still more romantic at heart than she'd have me believe."

"Has she never looked at anyone since the Martineau man?"

"Heavens, no! Why, you know my dear, how we none of us see a soul. Beth least of all."

"Is she a man-hater? Mi—something-or-other, I believe they're called?" asked Brigit with interest.

"I don't think so. That's to say, I don't believe she dislikes men more than women. She has positively no friends, you know, except your mother."

"Indeed, it is queer. And so deadly for you, poor dear! You must come up to stay with us again in the winter."

"I will if Veryan comes back. When he comes back, I mean. I couldn't very well leave poor Beth alone."

"Pooh! She likes it—must do. I should have no feelings on that score. Don't you long to have a home and babies of your own, Lerryn? I know I wouldn't be without my precious babes and Kenneth for anything in the world."

Lerryn sighed.

"I don't think I want children. Yours are very sweet, of course," she added hastily, "but I've no maternal urge in me. Beth has. She was like a mother to me when I was tiny and all the children in the village adore her. Which makes it so queer . . ." she stopped.

" Yes, go on."

" I was going to say it made her manner the more strange last year," and gradually she began to tell of the difficult times she had gone through with her sister. The other nodded her head sagely:

"All comes of being an old maid. I daresay I oughtn't to know about such things nor talk about them. 'Specially to you, my dear! But Ken is wonderful, he tells me everything. He's so unlike father. Much broader in all his views, you know."

" But Bethel? How d'you mean? "

" She is frustrated, poor dear. Poor Bethel was obviously cut out for marriage, and by bad luck the whole thing was nipped in the bud when she was madly in love. I beseech you not to follow suit. Indeed, you shall come to town and I'll make Ken find you a nice husband. He knows lots of awfully nice men."

Lerryn smiled at her.

" It's silly, isn't it, the way we just stick on here, the three of us. We're all very nice looking, and really you'd think we were diseased, or something! "

Lerryn told Bethel of Brigit's invitation to London, purposely leaving out the girl's intention of introducing her to young men. The elder girl listened without any great interest. Her mind was on other matters.

" I have had another letter from Veryan," she said. " He talks about some friend he has in Canada. Someone he met in the war."

" Oh ! "

" He hopes to be able to see him again."

" Well, that will be very nice. It must get a bit boring being with the same people all the time," Lerryn said.

" Yes. Yes, I suppose you're right."

Two things occurred during September which were to have great repercussions where Bethel was concerned, things which were, in fact, to alter considerably the trend of the lives of all three Treveryans.

In September, whilst in Canada, Veryan was knocked down by a cab and injured so severely that it was out of the question that he should return to England in the royal suite. Bethel, on first hearing the news, cabled her brother that she would come and join him if he wished. This, however, was not found to be necessary, for his Canadian friend was insisting on taking him to his own home immediately he was to be allowed to leave the hospital; and if Bethel was secretly a little hurt at her brother's obvious enjoyment at the idea of remaining in Canada, Lerryn did not notice it.

For Lerryn had fallen in love.

It happened during those warm September days when the harvest was being brought in and everyone, Lerryn included, was busily helping. Every day she helped Mrs. Mutton and her daughter Violet to carry the baskets laden with pasties and sandwiches, and saffron cakes and cheese, to the distant fields where all the men and boys were working. And in the late afternoon the women would make a second expedition, and Lerryn would find herself pouring out the strong brew of farm-made tea into blue mugs, and the men, a dozen or more, would collect by the huge stacks for a brief spell of rest, and all would be friendly and gay. Jokes would be made, and Lerryn knew that these people had a greater knowledge of freedom and the joys of happiness than she had known since she was a child.

Then one afternoon Ted Truscott got a thorn into his thumb and came to Mrs. Mutton with all the despair of a great boy, begging her to do her best.

"It's no good, Ted, I haven't my glasses on," she said after several minutes of probing and prodding. "You try, Vi," and the fifteen-year girl, all giggles and silliness, was so overcome with shyness that she, too, was forced to give up the attempt.

"You're a feeble couple o' women, I will say," said old Mutton. "I'm ashamed o' ye, Vily. No good askin' we men, m'boy. There's Miss Lerryn, she'll fix it, I don't doubt."

So Lerryn held his hand in hers and was aware of the power of Ted's strength, and felt the heavy breathing of the man as he stood close beside her, and smelt the sweat of the field work coming from him, and saw the thick hair on his arms, and the dirt, too, and her heart stopped beating for a moment. And suddenly she felt Ted's blue eyes piercing hers, and a wave of shame ran through her.

"It's mighty deep, that thorn o' yourn," laughed one of
the men.

"Aye, let it be, Miss. The silly fellow dursn't ought to
take up so much o' your time," twitted another.

Neither of them appeared to hear.

"I think it's out," she said presently. And slowly she
withdrew her own hand. He never spoke, but turned to join
the other men who were already on their way back across the
fields, and she watched him go after them, her heart amazed.
At the far end of the field he turned, and when he saw she still
lingered, waved.

"The cheek of that Ted," laughed Mrs. Mutton. "He's
just gettin' too big for his boots. But he's a good lad. I
never did believe these tales about him."

It was a strange coincidence that by the next post a letter
should come to Lerryn from Sally, enclosing a photograph of
herself and her baby. She wrote ecstatically, and was nearly
crazy with excitement at her husband's plan to take her and
the child out to Italy, where it appeared the climate and general
facilities made the lot of an artist's life a great deal easier.

How ridiculous to feel suddenly so shy of someone one has
known all one's life, thought Lerryn the next day as she made
her way to the farm, wearing a brand new sun bonnet that she
had bought from a peddling gipsy woman who had called at
the house after breakfast. The whole business was absurd—or
was it? After all, Ted was an old friend, she had known him
since they were children. What had happened yesterday, she
asked herself? What magnetic spark had suddenly flown
from Ted to her that could have ignited the strange new
—something—she had felt? When she reached the farm, a
little out of breath, she hardly knew how to hide her disappointment at discovering that, one of the horses having
cast a shoe, Ted had been given the task of taking the animal
to the smith, and was not expected back before the evening.
Mr. Mutton was grumbling, as well he might, for it could not
have come at a more inconvenient time, when all hands and
all animals were needed.

The next day, however, Ted was back again, and seemed,
Lerryn thought, to be avoiding her. This made the situation
a little more embarrassing.

" I've had a letter from Sally, Ted," she said as nonchantly as possible. After that, it was easier, for the young man was eager to hear his sister's news and pleased to discuss her.

" Aye, it's all turned out fine," he said happily, " and she's a real lady now, is Sal. I went up and saw her you know."

" Did you Ted? You never told me. How was she? "

" Oh, she's doin' fine. Has a maid of her own and wears pretty frocks all the time. She took me in a hansom cab to a theatre," he said, as if to prove that the peak of society had been reached.

" Oh, Ted! What fun! What did you see? "

But Ted had forgotten the name of the play which was, it seemed, a musical show. He had been very impressed, however, with London, and especially with a certain restaurant to which he had gone with his brother-in-law.

" Very different to what you gets in Cornwall," he remarked a little dubiously. " And they're going away, are they? " he said, " where are they going to? "

" He's taking her to Italy."

" Foreign parts. Fancy that! Aye, our Sally's a lady all right."

He scratched his head, then broke off a piece of straw and chewed it. He studied the photo of Sally's baby again.

" She's 'andsome, ain't she, little Lerryn? " he said.

" I told her I'd be her godmother if it was a girl. I'm so pleased she's called her by my name."

" Yes. She said she'd bring it here for her to be baptised. I guess they won't now," slowly he handed back the picture. " Lerryn . . ."

" Yes? " she said quickly.

He started.

" I beg your pardon, Miss. I wasn't meanin' you. I was thinkin' o' the baby. Sally's baby."

But he looked into her eyes as he lied.

" Why do you call me Miss? I wish you wouldn't. I call you and your sister Ted and Sally . . ."

" That's different. You know it is. What'd people say——"

" Sally's a lady now. You keep telling me so. I'll certainly tell her not to call me anything but my name now, so there! "

" It'd be wrong."

"Would it?" There was a pause. "Ted, you don't know what these days have meant to me. Being down in the fields with Violet and Mrs. Mutton and all the rest of you, being an ordinary human being, talking with you all like friends for once instead of being Miss Lerryn. Oh, Ted! If you only knew how I long for friends of my own. People I can talk to and think with. I can't explain . . ."

"You've always been a good friend to Sally and me, Miss. We've both known that and loved you for it."

Empty, cold words! Words spoken by a grateful servant . . . these were not the words she was wanting to hear.

"I must go back. It's getting late. Good night, Ted." She spoke wearily. Slowly she made her way towards Treveryan. When she reached the gate she turned. Violet Mutton was running over the field. She saw Ted wave and the girl join him. Feeling sick with jealousy and mortification Lerryn walked quickly to the house.

The next day she did not go to the farm. On the pretext of having caught a touch of the sun she remained up at the house. Bethel, fully occupied by troubles of her own, for she was deeply worried over the news of Veryan's accident, was not sufficiently interested to notice anything amiss with her sister. The following day, however, Lerryn could not remain at home, and when a message came to her through Prue, that Mrs. Mutton was wanting all the help she could get, waves of relief swept her as she realized a very real excuse must take her to the farm.

It was a glorious day, the sky was cloudless, and a scorching sun beat on the team of workers in the field.

"My! We've been lucky this year," Mrs. Mutton said to Lerryn, "we shall be able to get the whole harvest in by the week-end if it keeps like this. Are you coming to the dance on Saturday night, Miss Lerryn? Do now. We're clearing the big barn for it, it'll be ever such fun. Violet and the boys was only saying last night as how they hoped you'd look in, seeing as how you've helped so much."

Lerryn hesitated. Would she not feel rather out of it if she came? It would be distinctly dull to sit by and only watch the fun. Yet . . .

"I'd not thought about it, Mrs. Mutton," she prevaricated.

" Then you do, Miss," said the elder woman good naturedly.

She was keenly aware of Ted Truscott's presence when they took dinner to the men in the fields, and inwardly cursed the loud beating of her heart as she saw him walking towards her.

" Where were you to, yesterday—Lerryn ? " he asked quietly.

" I wasn't well. I think I had sunstroke," she said quickly.

" You didn't ought to get that," he answered, " you kept your bonnet on all day."

" Did I ? "

Slowly she poured out the ration of scalding tea from the can, hoping no one would notice her shaking hand. The other men came up, and there was no chance of further conversation alone with him.

" He's a fine-looking lad, is Ted," Mrs. Mutton began innocently later, as the women were gathering up the remains of the dinner things.

" Yes," Lerryn said vaguely.

Violet Mutton started to giggle.

" Oh, you get along with you, you silly great girl, you ! " laughed her mother. " She'd like Ted for a sweetheart. Did you ever, Miss ! At her age ! I keep telling her he'll not look at her for a year or two yet ! "

" That's all you know, Mother," the young girl simpered.

Lerryn longed to wring her neck. Of course they were ideally suited to each other, and the realization of it made the fact even less palatable. She glanced at the girl out of the corner of her eye, and thought what a great lump she was in spite of dark, curling hair and a quite pretty face. Large ankles showed below her skirts, and for a moment Lerryn wished ardently and shamefully that fashions and respectability were such as could have enabled her to show off her own exquisitely-shaped limbs. Doubtless, she thought crossly, a man of Ted Truscott's type would admire a great thing like Violet. She heard the girl and her mother talking of the dance, and the very thought of Violet being whirled gaily about the barn by Ted infuriated her. Almost at that very moment Ted passed, leading one of the laden carts. Unlike the other men he wore no cap, and his thick, red-gold hair was in wild confusion; bits of straw had fastened themselves about his head and person; weeks in the fields, working in the brilliant sunshine, had burnt him a dark tan, and his blue eyes seemed to poor Lerryn to reflect the sky more than ever.   He had on a shabby blue shirt, which exposed a very hirsute chest, and his corduroy trousers were fastened by a belt, and not by braces as the Mutton men's were. He smiled at her as he passed, and she noted with satisfaction that Violet was passed by without so much as a look.

"Is it true you're coming to the dance?" he asked at the end of the day.

"I don't know yet," she answered.

"Please come!" She felt a thrill of pleasure at the urgency of his tone.

"I don't know all the country dances; I'd hate to be an onlooker," she said.

"You won't be that," he said firmly.

"I must ask my sister."

He looked a little crestfallen.

"Will she come?"

"Goodness, no!   She's upset, anyway.   Mr. Veryan is ill in Canada and can't come back yet."

"That's bad.   I'm sorry.   But that wouldn't interfere with you, would it?"

"No, I'll come.   I'll come if you promise to show me how to dance properly," she said, greatly daring.

"What an extraordinary thing to want to do," Bethel remarked with surprise, when Lerryn spoke of the dance at the farm. "But by all means go if you think you'll enjoy it.   Take Prue."

"Oh!"   This was not at all according to her plan.

"You'll want to have someone to talk to," Bethel went on, seeing her sister's hesitation, "you'd be very bored sitting by and watching if you had no one with you."

"But I mean to dance."

Bethel looked startled.

"My dear Lerryn!   Have you no idea of your position?"

"I'm not going at all if it means standing alone, looking all stuck-up and ridiculous.   The whole point is to be one of them."

Bethel shrugged her shoulders.

"I give you up. I never heard of such a ridiculous idea. None of us has ever done it before. And how d'you know some of the men won't get very rough? And even perhaps drunk?"

"Mr. Mutton would see to that. He and Jack Mutton would certainly throw anyone out who misbehaved. Besides, Beth, it isn't a big village affair, it's only a harvest dance."

.   .   .   .

Lerryn wore a sprigged muslin frock and a sash. She looked upon the whole evening as a child might picture a fancy dress ball.

The party was in full swing when she arrived down at the big barn; Mr. Mutton supplied the music with a fiddle, and the place seemed crowded with the farm hands and their relations and a sprinkling of village youth. A long trestle table at the far end groaned beneath the spread, the like of which only a Cornish farmer's wife can give, and a huge barrel of cider had already been well tapped to quench the dancers' thirst. Mrs. Mutton stood behind the table to preside, and waved Lerryn a welcome. Suddenly overcome by shyness the girl joined her, glad of a chance to help and remain inconspicuous. The air was full of the smell of hay, sweat, and paraffin, for great lamps hung from the beams to light the barn. The big doors were flung open, and the harvest moon, in full splendour, made the romantic setting complete. Lerryn watched for some time with amusement and genuine interest, until the feel of a hand at her waist brought the colour to her cheeks as Ted Truscott's voice asked her for a dance. It was a polka, and when it was finished they both flung themselves down on a heap of hay at the end of the barn, exhausted and out of breath.

"My! That was something like dancing," she laughed.

He wiped his forehead with a handkerchief, and Lerryn suddenly realized his other hand still held hers.

"You do look pretty," he said quickly.

"Nonsense!" she answered, trying to keep her voice steady. "Where's Violet?" she asked, as casually as she could.

"I don't know. D'you want her?"

She shook her head. "I want some refreshment," she said.

They went over to the trestle table and were revived with mugs of cider and saffron cake. Mr. Mutton was now joined

by two other cronies and a country dance was called for.
Lerryn was unable to do this, and was forced to see Ted look
for Violet for his partner, and watch them for the next twenty-
five minutes twist and twirl and disappear at intervals, in the
sombre darkness of the barn.   It was evidently a dance of much
merry-making, and shouts of laughter and girlish shrieks kept
coming to Lerryn's ears, as once more she busied herself behind
the tables with Mrs. Mutton.

There was a long interval at the end of the dance, and then
young Jack Mutton came up with gauche politeness and heavy
feet, and asked for ' the next.'   By this time it was getting late,
and the noise and fun had intensified as the barn grew slowly
darker.   It was now difficult to make out from the shadows in
the middle and far corners of the barn, who was who, which
seemed to lead to even greater merry-making and laughter.
Ted Truscott had by now taken enough cider to forget caution,
and knew only that Lerryn was a mighty pretty girl who was
filling his senses with great excitement and even desire.   When
the music struck up again he seized hold of her and dragged
her into the rest of the fray, where the dancing was now rough,
to say the least of it.   Lerryn felt Ted's heart panting fiercely
against her breast.   He was dancing wildly now, and had
discarded the clean collar and tie which he had worn at the
beginning of the evening.   Gradually, however, his wild spirits
subsided, and when with calm deliberation he guided her to the
big doors, and pulled her gently towards the gate which led to
the garden, she felt a greater disquiet than she had known
inside the crowded and noisy barn.   The full moon lit up the
yard and the old grey farm-house, and Lerryn gave a little cry
as something black scurried out of her way towards one of the
lofts.   It was naught but one of the many farm cats, but served
the purpose for Ted's arm to encircle her waist with even
greater precision. . Neither of them spoke a word as they leant
on the little gate.   Presently the music stopped.

" We'd better go back," she said.   But, instead, she found
they wandered towards the bank close to the pond.

" It's hot and noisy inside," Ted spoke a little thickly, " stay
here a bit longer."

They stood beneath a gigantic walnut tree, and he suddenly
took off his coat and threw it on the ground.

" Sit on it," he urged, " you won't be feeling the dampness of the ground then."

Mechanically Lerryn obeyed him.   Once again she felt his arm go round her.   Then he kissed her.   She shivered.

" It's wild you're making me to-night, Lerryn, my 'and-some," he cried.   " I know as how I shouldn't be behavin' like this to you, but I can't help myself, like."

They lay beneath the giant tree awhile, Lerryn in full ecstasy of first love, while Ted Truscott dared not let himself think for fear the dream should cease.   Such things only happened in dreams or in books, he knew, and if, for an enchanted hour he could lie with his princess beside him, he must do everything in his power to keep the precious minutes undisturbed.   Like many Cornish folk, he was superstitious and ready to believe in the magic of fairies and pixies, and for a brief spell he frankly believed Lerryn to be some lovely immortal being.   Her fair hair now looked like spun gold in the light of the moon, and she let him run his fingers through its fineness, till once again her lips seemed to beckon his and she gave herself up to his worship.

" We must go," she said later as the moon dropped behind the elm trees and was hidden at last, leaving them in darkness. He rose and helped her to her feet.   Music still came from the barn, but she suddenly felt no desire to return.   What had happened to her, she began to wonder?   Had all sense left her?

" I think I'll slip away back to Treveryan," she said quietly.

Treveryan.   The very word brought the young man to his own senses.   He must have been crazy, right out of his mind. He looked at the girl beside him as though stunned.

" I'll—see—you back, Miss Lerryn," he stammered.   She turned sharply at his words.

" What's the matter? " she said.

He was silent.   She went up to him and shook him by the lapels of his coat.

" Have you forgotten already? " she asked in anguish. " *Miss* Lerryn? "

At the sound of her voice and seeing she was in earnest, he took her again into his arms.

" My God!   I'll never forget," he said fiercely, " but we're crazy.   What can the likes of me be to such as you? "

After a pause she answered.

" I don't know. I don't understand. But to-night I love you, Ted."

" We're dreaming."

" Then, dear God, let me keep this dream ! " she cried.

" Don't you see the madness of it ? "

" I neither see nor care. I only know that you have shown me a new life, you've made me realize that even for me there is love."

She spoke like one exalted. He was frightened. How could the magic of one night, such as this had been, continue? Outside the door he hesitated.

" Lerryn . . ." he murmured, " my-lady-Lerryn."

" Good night, my—dear," she whispered.

She opened the massive oak door and the lights from the hall lit their faces. Quickly and softly she leant forward and kissed his lips, and then the heavy door was closed. As in a dream he stumbled from the house.

PART TWO
5

THROUGHOUT THE AUTUMN and winter Bethel continued to hear quite frequently from Veryan. He wrote as affectionately as ever, but seemed in no hurry to make definite plans for his return. The royal tour had come to its brilliant end in October, and even Bethel felt sad at the thought of her brother's absence at the close, especially when Their Highnesses were formally created Prince and Princess of Wales as the climax to the trip.

Throughout the autumn and winter Lerryn and Ted Truscott continued to meet as lovers whenever it was possible for Ted to get off from the farm and for Lerryn to escape Bethel's unpremeditated vigilance. Lerryn soon realized that romantic meetings could only be held by stealth, and this was not always easy, for during the long evenings, when Ted was free, Lerryn herself could find no excuse to absent herself from Treveryan, and as he was busy at the farm there was very little time in the day when he was free. Sunday afternoons were the most possible times for the lovers to meet, and there again they had to be careful not to run into people, for though in

time past Lerryn's friendship for both the young Truscotts
had been acknowledged by all, the very nature of their meetings now swore them to guilty secrecy. It was Ted who
ultimately discovered a small disused cottage in the woods;
how much of a haven it was to be time was to tell. In the
past it had been used by old Simon Treveryan as a picnic
house for the big pheasant shoots for which Treveryan had
then been noted. It was now little more than derelict and
deserted, with a roof that needed mending and broken
windows. The inside, too, was damp and filled with cobwebs
and old leaves, and the furniture at first seemed too rickety and
hopeless for use. Lerryn shivered with dismay when Ted
Truscott, with excitement in his voice, showed it with pride
to her.

" Ugh! It's a horrible, sinister little place," she said. " I
should die of depression if I thought we had to meet here."

" You wait. I bet I'll get it fine in no time." And, indeed,
a fortnight later, when he showed the little house to her, she
had to exclaim in astonishment.

" But when did you do it? " she asked incredulously.

" Got up early and did two hours on it afore going to the
farm, and this last week-end I spent a brave while on it. Then
I can do a good bit in the evening with the aid of a lamp, see? "

She had to admit he had indeed made a good job of the
place, which now, as well as being habitable, looked even
pretty. He had found old covers, too, from some place or
other, and the little house hidden safely in the depth of now
unused woods became the refuge of their meetings. Perhaps
the very fact that they were unable to meet often kept the
affair at a height of passion and prevented the girl from the
inevitable awareness of sayings and traits due to his origin
and bringing-up that he could not have hidden for long. At
any rate, Lerryn continued during the winter and spring to be
madly in love with her Ted. Often she told herself that it
could not last, that someone would discover their secret, that
a scandal would, and must, probably, be the end. Ted, on the
other hand, in love as indeed he was, became as most men
become, gradually used to the strange romance that had come
into his life, and she became more woman and less immortal
to him. There were times when he cursed roundly the

difference in their stations of life, and would occasionally, in fits of sulky inferiority, pretend that things must end.

" What's the use of it all, really? " he would say. " I'm a man and you're a woman, we're not a couple of children playing fairy games. You're my woman now "—how she thrilled at his words—" I want a real home of my own and a wife in it. For always. These snatched meetings are damn silly, come to think of it."

A wife. Only sometimes did Lerryn think madly of suggesting marriage to him. Even she saw the impossibility. Then again, after an unexpected meeting in Tregony one day, with him in the company of Mrs. Mutton and Violet, she was filled with jealousy, and realized with horror the state into which he had dragged her. But for the most part they were happy and content, and perhaps the romantic excitement of it all prevented what would certainly have become dreary squalor if their state had been one of marriage. From an æsthetic point of view Ted Truscott was a glorious young animal, but socially the fact that Lerryn was Miss Treveryan, a daughter of one of the oldest families in Cornwall, put her attachment for him beyond the pale.

In the spring she received a picture postcard from Sally. It had been taken in Venice, and showed the girl with her husband and baby feeding the pigeons. No one would have known by her appearance that Sally was of humble origin, and from what she wrote it appeared that she was meeting all sorts of interesting people.

" You see she says Nigel has two pictures at the Academy," Lerryn murmured, " and that they may come to London in June."

Ted remained lost in silence.

In May Lerryn had a letter from Brigit Selworthy begging her to go up to town for a fortnight's holiday with them.

" Now that the war is over," she wrote, " you will find everything too delightful and gay, and even we in our humble way see the difference. Of course, if you would rather come for the Coronation we should love to have you then, but I can't promise we'd be able to have the fun we had at the Jubilee. Three children have greatly reduced our exchequer !"

With a feeling of guilt Lerryn realized that she did not really want to go up to the Selworthy's at all.   The idea of leaving Ted for a couple of weeks, just as the summer was beginning to deck Cornwall in full glory, filled her with dismay.

"Have you had a letter from Brigit?" Bethel asked at breakfast, "I thought I recognized her writing."

"Yes."

"I suppose she's invited you to stay?"

"As a matter of fact, she has," she replied, without much enthusiasm.

"You'll go, I suppose? It's ages since you went on a visit. Not even Exeter and Miss Garth have seen you for over a year."

At once Lerryn became wary. It would never do to let Bethel get suspicious. After all, she thought rapidly, a fortnight would soon pass, and in novels one read that men grew tired . . .

"Yes, I shall go up," she said.   "Brigit suggests any time, or during the Coronation week."

"You like shows, you'd better go then," Bethel answered.

However, Lerryn chose to go up to London the following week. Ted had been satisfactorily put out at her going, and had even shown signs of jealousy at the idea of whom she might meet.

"You'll not be wantin' *me* when you come back," he said moodily. "You'll meet a lot of fine chaps up along there, I know, as how'll make as want to marry you."

"Silly love!" Lerryn admonished. "I love you, I don't want anyone else but you."

"What d'you want to go leavin' me for then?"

"I think it will do us both good," she answered, surprised by her own lie.

So Lerryn went up to London and enjoyed shops and picture galleries and matinees with Brigit, and if the evenings were rather quiet, spent as a rule at home with the Selworthy's, she did not appear to mind; as often as not they were taken up with writing lengthy screeds to Ted. He, of course, was not a very satisfactory correspondent, half a page in rather illiterate handwriting would come, with a 'thanks dear for yours' and a few lines of meaningless scrawl.

"I'm sure you're in love at last, Lerryn," said Brigit, after the fourth evening, when her friend had excused herself from playing some game on the pretext of writing a letter. Lerryn blushed violently.

"Who is he? You are a little mean puss not telling me."

"It's all very difficult," Lerryn stammered.

"Why? Are you engaged secretly?"

"No, no!" And after a pause, "There are complications. We can't marry."

"*It's not a married man?*" Brigit asked with horror.

"Oh, no," Lerryn hastened to assure her, "it's really a question of—being poor."

"Oh, poor Lerryn!" Immediately Brigit was all sympathy. "How well I can understand that. But don't let it stop your getting married if you really love one another. After all, we manage, you know, and living in London with three children on what Ken has is not easy, I assure you. But it's worth it. Tell me, who is he, do I know him?"

"He's a sort of farmer," said Lerryn, not knowing where to look.

"What fun. A gentleman farmer's life would be really very nice, I often think. He must be new. Does he live near? I wonder Mother hasn't written of him. She's such an old gossip for anything of that sort."

"No, no," Lerryn lied blindly, "I met him when I was staying with Miss Garth."

"But I thought you hadn't seen her for ages?"

"I haven't. But that's how I met him."

"And I suppose he's been to Treveryan?"

Lerryn nodded. After all, that was the truth, if a rather distorted version of it.

"And what does Bethel think about it? And Veryan? Surely he could help financially?"

"They don't know." How Lerryn longed for someone to come into the room so that the conversation might be changed.

"Not know? Bethel not know? You mean he came to Treveryan and she never realized? She is an odd creature, I must say! You're so obviously head over heels!" Brigit laughed.

"He—he stays at the inn. I mean in the village. It's all

terribly secret. Brigit, swear, you must swear not to tell a soul. Not even Kenneth."

Brigit looked a little shocked.

" We have no secrets from each other," she began.

" But this is my secret. Oh, please, dear Brigit, you must promise me you'll keep it all to yourself. I wish I'd never told you now."

At that Brigit Selworthy seemed hurt.

" Now don't go getting upset. Of course I won't tell anyone. I promise. But I think it's all very strange."

A few days before she was due to depart, Lerryn felt a hand on her elbow whilst waiting for a 'bus. Swiftly turning, she found, to her amazement, Sally standing on the pavement.

" I had to speak to you ! " the girl said with a bright smile.

" Sally darling ! " Always fond of the girl, Lerryn felt doubly the bond of affection now.

" Where have you sprung from? We thought you were not coming till June ! " she exclaimed.

" We? "

" I showed your postcard to Ted," she said quickly. It gave her a thrill to say his name to someone.

" Dear Ted, how is he? "

" He's very well. You know, of course, he's working at the farm? But tell me how you are, Sally. Goodness ! You look smart and pretty."

It was easy to see that there was no truth—at least to the naked eye—in the old saying that a silk purse could not be made from a sow's ear, thought Lerryn, not, as she was the first to admit, that there had ever been much of the sow's ear about Sally. But how she had changed ! There was a new chic about her which was an added attraction to her prettiness, and the remains of any accent or dialect had completely disappeared.

" Come and have some tea," said Sally, " we're close to Fuller's, and I long to hear your news and tell you mine."

It seemed incredible, Lerryn thought later, that this charming, sophisticated person should be Ted's sister. Surely if Sally's Nigel had made such a metamorphosis of the sister, she too could work a like miracle over Ted?

Here she was, holding forth on the subject of art, as one

born in the milieu, and discussing her husband's pictures and others in the summer shows with every appearance of knowledge.

"We're having a tiny party to-morrow night," she said, "couldn't you come? And bring your friends?"

Lerryn suddenly realized she had forgotten to say with whom she was staying. When Brigit's name was mentioned Sally seemed taken aback.

"Did she—know—about—everything?" she asked, a little nervously.

Lerryn had to confess she did.

"Can't you pretend you've met an old friend and come along alone?" she begged.

"I'll see what I can do," she promised.

"Do. I want you to meet Nigel, and see my Lerryn. And we've taken the sweetest flat in Chelsea.

On the spur of the moment Lerryn told Brigit she had run into Miss Garth, up for only a few days, who had expressed a deep wish for Lerryn's company the following evening, and Brigit believed her.

Sally's party gave Lerryn a great deal to think about; she was, in fact, in no small way disquieted by it. She longed for Ted to acquit himself in as able and natural a way as his sister in like circumstances, and had to admit to herself that, given the same chances as Sally, there was very much less likelihood of this happening. Why was it, she asked herself? It was Bethel who confirmed her fears when, after her return to Treveryan, Lerryn told her of her meeting with Sally and the amusing party at Chelsea.

"Doesn't it show," Bethel mused.

"What?"

"How far cleverer women are than men. Can you imagine Ted Truscott, for instance, ever being anything but a labourer?"

"I don't see why——"

"You'll nearly always find it so. Women have a far greater imagination than men. If a woman wants to better herself she will go to any length to learn what to do, and whom to copy. Play-act herself into a character until she has become the very part indeed. And if she wants to become a lady, she's a poor actress if she can't convince the world sooner or later. Men are different. They have some sort of pride, some ego, that will always assert the true man he feels himself to be. John Smith may want to better himself just as much as his wife, but if he does so he will never forget John Smith, where she will be perfectly amenable to changing her entire identity. He will reach out with ambition of a different sort, money, power— she will want the niceties of what she considers the upper classes before all else. A woman will lose her accent long before her man realizes he has one. And there you have the difference between Ted and Sally Truscott. Of course she's been lucky enough to marry this man who, you say, is charming and a gentleman, and I suppose that's helped her a great deal. I expect he took trouble over her. After all, she's a very pretty girl, worth training, I daresay."

" But supposing Ted married a—lady ? " Lerryn asked.

" How likely ! " Bethel laughed.

" He's very attractive," Lerryn persisted.

" To one of his own class, perhaps. Personally I think he's rather coarse. Of course one hears of extraordinary people going everywhere nowadays ; people in trade get received who never would have done in Mama's day, for instance. And then there is the sort which climbs through politics. Some of the Radicals these days come from very humble homes. But Ted Truscott doesn't come into such categories."

" Yet he and Sally had the same education," said Lerryn, clinging to the memory of Ted's superficial knowledge of board-school Shakespeare, and his appreciation of music the one and only time he had heard her play.

" I don't suppose he could talk to one for ten minutes on any subject except farming."

" That's more interesting and more worth while than the small talk heard in most people's drawing-rooms, I daresay."

Bethel looked surprised.

" That may be. But the question in point is just whether he could pass muster in a crowd of small talk. And I swear he couldn't. Ted will talk with a Cornish accent all his life. And anyway, why not ? He probably eats off his knife, too."

"He doesn't!" Lerryn denied hotly.

"Really Lerryn! You're quite absurd where the Truscotts are concerned."

The younger girl, fearing she had said too much, hurriedly changed the subject.

She did not allow herself to worry long, and quickly realized that the very fact that Ted was unlike any of the men she had met either with the Selworthy's or at Sally's party, was in itself a reason for caring for him. To her, he was the fields, the country, the very Cornish air she breathed; she had been used to none other and found him natural, where the men in London had seemed either dull, or sophisticated and shallow. She forgot that friends of her own kind had always been denied her; in fact, she had forgotten the past entirely, her own irritation and restlessness included, so entirely wrapped up was she in her love for Truscott.

The fortnight away had been just enough to whet Ted's own desire and restlessness, and Lerryn was touched and a little frightened by his passion when she met him again.

Never had any summer seemed so beautiful to Lerryn; even Bethel remarked one evening :

"What's come over you, sweet? You look so different."

Lerryn could think of no adequate reply.

"It's just the fine weather," she said, hoping her sister would probe her no further.

The long evenings made lovers' meetings easier, for often Lerryn would make some pretext of taking the dogs for a walk after dinner when Bethel, tired from gardening, could be relied upon to excuse herself from any such outing. These were wonderful evenings for Lerryn and Ted Truscott, spent as often as not by some distant cove or headland. Sometimes on fine nights she would creep from the house and meet him, and they would wander to the sea and bathe off rocks, and later lie, slaking their love, under the stars.

When the serious illness of the King was announced, and for a few days it seemed as if England was once again to be plunged into national grief, it was Bethel who took her sister to task for showing no concern, and indeed so hopelessly in love was Lerryn that she had hardly realized the country's anxiety.

It was shortly afterwards that Bethel astonished and horrified her sister by saying one day : ·

" Do you remember that conversation we had about Ted Truscott? Just to show you what I mean I've asked him in to tea this afternoon when he's finished at the farm. I saw him this morning and we had a little chat, and I asked him to come along."

Lerryn felt as if her legs were giving way. Should she pretend she had some engagement and leave Bethel to entertain Ted? But such an idea was out of the question, for her sister would know it to be an excuse, and moreover it might only give rise to suspicion.

As might be expected the meal proved thoroughly embarrassing. Ted Truscott arrived late, wearing his best Sunday blacks, and was tongue-tied and unnatural, and Lerryn, who could have put him at ease, sat poker-faced, and seemed singularly lacking in conversation. Bethel talked about the farm and the weather and the harvest prospects, but there were a great number of awkward silences, and Ted was obviously ill at ease, and at sea as to why he should have been asked. Lerryn only spoke to him occasionally, and then was so palpably making conversation that even Ted grinned as he realized her unnatural behaviour. Only for a few moments were they alone when Bethel went out of the room for something.

" What did she ask me for? " he said quickly, " does she know about—us ? "

" S'sh, of course not. ·I can't think what's possessed her."

" And what's the matter with you? You're not acting a bit like yourself. I know what it is, you're ashamed of me."

" Don't be silly, darling, you must never say such a thing," but the tone of her voice lacked conviction, and a second later Bethel came into the room. She looked distrait, and conversation flagged even more than before. Shortly afterwards Ted took his departure.

It was after dinner that Bethel, looking pale and obviously worried, said :

" Lerryn, tell me if I'm wrong, did I hear you call Ted Truscott *darling?* "

For a moment the younger girl felt as if her heart had stopped.

" Yes," she said weakly after a pause.

" Had you taken leave of your senses or what? " Bethel had gone quite white.

" I love him," said Lerryn.

" You don't know what you're saying."

" Ted and I have been in love with each other for very nearly a year," Lerryn said slowly.

" My God! " Bethel sank slowly into a chair.

" Can you never understand that other people have loved besides yourself, or do you consider you had the monopoly, Bethel? " cried Lerryn, her eyes blazing. " I suppose you think I'm ashamed of Ted? Well, I'm not."

" Oh, God! Why didn't I forsee something of this sort was bound to happen? " Bethel groaned. " Why didn't I take Veryan's advice and tell you? It's my fault, all my fault."

" If you mean that by preventing me from ever meeting anyone else, then yes, perhaps it is your fault. I used to resent your attitude, oh, yes, I did, and Veryan knew it, but so potty has he always been about you, that he forbade me to grumble or talk about your own—attachment—to Oswald."

It gave the younger girl exquisite pleasure to see her sister flinch.

" Do you think all these years I've not known your jealousy? Realized how you loathed the idea that I might fall in love and marry, be lucky where you were unlucky, bring back to your memory all that time which you've done your best to forget and have not succeeded in doing? For years you've been more and more impossible and old maidy—yes, that's what you are for all your beauty. Even your beloved Veryan can't stick it any longer, or why do you suppose he took the first opportunity to leave England so soon after his return? Why does he remain in Canada? Because you, with your jealousy and possessiveness, have made Treveryan hell."

By now Lerryn was white to the lips and shaking as if with an ague. Bethel had covered her face with her hands, tears poured in abandon down her face.

" Stop, stop, you don't know what you're saying! " she sobbed.

" I'm not going to stop until I've made you see that I refuse to suffer as you let yourself suffer once upon a time. I know you'd have me give up Ted; I'm not going to. I don't care if he is not a gentleman—if it comes to that—have you or Veryan ever allowed me to meet one? I only know that for the last year Ted has given me more happiness than I've had during the rest of my life."

" Lerryn—Lerryn——" Bethel cried.

" In a way I'm glad you know. Because now we can have done with this hole-in-a-corner business. Oh! I've not enjoyed the secrecy of our love, believe me. But I knew if it were known it would create a scandal, as well as Ted probably being given the sack."

Bethel's sobs were beginning to subside, and she looked miserably at her sister.

" I know what snobs people are. But can't you understand that *I love Ted?* I don't care if he does talk differently from us, or look strange in his best clothes. And anyway, Sally has altered, so how do you know Ted couldn't? "

She looked at Bethel defiantly.

" You don't understand," Bethel said, " it's not Ted I mind, though I cannot believe that a girl like you could care for an uncouth creature such as he is, it seems fantastic. He's good-looking, perhaps, for his class——"

" *Class!* " Lerryn fumed.

" How you, a fastidious . . ."

" Shut up! Shut up! " Lerryn shouted. " I will not allow you to talk about the man I love like this. Am I child that you have no respect for my feelings? I've told you I love him, and I shall write and tell Veryan. He, of course, will take your side, he always does. But I don't see that either of you has any claim on me, or I on you any longer. By your own fault you force me into doing something I should probably have never had the courage to do. I shall marry Ted."

Bethel rose and went over to Lerryn and seized her hands.

" Oh, no you won't," she said.

" Nothing shall prevent it."

" Even Ted Truscott cannot marry you." She spoke slowly.

" Why are you looking at me as you do? And please let go my wrists, Bethel."

" Veryan always said I should have told you the truth. I

refused. I thought you could be spared the misery, the horror. But after all, I was wrong."

Her whispered words caused Lerryn to feel apprehensive.

"What are you talking about?" she asked.

"Why do you suppose I never married? Why do you suppose Veryan has never married? Why do you suppose we've gone out of our way to bring you up in so sheltered a manner that it has been possible for you to avoid meeting people?"

"I—don't—know," Lerryn answered in frightened tones, "I never thought there was any real reason."

"My poor Lerryn!" Bethel drew the girl to her. "I forgive you for what you've said to me. How could you know?"

"Know? Know what? For pity's sake tell me what this horrible secret is that you share with Veryan."

"You must be brave, my darling."

"Go on, go on!"

"I said just now that *even Ted Truscott* cannot marry you. Lerryn, no one can marry us."

"I don't understand," Lerryn stammered, "you speak in such riddles, Beth. I feel I'm going crazy. It's like some frightful nightmare, or a scene in a melodrama. You'll tell me next we're cursed."

"We are. You may one day be crazy. Our family is cursed with madness—Lerryn."

"It's not true," the girl whispered.

"That's the secret of Papa's death, Lerryn, he died completely insane. He tried to strangle Mama. And Papa's aunts were mad. There's a streak of madness which has run through the family for generations, our heritage from Tregony."

Her voice sounded old and weary. "Now you see, now you understand."

"Oh, God! Forgive me——" Lerryn dropped on her knees and buried her head in Bethel's lap.

"It's I who should ask your forgiveness. I've been wickedly, criminally wrong, keeping you in ignorance all these years. Believe me, dearest, I meant it only for your good. It never struck me——"

"Please!" Lerryn besought in anguish.

After a while she got up.

" After the things I've said to-night I don't deserve that you should speak to me," she said to Bethel.

" Don't——"

" I just don't know what I'm going to do. To be told suddenly that I—that any of us—may quite likely go mad . . . Beth, it's like a living death."

" I know,"

" It's so—*horrible*. It's the kind of thing that happens in books. I—I can't believe it. To us. Treveryan. The mad Treveryans . . ."

" Poor Lerryn. I prayed you'd never fall in love. I thought we had guarded against it so well."

" Beth, I know the subject is terribly painful to you. Could you—could you possibly bear to tell me how you've lived through these years? *Without Oswald?* "

The following day, a Sunday, Bethel felt deeply anxious as she watched Lerryn. She looked as if she had had no sleep at all, and Bethel tried to dissuade her from going to church.

" You look so ill, darling," she said.

" I'm all right."

But she sat through the service like a dumb creature, and hurried away at the end before the rest of the congregation had left their pews.

" I feel like a leper, as if everyone must know," she said later to Bethel.

" Mrs. Penrose is coming in to tea after Sunday school; would you rather I sent her a note saying you feel unwell? She thought you were faint in church this morning, so would understand," Bethel said after lunch.

" Don't bother. I promised to meet Ted." She looked wretched as she spoke. " We always spend Sundays together, but you've never noticed. Oh, heavens! Beth, what am I going to do? What am I to tell him? "

Bethel sighed. She could proffer no solution.

As the evening wore on and the girl did not return, she tried not to feel alarmed. She had no idea where they met, and told herself that often in the past, when aware that Lerryn was out with the dogs, she had gone to bed without bothering to wait

up for her sister. When eleven o'clock struck and there was
still no sign of Lerryn, Bethel, sick at heart and knowing there
was nothing she could do, went to bed.

She did not see her sister till the middle of the morning,
when she came upon her in the garden. She said nothing, but
her eyes spoke her unasked question.

" I couldn't," Lerryn said softly.

" You mean you told him nothing? "

" I funked it. I couldn't face what he might have said.
Beth, if you want to know the truth, I couldn't face the
expression I might have seen in his eyes once he realized."

Bethel sighed helplessly.

" Men are so queer," Lerryn said slowly. " I couldn't have
born to see his love turn to horror, repulsion."

" And are you not going to tell him? " Lerryn fancied she
detected censure in Bethel's tone.

" I've written to him. I've told him everything." There
was no hiding the abject misery in her voice. " Oh, Bethel ! "
and she flung her arms round her sister. " How could I spoil
that meeting? I'd die if my last memory of him was one of
scorn, disgust. Don't you understand? "

" Yes, I understand," she said.

*   *   *

PART   LERRYN RECEIVED NO answer to her letter, and a
TWO   week went by without news of Ted. Sometimes
          the wretched girl, distraught now by her lover's
6   silence, would wander to the cottage in the wood
          in the hope of seeing him or finding some message
from him. The little house, which had been so dear to her,
became repellant and hateful, yet day after day her feet seemed
to take her back as if by some insistent force, and she would
touch things Ted had touched, fondle old garments of his that
still lay about the place in casual disarray, caress the cushion
against which his head had so often lain.

There was no one with whom she felt she could share her
suffering. To Bethel, who was kind and so obviously understood her agony, she could not turn, for she still felt ashamed
of the things she had said in anger. There were times, too,

when she felt shy with Bethel, feeling her sister's eyes upon her, as if the latter were trying to read the secrets in her heart, precious, sacred secrets shared with Ted, now to be destroyed for ever.

So many days went by, and Lerryn's icy reserve seemed to create a new barrier between the sisters, until at last Bethel could bear it no longer, and said :

" Did Ted Truscott answer you or see you——? " she hesitated.

" No."

" Then you don't know——? "

" What? What have you heard? Tell me for mercy's sake ! " Lerryn turned sharply and besought her sister.

" Lerryn, my dear. He's gone."

" Gone? " The younger girl looked at Bethel blankly.

" The Muttons told me. In fact, they asked to see me about it. They couldn't understand his disappearance, and could get nothing out of Mrs. Truscott, so they asked me if I could throw any light upon the matter. Of course I said I barely knew him. They knew he was a—friend," she paused, " of yours, in a manner of speaking. Everyone in the village, of course, has always known you were fond of both of them. I said I was sure you knew nothing."

" But where is he? Where has he gone? Hasn't his mother any idea? "

" I went to see Mrs. Truscott. Poor Lerryn, I'm afraid what I heard will be a shock to you."

" Go on, tell me. For God's sake tell me ! "

" I found Mrs. Truscott in the throes of despair, naturally. Those children were all she had, and now they've both left her. She could not make head or tail of why Ted had thrown up his job at a moment's notice, but anyway he's gone to an uncle, a brother of hers, who had promised him an opening if he should ever want to leave England . . ."

" Leave England? " Lerryn's voice was a bare whisper.

" The uncle lives in Australia. He went up to London some days ago, and has sailed. I suppose he went steerage. Of course he had letters from his uncle promising a job so I fancy the authorities made no fuss."

There was a long silence. Presently Bethel noticed two tears

well up in her sister's eyes and overflow. Lerryn made no
sound, and her quiet sorrow upset the other woman deeply.

"Darling, my poor darling," she murmured, taking the girl
into her arms.

"He couldn't even come and say good-bye!" Her words
came falteringly. "Beth, he loved me so much. Is it possible
for love to turn to hate so quickly? To hate and loathing and
disgust? Do you suppose he looks on me already as something foul, diseased? Oh, God!" She hid her head against
Bethel's breast.

"I've seen his ruthlessness with sick animals which have
been incurable. I know what he thinks and feels about anything that is unhealthy. This is what I was frightened of, and
what, in my heart of hearts, I believed impossible. Bethel,
how am I going to go on?"

"You will, dear one. I've had to. In time you'll get used
to the idea that we belong to no one but ourselves."

She tried to prevent bitterness from creeping into her voice.

"Thank God we have each other," Lerryn answered.

"We have so much, really. We have Treveryan. And
above all, there is Veryan. Oh, darling, I've not told you
before, I had a cable from him yesterday. He's expecting to
sail any day."

Lerryn glanced at her sister. Bethel looked transformed, she
thought. Perhaps in time she would also find Veryan's
affection enough. But even while she thought, she remembered how, in their childhood, Bethel and Veryan had been
wrapped up in each other. She had always been very much the
third, the petted baby sister, rarely the companion. Never to
Veryan had she been the comrade Bethel had been.

As the days passed, Bethel did everything in her power to
distract Lerryn from the misery which she knew only too well
she was suffering. She was alarmed, too, by catching glimpses
of terror in the girl's eyes, and realized the morbid fear and
anxiety through which her sister was bound to pass before she
became inured to their fate. She had almost forgotten her own
shock and past sorrow, so determinedly had she striven to live
anew, and make a life of Treveryan and her brother. How
long had it been, she tried to remember, before she had been
able to look on their lives calmly, and, as it were, detached

from the outside world? The past, her love for Oswald, all
that which should have been so beautiful, had been as some
fearful cancer in her life, to be cut out ruthlessly and utterly
destroyed. The very memories she nursed were but vile
adhesions to one as unfortunate as she, and therefore to be
dealt with as stringently. Thank God! Veryan was on his
way back. She wondered why his last message had given so
little news of his actual plans. He had given neither the name
of his ship nor the port at which he expected to land, only the
surprising information that he would arrive in time for the
Coronation, which happily was now to take place on August
the ninth, and would return to Treveryan immediately after.
She had had nothing but wires and cables of late from him,
and longed for a letter.

Would Veryan blame her for Lerryn's calamitous affair,
Bethel wondered? It was unlikely, though she was ready to
take full responsibility. She felt horribly guilty in that the
business would never have happened if, as Veryan had always
advised, she had told Lerryn the truth long ago. It was no
use bewailing her lack of forethought now, what was done was
done, and the real blame lay on the shoulders of their ancestors,
she thought bitterly.

Lerryn's shattered romance was likely to bring the girls
closer to each other Bethel fully realized; already she knew
herself to feel more tender towards her sister; the wish to
protect and cherish the younger girl against any evil to which
their common heritage might lead them, reminded her of the
old days when she had loved her with almost maternal
devotion.

Gradually as the weeks passed, bringing them nearer to
Veryan's return, Lerryn began to feel less strained with Bethel.
It was almost as if the past had not been, and they were back
in the years that followed Anna Treveryan's death when no
barriers had existed between them. If Bethel had taken in the
words Lerryn in her blind rage had uttered, she never alluded
to them, and the girl, filled with remorse, prayed that they had
been ignored and forgotten.

She tried to take the interest in her brother's return that
Bethel was feeling, and any other time this would have been
possible. But her tortured spirit still felt too numb to share

the other's excitement, and although she looked forward to seeing him, it was impossible to appear the bright-eyed vision that Bethel now seemed.

At last a letter came from Veryan. It was very short and had been written on the boat. Apart from saying he was better than he had ever been, and how he was looking forward to his return to Treveryan and seeing both Bethel and Lerryn, he gave no news at all beyond the fact that he should stay in London, where he hoped to see the Coronation procession and would come down the following day.

"I wish he had told us a bit more about himself and what he's been doing," Lerryn remarked, handing back the letter to her sister.

"Bless him! I expect he realized we should plague the life out of him with questions when he's back," Bethel smiled happily.

As bad luck would have it the day before Veryan's return Bethel was seized with a violent chill. The doctor, a young man named French, old Dr. Pearce's successor, pronounced it out of the question that she should go to the station to meet her brother.

"I may be as fit as a fiddle to-morrow," she stormed impatiently, but the doctor remained adamant.

So last minute preparations fell to Lerryn, who tactfully suggested next day that, what with so much to see to and Bethel still feeling poorly, the carriage should go alone to the station.

At lunch time rain began to fall, and by the middle of the afternoon a veritable downpour gave every promise that the bad weather had come to remain for the rest of the day.

"It's too bad," Bethel fretted, "when everything has been looking so lovely. The garden has never looked better."

Neither of the sisters seemed able to settle down to anything, and Bethel kept going from room to room, to see that everything was 'just so,' in spite of Lerryn's protestations that all her sister's orders had been carried out in exemplary fashion.

So it was that neither Bethel nor Lerryn heard the approach of carriage wheels, and it was not until the dogs barked and they heard his voice call for them, that they realized Veryan had returned.

Lerryn ran downstairs, quickly followed by Bethel, who threw her arms round her brother's neck.

" Darling, darling," she cried. " Oh, let me look at you." Then she held him at arm's length as if to see him afresh.

" Oh, to think you're back, my darling Veryan ! " She was as excited as a child. The doors of the drawing-room were open, and as Veryan, with Bethel and Lerryn each side of him entered the room, Lerryn gave a start of astonishment. A young woman was standing by the fireplace. She turned and came towards them.

" I'm Lucy," she said.

Veryan quickly intercepted.

" I've not told them yet," he began.

His sisters looked at Veryan. Bethel had gone deathly white.

" This is Lucy. We were married a month ago," he said.

PART THREE

I

" WHY IS BETHEL so extraordinarily unfriendly to me ? " Lucy Treveryan asked her husband after she had been in Cornwall about a month.

" Is she ? " Veryan tried to sound casual.

" You must have noticed it. Not once since I arrived has she made any pretence of welcome, nor gone out of her way to show me even common politeness."

" Come, my dear, you exaggerate," he remonstrated half-heartedly.

" No, I don't, and you know it. Indeed, I do blame you for never warning your sisters you had married, and I realize it must have been a great surprise to them, but I didn't bargain for the unpleasant shock they consider it to be."

" Surely Lerryn is friendly ? " he said.

" She's the better of the two, I admit, but even she seems unnatural and her good manners appear to me at any rate a trifle forced."

Veryan sighed.

" I expect our English ways are difficult," he prevaricated, " we're altogether different."

"Nonsense, Veryan! I've been to England before, and I've met English girls in Canada. Bethel and Lerryn are unique in my experience."

He went over to her and kissed her.

"Try to put up with things, darling," he begged. "For my sake. I realize it's not easy."

He paused. Lucy's eyes filled with tears.

"It makes me feel so dreadfully homesick," she said. "You know what lots of girl friends I have at home, I can't understand your sisters' attitude. Why, you know darling, how we go out of our way to make strangers feel at home— you'd think they were jealous. Honestly, Veryan, I some- times wish——" she hesitated.

"What?"

"That we hadn't got married."

"You're not to say things like that, Lucy. It hurts me terribly. I'll talk to the girls." His voice was stern.

"If only we were alone," she continued tearfully. "You know how I love you. It would have been different if we could have stayed at home. Had our own house."

She sniffed. Veryan looked horrified.

"My dear girl, you're absurd. This is our own home. And you know how excited you were at the idea of Treveryan. It's your house, you're its mistress."

"I'm not. And I never shall be as long as Bethel's here."

Veryan strode angrily about the room.

"Oh, God!" he muttered.

"You're different, too, over here," she said in her plaintive voice, "you don't talk to me as you did way back in Canada. At meal-times you talk much more to Bethel than you do to me, and you're out nearly all the rest of the time."

"Now who's talking like a child? Really, Lucy darling, you're making a great deal out of nothing. As you know, Beth has always helped me to manage the estate, naturally we have lots of matters to discuss."

"And so you both ignore me."

"But dear, you don't know a damn thing about Treveryan."

"And how am I going to learn? Isn't it a wife's place to help her husband? I mayn't even run the house. And yet you say I'm the mistress of it."

He sighed wearily.

" Be fair, pet," he began, " we can't suddenly take Bethel's life-work from her. She'd not understand and she'd be perfectly miserable."

" It's always Bethel. Bethel this, Bethel that," she cried. " Which of us do you love the most? "

He took her into his arms.

" You. You know I'm mad about you," he said. " You shall have everything you want in time, never fear. But you must be patient, lovely one."

She pouted.

" I'll try," she answered, " but I just don't understand them. After all, they must have expected you to marry one day, and I've gone out of my way to be nice to them, darling. Most women would show their resentment at having to share a brand new husband and home, and never once have I let them know it's not really their home any longer."

Veryan by this time had ceased to listen to his wife with all his attention, and did not hear her last words. Of course it was madness to have brought her to Treveryan with his sisters living at home, a crazy idea. Madness . . . crazy . . . He swallowed hard and turned his thoughts quickly to other channels. He could still scarcely realize that Lucy was actually his wife. Sometimes the whole business seemed like a fantastic dream. Who could have believed that such an exquisite little creature as Lucy Hervey would ever have consented to leave the luxurious home of her parents, braving the Atlantic crossing, of which she boasted she was petrified, to settle in the depths of the Cornish countryside for sheer love of him? Poor darling, of course the place seemed strange after the gaiety of Ottawa. What an oaf he was, that he had not realized that she was pining for more amusing society than Treveryan had been able to offer. The truth was that, in spite of the gay entertaining to which he had been used abroad, he had slipped back unconsciously to his old routine at Treveryan, and it had never dawned on him that matrimony might alter life altogether. As for his sisters, and Bethel in particular, some odd, ostrich-like psychology refused to allow him to think of the real issue at all. He had been completely swept off his feet by Lucy. She was an exceptionally pretty girl, utterly different from his sisters; but she was very young, and spoilt, as only children often are. Lucy was petite, indeed she was barely more than five feet in height, with raven hair and Irish blue eyes, which she inherited from her mother. She looked like a delicious doll, and Veryan had fallen in love at first sight. So badly had he wanted her that he had managed to convince himself that he was harming no one by marrying her. Conveniently he had found it easy to forget Bethel's tragedy.

The years away from Treveryan had altered Veryan more than any of them had realized or could have foreseen. He had been extremely young when the shock of his family's tragedy had been broken to him, the nature of it helping to retard, almost to kill, natural feelings which are man's birthright. Bethel's despair had also kept at bay any further interest in people outside his own home, and, in the years that had followed, her strength and will-power had done more than anything else in keeping brother and sisters inviolate from the outside world. For years he had accepted the fact that women, in that they meant love and marriage, were not for him, and circumstances being what they were at Treveryan, thoughts of entering into any form of intrigue had never crossed his mind. So it was that he found himself particularly unsophisticated amongst his fellow men, a state from which it had not been easy at first to break away. The war did its best to make him see everything in a clearer, or at any rate more usual, perspective, and, too, gave him the comradeship of men, which for so many years he had forced himself to be without for his sisters' sake.

The months in South Africa had been just enough to unsettle Veryan, giving him a taste for not only men and women, but travel as well, and Lerryn had, with perspicacity, noticed his new restlessness. Therefore, when the chance of the appointment on the royal tour came his way, he had eagerly seized it, and few would or could have blamed him.

Gradually the hideous nightmare of his family's past began to fade. New interests, new people, new things took shape, and by the time he met Lucy Hervey he had begun to look upon himself as no different from other men. If he sometimes forced himself to think of his heritage, he would quickly tell himself that there were plenty of families the world over bearing the same unfortunate taint as his own, and not making the song and dance of it that they had done. Yet there must have been some streak of guilt in Veryan's heart when he asked the Hervey's consent for his marriage to Lucy, for he took great care to omit all reference to health. Guilt there must have been on his conscience also where Bethel was concerned, else how keep his sisters in such ignorance of his plans for marriage? It was Lerryn who noticed that though his manner to Bethel was nearly, if not quite, as loving as in the past, he never seemed to look her in the eyes.

And it was Lerryn who saw a new Bethel come into being.

PART IT WAS STRANGE, even a little frightening, Lerryn
THREE thought one day in the following autumn, that not
       once since Veryan's and Lucy's arrival had Bethel
2   discussed the marriage. Perhaps it was strange
       that she herself had not discussed it, but where
Veryan was concerned it had always seemed Bethel's right to bring up the subject; therefore, as in the past, she had left it for her to do so. Somehow she found it impossible to speak of it to Beth; even she herself hardly knew what to make of it. She supposed she had every reason to be bitter against Veryan; but just for that very reason she felt she could afford him the sympathy he had not asked.

Of course he knew nothing about Ted, for before her brother had returned Lerryn had begged Bethel to keep her unhappy love secret from him.

True, Lerryn had asked Bethel diffidently whether she did not think the girl pretty, to which she had replied in icy tones that she had not noticed, and again later Lerryn had let slip the remark that their sister-in-law seemed quite a nice little thing; but Bethel's expression of outraged surprise was one that had not tempted her to discuss the girl further.

Personally she felt sorry for Lucy.

She was obviously homesick for her parents, was finding the wet autumn, far from city gaiety, extremely unpleasant, and could hardly be blamed, in view of Bethel's behaviour to her, for adopting an antagonistic manner in self-defence.

Lerryn did her best to interest her in whatever ways she could; but, as well as incurring Bethel's displeasure for this, it was uphill work, as Lucy seemed to share none of their tastes. Lerryn generously blamed a spoilt upbringing when, in bored accents, the young bride bemoaned the absence of a continual house-party atmosphere. It was hardly poor Lucy's fault that she was unable to appreciate the countryside when, day after day, a wet mist would come in from the sea, blocking from view everything there was to be seen, followed, as likely as not, by ceaseless days of rain. Indeed, Cornwall and Treveryan had seldom put on a more dismal appearance, and the beautiful trees in the park and avenue, which as a rule glorified the surrounding land until nearly Christmas, were bereft of leaves which lay in black and sodden masses by the end of October. By November winter seemed to have settled in; not the crisp Canadian winter to which Lucy was used, but raw, damp weather; and in spite of large log fires in most of the rooms the passages struck chill and unfriendly to Mrs. Treveryan, who would huddle in a coat as she walked from library to dining-room, fully aware of Bethel's look of contempt.

" What a fuss you make ! " she said one day, coming across her sister-in-law crouching over the fire in the dining-room. " You should go to Yorkshire or Scotland. We consider Cornwall to be our riviera. And anyway, I thought all Canadians were hardy creatures, used to a freezing climate. This isn't even cold."

" Canada may be colder, but it's fine. We have snow, not this interminable rain, rain, rain. And our houses are centrally heated. With pipes *everywhere*," she ended with spirit.

" You had better get Veryan to take a house in town for you. I daresay you'd find one with radiators." Bethel answered.

" I don't know how you live through the winter. My God ! I wonder what my folks'd say at home ! The size of a house like this and only lamps to light you ! One bathroom ! I just can't get over it. It's so big, and you don't seem to mind all the discomfort. I think you must be crazy ! "

There was an ugly glint in Bethel's eye.

" Perhaps we are. At any rate in England we don't think

it necessary to spoil the beauty of old houses by adding all the horrors which go by the name of modern conveniences. Ridiculous fads, most of them."

Things were generally a little better when Veryan was in the room. Lucy would curl up quietly and sit on a cushion at his feet, talking very little and embroidering countless articles of lingerie, and the others would read, or occasionally Veryan and Bethel would play a game of piquet. But this frequently finished before it should have, as Lucy, prompted by jealousy or devilry of some sort, would begin to chatter to her husband, or go over to the piano and start to strum.

"You're a baby," he said one evening, as some game had been hopelessly spoilt and Bethel had left the room. "Why do you go out of your way to antagonize her? Beth is nearly twice as old as you are, you ought at least to respect her age, even if you don't care for her."

"Silly old maid," she pouted, "she treats me as if she were a school marm and I an unruly child instead of being . . ."

"An unruly little baggage of a wife." He caught her up in his arms, holding her as if she were a baby. Lucy giggled.

"Great big thing, aren't you? I'm glad I have you to protect me against the ogre."

"Lucy, you're not to talk of my sister in that manner. It's not at all becoming. I don't care for it, and it's not amusing."

"Darling!" She brought his head down to hers and softly kissed his lips. "I'll try to be good. I'll try to behave. Tell me you're not really cross with me!"

God! How could he be angry with such an absurdly adorable little creature? he asked himself, feeling himself aquiver as she lay without resistance in his arms, looking for all the world like a mere child. Might as well be angry with Lerryn's small kitten, he thought.

"Where are you taking me?" Lucy asked, as he strode across the room with her in his arms.

"To bed. It's late." She chuckled deliciously and whispered nonsense into his ear as he kicked open the door. On the threshold stood Bethel. Veryan saw her flinch, and he also felt Lucy's arm about his neck and the feel of her hands.

"Good night, Beth," he said shortly, and walked towards the staircase.

" Good night, Bethel," called Lucy, and in a voice calculated to reach her sister-in-law's ears, cried softly, " Hurry, my darling."

Bethel was still standing by the dying embers an hour later when Lerryn came into the room.

" Oh ! " She started. " I didn't know you were still down here. I thought the others must have forgotten to put out the lights."

" He was carrying her in his arms. As if she were a child. What a fool he has become ! "

There was so much scorn, so much venom in her words, that Lerryn stood speechless.

" How—I—hate—her." Bethel spoke so quietly that Lerryn could only just catch the words. She went over to where her sister stood, and sat down on the low stool in front of the fireplace.

" You must try not to hate her so much, Beth," she said softly. " She's so young."

" Young ! " It was like a cry. " I was young once."

" Veryan loves her——"

" So Oswald Martineau loved me. So Ted Truscott . . . You, Lerryn ! How can you take her part ? " Indignant anger rang in her voice.

" I don't. Heaven knows I don't take her part. I only ask you not to hate so—terribly. That can't get any of us any-where, and will only, in time, alienate you from Veryan. Then what is your life to be ? "

Bethel sank to her knees.

" How could he ? " she whispered.

Lerryn felt powerless. What was there that she could either say or do that could help Bethel ? In her angry misery the younger girl found her sister strangely pathetic.

" Do you find Veryan changed, Beth ? " she asked after a little while.

" Changed ! He's a different being. And it's her fault."

Lerryn sighed.

" One's bound to be different when one marries, my dear. One's whole perspective alters. Naturally he will be very wrapped in Lucy for a while. Marriage, being a husband, is new to Veryan we must remember," she said.

" I'm not likely to forget," Bethel replied. And then, after a pause she went on, " He forgot—as you seem to be forgetting—that marriage is not for the Treveryans. Even now I can't bring myself to ask him whether he betrayed our promise deliberately, or whether he married her in a fit of—madness." She lay back, her eyes closed. " In either case, what he has done is unforgivable."

" Perhaps," said Lerryn slowly, " we've made too much of it always. Perhaps, since he's travelled, Veryan has come across lots of families who suffer from—madness. He may think it doesn't matter so much after all."

" What about my life? What of Oswald's and my wrecked happiness? Even if it were true, and it's not, what future have I, either of us, can you tell me? Veryan knew as well as I did fifteen years ago that marriage undertaken by any of us three would be criminal. You were a child, you didn't know, how should you? When Veryan and I made our decision we vowed our lives to each other and to Treveryan. And now that little girl is brought here to be the mistress of Treveryan." Bethel's voice rang with contemptuous scorn.

" No, no, Beth," Lerryn said quickly, " Veryan would never dream of letting Lucy run the house."

" Do you think she will be content to play second fiddle in her husband's house? You're more fool than I took you for, Lerryn. Oh, no ! She will do her damnedest to oust us from the house that is ours, and only ours. But she shall never be mistress of Treveryan."

The words were cold, calculated. Bethel rose slowly and shivered.

" It's cold, the fire has gone out. It must be getting late, too. We must go to bed."

She walked across the room as Lerryn turned down the lamps and blew out the candles. As she reached the door Bethel turned and spoke again.

" Perhaps I forget that you've only had four months to realize things. Good heavens ! What are four months? Perhaps you will remember that I have had to live through fifteen years."

.   .   .   .   .

" Well, my dears ! " said Veryan brightly, one morning a few days later, " I've decided to have a party for Christmas. Lucy rightly says she's meeting nobody, and how can she, bless her! if nobody realizes the sweet pet is hidden away from sight. We've all been very remiss. My fault, of course. Anyway, it's going to be remedied, and my wife shall receive and entertain to her heart's content!"

Lucy glanced at her husband and smiled like a child who has been promised the largest sugar-plum at the party. Neither she nor Veryan looked at Bethel, who remained as though carved in stone.

"Lerryn will enjoy it, won't you my love?" he said lightly. "You've no idea, darling, how we used to have to scold her in the old days for spending all her money on dresses." He finished peeling a pear and passed it to Lucy.

"Really? How surprising!" Young Mrs. Treveryan sounded disbelieving.

"Yes, I—I used to love pretty frocks," Lerryn said, feeling she must contribute to the conversation.

"You must both have been very pretty when you were young," Lucy said.

There was dead silence, and then Veryan scraped back his chair from the table and said a trifle awkwardly:

"I must be getting down to the farm. There are things Mutton wishes to see me about."

He left the room and Lucy hurried after him.

"Do I look awfully old?" Lerryn asked presently. Even Bethel laughed.

"No, darling! Moreover our Lucy will be a fat little pudding in ten years time when you will look like a silver birch."

"What do you feel about this party, Beth?" Lerryn asked anxiously.

"Does it matter what I feel?"

"It's going to be so embarrassing meeting people I knew when I was a child. What on earth will they think? I mean, why after years of silence are we to be shown off?"

"Don't delude yourself, my dear. This is for Lucy."

"All the same, they'll meet me. They're bound to wonder where we've been hiding all this time."

"If they see us," Bethel remarked, "personally, I've no intention of being present."

"Oh!" The older woman thought she detected disappointment in Lerryn's voice.

"To what end should we put ourselves out?" she asked.

"It would be fun to dance," Lerryn said.

"And meet a lot of people? Find another man to fall in love with you? Undo the work of all these years? Oh, if you want to be so foolish . . ." she sighed impatiently.

"You don't understand, Beth, I'm only trying to help."

Bethel lifted her eyes ironically.

"Now that I know what there is to know I shan't allow myself to think of—men and marriage. Besides, I love Ted. I shall always love him." After a pause she continued, "One can dance and be gay and meet people without falling in love, surely, Beth?" She tried to speak lightly.

"Certainly, if you've the heart. I can see you and I are very different, that's all. I should have realized that ages ago, and saved you many years of boredom."

Lerryn sighed. She wished Bethel were not so bitter, and that she would try to take Veryan's marriage more philosophically.

"Lucy will fancy herself enormously receiving all the guests," she said.

"Standing by Veryan at the foot of the staircase, dead Treveryans looking down on them. No, Lerryn. You are right after all. If she stands there, I shall also."

⋇⋇⋇

PART THREE 3   THE REOPENING OF Treveryan gave the county something to talk about for many months. Rumours had got about that Veryan had married, but, as no one saw the bride, word again went round that the story must have been a rumour after all. Then came the invitations to a ball on Christmas Eve to meet Mrs. Veryan Treveryan and all were agog once more.

"It was a most extraordinary affair in a way, Mama," Mary St. Hilary said to her mother the following day; she had taken the children down to old Lady Rogers for Christmas luncheon. "I only wish you had been well enough to go."

" You know what my gout is, child," grumbled her mother, " and anyway, who wants a lot of useless old dowagers these days, unless they've girls to chaperone. But tell me, what's the girl like? And were his sisters there? "

" I'm just going to tell you, Mama. She's a Canadian, he must have picked her up when he was over that time with the Prince."

" Picked her up? Isn't she a lady? " Lady Rogers asked.

" Oh, yes, I was only speaking vulgarly, Mama. She's very pretty in a chocolate-boxy way. He dotes on her, it's obvious, and she looked very fond of him. Of course, I didn't have very great opportunity of talking to her, one doesn't, though I had supper at their table and sat next Veryan. I've asked them over to St. Hilary to shoot woodcock, so you must meet them. But it was Bethel and Lerryn who astonished me more than young Mrs. Veryan, Mama."

" Go on, tell me about them."

" Well, to begin with, Bethel received the guests along with Veryan and his bride. I suppose, in a way, it was natural, as she lives there, but I should hardly like to have done it in her place. However . . . Mama, I kept watching her; it was like looking at a ghost, or watching a play, or—or something. She just never seemed real."

" What on earth do you mean, Mary? Don't be absurd ! "

" Well, Mama, after all these years wouldn't you have thought she'd have been pleased to see her old friends? Smiled at them, welcomed them? I tell you, she went through her ' how d'you do's ' as if she were in a trance. I never felt more bewildered in my life. She never spoke to her sister-in-law—"

" Probably loathes the sight of her, m'dear. And there, as likely as not, you have the whole tale in a nutshell."

" I wonder. I wonder," Mary St. Hilary pondered.

" Has she aged a lot? She must be well over forty. I wonder she was there."

" I was amazed. She looked really beautiful. Of course the little bride was pretty, but lacks the Treveryan breeding. Bethel looked like a queen. I must say, if what you suggest is true and she dislikes the marriage, I'd be petrified of Bethel if I were that little wife."

" What did they wear? Go on, tell me everything, I'm

enjoying this." Lady Rogers drew her shawl across her knees and reached out for a caramel.

" Bethel had on a claret velvet gown—as I say, she looked quite glorious. Oh, of course she looks infinitely older than when we all last saw her, but heavens ! she's kept her looks and her figure. What a pity she's never married," she sighed. " However, I suppose one will never know the ins-and-outs of that. But there's nothing old-maidy about Bethel. She looks dreadfully hard, though."

" What about the younger girl, was she there? "

" Lerryn? Yes, indeed, and looking lovely. So like their mother, but such a much more charming face. I cannot imagine why *she* hasn't married now. She made a great success, I think people were very taken with her."

" And what are they going to do now? "

" I wonder, Mama. Obviously Veryan and his wife mean to go about and entertain, but I don't know what to think about the girls. After all, pretty as Lerryn is, her age is rather a handicap. I mean, I don't see her fitting into house-parties. She's much too old to mix with the debutantes, and yet you can't put her alone with the married lots. I do think they've been most astonishingly remiss in not bringing her out properly years ago. I don't know who there is for her now, do you? Most of one's eligibles are younger than she is."

" Perhaps she doesn't want to marry," said old Lady Rogers.

" Come, Mama ! Don't be ridiculous ! All girls want to marry, and pretty girls like Lerryn Treveryan should have done so years ago. But," she added a few minutes later, " I can't help wondering about Bethel."

The Treveryan ball had proved an enormous success and soon Veryan and his young wife were to be seen all over the county and beyond. The yoke of her sisters-in-law shed, as it were, Lucy blossomed into quite an entertaining young woman, and her Canadian accent, rarely before heard in the county, was thought by a number of people to be most effective and attractive. Her looks were greatly admired, and indeed she made an extremely pretty picture in those early weeks of nineteen hundred and three, driving about the countryside in the smart new car which she had begged Veryan to buy, snugly clothed in Canadian mink coat and cap, wedding present from her parents.

" You are settling down now and really enjoying England, my pet? " Veryan asked one day. She squeezed his arm.

" Yes, Veryan darling. Of course I am. And you will admit, honey, that life is much greater fun now that we meet everybody and go places, and have the car."

" You're talking like an American," he teased.

" I'm not !   Darling, I just can't think why you shut yourself up all those years. Did you never want to go places and meet nice girls, or have them here? My ! If this had been my home and I'd been you, I'd have had people here all the time. You must have been so bored you poor darling."   She put her arms round his neck and kissed him.

" No, I was never bored. Not at first, at any rate."

" But it got you down later? I guess it'd get any man down."

She climbed on to his knee.

" When I came back from the war I got a bit restless."

" 'Course you did.   Lerryn's pretty you know, in her own way."   She spoke with patronizing kindness.   " She ought to be able to find a husband. Somewhere."

" Neither Beth nor Lerryn want to marry, Lucy."

" They might think of you then.   I call girls pretty selfish who expect to share their brother's home for life."

" This is their home, you mustn't forget, as much as it's mine."

" Anyway, we shall have to make different arrangements. You'll have to tell Bethel I want her room."

Veryan looked aghast.

" I can't possibly do that," he said, " she's had it all her life." Lucy bit her lip.

" Besides, what on earth do you need it for? Now that we're in my father's and mother's rooms, you can't possibly want any other."

" I like the light," she said peevishly, " I want a boudoir of my own.   And Bethel's would be the most suitable."

For once he was adamant.

" I'm sorry, darling. I'll give you most things, but I'm not going to turn Bethel out of her room for you."

Lucy got up and shrugged her shoulders.

"I wonder if you'll ever realize how your sister hates me?" This was a different tack. A fine sense of injury sounded in her voice. "Other people don't look down on me as Bethel does. She poisons this place for me. Sometimes I feel I can bear it no longer."

"Oh, God! What with the two of you," Veryan muttered.

"Can't you find some place else for her to go, Veryan? I tell you, it gets on my nerves till I could cry. I don't mind Lerryn, she's always been much kinder to me. If she weren't under Bethel's thumb I could get quite friendly with her I daresay, in spite of her being years older than I am."

"I've told you once and for all, Lucy, this is their home. Don't let us have any more words about it. It's damnably selfish of you."

"Oh!" She burst into tears. "I like that! I wonder how many wives would be content to live with sisters-in-law bossing them. If it's a case of selfishness, you can't talk."

"What am I to do?" Veryan turned to her weakly, and she clung to him.

"It's only because I love you so much, darling. Only 'cos I long to be with you alone. Alone. Alone. Alone. I won't be at you again, darling, if only you'll promise to think it over. I know there's no place for the poor things to go to right away, but before next winter. Veryan, say you will, or I swear I'll . . ."

"All right, all right," he said hurriedly, "I'll see what can be done."

"Promise?" She nestled closer.

"Yes, I promise," he answered wearily.

"They'll be much happier on their own, you know," she said, all trace of tears miraculously vanished. "It must be very boring for them watching us. Must make them feel what they've missed."

Veryan broke away from Lucy.

"I do wish you'd stop talking of my sisters as if they were two old frumps, old enough to be your mother," he said crossly.

"Bethel is," she said.

"Lerryn isn't, anyway. You're always talking as if both of

them had one foot in the grave. It may astonish you to hear that a great many people were bowled over by Lerryn on Christmas Eve. One or two fellows thought she was the same age as yourself."

" I'll bet none of the women did," Lucy replied tartly.

" You've got so little rhyme or reason to carry on as you do, Lu. You're twenty, you're lovely, the county has fallen in love with you—they see a very different you, I may add—and I worship you when you behave yourself—and love your beauty damnably when you don't. So why these endless scenes of jealousy ? "

" I don't know. Yes, I do. I told you why. It's because I love you. And because I want to feel that I'm altogether your wife."

" Surely, sweetheart, you're convinced of that by now ? " He laughed once more and pulled her over towards him.

" I want to run Treveryan," she said quietly. " I've been married to you for eight months now, and I've been here for seven. I've never even seen the kitchen. I've not been allowed to."

" Most women would thank their stars to be relieved of the housekeeping. Why dearest, my mother never did a stroke of work. A funny old body called Mrs. Mitchell ruled the house with a rod of iron."

" She's dead. I've heard all about her. And Bethel has ruled it with a similar rod ever since. Be that as it may. If Bethel is lucky enough to live here now that you're married, then she must at all events allow me to run the house. Our house." She longed to add ' my house,' but refrained.

" Well, I'll see what she says," said Veryan.

" Oh, no, darling. You'll tell her you want me to. Tell her to teach me if you think she'd prefer it. Somehow I don't believe she will."

The next day, however, Lucy once again changed her plans when a batch of letters arrived bringing further invitations to go visiting, and as she made no further allusion to the conversation of the previous day, Veryan let the subject drop.

The spring was early that year and the fine weather and prospect of seeing people appeared to cheer Lucy. She turned an affable side to everyone, even to her sisters-in-law. It almost seemed as if she were determined to keep her temper at all costs, and put the onus of any unpleasantness that might occur on to Bethel's shoulders.

In spite of the fact that they were now keeping open house and entertaining on a lavish scale, Bethel still continued to refuse all invitations. Old friends of the past did their best to try and persuade her to visit them, but she invariably refused on some pretext or other.

"I don't understand her," said one of the Tremaynes, "she's quite genial when one lunches at Treveryan, but nothing on earth will get her to budge from the place. I always feel she is being polite and really longs to see my back."

"I suppose the fact of the matter is that she's never got over that odd affair, and hoped to live forgotten and alone, and now that Lucy's taken over the reins that's out of the question."

"One always feels a bit diffident asking Lerryn without Bethel," someone was heard to say, "and wonders whether it'd be a popular move or not."

"Is she her sister's keeper? Old Bethel's a handsome wench, but I should say rather a dragon of a sister!"

Possibly if Bethel had known the remarks caused by her rigid, and to most people, inexplicable behaviour, she might have accepted the friendship and invitations proffered her, but she was deaf and blind to comment from the outside world; and had the rest of her family known, it is doubtful whether they would have cared to break down the reserve which was her defence, and have told her the truth.

Poor Bethel! Many a worried hour Lerryn spent wondering what was to be the outcome of it all. She saw all their points of view so fully. The love she had known for, and given to, Ted Truscott had opened a wider knowledge of men to her. She could understand only too well how helpless her brother had been where Lucy was concerned, and in spite of the wreck of her own love affair, she felt no bitterness or jealousy over Veryan's happiness. She tried to like Lucy for her own sake, for it was not going to be easy, as well she realized, to live on terms of veiled enmity with one's sister-in-law. Besides, she did not mind Lucy. She interfered in no way with anything she did, and sometimes showed signs of friendliness. She quite frequently asked Lerryn to accompany her to Truro or St. Austell in the car on shopping expeditions, and if there was a hint of patronage in the younger girl's manner Lerryn did not bother to notice it. Sometimes Lerryn would go with Veryan and Lucy to luncheons and an occasional week-end party, and away from Treveryan and Bethel she became a different person, gay, animated and radiant. Then, alone in her room at some strange house, at St. Hilary, or at the Tremaynes or glorious old Poluan Abbey, remorse would seize her, and guiltily she would remember Bethel at Treveryan, alone of the three of them remaining true to their pledge.

Yes, she understood Bethel as well as she understood her brother. She knew that many years of suffering had made her into the woman she now was, and that the pent-up emotion of years, centred as it had been in Veryan, had burst in a torrent of almost superhuman bitterness, at what she considered his base betrayal of their lives.

If only Lucy would treat Beth with a little more understanding, she thought . . . but how should she, knowing nothing, and only seeing the older woman as a jealous, intolerant spinster. Lerryn had no illusions as to Lucy's opinion of themselves. Sometimes she longed to tell her of that year of perfect romance with Ted, when her sister-in-law had been in a particularly trying mood, patronizing her more than usual; but Ted was too sacred a subject to use as an excuse; moreover she neither cared for, nor trusted Lucy sufficiently. She most certainly would have scorned Ted's humble origin, and would probably hint, with a certain perspicacious truth, that Lerryn had been so hard up for a man that she had taken Ted *faute de mieux*, which possibly may have been the case psychologically but not, certainly, in actual fact.

It was after Easter, when Bethel was particularly engrossed in helping to arrange a school outing for the village children, that Lucy once again attacked Veryan on the subject of household management.

" Now, darling, I've been a sweet, good little sister-in-law for months now. Even you will agree that I've kept my mouth firmly closed in the face of all *dear* Bethel's snubs. But I want to take on the housekeeping. I know quite a lot by now, I've kept my ears and eyes open, and there's not much that goes on that I don't know about really. So be a good boy and let me try. Go to her now while she's worked up over her old school treat. Lord! What a thing to bother about! Let her carry on with her good works by all means, dearest, and leave me to go ahead with my own house."

Lucy looked up at her husband and smiled. When she smiled she showed two dimples, and . . .

"When you show those dimples you know I can refuse you nothing, monkey."

So that afternoon when Lucy was 'resting,' a habit she had lately acquired, Veryan approached his sister.

"How's the school treat going?" he asked brightly.

"I think it'll be a great success this time if only we have a good day. You know we're taking them in waggonettes to Gerrans Bay; but I'm up to my eyes over it all because poor Mrs. Penrose is *not* up to it all these days, all the organizing I mean, and now I've got the summer outing to arrange for as well as this affair next week. That's going to be much more ambitious as they're going by train to Penzance for the day, and it means writing endless letters arranging one thing and another."

"You're certainly busy," he said.

"I am. There are several things I mean to do in the house which I keep neglecting, they'll have to wait."

There was a pause.

"Beth, I want Lucy to take over the reins of the house-keeping. She's been here nearly a year, absurd as it seems, and it is her house after all."

"Her house?"

"Yes. I know my dear you've done it for years, but, as you say, you're terribly busy——"

"Not too busy to run my own house——"

"I think it's a very good opportunity to let Lu try her hand. Anyway, I want her to."

"I see."

Veryan walked across the room, carefully avoiding Bethel's eyes.

"If you imagine a child of twenty can know anything about the running of a house the size of Treveryan," she began. Her eyes were smarting and she suddenly felt very old.

"She must learn. Besides, she helped her mother at home pretty often. She's no fool, is my Lucy."

"Some little flat in Ottawa? A very different state of affairs."

"Lucy's family live in one of the largest houses in Ottawa, they keep plenty of servants and entertain a great deal oftener than we do. If you'd try to take the smallest interest in her you'd not sound such an ignorant and jealous fool, Beth." His eyes blazed.

"Veryan!" she cried.

"You make me furious. You've never attempted to show one single sign of friendly feeling to Lucy since she arrived. She's right about you."

"Oh, God!" Bethel had by this time gone deathly white, and she leant against the table, clutching at it as if to keep herself from falling.

"Don't be so dramatic, and try and pull yourself together, for heaven's sake," Veryan said.

"You called me a fool. You listen to that chit of a child . . . I don't care if she is your wife! You know as well as I do you had no right to marry her, but have I ever said one word——"

"You've done your best to throw it in my teeth ever since I brought her here," Veryan said furiously.

"And haven't I the right? Who made me throw away the all-absorbing love . . ."

"Oh, for God's sake stop it! I made you, I know, I know. And that silly old doddering Pearce persuaded me into thinking it a criminal act if any of us married. Well, he's wrong."

"Who told you? How d'you know?" There was agony in her voice.

"I don't know. But from the amount of people I've seen in the world who don't care a row of pins about their antecedents' state of health, I can only think we were a couple of fools to be taken in so easily. We were young, of course, and I grant it's been a bit of a mess up for you."

"*A bit of a mess up.* Thank you, Veryan. All right, I won't be dramatic again. But if you think I shall ever forget your words . . . Certainly let Lucy take on Treveryan. It no longer even interests me."

Veryan kicked a chair impatiently.

" Do try and be a bit reasonable, old girl. I'm sorry if I sounded unsympathetic. God knows I minded like Hell about your rotten old business with Oswald."

Bethel closed her eyes and clenched her hands. Could it be Veryan, her once so beloved Veryan, talking?

" Try and get the thing in its right perspective if you can. I only ask you to be a little lenient, more friendly as it were, with my poor Lucy whose only fault is her extreme youth, the darling."

" I've said I'll stand down, Veryan. Need we go into it all again? " She spoke wearily.

" You'd love her if you only got down off your perch and tried to understand her," he continued in a tactless manner.

" Veryan, is there any need to prolong this conversation? I've done as you asked, more I cannot do. Doubtless Lerryn will help Lucy if she needs any advice, which I doubt," she added a little bitterly.

" I don't suppose Lerryn knows a leg of mutton from a tin of furniture polish. There never was such an undomesticated girl! However, she's at least kind to my wife, and I must be grateful for that, yes? "

But Bethel left the room and his remaining words were lost in space.

Shrugging his shoulders impatiently, he went in search of Lucy.

For the most part the servants took to ' young Mrs. Veryan's ways ' at once, without giving Bethel so much as a thought.

" It's natural she'd want to be looking after her own house, Miss," Prudence remarked to Lerryn after the news had gone round that Bethel was handing over the keys to the younger woman. " I expect Miss Bethel will feel it a bit strange at first like, but she'll get used to it. I should think she'll be glad of the change. But it's a pity she doesn't like 'er."

" Oh, Prue, you shouldn't jump to conclusions. You know Miss Beth is only very reserved."

" So's me Aunt Fanny, if you'll pardon me, Miss. I've been here too long not to know Miss Bethel by now. And you, too, Miss Lerryn. And everything else as goes on. Not much of the goings in and goings out *and* goings on, that escape me,"

Prue said darkly. Lerryn blushed and changed the subject.

"Mrs. Treveryan comes from a very smart home in Ottawa. I expect she'll soon pick things up."

"So I gathered from her. She was asking me if I didn't know of any girl who we could engage to look after her. As a personal maid. You know, Miss, a proper lady's maid."

Lerryn had noted a new tone of respect in Prue's voice of late when referring to Lucy. Obviously, like most other servants, thought Lerryn, she was snobbish enough to be more impressed by her mistress since hearing she came from an affluent home.

"Young Violet Mutton might suit, I thought, Miss. She comes of such very respectable people, and I've heard they'd like her to go into service provided it was a big house like this."

Lerryn's brows contracted.

"Don't get Violet, Prue. I—I don't care for her. That's to say, I know she's a nice girl and all that, but——"

"You've been listening to gossip, Miss. I'm surprised at you! There's nothing against Violet, though she is a bit silly and giggly like. Her people brought her up nice and proper, and she's a regular communicant, that I know. A shame all the stuff they started putting about her, and not a word of truth, I'll be bound."

"What?" Lerryn was not paying very much attention, but she knew that it was hopeless to try and stop Prue once she had started in one of her garrulous moods.

"They do say as how that Ted Truscott left all along of Violet. She was a bit sweet on him, but it was silly. Putting two and two, Violet's too young for that sort of thing really. Anyway, her dad and her mum wouldn't hear of it, and they say Ted went off out of pickwe."

"Pique," Lerryn corrected her mechanically.

"Oh, well, that's what they said. Whether it's true or not I don't know. That old mother of his at the lodge is ever such an old bear, won't answer your questions. Are you feeling all right, Miss? You don't look so well." She was now all concern for Lerryn.

"I've got a bit of a headache, that's all. I think I'll lie down for a bit. And Prue—try and get anyone but Violet for Mrs. Treveryan. D'you understand?"

" Yes, Miss. Though I don't know why you should be down on her, I'm sure."

After years of the same sort of food, a new and excitingly varied assortment of dishes would now come to the table. All sorts of American and Canadian menus would appear, and guests at Treveryan would invariably exclaim at Lucy's delicious luncheons and dinners.

" She's a born manager and housekeeper," Veryan would say, if his sister was out of earshot, and often enough a visitor would groan disconsolately——

" Lucy darling! I beg you, come over and tell my wretched cook the secret of that divine sweet," or " enchanting fish soufflé,"or any other recipe new to the guests and to Treveryan.

" What a glorious holiday after all these years for you, Bethel," someone tactlessly remarked once, and made matters worse by adding, " But I don't suppose you bothered about things, did you? You must love having such a clever and attractive sister-in-law."

As the summer months went by Bethel found herself more alone than she had ever deemed it possible to be. Pride, hatred of Lucy, contempt for Veryan, all kept her from accompanying the others about the county to cricket matches, garden parties, country shows. And she found herself now at home with less to do than ever before. There were still things to do for the village, of course, and Mrs. Penrose was only too thankful to be able to lean on her more. And there were the gardens at Treveryan. Those, at least, had not been taken from her by Lucy, but there were gardeners enough, and the work Bethel put in was more to occupy herself than of necessity.

Yet another blow to her pride and memory was to be struck however, when Veryan announced that Lucy wished to give another ball for her twenty-first birthday, preceded by a dinner party.

" Isn't that going a little too far? "

Even Lerryn had the courage to question her brother. He looked surprised.

" Poor Beth! It must bring back that wretched time so very vividly," she said. " Couldn't you do without the dinner first? Speeches and all that kind of thing? "

" Lucy's set her heart on it all," her brother said. " Surely Beth is old enough and unselfish enough not to grudge the child this ? "

" I must say, I don't understand you, V.," Lerryn replied with more spirit than she usually showed to her brother. " I should have thought you could have put it to Lucy, let her understand what happened. And I should have thought, too, that even you wouldn't want to be reminded of that unhappy time. Lucy and I get on all right together as you know, so I don't feel any qualms in talking to you. I honestly do think you treat Beth in a very cavalier fashion these days. Considering the amazing friends you were to each other."

" I hate to ask you to mind your own business, my dear, because I believe you think you're speaking to some purpose. It's no good. I expected Beth to have been—bigger—than she has about everything. You'd have thought her brief love and engagement to Oswald Martineau would have helped her to understand how I feel about Lucy, but not a bit of it."

Lerryn sighed.

" I'm sorry," she said. " You don't understand Beth, do you ? "

Strangely enough, Bethel made no untoward fuss about the celebrations for Lucy's birthday when Lerryn warned her what to expect. Merely shrugging her shoulders, " I'm not surprised," she said. " I wish I could go away for a bit. Isn't it silly to think I've never been away ? I've no friends, you see."

" I suppose it would hardly be considered proper for you to go off by yourself? To London, for instance? "

Bethel looked amused.

" Hardly," she said.

" I don't see why you shouldn't, all the same. Take Prue, that'd make it look quite convenable."

" I wonder. You wouldn't come, too, I suppose? "

Lerryn hesitated.

" I think it would look rather odd if we were both away for the occasion, wouldn't it ? "

" Perhaps you're right. I'll think about your idea, anyway."

If Bethel expected the announcement of her proposed trip to cause surprise or comment she was to be disappointed. Lucy, though palpably relieved, said nothing at all, and Veryan had the grace to ignore the obvious reason for the visit.

The birthday fête was to take place in the middle of August, and Bethel, accompanied by Prue, went up to London several days before. She had arranged to stay at the Langham Hotel.

How thankful Lerryn was that her sister was away when the night of the party came round. For although the time of year was very different from that occasion of nearly sixteen years ago, and the guests wandered freely in the garden between the dances, there were moments during dinner which vividly brought the other back to her memory, and references were made in one or two of the speeches to Veryan's own coming-of-age.

"'Jove! I can't think it was all that time ago, old man!'" said one guest, slapping his host on the shoulder. "Who'd have thought the next coming-of-age would be your charming lady wife's? Nearly twenty years on, forsooth." Followed ribald digs in the ribs and a few stories before Veryan remembered that the main entertainment of the evening was only just about to begin.

As ever, Treveryan looked beautiful for the occasion, and Lucy, flitting about in pale blue chiffon, was for once complete mistress of the place.

"I remember the night your sister came out," said old Squire Trewinnow to Lerryn, as they sat out a waltz together on the terrace. "I don't expect you can remember that."

"Yes, I do," she answered. "I remember peeping at everybody from one of the landings upstairs."

"She was a lovely girl, your sister. I don't see her to-night."

"No. She's—she's away at the moment."

"I'm sorry. I should have liked to have seen her again. I see you about quite often, how is it she shuts herself up?"

"She's—rather a recluse," Lerryn faltered.

"Never married, did she? Pity! Some man missed a good thing there."

PART
THREE

4

IN LONDON, BETHEL was emerging from the chrysalis stage. She felt like someone learning to walk after living for years bedridden. She found she enjoyed going on expeditions alone, peering into the windows of curio shops in the King's Road and Church Street, going once again to picture galleries, exploring the City churches. The loneliness she had feared evaded her, as also the ghost of Oswald which she dreaded might haunt her. Many changes had taken place since she had visited London in 1887, and she realized after she had been there a week that she was actually enjoying life. It was Prue who remarked one morning:

" You're looking a different person, Miss Bethel. I declare, London suits you."

" I feel well, Prue. I expect I've been silly not to do this before. I shouldn't have come now if Miss Lerryn hadn't persuaded me to."

" I wish Miss Lerryn was here as well. She loves London," Prue informed her mistress. " It is very enjoyable, though I won't say I'd care to live here, would you, Miss; all the smoke and the noise."

" I don't believe I should mind having a little flat somewhere. Near the Park or Kensington Gardens."

" Oh, go on, Miss. You'd get ever so lonely after you'd been there long. That's what I always say about places like London—all right for a visit, very nice indeed, in fact. But not to live. Not for country people like us, Miss. You'd miss Treveryan no end."

" Treveryan isn't what it was, Prue," Bethel sighed, and then quickly, as if ashamed of having allowed the servant to see what was in her heart, added, " I thought I'd go to the Zoo this afternoon, Prue. Would you like to come with me? "

" It's a pity you don't like music like Miss Lerryn does," Prue remarked the next day, " there's ever such lovely concerts coming from the Queen's Hall."

Music . . . Bethel wondered if it would be possible to sit through an evening listening, without feeling her heart being torn to shreds. Music more than anything else seemed to bring the presence of Oswald nearer. If only she could slay that bogey it might open new fields to her as she had once hoped in the past. She told Prue that she could have the evening off a couple of nights later, and, when sure of being alone, slipped into the Queen's Hall.

The programme was one of Beethoven, and Bethel soon found herself lost in the greatness of the music. No ghost of Oswald Martineau appeared beside her, and she left the hall feeling cured for ever of one of the worst of her fears.

This destruction of what had been merely a myth, as it were, had a psychological reaction on Bethel. She did in fact feel cured of some illness, of some mental aberration. It was as if she wanted suddenly to become an entirely new person. Twice again she went to the Queen's Hall, each time returning with the blessed knowledge that music in the future was to be her friend and not the spectre she had found it all these years.

The following Sunday, after attending the morning service at St. Paul's Cathedral, she was surprised and touched by a note which was handed to her by one of the pages. It was from an elderly clergyman who lived in the hotel with his invalid wife, enclosing her two Fellow's tickets for the Zoo for that afternoon. She had spoken to them several times and struck up a slight acquaintance with them.

" I wish I could take you myself," the letter ran, " but Sundays are never my days of leisure. I hope you can make use of the tickets, as it is the nicest day of the week at the Zoo, and only Fellows and their friends are allowed."

Bethel was delighted, as the short visit she had paid the gardens the previous week had been all too brief. Prue, when asked if she would care to go again, excused herself with a sick headache, and Bethel set off alone. She spent a long time in the Small Birds' house, which she had not seen before, and after watching the antics of the monkeys for another half hour wandered off to the Lion house. She soon became engrossed by a litter of cubs, and was paying no attention to the people round her, when she was suddenly aware of a man's voice saying :

" They're doing fine, Sir Oswald."

A keeper was talking close by, and a few seconds later a tigress and her cubs romped out into the open playground.

" They're the best we've had born here for a long time,"

the man was saying, " and she's certainly a lovely creature. Ain't you, Dido? "

" She doesn't appear to mind her captivity? " the other asked.

" Not unduly, Sir Oswald, not unduly.   In fact, you might say she's settling down very comfortable.   Most docile, she is, most docile."

Oswald Martineau slipped something into the man's hand and a second later was outside the barrier.

If Bethel had looked closer she would have seen the label with the words ' Presented by Sir Oswald Martineau, K.C.,' on the bars of the cage.

For a moment she thought she was going to faint.   Exerting all the will power of which she was capable she clutched the barrier, and then after a moment turned blindly to go.   Oswald Martineau, after one more glance at the tigress, also turned to leave and knocked into her.

" I beg your pardon," he said, raising his hat.   Something about the woman was familiar to him, however, and he turned and looked again.

" Bethel! " he ejaculated.   And then, " My dear . . ."

For a few seconds they looked at each other without further words.

" What an absurd place to meet in after all these years," she said tremulously.

" Do you often come here?   Are you living in London?" Martineau asked.

Bethel told him she was up for a couple of weeks or so. She did not add that it was her first long visit since that time sixteen years before, when they had met.

" It's the most amazing luck running into you, Bethel," Martineau said.   " I'm only in London for the week-end, staying at my club.   Going up to Scotland to-morrow night."

" I thought you were in India," she said.

" My dear, my health has broken.   It's damnable, but here you see me a broken down old man! "

" Don't be ridiculous, Oswald! "   Oh, God, the sweet agony of saying that name again!

" It's the truth.   Malaria has played havoc with me.   I've finally had to chuck it all and come home."

" I'm terribly sorry." They walked on in silence.

" Won't you let me give you tea somewhere, Bethel? It—it would give me such pleasure, my dear."

" I—should love it."

Hailing a hansom, Martineau directed the driver to go to the Carlton.

" It's almost like old times," he said lightly. She could not reply.

" I ought to congratulate you on your knighthood, Oswald. Somehow I've missed it. I don't read the papers very much, I'm afraid."

" It's very recent," he smiled. " Part of the Durbar trappings."

" I see. Anyway, I'm awfully glad."

" It's wonderful to be back in England," he said, as they drove along past Regent's Park, " everything so green and glorious."

" It looks very dusty to me."

" Wait till you've lived in India as long as I have! You're spoilt. All you lucky ones who live in places like Cornwall. Cornwall! Tell me about it. Is it as lovely as ever?" Had he forgotten? she asked herself. Did he realize that he was making her undergo a process of slow torture?

" It's still very lovely, yes." And she proceeded to direct the conversation to impersonal channels. They talked of old mutual friends, of poor Nicolas Rogers whom he'd come across fairly frequently in India, before he'd been killed in the war. He told her about India and his life there, of the Chitral and Afridi risings, both of which he had witnessed. As they sat together in the Palm Court she listened spellbound to his accounts of the appalling famine which had devastated vast tracts of India four years before. The years seemed to recede and it seemed as if they had been parted only for months. Gradually the pain left her heart and a new self-confidence filled Bethel, helped by the natural ease and lack of self-consciousness on Martineau's part. He had left a girl sixteen years ago; it was a woman who listened to him now, a woman who had suffered bitterly and miserably, but who, with the experience of age and sorrow, was able to meet him without hysteria, without fear.

Presently a waiter brought him the bill.   Bethel looked at her watch.

" Must you go? " he asked regretfully.

" I really think I must," she answered, her heart sinking at the thought of a lonely dinner at the hotel.

" What are you doing?   Where are you staying?   Good heavens, Bethel!   There's so much I want to know.   Here have I been yarning on in the most insufferable way about myself, you've not told me a thing about you."   He paused, and she smiled wanly.

" I've not much to tell," she said.

" Bethel, I believe we're both going home to lonely dinners. I know I am.   Am I right? "   She nodded.

" Then I beg you to dine with me.   Will you?   They give you a very good dinner at ——'s," he mentioned a very noted club, " and it's the only night they allow ladies."

What was the sense of refusing when all she wanted was to be with him?

" I should like to go back to the Langham and change into something else," she said.   " D'you mind?   I can easily get a cab, and I'll be back at your club soon after eight."

As Bethel drove back to the hotel she felt caught in a vortex of emotions.   She realized that, far from being dead, her love burned more fiercely than ever.

Oswald had altered a great deal, his life in the East had aged him more than she could have thought possible.   Women-like, she hoped he was not thinking the same of her.   Where age may add to a man's dignity as likely as not it only draws attention to the fact that a woman has become plainer and dowdier—at least, so women think—and Bethel found herself taking extra care with her toilet.   As she dressed the vision of Oswald was ever before her eyes.   Indeed, he looked every inch of his fifty odd years.   His hair was now iron grey, and he looked what he was, a distinguished member of His Majesty's High Court.   Queer to think of Oswald as a judge, and queerer still to think that he had retired from India for good.   What was he going to do? she wondered.   He had said something about being under doctor's orders.

She called a cab and was soon making her way through the empty streets to Oswald's club.   It was no good; in fact it was useless to try and keep at bay the excitement she was feeling. It was all so strange. If it was only a dream she prayed it might continue indefinitely. She began to think of her family, of Veryan and his wife. Of Lerryn—oh, how she blessed her sister for suggesting the visit to London. She began to realize, too, at first unwillingly, that the very fact that Veryan had married and Lerryn had had a love affair were helping her to-night to face an ordeal with far greater aplomb than she would have found possible a few years ago. Was it so very wrong for her to have a share in love? True, she did not know whether Oswald Martineau still cared for her, but surely love such as theirs had been was timeless? Veryan had basely betrayed their lives, and Lerryn in ignorance had allowed passion for her Ted a free rein, surely in the secret places of her own heart she, too, might at last be allowed to indulge in thoughts to which she had long ago bidden adieu . . .

The cab stopped and Bethel realized she had arrived. Oswald was waiting for her on the step.

" You look as—charming as ever," he said. " Time has stood still with you."

" Oh, Oswald ! " Tears leapt foolishly to her eyes. " How nice you are, and how untrue ! I'm so old now."

He led her through the hall and up the shallow, wide staircase confronting them.

" You could never be old," he answered. " I was almost hoping yours would keep my grey hairs company. I deserve my punishment for such an ungallant wish. Go and leave your coat and we will go straight in."

She rejoined him a few seconds later.

" It's generally fairly quiet, and of course at this time of the year there are very few people anyway. Birds of passage like myself, for the most part. But I like it because in spite of the quiet one can talk without being overheard. I can't stand that atmosphere one gets so much of in England, of whispering in public rooms. I'm never certain if I'm at somebody's funeral or whether I'm supposed to be listening to a risqué story. Nice room, isn't it ? " He led the way to a table in the corner. " That's one of the finest Adam mantel-pieces in London. Always used to remind me of the one in the library at Treveryan."

It was odd, Bethel thought, that when Oswald mentioned the past she did not seem to mind. Perhaps it was because the past was momentarily lost in the present. All the same, she hoped the conversation would not take too personal a turn, for she felt unsure of herself. And for a time the topics chosen were impersonal enough. But a long pause ensued as they were nearing the end of dinner, and then Oswald Martineau said quietly :

" I can't believe we're really here, you and I. It's too fantastic when one thinks that out of all the years we should both have chosen this minute to be in London. And to meet at the Zoo of all places ! "

" Yes . . ."

" You've not changed. Not really. Of course we're both older," he sighed, " but age becomes you, my dear. The pretty girl has become a beautiful woman. Tell me, are you happy ? What do you do with yourself these days ? I suppose a lot of your time is taken up with helping Veryan. How is he ? And Lerryn ? "

" Veryan married, Oswald." She spoke slowly, and watched his expression change to one of incredulous indignation.

"*What* ? "

" Yes, he married a year ago. A Canadian girl he met when he was over there." And she started then to tell him of their lives, how Veryan had gone on the royal tour; how, in fact, he had seemed restless ever since his return from the Boer War.

" I wouldn't have believed it possible of him," he said, when Bethel described his homecoming with Lucy. " He must have been mad ! "

The words were out before he could stop himself. Quickly he asked, " What's she like ? "

Bethel shrugged her shoulders.

" Oh, Oswald . . ." she sighed.

Without thinking he took her hand. " Poor darling ! " he murmured. His touch unnerved her. She had begun to hope as dinner progressed that the physical attraction she had felt for him had died. She knew now that this was not so.

" I was very ill after you went away," she began.

" Why didn't they tell me ? "

" I suppose after what had happened it would have seemed

pointless. But when I was all right again Veryan and I dedicated our lives, our future, to each other. I hoped he would take your place in as much as any one could. I did my best to forget about you and the past and the hideous reason that had separated us." She paused. "Ought I to talk to you like this?"

"Please go on."

"Treveryan and V. were my entire life, Oswald. I suppose I must have become terribly narrow, terribly hard."

"No, no," he said quickly.

"Veryan was everything to me that a human being could be to one as unfortunate as I was. He was father, brother, son, friend . . . or so I foolishly thought."

"What about your sister?"

"There were times when I'm afraid I neglected Lerryn, though I swear I never realized it. Poor sweet . . . I injured her—yes, it was my fault!"

It was as though she were talking to herself.

"I insisted to Veryan that she should never be told the truth about everything, much against his advice. When he was away she fell desperately in love with someone; she kept it from me for a year. I could have spared her that."

"Lerryn, too," he mused.

"He was unsuitable in every way, as it happened, but that does not absolve me from blame. Of course, she went crazy when she learnt the truth. He went to Australia, without even saying good-bye to her. A month later V. returned with his—bride."

Her voice shook bitterly.

"What on earth did he offer as explanation? What could he?"

"He never has," she replied. "He's a changed creature, Oswald. Sometimes I wonder if the man at Treveryan can be my Veryan."

Gradually he dragged other things from her, he learnt of the way Treveryan had been wrested from her, he learnt of the birthday festivities that had finally driven her to London. By this time they were the only people left in the dining-room, and Bethel became aware of the waiter's apparent desire to get rid of them both.

" It's getting late, Oswald," she said, as they made their way across the room, " I think I ought to be going back to my hotel."

" Can I see you again? " he asked.

" I thought you were going to Scotland," she said.

" I am, damn it. To-morrow night. I can't let the fellow down either. But I'm free at lunch time. What about it? "

" Why not? " she said, " who knows when we shall meet again."

Bethel hardly slept that night. The woman she was longed for Oswald more than the girl had done. Awake or with closed eyes his face was before her. Once or twice the vision of Veryan with Lucy would haunt and torture her, and she would realize with greater passion her brother's betrayal. In a mad moment she wondered if Veryan had been right, whether it were possible that their fears had been groundless? But she knew such temptation to be against every decent feeling she possessed, and in agony of despair she told herself she was doomed and damned.

For Martineau also the night was one of torment. He had put Bethel Treveryan from him so many years ago that he thought he had succeeded in forgetting her. But for this chance meeting he could have believed the old adage, of time's power to heal, correct. Last night had been fatal, however, and he knew he longed for Bethel as much as he had ever done. Moreover, she had shown all too plainly by the story she had told him that she had never ceased to care for him, and what man is proof against such words? Cruel as the knowledge was, he knew he must not see Bethel again. After he had bidden her farewell to-day they would have to abide by that decision for ever. What was the point of seeing her in the future? To what end prolong what could only be agony to both of them? There were complications in his own life, and, even if Bethel had not been doomed by the appalling possibility of insanity, one did not propose entering into a *liaison* with the only woman one had ever loved. Marriage was the only possible life for himself and Bethel, and that was impossible.

She found him distrait at luncheon, and with a woman's usual intuition divined the reason and spoke little herself. It was not necessary to talk when one was with Oswald. The perfect understanding of being together was enough, even when one knew, as she knew, that time was so fleeting.

Afterwards they strolled out into the Park and presently found two chairs facing the Serpentine.

" Funny ! I haven't been here since I first fell in love with you." He sighed. "A long time ago, Beth."

" Oswald . . ." she touched his arm and spoke impulsively. " I know I oughtn't to ask you such a thing—it's despicable, cheap and altogether dreadful of me, but do you still care? "

He turned and looked into her eyes.

" Oh, God, yes ! " he said quietly.

" My darling . . ."

For a long time neither of them spoke.

" I did my damnedest to forget you," he said, a little while later. " I thought I'd succeeded. I knew my love for you could never die, but I thought I'd managed to banish you from my memory. But the last twenty-four hours have brought back the past so vividly, so hopelessly . . ."

" Is it so hopeless? Must it be? " Unabashed she began to speak of Veryan's excuses, of how he had refuted all the statements and reasons that had been brought up nearly two decades ago, as being old-fashioned and untrue.

"And do you believe him? " Martineau asked.

" I don't know," she said faintly.

" Even if it were so, Bethel—I myself believe Veryan to be lying—I'm no longer free."

Slowly the colour drained from her face.

" What do you mean? " she whispered.

" I married, my dear, fourteen years ago."

For a minute or two she was so stunned that she could not think or speak coherently.

" Why didn't you tell me earlier? " she presently asked. " Why have you let me make such an—exhibition of myself? It was unkind of you. Oh, God! I feel so ashamed! " Her last words were so whispered that he could barely catch them.

" Because I love you and have always loved you, of course. Because it was like receiving new life to hear you still loved me. Bethel, beloved, never regret these few hours. Never regret that you showed me that all these years——"

"I was the only one who remained faithful. Oh! I don't blame you. Even last night, when I realized I loved you as much as I ever did, I hardly expected you to care still. But somehow I didn't think you would have a—wife."

"Believe me, my dearest, when I tell you our marriage was a mistake from the first. Laura and I haven't been together for nearly twelve years."

"You're divorced?"

He shook his head.

"She's a Catholic, so that's been out of the question."

"Tell me about it, please."

"I met her when I was in Madras. She was helping the R.C. Mission out there . . ."

"A *missionary*?"

He smiled slightly.

"I can scarcely describe Laura as a full-fledged missionary, no! She was the niece of the Abbott in charge out there, and her people were Anglo-Indians anyway, and somehow or other it seemed natural for Laura to be in that set. I met her, she was kind and interested in my work—which meant a lot to me. I was attached to the Indian Bar at that time, which dealt almost entirely with Indian and Eurasian cases, and few English women were interested in it. Anyway, Laura was, and I was desperately lonely, longing for you with every fibre of my being, and refusing to let myself think about you. So we married."

"Was she pretty?"

"Laura? I don't know. No, not really. Quite nice looking."

"Go on."

"It was a failure from the start. I'd have given anything the night before our wedding to have got out of it there and then."

"Then why didn't you?"

He shrugged his shoulders.

"Why do so many behave as I did? And they do, believe me. Line of least resistance, perhaps. I thought after I'd had a few drinks that it was all nonsense, told myself most men felt that way. And that was that."

"You must have loved her some of the time, Oswald."

"It was ghastly, I didn't. I had liked her tremendously, or thought I had. I was fool enough to imagine love would come automatically. It was criminal of me to have married her, knowing that her religion would never countenance a divorce if it went wrong."

"Did she love you?"

"She wanted to get married; she was nearly thirty and she felt she could help me with my work. But she seemed to change after we got married; I expect it was entirely my fault."

"Why was it a failure?"

"Need you ask, my dear? Your vision came between us from the first. I couldn't . . . but I can't talk about it. She didn't know about you, but gradually wormed it out of me. In a way I felt I owed her some sort of explanation. Instead of it filling her with hatred for me it merely worked her up into a frenzied state of jealousy. Life became intolerable. She got very ill and had a nervous breakdown, and I had to take her away for a holiday."

"Why did you have to go?"

"My dear, I had married her, she was my wife. I tried to begin again, and for a time things did go much better. She seemed more as she had done before we married, and I—well, I realized it was up to me to try and make our marriage a success."

"And then?"

There was a pause.

"We had a son, Bethel. He only lived five days. Laura nearly died. After that I think we both realized it wasn't much use going on. We both tried, but it was hopeless. We finally decided to separate."

"Where is she now?"

"The last I heard of her, some years ago, she was thinking seriously of entering some sisterhood or other. Bethel, at the risk of your thinking me a cad for saying this, I have to tell you that my marriage meant nothing to me. The two or three years I was with Laura are nothing in my memory compared to the four months I knew and worshipped you. Please believe this."

" I do, Oswald. And I'm glad you have told me the whole story."

Presently they got up and walked back across the park. In Knightsbridge Martineau hailed a cab.

" I'm going to drive you back to the Langham and then I must get back, as there are some important things I have to see to before I catch my train to-night."

They drove in silence for some time, each aware of the bleak misery in the other's heart.

" This, I suppose, is our end," Bethel said presently.

" Darling, there's no end for us. Not really. I shall love you for all time . . ."

"And I you."

" But I think we should be foolish if we tried to see each other. Let us be wise. We're older, a good deal older than we were when we last said good-bye. If our love were not so great, if we could settle down to an old age of friendship and sweet memories, I would suggest we tried it. But we're neither of us old enough for that. I love you, am still passionately in love with you. I know I could not stand seeing you, meeting you, knowing you cared for me, too . . ."—and as he looked at her she pressed his hand—" all the time wanting you for my own and not being able to have you. If, my Bethel, you feel as I do, then you will agree that it is best we should part."

" I wonder if the next seventeen years will be the same hell? " she said.

" Sweet, have you ever read ' Peter Ibbetson '? "

She shook her head.

" If I send it to you, will you promise to read it? "

" Perhaps. I don't read much."

" George du Maurier wrote it."

" The man who wrote ' Trilby '? "

" Yes. It's the greatest love story I know. The greatest and most tragic story of lovers' separation in modern fiction. You'll understand what I mean when you've read it."

" Send it to me. I'll read it."

All too soon the cab turned into Portland Place.

" Drive to the top first and put me out there." Martineau leant out and spoke to the driver.

"For all we may be going to suffer for this in the future, I still thank God for these few precious hours of you," he said, as he took her in his arms.

"Beloved, Bethel beloved," he said brokenly.

A few minutes later she was alone.

The Past had now merged into a new and hideous Present for Bethel. White-lipped and haggard, she made her way slowly to her room.

"Pack our things this evening," she said to Prue, "for I want to go back to Cornwall to-morrow."

"Oh, Miss!" began the maid, but a look at her mistress's face stopped her from further speech.

PART THREE

5

"GOODNESS! SHE LOOKS more like a thundercloud than ever," was Lucy's private opinion of her sister-in-law as she watched her at dinner on Bethel's first evening home. Very soon afterwards, on the pretext of having a bad headache and feeling extremely tired from her journey, Bethel excused herself and retired to her room.

"Bethel's trip doesn't seem to have done her much good," said Veryan the next day to Lerryn.

"I can't understand it," she shook her head. "I had such contented letters from her from London, you know, I was rather surprised at the time."

"Pity she didn't remain, if we please her so little," he remarked.

"Veryan, Prue says she's sure something must have happened. Suddenly. She told me that Beth was like a different person up there, almost gay. And the last two days she says she was in extraordinary spirits. She went out to dinner on Sunday night—and seemed rather mysterious altogether, Prue thought. Then she came in on Monday before dinner, looking simply ghastly, and told Prue to pack. And that's all we know."

"Very odd. Have you said anything to Beth?" he asked. Lerryn shook her head.

"I don't like to. Why don't you?"

" I'm afraid Beth and I are not the friends we were, my dear. You know that. Indeed, she seems to resent anything I say or do now. Perhaps it's her age. They tell me your sex is strangely tricky, Lerryn. You ought to manage her, you're a woman."

" It's a bit late in the day to shelve all your responsibilities, you know."

" Don't you start on me," he said.

For a few more weeks life at Treveryan went on very much as usual. Veryan held several partridge shoots, and later, when the pheasant shooting began, Lerryn and Lucy would join the men for picnic lunches. Occasionally Bethel would join the party if, as sometimes happened, Lucy excused herself from going at the last moment.

Towards the end of November Lucy came into Bethel's room one day; Bethel arrived to discover her peering at her knick-knacks and behaving as if the room belonged to her. Veryan had gone to Falmouth for a couple of days on some business.

Bethel started when she saw her sister-in-law, who made no attempt to apoligize for her intrusion.

" Did you want to see me about something, Lucy ? " Bethel asked.

" Oh, Bethel," her voice was studiedly unconcerned, " I was only having a look at your room. Yes, it's very nice." She seemed to be speaking to herself.

" I'm quite capable of looking after my own room, I think," answered Bethel. " In fact, I doubt if you'll find anything the matter with any of them. The ceilings are all sound, and the chimneys were swept not so long ago—you overlooked that item, I heard. I gave the orders in September when I heard you'd forgotten."

" My dear Bethel, I'm not the slightest bit interested in your ceiling, nor Treveryan's chimneys, nor the possibility of damp patches in some of the upstairs attics. I don't consider that sort of thing comes into my ken. No, I was wanting to see your room with a view to aspect and size, and various things. It's nice and airy, too. In fact, altogether most suitable."

" Perhaps you'd tell me what you're talking about ? " asked Bethel.

" I shall want this room next year. I'd like you to be out of it by the spring, if you'd be so good."

Bethel looked at Lucy with amazement.

" I think you must have taken leave of your senses, Lucy. If you imagine that for a moment I have any intention of clearing out of the room I've had all my life for a mere whim of yours, then you're mistaken."

" There are plenty of others very nearly as nice," said Lucy.

" Then why can't you use one of them, pray? Anyway, why should you want this? It's in this wing of the house, very much by itself, near the old nursery, not a bit suited as any sort of spare room——"

" You're extraordinarily dense, Bethel. Those are the very reasons why I want it. I'm going to have a baby next summer."

After a long pause, Bethel exclaimed, " No, no ! " in tones of such horror that it was Lucy's turn to look amazed.

" You're the most unnatural woman I've ever met," she said. " I don't begin to understand you. You're one colossal lie; you pretend to live for the good works you do in the village, you make a song and dance over the school children, and yet you won't even give over the sunniest room in the house for your own brother's child ! I've never heard such selfishness, upon my word ! You pretend to be so fond and so proud of your precious Treveryan; does it mean nothing to you that Veryan will probably have a son to carry on the name and succeed? "

" Does Veryan know? " she asked.

" Of course he knows."

" He did not dare tell me."

" If I didn't know Veryan as well as I do, I should think your love an extremely horrible and unhealthy thing," Lucy said. " As it is, I'm just beginning to understand you. I'm beginning to realize at what Veryan has hinted. All his life until he met me he was at your beck and call. Veryan may have inherited this place, but it's been you who ruled it as you ruled him. You're warped, unnatural, horrible. In love with your own . . ."

Before she could finish the sentence Bethel had caught her a hard smack in the face, which sent her tottering across the room.

" How dare you," she hissed.

" Veryan will never forgive you for that ! " said Lucy slowly, as she picked herself up with as much dignity as possible.

" Stop ! You're not going till you hear things which will make you wish you'd never set foot in England."

There was something in the cold fury of Bethel's voice and the blaze of her eyes that made Lucy turn to the door.

" You've got to get rid of this child, Lucy," she said slowly.

" Are you mad? " the other cried.

Bethel started to laugh. As she saw the effect this had on her sister-in-law she could not stop and for several minutes became hysterical.

" Yes," she gasped presently, " that's exactly what we are. Mad. Mad. Mad."

She strode to the door and quickly locked it, thus preventing Lucy from making her escape.

" Bethel, what do you mean? "

There was fear, deathly fear in her expression and in her voice.

" We're mad, Lucy. The Treveryans are all mad." Bethel spoke calmly now. She saw that Lucy was very frightened.

" Our father died totally insane, and he tried to strangle our mother. Most of our ancestors were insane, too. We shall be before long," and she started to laugh again.

" I don't believe it. I don't believe a word you're telling me. It's a lie, a hideous, foul, frightful lie," Lucy cried.

" Oh, no, it's not. It's the truth; ask Veryan, he can't deny it. Why do you suppose his marriage was such a shock to us? " She paused. " We never knew the truth as children. When I was twenty-five I was engaged to be married. It was announced at Veryan's coming-of-age dinner, we had a joint party for the celebrations. Two days afterwards Veryan learnt from the old doctor that Papa had died a madman, that there was incurable insanity in our family, that it would be fatal and criminal of us to marry. I had to give up Oswald Martineau, and all thought of love for ever, Lucy. We all had. We pledged our lives to each other and to Treveryan, the three of us. Poor Lerryn was only a child, she knew nothing about it until a month before Veryan returned with you. I had to tell her because she, too, had fallen in love with someone. That, too, had to be broken. The man I loved went to India, the man she loved, to Australia. Lerryn's pretty, isn't she? She adored this man, but it had to be smashed, and when he learnt the truth he was so shattered by the horror that he left without any word to her. Then Veryan came home—with you. He'd married you. You wondered why I didn't receive you with open arms, didn't welcome you to Treveryan. Well, Lucy, you know now. Lerryn's and my lives have been wrecked, and we've been betrayed by our brother. You've wondered why we led sheltered, isolated lives. Ask Veryan, his was the idea. Any time, anyhow, the madness of our ancestors may fall on any one of us. Papa nearly strangled Mama, and he loved her. *He loved her, Lucy.* What are you going to do about it? You're carrying a madman's child, Lucy. What are you going to do about it?"

But just then Lucy could do nothing about it, for she had fainted dead away on to the floor. Lerryn found her thus when she came to look for her sister a quarter of an hour later. Horrified by the sight of Lucy unconscious and alone, she rushed to her side and tried to revive her. Presently the girl began to come to, but realizing someone's arms were about her, cowered with revulsion, presuming at first that it was Bethel. When she saw it was Lerryn, she relaxed slightly and moaned.

"Lerryn, tell me it's not true."

Gradually Lerryn dragged out from her the story of the scene.

"It's true, Lucy, I'm sorry," and her heart filled with remorse and pity when Lucy told her between broken sobs, that she was expecting a child.

All the next day Lucy remained upstairs in her own room, refusing to allow anyone near her but her maid, a new servant who was fresh to Cornwall and knew nothing of the family, and was ready to give all her attention and devotion to her young mistress.

Bethel was out when Veryan came home the following day, and the first she knew of his return was the sound of raised voices coming from Lucy's bedroom. Lucy sounded as if she were in hysterics, and she could tell from the way Veryan was shouting that he was both angry and afraid.

Presently she heard the door open and then she saw her brother. His face was like chalk and he was shaking. He stopped dead when he saw her beneath him at the foot of the stairs.

" God damn you for an interfering bitch ! "

She said nothing. Very slowly Bethel smiled.

" What did you do it for, what the hell had it to do with you ? " Veryan was still standing at the top of the stairs.

" You know all the servants can probably hear you," she said, and started to move away.

" I've got to talk to you, d'you hear me ? I've simply got to talk to you," he called out.

" Very well V. There's nothing to stop you." She went into the library, where in a few minutes he joined her.

" How dare you," he began, " how dare you terrify Lucy ? "

" I'm sorry I hit her. I admit I lost my temper, but she said something that I considered unpardonable and for a moment I was beside myself."

" You know that's not to what I'm alluding, though for that alone I'd like to turn you out of the house."

" Just exactly what d'you mean then, Veryan ? "

He began to get flustered.

" Telling a highly strung girl in her condition a pack of lies——" He could proceed no further.

" Don't be such a fool, V. I told Lucy what I'd tell any woman in the same circumstances, that it's criminal to bring a child into the world with a heritage such as you have to offer it. I told her no lies. I told her that madness is in our family, and that many years ago we pledged ourselves never to marry because of it. I let her know that Lerryn and I had to see our own lives and loves wrecked . . ."

" That's a lie to begin with. Lerryn never had a love affair."

" It's over and done with now, it happened when you were in Canada."

" I don't believe a word you're saying."

" It's perfectly true, what should I want to make it up for ? And, anyway, it's neither here nor there. I thought it only fair to let Lucy see that we thought enough of our pretty little mad streak to make sacrifices, and that you had not."

Veryan paced the room.

" God ! I wish I'd never interfered with you and your wretched lover when I was an ignorant young ass of twenty-one ! "

" It's a little too late to start being sorry for my wrecked happiness."

She spoke bitterly.

" There never was a woman so eaten up with self-pity as you, Beth. Anyone'd think you were the only woman in the world whose love affair had gone on the rocks."

" I doubt if many women have been so deceived by a brother as I have been by you."

" This isn't getting us anywhere. Beth, somehow or other, you've simply got to convince Lucy that you were not telling her the truth."

" I fail to see why I should do that," she answered.

He looked at her.

" You're cruel. God ! How cruel you are. And wicked, too. Why should you vent your anger on poor, pathetic Lucy . . . ? "

" Poor ! Pathetic ! Really, Veryan, that girl has made you into a drivelling idiot. Anything less poor and pathetic ! "

" Listen, Bethel. That girl, whether you hate her or no, is having a child. I appeal to any decent feelings remaining in you to have pity on her. I don't ask you for my sake, but for humanity's sake . . ."

" Then for God's sake, don't ! "

He started back as if struck.

" Do you think humanity wants another insane person born into the world? If it's for humanity sake you're pleading, take your wife to a doctor and tell him the truth. Don't be such a hypocrite, Veryan."

" I'm as sane as any man living," he answered.

" So was Papa at your age," she retorted.

" Bethel, if you don't give me your word to undo the mischief you have done I'll not be answerable for what I may do myself."

" My dear boy, do you suppose threats can frighten me ? And won't Lucy believe what you tell her ? Has she also lost her faith in you, her trust in you ? "

Veryan came over to where Bethel stood and shook her.

"Lucy was still so upset when I saw her that she could hardly speak coherently. I'm going to her again now. But, by heaven above, if my marriage is going to be ruined by you, you shall pay for it!"

He went out of the room.

That night at dinner Veryan addressed himself almost solely to Lerryn, who, aware of the tension in the atmosphere, spent a miserable evening realizing how near to breaking point Veryan's relations with Bethel had become.

"Oh, dear, I wish in a way you'd never told Lucy," she said later, when Veryan had left them.

"Why? I don't regret it. You're always one for taking the line of least resistance, Lerryn."

"I don't think I am. Not always," she said.

"Well—perhaps not always," Bethel replied, smiling slightly.

The next morning, when Bethel went downstairs for breakfast, she saw that Veryan had already taken his, but when later she left the dining-room she heard his voice calling her into the study. She found him standing in front of the fireplace. His face was drawn and haggard, he looked as if he had slept little.

"It may interest you to know, Bethel, that Lucy won't allow me to go near her. Not only did I have to sleep in my dressing-room, but the door between our rooms was locked. Thanks to you, I'm barred from my own wife's room."

"Really, Veryan, I'm sorry, I don't see what I can do about it."

"I'm not allowed near her. She won't let me go anywhere near her. She's terrified. Of me, her husband. I tried to take her in my arms, to kiss her, to show her that I'm no different . . ."

"Well?"

"She started to scream."

"You should have told Lucy the truth before you married her. Why didn't you?"

Veryan could not answer.

Again the day passed in an extremely unpleasant atmosphere, Lucy still preferring to keep to her own room.

As Bethel passed her room in the late afternoon she heard

once again voices coming from within, her brother's beseeching tones, her sister-in-law's high-pitched hysterical ones. Suddenly the door opened and Veryan saw her. Catching her by the arm he dragged her inside. Lucy, fully dressed, sat huddled in a chair by the fire. Her face looked blotchy and her hair unkempt. Even Bethel was shocked by her appearance.

"Look at her! Look what you've done to her," he said angrily, as he more or less pushed his sister over towards his wife.

"Really, Veryan!" Bethel exclaimed. "You're being a little crude, and I am not to blame. Women in Lucy's condition do look like that."

"You beast!" he said.

"If you only brought me in here to insult me I've other more important things to do with my time."

"Bethel, you'll tell Lucy here and now that you very greatly exaggerated our family—misfortune."

She shrugged her shoulders.

"If by telling Lucy Papa died mad, as did many of his relations, I exaggerated—very well, I exaggerated. If by telling her that old Doctor Pearce told you that I must not marry Oswald, that it would be criminal for us to marry as any one of us might inherit the disease *or pass it on*—if by telling her that I exaggerated, then I plead guilty."

"Deny it, Veryan, deny it, then," cried Lucy.

"He can't," said Bethel.

"Darling Lucy!" He went across to her, but she shrank back into her chair, and a look of horror came over her face.

"Don't come near me, I can't bear it. I can't bear you to touch me," she said.

It was Veryan's turn to start back now, which he did as if he'd been whipped.

"Darling, my sweetheart! Surely her lies haven't killed your love?"

"I don't know, I don't know," she moaned. "They aren't lies. I know they aren't. Something tells me she's speaking the truth. I hate her and she hates me, but I know she's speaking the truth."

"Oh, my God!" Once again Veryan tried to go near her,

but " Don't come near me," she screamed, " I can't stand the thought of your touching me. I love you, it's awful, it's vile, I don't understand it; I do love you, but I simply can't bear the thought of you near me. Go away, get further away. Oh, Bethel, make him go further from me."

Was this her hour of triumph? Had she really heard the enemy call on her for help? Bethel looked at Veryan and smiled.

" You heard what Lucy asked? " she said.

" My God! I'll never forgive you. My whole life's happiness wrecked by you, the sister I've loved as probably few brothers love their sisters."

" Shall we cry quits then? You bade me wreck my life's happiness in 1887, Veryan. You promised to stay by me, and I swore to stay by you, for the rest of our lives. We had no child but Treveryan. You've broken your word, you've married Lucy; you've given her a child with the diseased blood of our cursed family in its veins. Mad, insane blood . . ."

" Christ! I could kill you for this, Bethel . . ." He strode across the room and seized hold of her. With maddened anger he started to shake her, but she only laughed. The more she laughed the more infuriated Veryan became until at last, his anger spent, he let go of her and she dropped exhausted to the ground, while Veryan sank into a chair and began to sob.

Presently Bethel looked up. She saw they were alone.

" Where's Lucy? " she asked a few minutes later. That roused him. He got up from the chair and went into the next room, only to return a moment later with a blank expression in his eyes.

" She's not there," he muttered. He went to the door and opened it. " Lucy! " he called.

There was no answer.

" LUCY! " he shouted.

And presently Treveryan echoed with the distraught cries of the unhappy man.

" Lucy—Lucy—Lucy . . ."

LUCY HAD GONE. After an hour's fruitless search by Veryan with the help of Lerryn, there was nothing to be done but tell the servants and institute a general hue and cry. By this time it was dusk, and even with the aid of lanterns and lamps it was soon obvious that the search would not be easy, especially as Lucy had disappeared apparently by her own wish. Luckily it was a dry night and no sign of rain, but it was pitch dark, without so much as a star in the sky, and bitterly cold, with a wind getting up.

"One feels so utterly at a loss," Veryan said, when at nine o'clock there was still no sign of his wife. "Not a soul in the village has seen her, I've been down there. She's taken nothing with her; she must have slipped out of the room when we were talking. God knows what she's got on! For all we know she mayn't even have on a thick coat or decent shoes."

"Surely she wouldn't be so silly as to go out improperly clad," said Lerryn, "a cold evening like this? It's been cold all day. I'm certain she'd have wrapped up."

"How can one know or be certain of anything. You weren't there, Lerryn. I can't tell you what it was like, but Bethel and I had the most shattering row in front of Lucy. Then, suddenly, she was not there. God knows what possessed her, but I can only think we frightened her and that in a moment of hysteria she rushed out. She's been completely hysterical ever since Bethel spoke to her, damn her! Heaven knows where she may be, what may have happened. In her condition . . ."

"Have you tried looking for her at any of her friends?"

"No, I hadn't thought of that. I'll get the carriage harnessed at once. The only thing is that everyone lives such a way off. But it's worth trying the Tremaynes, perhaps. I'll tell some of the men to scour the other roads, all the Muttons are out looking for her in the woods. It's all so beastly, Lerryn, apart from the sickening worry of it. What on earth are they all thinking? What can I tell the Tremaynes, for instance?"

"Poor Veryan! You'll simply have to explain that Lucy's going to have a baby and that somehow or other it's unhinged her. Women sometimes do get very odd, you know."

"I only hope she doesn't tell the truth to anyone. I don't care if she curses Beth, but we don't want everyone to know the other damnable business after all these years."

"I do hope we shall find her soon. In the meantime I'll take a lantern and search the gardens again."

Bethel alone, out of the entire household, refrained from helping to look for her sister-in-law.

"Why should I?" she asked, when Lerryn hinted that it looked a little strange to be sitting in her room reading, when every man and woman was making some sort of effort to help to trace Lucy.

"I'm not such a hypocrite. We hate each other, why should I now pretend to be worried about her? She's probably walked to the station and has got a train."

"I haven't thought of that," said Lerryn. "I'd better go at once and tell one of the men to saddle up and ride over. It's a longish way, Beth. Lucy never walks a yard if she can help it."

"I'm pretty sure she's safe and comfortable enough somewhere," Bethel said.

"It looks so bad, your sitting here doing nothing, I mean," Lerryn remarked. "People are sure to put two and two together, you know how everyone gossips. And, after all, if she is unhappy and ran off in a fright, as V. seems to think, one can't be absolutely heartless, Beth. Even you must have some pity, I should have thought."

"You're absolutely wrong. I have no pity for any of them."

"Veryan . . ." Lerryn began.

"Veryan least of all."

Lerryn sighed and left the room.

In the meantime, footsore, weary, hungry and at last thoroughly frightened, Lucy was plunging through the undergrowth of the old Pendragon Woods. She could not have said how long it now was since, bewildered and terrified by the quarrel she had witnessed between Bethel and her husband, she had rushed from the house, convinced that both of them were insane, determined somehow or other to escape and never to return. In such a hurry had she left Treveryan, in order to avoid being stopped or seen, that it was not until she had run a mile or more, and in a sudden attack of giddiness been forced to

rest, that she realized that not only had she run away
with inadequate clothes, but had brought no money with
her.

She felt too frightened to return, and too stunned for the
moment to pull her scattered wits together. She only knew
that she MUST GET AWAY. She cursed herself for having
in the past taken so little notice of the countryside, one lane
was the same as any other to her, and she had invariably refused
to go for rambles with Lerryn or Veryan, preferring always to
remain in the garden if the carriage or car had not been avail-
able for trips farther afield. She had purposely avoided the
village and had struck out, as she had fancied, in the direction
of Port Holland, where it had been vaguely her intention to
have got some trap to take her over to Mary St. Hilary. But
sense of direction was not Lucy's strong point, and very soon
dusk began to fall, and she found herself completely lost.
Presently she realized by the sound of breaking surf that she
must be nearing the sea, and she began to hope that after all
her surmise had been correct, and that the semblance of a path
that she had followed was bringing her to her goal. But in a
few minutes she realized to her dismay that the path had
brought her out on to the cliffs, and that it ended abruptly
there. She peered through the light which was fast diminish-
ing, only to realize that there was no sign of habitation;
moreover, the coast was a part utterly unknown to her.
Jackdaws and gulls screamed and wheeled beneath her on
hearing the sudden approach of a human being, and a bat
suddenly flew out from somewhere, brushing her face. The
wind was blowing in hard from the sea, and although the cliffs
were high, she caught the spray in her eyes. There was something eerie and bleak about the place; it grew darker every
minute, and she was aware of great shapes looming out of
nothingness, as it were, which she discerned later to be sheep.
Surely in that case there must be a farm nearby, she thought,
but there were no signs of light or habitation. She called, but
not even the echo of her own voice replied. Wearily she
retraced her footsteps, since the idea of remaining out on the
barren headland was even more unpleasant. On and on she
wandered, and soon darkness had completely fallen. She
realized after a while that she was on yet another path, for a

tiny stream ran by her which she had not been aware of before. Presently she stumbled, and was forced to sit down. Dew had fallen and she soon began to notice the damp cold, and staggered to her feet again. Her feet were now icy cold and wet as well, for her shoes had only thin soles, and already showed signs of wear. She shivered and was unable to keep back her tears. Soon she was whimpering loudly, and thoughts of Treveryan madness began to recede as she ached for the warmth of the fire which she knew would be burning in her room. Somewhere a dog began to bark furiously and a new terror was added, for poor Lucy was frightened to death of dogs, and it suddenly struck her that even if she found herself outside some farm, she would be far too petrified with fear to penetrate near a house at this time of night, when the animals would probably be wandering about, ready for any poachers or prowlers who might be venturing nearby. She stopped still and waited, but the barking ceased and she trudged on. If only the stars would shine or a moon come out, she thought with desperation, but there seemed little likelihood of her wish being granted. Suddenly she came to an open space; it smelt in the darkness like a stretch of moorland. She had no idea of the time, and was beginning to feel at the end of her tether, when close by she heard coming towards her the ambling hoofs of some animal. She could not tell what it was, but ran blindly in the opposite direction. Once again she tripped and by a miracle found a big gate which stopped her fall. She leant against it panting, and then, as once more she thought she could hear some animal approaching, she hurriedly climbed it and dropped to the other side. Lucy did not know it, but she was now inside Pendragon Woods, a small forest belonging to the Duchy, rarely visited during the winter months, but the scene of many a picnic and haunt of trippers in the summer. A veritable maze of winding paths and pretty glades, with a rivulet having the biggest ' falls ' in Cornwall, Pendragon was also a wilderness, and even in daylight it is easy enough to lose one's way in the thickness of its undergrowth. Before long, Lucy was properly entrapped, and found herself stumbling or falling every few yards. Thorns and brambles caught at her dress and would hold her in their cruel vice, and when she finally extricated herself from these horrors, as likely as not a remaining bramble would trail on the hem of her garments to trip her up before she had gone many feet further. By now her skirt was torn, her stockings in shreds, and her hands and legs bleeding from the thorns, and the ice-cold of the air enhanced the pain. Sometimes she began to wonder if it were all some hideous nightmare, but when she fell against a huge beech tree and nearly knocked herself unconscious, she realized only too clearly that it was all true, that she was fully awake, and that this was all really happening to her. She had no idea how long she had been walking, nor how far she had come. She felt lightheaded for want of nourishment and the cold night air and her wretched condition were now starting to take physical effect on her. Violent pains started, and in a moment the delirium which had subconsciously taken pity on her brain, left her, and suddenly alert, she was aware only of real terror. What if during the night she became ill, lost as she was in the midst of this ghastly wilderness? She knew very little about childbirth and confinements, and was overcome by fear. What would she do if the baby were born in this wood, presently, now, without doctors, without nurses? Why, oh why, had she left Treveryan, because in a moment of hysteria she had been frightened of Veryan and Bethel? Anything was preferable to the ghastly fears she was undergoing now. Even madness was preferable . . . and the Treveryan madness was only a possibility, so Lerryn had tried to persuade her into believing. Convinced as she had been those few hours before of her husband's insanity, Lucy was now as fully convinced that she was about to give birth to her baby. She knew that she wanted Veryan now as she had never wanted him before.

Suddenly she found her voice and started to scream.

" Veryan . . . Veryan . . . Veryan . . ."

' 'Eryan . . . 'Eryan . . . 'Eryan . . .'

From the distance the echo of her cries returned to her from the rocky chasm of Pendragon Falls. She tried to push on and found to her relief that she was able to move. Blindly she started to run, crying, sobbing, and calling on Veryan as she did so. In the dark she could not see the wide ditch which was waiting for her, and she fell. Only for a moment did the pain in her leg register, for her head struck against a stone and she was knocked unconscious.

It was about eleven o'clock the following morning when the village constable came up to Treveryan and told them that he believed Mrs. Treveryan had been found.

" Is she alive? " Veryan cried.

" The poor lady's alive, but in a bad state. One of the woodmen at Pendragon discovered her this morning, sir. You'd better come right away."

" *Pendragon*? " Veryan and Lerryn exclaimed, " but that's miles away, she's never been there, are you certain it's Mrs. Treveryan? " the girl enquired.

" I've not seen the lady myself," the constable replied, " but from enquiries I made it sounds like Mrs. Treveryan."

When Veryan arrived at the cottage where Lucy had been taken, he found her bruised and still unconscious and a strange doctor with her. The woodman, a young fellow called Trenance, told them that it had been a miracle that he had gone along that particular pathway during the morning, and it was evident from what he said that Lucy might well have lain there for days.

" In which case the pore thing had been a corpse," said his wife, " for if ever a body would have passed away from exposure, that pore lady would 'ave done."

" How is she, doctor? " Veryan asked with anxiety.

" We must get her home at once," he said. " It's her leg that's fractured. I've sent for an ambulance and she ought to be all right. Obviously she can't remain here, and we must risk moving her. She's got a nasty knock on her head and slight concussion, but I'm not worried about that."

" And the child? "

The doctor at once reassured him, that as far as could be ascertained at the moment there was nothing to fear.

" Of course she'll have to be nursed and kept absolutely quiet for a very long time. But if nothing happens within the next month she should be all right. Mind you, I can promise nothing, but I think she'll be all right."

" And she's not caught cold, you are sure? "

" Your wife must have a wonderful constitution," the doctor said, " there seems nothing wrong with chest or lungs this morning. Luckily it was a dry night, though so cold. Whatever could have possessed her to go off on such an escapade. Do you know?"

Veryan replied as evasively as possible, telling the doctor that Lucy had been hysterical and depressed for some days.

"Get her own doctor as soon as you can. Luckily the fracture is a simple one. If, however, your wife is inclined to be hysterical, with her condition it's very important that she does not suffer from shock."

The doctor returned to Lucy, and with the help of the district nurse, who arrived at the same time as the ambulance, went in to set the fracture. Meanwhile Veryan went into the other room to express his gratitude to the Trenances for all they had done.

"My wife owes her life to you. I fully realize it," he said, "and not only her own life."

"Ah! So it's that as well?" Mrs. Trenance chipped in. "Pore, pore lady! I knowed who it was direckly I seen her, sir. When Will here brought her in, I said to him, Will, I said, that's young Mrs. Treveryan from Treveryan, what I had seen at the big fete way back in the summer. But sakes alive, I said, whatever is she doing over here, her clothes all torn, and her pore head cut and bleeding, and found in a ditch like Will found her? It looks like foul play, I said, but there! if it's a little one on the way! And her first I expect? Sometimes the queerest fancies comes over some women at such times. High-born ladies and pore alike, it's all the same. Indeed, sir, I hope the lady won't take too much hurt from all she's been through."

"Indeed I hope she hasn't," he answered, when at last she drew breath.

Here Trenance himself, thinking his wife had had too long an innings, began to tell Veryan again the full story of how he had found Lucy in the early morning.

It was afternoon before they were able to move Lucy, and the doctor and nurse drove back to Treveryan with her. Lucy's own doctor was already waiting at the house when they arrived, as Lerryn had had the foresight to send for him. At once he took a more serious view of the case.

"I'm not worried about the fracture nor your wife's concussion, it is her general condition and, of course, the child," he told Veryan. "We shall simply have to await events. In a way I can't help hoping for a miscarriage. She's not far enough gone for that to be too serious, whereas——" he hesitated.

"Yes?" Veryan enquired anxiously.

"One can't tell what effects this may have on the child itself. I have to warn you that I do consider it a grave business. It's not unlikely that your wife will give birth to a stillborn infant, and she may have a bad confinement."

"The child may have been killed, you mean?" Veryan said.

"It's possible it may live until the time of birth, and be stillborn, yes. Or it's possible she may have a miscarriage. In any case we shall have to go very, very carefully indeed. I shall send you two excellent nurses over immediately, it's best to be on the safe side for the time being. In the meantime Nurse Brown can remain till to-morrow, she tells me. I hope I can get in touch with one of my best private nurses when I leave here; unfortunately there are no telephones near here. Let us hope it will not be long before more general use is made of them. What a splendid invention! We doctors bless them hourly. Unfortunately they don't seem to progress further than towns."

"Doctor French—there's something I feel I ought to tell you. My wife has been a little hysterical of late. In fact, to put it mildly, she has taken a strange—aversion—to myself. D'you think I should keep away from her?"

The doctor looked thoughtful.

"I'm very glad you told me. As long as she's unconscious you can go into her room as much as you like. But don't attempt to see her when she regains consciousness unless she asks for you. We must keep her as quiet as we can. I don't want her to be upset in any way. But tell me," by this time the two men were downstairs in the hall, "she's quite glad to be having a child, isn't she?"

"She was." Veryan spoke as calmly as he could.

"Has anything happened to have upset her? Anything which has made her alarmed? Women are queer you know, Mr. Treveryan. Inclined to be highly strung and more sensitive at these times."

"She and my sister had a rather violent quarrel," he began.

" A pity. But still . . . that would hardly account for everything that has taken place. Unless, of course, you took your sister's part? "

" Indeed I did not! I gave her a piece of my mind, and in no uncertain way. We had a hell of a row, I don't mind telling you. Lucy, my wife, was in the room at the time."

" I see. I see. You never know, that in itself might have alarmed her. She's probably never seen you in a temper before? "

At that moment Lerryn came into the hall, and Veryan changed the conversation.

" Where is Bethel? " he asked when the doctor had left.

" She's dining at the vicarage with Mrs. Penrose," he was told.

" She's been quite extraordinarily conspicuous by her absence," he said. " Has she no conscience about this? Or is it such a guilty one that she's deliberately kept out of my way? "

Lerryn said she did not know.

He gave orders when dinner was over that he wished to see Bethel in his study directly she returned.

If Lerryn had only watched her brother with more care, she would have noticed that he was drinking considerably more than usual that night, and she would have been able to warn Bethel of the sort of mood in which he was likely to receive her. But she was too worried to take in more than the very understandable fact that he was extremely anxious about Lucy, and she fully expected him to be unpleasant, to say the least of it, to Bethel.

Veryan was not drunk, but he had taken just enough to upset, finally, nerves already frayed. Moreover by nine o'clock he had fully convinced himself that Lucy and his unborn child were near to death, and that Bethel was to blame. By the time his sister eventually arrived he had, with the help of half a bottle of brandy, accused her in his heart of murder. She came into the room and saw him standing, none too steady, in front of the fire. She noticed at once how pale and weary he looked, noticed the dark lock falling untidily about his forehead. For a moment her heart contracted with pity. For a moment she

was a girl again, and saw him as the small dearly loved brother,
worried because he was unable to construe some Latin verse,
and she would try to help him, and would gently smooth that
troubled brow and unruly lock of hair.   But in a moment she
was back again in the present, for a man's severe and rather
thick voice was speaking.

" You must leave Treveryan," he was saying.

For a few seconds she stared at him, as if uncomprehending.

" You heard what I said.   This house, my house, is not big
enough for my wife and my child's murderess."

" I think you're drunk, Veryan," she answered coldly then.

" Drunk, am I?   And would it be surprising if I were?   It
happens, however, that I'm not.   Do you know, Bethel, that
Lucy is likely to lose her child? "

" Veryan be sensible.   I beg you.   If this is the last conversation we're ever to have, I beg you to be sensible.   Surely
you see that if Lucy's baby dies it's by the mercy of Providence,
and can only be a good thing? "

She had forgotten her quarrel with Veryan, she had forgotten
she had so recently come to hate him.   She only saw a possible
way out of what had haunted her of late as being the climax of
the tragedy of Treveryan.   Surely he could see she was right?
But Veryan was obstinate, and Bethel's answer only seemed to
anger him more.

" I see nothing of the sort.   I see, in fact, that if our child
dies you have killed it.   You're nothing less than a murderess
if anything happens to Lucy's child, Bethel."

" You're exaggerating cruelly, V.   To begin with, Lucy's
in bed with a broken leg and concussion.   There's no question
about the child having been injured, or anything else."

" You've been out for God knows how many hours, you
don't know what you're talking about.   Doctor French himself
is very concerned about the whole affair.

" That may be.   He's her doctor, he should be concerned.
A broken leg and concussion are both enough to worry him.
I refuse to be called a murderess by my own brother, because
Lucy, in a fit of hysteria, runs away, gets hopelessly lost and
has a bad fall.   The whole thing is fantastic."

" Have you forgotten so quickly why she ran away? "

" I should imagine she was terrified at the sight of you

shaking me. You were beside yourself with rage. She probably thought you were—mad."

Whether it was the scorn which Bethel managed to heap into her voice, or the hideous supposition that her idea was the right one, Veryan, at any rate, started back and looked at his sister with real hatred.

"I don't care what happens to you, but you go. D'you understand? You leave this house to-morrow, and I don't want to see you again. Go."

For a few moments she felt at a complete loss.

"Where shall I go?"

"I don't give a damn as long as you keep clear of Treveryan. Yes, by God! No lingering near with the Penroses. Understand that. I'll not have you putting your stories round the village, mind."

Bethel remained silent. Surely this wasn't really happening to her? It couldn't be that she, Bethel Treveryan, was being turned out of the only house she knew, for a mere crazy whim of her brother's? Crazy . . . yes, that was it. Already the blood of their fathers was beginning to tell on their own generation. No sane man would turn his sister out of the house at a minute's notice because of a mere quarrel. When she looked up again he had turned his back on her, and was gazing moodily into the fire.

"Good night," she said.

"Good-bye."

Sick at heart she left the room. For a while she remained in the great hall. It was as if her feet were suddenly powerless to take her farther, and she turned, first to one side, then to the other, trying to visualize every picture, every piece of well-loved furniture, the wide, twisted staircase, the tall vases of beech leaves gleaming red in the light cast on them by the burning log fire, telling herself that after to-morrow she would see them no more. Then a sound caught her ear. Very softly Lerryn was playing Bach in the drawing-room. Bethel went and joined her sister.

"What's the matter, Beth? You look so tired. Was Veryan very—difficult?" She stopped playing and came over to the other.

"Go on playing, I don't mind," she said mechanically.

Lerryn looked astounded.

" But you hate it," she said.

" I don't. Not really. It was so connected with Oswald that it used to upset me. It was easier to pretend I loathed it than go into all sorts of weary explanations."

She sank on to the sofa, closing her eyes, and Lerryn went back to the piano.

Much later, after old Hockin had been in with their usual hot lemon water and bade them good night, Bethel opened her eyes again, stirred, and said :

" Veryan has ordered me from the house."

Her voice was weary, but there was no trace of tears or bitterness.

Lerryn caught her breath.

" What shall I do? He says I'm not to stay in the village. So that rules out the vicarage. I can't go to any of his friends. Lerryn, what on earth am I to do? I can't live by myself, suddenly, at my time of life. I can't take a house or a flat on my own. I couldn't afford it for one thing. Lerryn, supposing he stops my allowance? Good heavens, how utterly foolish I've been never to have insisted on having my own money. There's never been any reason, has there? "

She got up from the sofa, and paced the room, looking at Lerryn with worried eyes.

" Could you go to London again," Lerryn asked.

" No." Why did that hurt her, Lerryn wondered, noticing an expression of anguish in her sister's face.

" No," she repeated. " Besides, I can't afford it for more than a few weeks. Two or three months at most. I wonder if Oswald would help me."

Lerryn started. Was her sister going out of her mind? For a moment she was really afraid.

" It's all right," Bethel said, noticing Lerryn's look of amazement, " I've not gone mad. Yet."

" What did you mean? "

" Lerryn, I saw Oswald in London."

" Beth ! "

" We ran into each other quite by accident."

" Tell me," the younger girl begged, and Bethel for the first time unburdened her soul to her sister.

" But it's useless," she said, much later, " I can't worry him. What could he do? It would only make him wretched to know I was unhappy or distressed."

" Beth, I have an idea. It's the maddest one, but as we are mad, what does it matter? Beth, did you ever wonder where Ted and I met?"

Bethel shook her head.

" We made a cottage in the old wood which Grandpapa used to shoot over. It was practically derelict when Ted found it, and is hidden in a dell. I don't believe anyone knows of it now. We made it quite comfortable, we used to go there. I thought I'd never be able to face it again; but Beth, that's where you must go."

" Can I? I mean, could I?"

" Of course. It's very small, only two rooms and quite easy for one person to keep clean. Ted and I got to love it very much, Beth. There's a spring at the back where one can get water, and although I know it's lonely I believe you'd get used to it, darling. You're not nervous either so you would not mind that, would you? Somehow or other I'll try and come over every day, and I can bring food. Can you cook at all, Beth?"

" Of course I can. I've got out of the way of it, but I remember I used to love making cakes and things."

" But you can't live on cakes," Lerryn objected.

" I shall have to learn to do other things. Oh, Lerryn, it's a wonderful idea. You're a darling to think of telling me. I know how you must feel about it. But you see it means I shall still be here, still be at Treveryan. I shan't have to go . . ."

" P'rhaps he'll be himself again one day, Beth. If the baby's all right . . . you never know."

Bethel shook her head.

" Things will never be the same again. I know it. If the child dies, even if Lucy were to die, Veryan would blame me for everything. He sees no guilt in himself nor ever will."

Lerryn moved nearer to her sister and pulled a cushion to the floor and sat down.

" It seems so dreadful. So unutterably sad to think that you and he of all people should feel as you do, when one thinks of the past."

" Sometimes I think I no longer care about anything," Bethel said slowly. " All the things I love are slain or taken away from me one by one. Yet something prevents me from making an end to it all."

" Beth! You'll never do anything terrible like that? Promise? Swear you'll never try to kill yourself? "

For a long time the older woman gazed in front of her into the fire and made no reply, then she slowly turned and looked at Lerryn with a strange expression in her eyes.

" No, my darling," she said, " I'll not kill myself."

PART THREE

7

BETHEL'S SUDDEN AND strange departure was acknowledged with silence by everyone. It had long been realized amongst the servants in the house that she was barely on speaking terms with her sister-in-law, and gossip had been rife in the village that she and Veryan were no longer the friends they were. When, however, it became known that she had mysteriously vanished all talk ceased. It was almost as if the people of Treveryan imagined that, by ceasing to chatter about the ' goings-on ' at the ' big house,' they acknowledged their partisanship for Bethel.

Although they looked on Veryan as the squire it was Bethel they had always loved, and from the beginning ' young Mrs. Treveryan ' had unconsciously antagonized them, and alienated herself from the village by her refusal to be ' dragged in,' as she called it, to help local activities, and by her palpable lack of interest in anything outside the immediate house. When it was heard that she was seriously ill they shrugged their shoulders and showed no outward sympathy. They missed Bethel's kindly visits, and in their hearts blamed the young mistress for her strange, unexplained absence. One or two of the older women plucked up courage to ask Mrs. Penrose if she had news of her; but, sighing sadly, the vicar's wife was forced to admit that she had heard nothing beyond what Lerryn had told her, that owing to unforeseen circumstances she was having to leave Treveryan at a moment's notice for an indefinite period.   Those who would have hung back after church on a Sunday to enquire of Lerryn herself found themselves unwilling at the last minute to incur Veryan's probable displeasure.   A few even went so far as to say that the squire's new regularity in attendance was due to the fact that he did not wish his younger sister to be drawn into any form of discussion.   But for the most part they kept a rigid silence about the whole matter.

At Treveryan itself a new, strange atmosphere seemed to pervade the place.   For years Bethel had impregnated the house with her presence, and if it were not a particularly joyous or even happy one, it had nevertheless made itself felt as the one of most importance.   The place now seemed haunted by the very lack of her, and although her name was never mentioned the family continued to think of her in their hearts.

Gradually Lucy recovered and no more was heard of her antipathy to Veryan.   She continued to remain upstairs, and began to form a strange, unfathomable attachment to Lerryn, much to the latter's embarrassment, who felt that, by enjoying even the slightest friendship with her she was being disloyal to Bethel.   The doctor strictly forbade any visitors from outside during the winter months, which may have accounted for her newly formed affection for her sister-in-law.

Veryan struck Lerryn as becoming daily more morose, and she was sure he was not happy.

'Whatever he may like to imagine, he misses Beth,' she wrote in her diary.   'It's terrible to see anyone so changed. He looks years older, and so careworn.   I noticed there were grey hairs near his temple.'   And again: 'What have they done to each other, Veryan and Beth, to produce this dreadful Jekyll and Hyde aura about themselves?   Is it part of the whole horrible business, I sometimes wonder?   I sat in Lucy's room after lunch to-day; the three of us were drinking coffee, and I could not help watching V.   He was looking at her with such adoration in his eyes.   Alas! an expression he rarely lets one see these days.   He is so happy with her.   And she —how I hate to have to admit it—is completely altered now that Beth is no longer here.   All charm and sweet gentleness. To-night Bethel's name came up *à propos* of some local organization that she used to undertake, and I had to turn away, so hideous a look of hate was upon his face. If he were not my brother I should have to run from the room in fear. Bethel, too—so sweet to me nowadays, so pathetically grateful for all I do and am able to take to her. Yet when she speaks of V. and Lucy her expression also turns to one of such loathing that it is really frightening. Sometimes I believe she feels greater anger towards Veryan than she does for Lucy. Lucy's name makes her lose her temper, and she curses her roundly and, of course, blames her for everything; but when she speaks of Veryan it is with a cold, calculated hate. It is indeed horrible.'

Bethel was leading the life of a hermit in the cottage in the woods.

As an existence it was not helpful to one whose mind was becoming daily more and more introspective. Lerryn did her best to go to her sister most days, but it was not always easy.

The cottage was quite comfortable. By degrees Lerryn would bring things from Treveryan. She had been given the keys of the linen cupboards and storerooms, as Lucy was too unfit to manage the affairs of the house. She also offered to take Bethel's place in the village and help Mrs. Penrose; so nobody questioned her when she left the big house laden with food and comforts. For some time past Bethel had been in the habit of providing one or two ailing villagers with milk, and it was easy enough for Lerryn to smuggle the necessities of life to the cottage.

There was still the remains of a tiny garden that she and Ted had amused themselves with planting, and the few trees which he had felled in order to let in a little more light lay near enough for the girls to chop logs for the fire. At first Bethel had found this an arduous and back-breaking business, and had been astonished by the ease with which Lerryn had tackled the fallen trees.

" Ted showed me," she said. " You'd be surprised at the manual jobs I can do. We found such things exciting and rather fun. You, poor lamb, will think differently ! All the same, I wish there were someone we could trust sufficiently to look after you."

But in spite of feeling tired, unused as she was to doing for herself, Bethel refused to contemplate the idea. Once a third person was let into the secret of her hiding place and way of living the truth would out, she was sure, and that would be the end.

" I'm always terrified of the smoke giving me away," Bethel said one day.

" It's a miracle, but it never seems to rise above that cliff, and you're so far down in the dell, anyway. Besides, no one ever dreams of walking through these woods."

But in bad weather, when Lerryn found it impossible to get to her, she spent miserable hours worrying over Bethel, in anguish lest her enforced solitude should begin to prey on her nerves and unhinge her mind. Always now was the fear uppermost with Lerryn that, sooner or later, one or the other of her brother and sister would become affected by the family curse.

" I wish you'd go away for a bit," she said to Bethel one day after her sister had been at the cottage a few months.

But the other refused emphatically.

If Lerryn had been able at that time to look into her sister's mind she would have been far more terrified by what she would have seen there.

Left alone, to brood over what she considered to be a great wrong done to her, and able to dwell without interruption on the hate she now felt for Veryan, there was only one thought uppermost in her mind. She meant to kill her brother and Lucy. Fantastic as it was, the seed of the idea had been planted by Veryan himself. In his anger he had said she was a murderess; in a bout of rage he had gone so far as to use the very words, ' I could kill you for this.' Subconsciously those words had sunk into the fertile ground of Bethel's imagination, watered as it were by a sentence spoken by Lerryn, during her last night at Treveryan. Lerryn, in a moment of panic, had begged her never ' to do anything terrible,' had made her swear never to kill herself. Again that word *kill*. A sudden flash lit up and stirred anew that imagination, and from that very moment, at first subconsciously and soon deliberately, she began to plan some way of ridding the world of the evil creature she now seriously considered her brother to be. That the luckless Lucy was to be a pawn did not appear to worry her, since it was the child above all that was the cause of the crime which she intended to commit. As a family they must be stamped out. For herself, what matter if they hanged her? She knew her life was useless, she had no future, she told herself, to look forward to, then let her be the tool by which the curse should end for all time. There were times when she thought of Lerryn. She was even sorry for her, knowing there were bound to be bad times ahead for her. But she trusted her enough to be certain that, whatever happened, Lerryn would never marry.

It was Veryan who had betrayed them, therefore it was only right that he should pay the price. Even if this first child should be born dead or crippled as the result of Lucy's mis-adventure, she could never be certain that Veryan would have no other children, especially as, according to Lerryn, Lucy was no longer afraid of her husband, and appeared to look on that disastrous scene of the past as a bad dream. It was up to her then to see that no heir should ever cross again the threshold of Treveryan. She was helped in her ghastly project by disturbing and haunting dreams of Oswald Martineau which did nothing to abate the rapidly-growing hate against her brother.

By March Bethel had become such a creature of thwarted passion and insane jealousy that it was only a miracle that kept the truth from her sister. A sadly misplaced miracle, for had Lerryn been able to guess one iota of what was passing through the other's mind, the ultimate tragedy could scarcely have happened.

As it was Bethel's extreme pallor, which enhanced the heavy shadows beneath her eyes, was put down by the younger girl as the result of sleepless nights, lack of exercise, and not enough nourishment. She was worried sometimes by Bethel's seemingly distracted air; as often as not it seemed that she paid scant attention to what was being told her, and she noticed that her sister had formed the habit, hitherto so repugnant to her, of biting her nails, or, if she were not actually biting them, of tearing the skin till sometimes they were raw and bleeding—Bethel, whose hands and nails had always been her chief source of pride.

" Dearest, I know you're lonely here and you won't admit it. Let me come to you for a bit; I can easily pretend I'm going to Miss Garth."

But quickly Bethel vetoed the idea, and said she was perfectly all right.

"I know I couldn't do it," said Lerryn. "I really would go off my head. You know, Beth, when I originally suggested this idea I never for a moment thought it'd go on all these months. I hoped Veryan would relent, or something."

"Did you, Lerryn? I knew he never would. The Treveryans are pretty good lovers, and pretty good haters, too."

Bethel's greatest difficulty was discovering some manner by which she would be able to kill Veryan and Lucy. It wasn't easy. If she were only living at home the task would have presented fewer difficulties. She tried to remember historical murders of the past, and murders which had become *causes célèbres* during the past fifty years or so, but most of the ways and means seemed impracticable. Moreover, there were the two of them that must be killed. She wondered how it would be to express a wish for some chocolates to Lerryn, and then later to ask her to bring rat poison, and fill the sweets with the stuff, and somehow or other walk to a distant post office from which to send them to Lucy. The trouble would be that not only would she herself not be immune from detection—known as she was for so many miles around—but that other people, most probably Lerryn, would as likely as not be poisoned. No, she must rule out poison. She had no gun at the cottage, and although she might persuade Lerryn into bringing her one on the pretext that she had suddenly become nervous, she knew she was not adept enough to be certain of killing; moreover, how would she be able to come in close enough range to fire without being seen? So that also looked a hopeless proposition. She began to wonder if there was any way by which she could set a trap for Veryan whilst he was out riding, but she realized that Lucy would not be with him, and she had no wish to injure an animal. It looked as if a gun at close range was the only feasible way; if only she could practise somehow. But that would be dangerous, for any shots heard would be enquired into. She must get it over soon before the child was born. She would persuade Lerryn to go away, and she would do it then. Yes, that would be best. She certainly would prefer Lerryn out of the way.

And then one fine evening she would steal up to the house, and in a very short time it would all be over. If any of the servants saw her she could say she had returned to Treveryan. But what of the gun? Possibly by creeping back to the house the night before she might be able to hide it somewhere close to the house, so that, if seen, her story would not arouse suspicion. Yes, that would be the best way. Not for a long time had she shot, so that the excuse that she was after rabbits on her first evening back would be silly enough to hang her before she had accomplished her task. Besides which, from what she could remember, April and May were considered close months, in any case. Yes, she would hide the gun in the old derelict tower, nobody ever went into the bat-infested ruin, close as it was to the house. She would choose the time Veryan chose to be alone after dinner; she must remember to probe Lerryan as to Veryan's and Lucy's usual habits and movements.

One day after Lerryn had left her and she was reading the paper which Lerryn generally brought her, she became immediately engrossed in the account of a current murder trial. A woman had been found guilty of killing her husband, but she had been proved insane.

But, of course; why had it not struck her before? She herself was insane. She went to the little mirror that hung over the mantelpiece and peered at herself. She started to giggle. Mad, mad, mad at last! Now she knew what it felt like. It was no different really. Funny, that now she knew she was mad, it didn't seem to matter any more. Moreover, there were certainly advantages; she was going to kill and get away with it. She took up the newspaper again and began to read with avidity the story of the insane murderess. Yes, there was insanity in this woman's family also.

And now Bethel began to look upon herself in the light of a heroine. She told herself that what she was about to do was pre-ordained. It had been given to her to understand and ultimately to fulfil Treveryan's destiny. Mad they had become, mad they must finish. Through Tregony Treveryan had this foul disease been bred into their family, through Bethel Treveryan it should be wiped out. She became exalted with what she now firmly imagined to be her mission and purpose.

"Lerryn," she said a few days later, "do you remember that little pea-rifle I used to have?"

"No, I don't think I do. I certainly never remember your shooting."

"I suppose you were a child, I think Mama was still alive. I used to shoot rooks with it. Veryan used to get so cross because I hated killing rabbits. Anyway, I want you to see if you could find it for me."

"What on earth for?" Lerryn asked.

For a moment Bethel hesitated, then——

"I'm always hearing queer noises at night," she replied. "It may be only rats, I've certainly seen one or two——"

"Darling, surely a trap would be better? Or even some poison?"

"I'd much rather have that little rifle. I loathe traps, and there's something rather nasty about poison, too. Besides, I feel I'd be safer with a gun of sorts. Sometimes I've even thought I heard footsteps——"

"Ah, there! You *are* nervous," Lerryn exclaimed.

"No, sweet, I'm not really nervous. But I think a woman on her own should have some sort of protection. I've no dog, you see."

"But supposing anyone hears your shots?" Lerryn objected.

"I must risk that. You can bring me a trap, too, if you like. I'll try that first. I'll keep the rifle for emergency. Anyway, see if you can find it."

"What shall I say if V. notices its disappearance? I shall have to ask him which it is in any case."

"You mustn't do that," Bethel said quickly, "it would only rouse his suspicions. I mean, he'd wonder why you asked. Besides, that's unnecessary, it had my initials engraved on it."

"Well, I'll see what I can do. What shall I bring in the way of cartridges?"

"Oh, heavens!" This indeed was a difficult question to answer.

"None of Veryan's will fit it. I'd forgotten that. No, after all, you must be clever Lerryn, and somehow or other inveigle Veryan into the gun-room and start questioning him."

"It all sounds very silly and unnecessary, Beth, to me. V. never goes into the gun-room at this time of the year anyway. Do let me bring a couple of traps. And try and forget about the other noises. I expect they were rats."

" I want that rifle." Bethel spoke stubbornly.

" Couldn't you manage with another one? One of V.'s? Or what about that old pistol he had at the war which he's so proud of? I don't suppose there's any ammunition for that, but the look of it would probably scare any tramp away. And I'm sure, dear, it's only your nerves."

" His revolver, yes. That wouldn't be a bad idea." Bethel spoke slowly. " But I must have ammunition for it. You're quite wrong in saying the look of a gun frightens people, sometimes it does the reverse. They kill first."

" Beth, your nerves are in a shocking state," Lerryn said, with her voice now ringing in alarm. " Really I hate to leave you."

" I'm all right. I promise. It's only that I like to be prepared. Just in case. To have things by me, handy, so to speak. Prevention is better than cure, forewarned is fore-armed and all that sort of thing."

Lerryn sighed.

" Well, I'll do what I can," she said, " and now I must get back. The Tremaynes are dining to-night."

" Oh."

" Why d'you sound so surprised? "

" I didn't think you ever had people in the evening."

" We don't very often. When Lucy was so poorly we never entertained at all, but she's been so much better lately and likes to see a few of her friends."

" How is—Veryan? "

Lerryn was surprised that Bethel should mention her brother, for a long time now neither sister had mentioned him.

" He's all right," she said.

" Does he ever speak of me at all? Or old times? "

Lerryn shook her head.

" I'm afraid not," she said apologetically.

" When is it that Lucy expects the baby? " She spoke so casually that once again Lerryn was astonished.

" Sometime in May," she said.

Three days later Lerryn arrived with a heavily laden bag, panting under its weight.

" As well as all your food I've got you two huge rat traps and your beastly old gun," she said, and sank into an armchair.

" You angel ! " Bethel cried. " But where? I see no sign of the little rifle."

" I've brought V.'s pistol after all. I thought it'd be easier to carry. And I managed to get hold of it without bothering him, moreover. Haven't I been clever? "

Bethel went to the bag, the contents of which Lerryn was emptying, and immediately seized hold of the revolver.

" Be careful, for heaven's sake ! " the girl said, " I don't know in the least if it's loaded."

" It's terribly heavy, isn't it? " Bethel remarked.

" Yes, I shouldn't think for a moment you'd ever be able to aim properly, let alone hit anything. Look," here she handed Bethel a little case, " I think these must be its bullets or cartridges or whatever they call themselves. I found them on a shelf in the cupboard of the gun-room."

" Yes, those are the right ones. I remember V. showing them to me a long time ago."

That evening, after Lerryn had left, Bethel took out the revolver from the drawer in which she had hidden it. She walked about the room holding it at arm's length, aiming it at different objects. At first it was impossible to keep her arm from wavering, it seemed such an incredibly heavy weapon. But after two days' time, with much practising, she could hold the gun as firmly as if it had been a shoe-horn.

She stood one evening facing herself in the mirror, and pointed the revolver at her own reflection. Suddenly a wave of nausea swept over her, and for some time she was so upset that her heart almost misgave her. But, " no, no," she whispered to herself, " I must do it. I can't be weak. We don't matter any more. He must die. They both must die. It can't go on. We must not go on "; and, pulling herself together, she got up from the bed, and once more cocked the revolver into the looking-glass and pulled the trigger.

The freak storm, which wrought havoc about the whole countryside, took place the following week.

It had been hot and sultry all day, with a damp, cold wind at the same time, blowing in from the sea. By the middle of the afternoon lamps had to be lit at Treveryan, and Bethel's cottage had all its candles burning when Lerryn dropped in to see her sister at tea-time.

" Did you ever see such an extraordinary day for April? " she said.

" Do you think it's going to thunder? " said Bethel.

" I should think anything might happen, though I don't ever remember thunder so early in the year, do you? I hope it doesn't. You know how I hate it ! "

" I do. I always find it rather thrilling and exhilarating myself."

" Poor Lucy ! I hope for her sake it doesn't get bad. She's simply terrified to death of thunder. I won't stay after I've finished this cup of tea. It's getting worse—so black. The air is the colour of a London fog. I declare, it's really frightening."

" Perhaps it's the millenium," Bethel remarked lightly.

" Well, if it is, I'd rather be at home at Treveryan than in this wee cottage. Oh, darling, I do hope you'll be safe."

" Of course I shall. Now run along back home. I should hate you to be caught if it breaks."

About an hour later the most alarming wind started, and by seven o'clock the noise was so deafening that even Bethel began to wonder if the roof of her little house would be blown away. The first crash of thunder came about an hour later, and for the rest of the night it seemed as if Walpurgis terrors must be let loose. Bethel realized before many hours passed that the cottage owed its safety to the dell in which it was situated, and if the high rocks nearby exaggerated the noise, they certainly helped to keep it safe from falling trees and other terrors. During the whole of her life Bethel never remembered a worse storm, as hour by hour went by, accompanied by high scream-ing wind, flashes of forked lightning, and peal upon peal of ear-splitting thunder. It was not until after the dawn had broken that the thunder abated and the rain, hitherto kept back by the extraordinarily high wind, at last fell in torrents.

When Bethel finally arose and was able to go outside she was horrified at the sight which met her eyes. Branches lay scattered pell-mell about the ground close to the cottage, several great trees were down, and what as a rule was a tiny trickle from the rocks, now gushed forth a mighty stream, and Bethel soon found she was wading ankle deep.

It was not until nearly the close of day that she thought she heard the sound of running feet, and a few seconds later the door opened and a wet and bedraggled Lerryn stumbled into the room. She looked completely exhausted, and Bethel saw at once that something was amiss.

" What's happened? " she asked quickly.

" Oh, I can't tell you what's been happening ! " murmured the other, still out of breath. " What a ghastly time it's been ! I never thought I'd find you here alive."

"I'm quite all right, but do tell me what's been upsetting you."

" I don't know where to begin, Beth. Everything's all so extraordinary. But first of all, Lucy's had her baby——"

" What? " Bethel cried.

" I knew something would happen when that ghastly row started last night. Anyway, to cut a long story short, the baby was born at lunch time, before it should have been, of course, and it was dead."

" Thank God ! " whispered Bethel.

" As it happens, you're right. The poor little thing was hopelessly crippled, and that would have been frightful for it. It was a girl, by the way."

" How's Lucy? "

" Very ill, but not dangerously so. It was a miracle we got Doctor French. Toms drove like a madman for him as soon as nurse saw something was going to happen. Poor Lucy, I couldn't help being sorry for her. It really was terrifying up at Treveryan, chimneys falling, and as I told you she's frightened of thunder anyway."

" What has Veryan got to say about it all? " Bethel asked after a pause.

" He was stunned at first. Didn't seem to be able to take it in."

" Yet he must have expected something like this might happen."

" Lately Lucy was much better, you know. I think they both forgot to worry. I've scarcely seen him since the doctor came in and broke the news. But Beth, I've not told you the other thing."

" What ? "

" The yew has been uprooted ! "

" You mean our yew, the Treveryan yew ? "

" The one about which the superstition is. When the yew falls no more Treveryans shall be here. It's rather significant, isn't it ? I mean that it should be blown down after centuries the night Veryan's child is born *dead*."

" Very significant, indeed," Bethel replied, a strange look in her eyes.

" Of course there's probably nothing in it. On the other hand there would probably have been this storm and the tree would have fallen had Veryan married or not. If he hadn't, then he would have been the last Treveryan. D'you see what I mean ? " Lerryn ended breathlessly.

" Yes, I see. A little involved, but I understand ! Superstitions are always right, Lerryn," she said quietly.

" How frightening ! But let us forget the horrid things that have been happening, and give me a cup of tea for pity's sake."

" Weren't you in the least frightened by last night ? " Lerryn asked a little later.

" Not really, though I grant it was rather alarming."

" How funny you are, Beth ! In such a state over rats and unknown noises, and fearless when you might have been killed by a falling tree at any moment. I was horrified by the damage that has been done."

" You say Lucy isn't dangerously ill ? " Beth asked presently.

" They don't think so. Of course, she's pretty bad."

" I see." Bethel appeared wrapped in thought, and soon Lerryn took her leave.

" V. might think it unkind of me to have gone out. I think perhaps I'd better go back."

"All right." Bethel kissed her sister. " Tell me," she said, " have you no bitter feelings against him ? Do you never feel that by his marriage he has betrayed you and Ted Truscott ? "

" No, I don't think I do," Lerryn said after a few moments' thought. " If V. wishes to bring diseased children into the world, that's his affair. For myself, now that I know the truth, I'd sooner die. I don't believe I was ever cut out to be anybody's wife, Beth. That's where you and I are different, perhaps. God knows, I loved Ted—as I might have loved some other man if I'd met one before I met him. But I never have wanted children . . . Am I unnatural? I suppose V. wants a son to come after him at Treveryan, and is willing to take the risk. I wouldn't; I couldn't. It's a wife's duty to give her husband children, and I would never have shirked the responsibility, but for these very reasons I believe I'm less bitter about Ted than you have always been about Oswald. And yours has been a different case in many ways—Veryan knew Oswald and made you give him up. If I wished to be bitter, I think I have greater cause against you, for it was you who made me give up Ted, not Veryan. But don't look worried, for I'm not. Nothing would induce me to marry now. Apart from the children one might or might not have, I always remember what you told me of Papa. We might go insane ourselves. We might kill the person we loved, or try to. Poor Papa, how could he have tried to strangle Mama?" She shivered. "I'm going now. Good night, darling."

For many hours that night Bethel thought of Veryan and Lucy. It seemed that fate had stepped in ahead of her; snatched at the angry elements for a tool and relieved her of her task. Was she to take it as a sign that her plans were not to materialize after all? Surely she could not want to kill Veryan? Or was there, deep rooted in her heart, the unconscious desire of revenge? Was her soul all the time crying for vengeance for the wreck of her own romance, for which she still blamed her brother, since she considered his happiness a betrayal of her own?

It was a week later when, one evening about an hour after Lerryn had left her, Bethel heard footsteps again outside the cottage.

"Have you left something behind?" she called. A shadow darkened the window, and when she turned she saw Veryan framed in the doorway.

"You . . ."

For a moment her heart seemed to stop beating.

"So this is where you've been hiding all these months, and this is where Lerryn creeps off to like a thief in the night."

"What do you mean?"

"I've often wondered why she seemed so secretive, where she used to wander off to so mysteriously. At one time I did suspect it was connected with you, but as so many months passed and there was never a sign or mention of you in the neighbourhood, I thought I must have been wrong. I remembered what you told me about her and some man or other. I began to think she had some lover. So to-day, when I saw her disappear, I thought I'd follow her. The little sneak!"

"How dare you blame Lerryn for being loyal to me? Why on earth should she be brought into a quarrel which concerns no one but you and me?"

"She knew perfectly well that I'd ordered you to leave Treveryan. I suppose she brought you food and looked after you? Whose is this place, anyway?"

"Lerryn says Grandpapa used it in the old days."

"I see. Well, you can clear out of it."

"Oh, no, Veryan. You'd never have found it or me if you hadn't meanly followed Lerryn like a spy. I've lived here nearly six months without your being aware of it, I'm damned if I'll leave it now."

"I'll not have you at Treveryan, and you know it."

"I've not been to Treveryan since the night I left it."

"Did Lerryn tell you Lucy's baby died?"

"Yes. It was a girl, I hear."

"How does it feel to be a murderess?"

"I don't know yet," she said slowly.

"You killed that child as surely as there's a God above," Veryan cried.

"Don't be such a fool! You'll blame me for the storm next. Your child was born a month too soon because Lucy was frightened of the thunder. Anyone can tell you that an eight months' baby seldom lives. I hear the poor thing was crippled, too. Good God! Veryan, even you could not wish a crippled daughter about the place!"

"That certainly was the result of Lucy's appalling night in the woods and her accident. And if that wasn't your fault, I'd like to know whose it was."

Bethel did not reply, but continued to stare at her brother.

"Take that self-satisfied look off your face. My God! I hate you, Bethel! D'you think I don't know what you're thinking, standing there gloating, pleasure written all over you? D'you suppose I don't realize Fate's given you a feather to wear in your cap about this? But you needn't think it's the end. By Christ, no! Lucy will have other children, and nothing you can say or do now can prevent it. You've shot your bolt as far as threatening her is concerned; she's game to try again. It's been a bitter blow for her losing this one. I daresay you hoped she mightn't be able to have other children. For once you've lost, Beth. I asked French myself; he told me there's no reason on earth why Lucy shouldn't have a splendid family in time."

"No reason on earth, eh? I think you—or I—could furnish him with reason enough, even if Lucy has forgotten her fears. I think you—or I—could tell him that there's every reason why you, Veryan Treveryan, should not be allowed to breed. Did you by any chance speak to Doctor French of our—misfortune?"

"You're revolting!" He turned away from her in disgust. "You talk as if we were farmyard animals."

"And more's the pity we're not. Some use could be made of us, perhaps. At least they could kill us for meat."

Veryan turned again and looked at Bethel with horror.

"My God!" he stammered, "I believe you have gone crazy. Only a mad woman would have such filthy ideas."

"Yes, V., I think I am. I've thought so for quite a long time now. It won't worry you for long, that I promise you . . ."

"By heaven, it won't. I'll have you put away."

"And will you tell the doctors why I'm insane? Will you tell them it's hereditary? Veryan, if you'll be certain to tell them the truth, I'll go quietly. Because then I shall know that no doctor on earth will allow Lucy to have any child of yours. Will you tell French, V.? Will you, will you?"

"I'm damned if I will!" he replied roughly, "you'll see a specialist, not a country fellow like French."

"How frightened you are of me, Veryan! How frightened you are that I shall outwit you somehow or other. You selfish beast. Only thinking of your own ego, utterly careless of any responsibility you owe to mankind."

"Ego! That's a good one coming from you! For years you've thrived on your own self-pity . . ."

"Have you forgotten the years I gave to you and Treveryan?"

"What else was there for you to live for?"

"Out of your own mouth you convict yourself, V." She faced him triumphantly. "What else had I to live for. Yet you—*you married*."

Veryan started to bluster.

"Just because you never married and had children of your own you've nursed this bitter, criminally bitter, grievance against me. I wish to God you'd find Martineau again and marry him. Believe me, I'd wish him well of you this time."

"I have seen him. I saw him in London. He's married."

"O-ho! Things indeed become clearer. They show you at last for what you are, my dear. Just a thoroughly warped, disappointed woman. So out of revenge for what you cannot have, you'd do me out of my rights. All this talk of responsibility! Responsibility, my foot!"

"You have no rights, Veryan. We none of us have. I know that you have either forgotten or are determined to live as you please, in spite of the fact that you said a few minutes ago that I myself am insane. Very well then, I must prevent you."

"How are you going to do that, pray?"

Bethel went across the room and opened the drawer in which she kept Veryan's revolver.

"I'm going to kill you," she said quietly.

For a moment Veryan stood stock still. Then he noticed the gun in her hand.

"Don't be silly, Bethel." He tried to speak gently, but he could not keep his voice from quavering. "It's stupid to play with firearms, you never know if they're loaded."

"Did you know the yew had fallen?" She suddenly asked.

His face went ashen pale.

"Stop this play-acting and don't be an idiot!" he said, and started to come across the room.

Bethel fired.

It all seemed a very long time. Why didn't Veryan get up? He lay so still.

She remained standing with the revolver hot and smoking in her hand until, for no apparent reason, it dropped from her fingers. That seemed to wake her.

. " V. ! " she called.

She went over to where he lay and knelt down. He had fallen on his face and carefully she turned his body over. She had shot him through the heart; she saw the sodden blood which was fast saturating his jacket. He was quite dead.

" I've killed you," she whispered.

Mechanically she pushed back the black lock which had fallen, as often in the past, across his forehead.

" Veryan," she whispered, " Veryan ! "

PART THREE

8

" THERE'S A GENTLEMAN to see you, Miss Lerryn," Prudence said, still speaking in the hushed whispers that all the servants had used for the past few days.

"I told Hockin I'd see no one," Lerryn answered.

" Hockin's resting, Miss. It was Paul who answered the bell."

. " Then tell him to tell whoever it is that I can't be seen. Will nobody respect one's wish to be left alone ? "

" The gentleman said you were to be given this, if you didn't wish to come downstairs." Prudence held a note in her hand.

" Give it to me then," the girl said wearily. She opened it and started violently.

" It's from Sir Oswald Martineau. Didn't you recognize him, Prue ? "

" I never saw who it was, Miss. Paul gave me the message with the note. He didn't know the gentleman either, though he did say it didn't look like an ordinary reporter. Would that be the gentleman Miss Bethel got engaged to ? Just fancy him turning up at this moment. What a thing ! Did you say he's a ' Sir ' now, and all ? "

" He's very important, I believe. Show him into the library at once and tell him I'll be down.

Her prayers had been answered then!

As by a miracle God had sent the only man alive who might be able to help Bethel. How did he know? What could be the reason of his coming? She ran downstairs and found Oswald Martineau in the room waiting for her.

"Lerryn! My dear! I came as soon as I heard."

"Oh, Oswald!" Lerryn tried to keep the emotion she felt from her voice. How was she going to talk to this stranger? It was Oswald right enough, but how changed. Of course she had been a mere child when he had been engaged to Beth, but for some reason or other she had expected to see him as he had been then.

"How did you hear? What exactly do you know?" she asked.

"Only what everyone has seen in the papers——"

"Papers! Of course! I've not read them. Oh, Oswald, how ghastly. Are there huge headlines and pictures of Bethel? Oh, I can't bear it." She broke down and began to cry bitterly.

"Lerryn, there's no time to lose. You must tell me everything. First of all, who's taking care of her?"

"Of course you don't know! They've taken her away, Oswald. Taken Beth! To Bodmin."

"I guessed that. That's not what I meant. Who's seeing to everything for her? Has anything been arranged? Because I must defend her. There's only one man on earth who knows your family's history sufficiently to get her off, and that's myself."

"Oswald? You will?" She tried to find words of gratitude, but her mind was still numb with shock and misery and none came.

"The papers say that at the inquest she pleaded guilty to killing Veryan. There was little else except, of course, long descriptions of Treveryan and your family, and accounts of Veryan's war record and travels. Nothing as to motive, of course. What happened?"

"She came up to the house, this house I mean, and told me she'd done it. That she'd shot him. She said she had done it intentionally, and that someone must go for the police." Tears started to run down Lerryn's face.

" Go on."

" Am I helping her if I talk to you professionally? Oh, God . . ." She broke down, and Martineau came over to her and patted her gently on the shoulder.

" You and I must keep nothing from each other. I love her, I know I'm the only person you can talk to. You can help me a very great deal."

" Will they let you see her? " she sobbed.

" Of course ! I shall see your solicitors immediately I leave you. But I want to hear a little more from you. So be brave, my dear, and tell me what you can."

" Lucy—that Veryan's wife—had a baby. It was born dead. It was born prematurely. But you see Veryan turned Beth out of the house in the autumn because they had a terrible quarrel, and she's been living in a cottage in our woods ever since."

" Alone? "

" Entirely alone. I knew something like this would happen."

" What do you mean? "

" I knew that living alone as she was doing would make her do something. I just felt it. I was terrified she'd kill herself."

" You never heard her threaten Veryan or his wife? "

" No, but she was violently opposed to Lucy. And she was mad with anger at their having a child. That was why V. turned her out eventually."

" Why was she so angry, did she say? "

" Because of the—madness in our family."

" Yes, I see."

He walked to the window.

" Yet she shot Veryan after the child had died, you say? "
Lerryn nodded.

" Yes, I don't know anything more. She told me nothing."

" How on earth had she managed to get any firearms? "

" I took her V.'s revolver." Here Lerryn burst into tears again.

" You did? "

" She asked for something to kill rats with. And she said

there were noises outside the cottage. It never struck me
that she could——" but again her tears were too much for
her.

"I'm going to get in touch at once with your solicitors.
You're not to worry yourself ill, Lerryn. I shall need your
help. I shall need all the help you can give me. I suppose it was
well known that Beth and Veryan were on bad terms latterly?"

"I expect so. But Lucy isn't popular in the village, and
they all adored Beth. Oh, Oswald, you won't let them hang
her?" She ran to where he stood and flung herself in his
arms.

"Bethel shall never be hanged," he said quietly, "but——"
and he hesitated.

"Yes?"

"You may as well know what the alternative will be. Be
brave."

"Go on," she whispered.

"Bethel's life will be spared her on the grounds of insanity."

"You mean Bethel's mad? Really mad? At last?" She
looked at him fearfully.

"That's what we shall have to prove."

"What'll they do to her?" she whispered.

"Lerryn——"

"You mean . . . you mean . . . she'll have to go to an
asylum?"

He nodded. He looked worn, and Lerryn realized the
misery in his eyes.

"She's not mad, Oswald. She's no more mad than I am,
or Veryan himself. You can't send her to a lunatic asylum for
the rest of her life! It's a ghastly thought."

"Bethel has killed a man. She's admitted it. If she pleads
guilty to murder——"

"Murder. Veryan murdered. Oh, Oswald! This is worse
than anything any of us could have ever imagined."

"Tell me the name of her solicitors so that I can get in
touch with them right away."

"Pennelly, Trelithick and Pennelly. At Truro."

"Thank you." He wrote the names down.

"I thought Beth told me you were a judge now. How will
you be able to defend her," she asked presently.

" By God's mercy I have had to chuck India because of my health. At the moment I'm supposed to be a sick man."

" Will you be allowed to defend her? "

" There's nothing to stop me. And now, my poor dear, I'm not going to keep you any longer, for I want to get to Truro at once. I shall be at the hotel there to-morrow and probably to-morrow night, unless I can push on to Bodmin. Remember what I said, you're not to worry, for Bethel's life may depend very much on you."

" Shall I have to go into the witness box? " she said, horror in her voice.

" I'm not going to tell you any more, my dear. Rest assured I shall look after you."

Lerryn sank on to her knees when Martineau left the room.

" Oh God," she prayed, " spare her life ! "

Glancing upwards, she saw the cold, soulless eyes of Tregony Treveryan staring through her.

PART
FOUR

I

AS ON THE previous day, the court room was packed to suffocation. Not for many years had a case like *Rex* v. *Treveryan*, as it was listed, caused such frantic commotion in the county. Indeed, the whole country was absorbed in the trial of Bethel Treveryan, charged with the murder of her brother; and cities as distant as Liverpool, London and Glasgow, rang with the cries of newspaper boys as they ran through the streets, hawking their latest editions, yelling ' all about the Cornish murder,' ' latest news of the Treveryan case.'

The news of Veryan's death and the manner of it had frankly stunned the people of Cornwall. For days no one talked of anything else, and a good many people unwittingly and unconsciously remarked, ' she must have been mad.' But Lucy Treveryan had made enough friends during the time she had been in England for a certain amount of gossip to have filtered through as to the bad relationship which existed between herself and her sister-in-law, and there were plenty of people who, although not wishing to harm Bethel, spread the rumour about the country that brother and sister had not of late been on the loving terms which they had been in the past. Veryan's death, coming as it did, on top of the birth of Lucy's stillborn child, also greatly added to the wave of sympathy which was fast spreading in her favour; and to the more general public Bethel appeared nothing less than a cold-blooded, heartless murderess, fit victim for the gallows.

More than one family was soon engaged in heated arguments that led in some cases to open quarrels.

" I tell you she did it a' purpose," one girl was overheard to say in Port Holland, " everyone knows she and Mr. Veryan quarrelled and that he turned 'er out of the house."

" Don't you go spreadin' such lies about Miss Bethel," her mother answered, fetching her daugher a hearty box on the ears. " If she killed him it was a mistake, and when she owned to it she only meant as how she admitted her gun went off. A' purpose indeed! Thet'll learn you to talk of ladies and gentlemen like you're gettin' to do."

The gossip and talk died down somewhat for a few weeks, except in the immediate neighbourhood, everyone waiting until the trial should take place, which was listed for the next Assizes. Interest grew when it was announced that Bethel's Counsel was to be Sir Oswald Martineau, who had lately retired from the Indian Bench on the grounds of ill-health. Martineau was not very well known in England owing to his absence from the country for so long, but the Press soon had his life's work printed fair and square for the public to study, and before long most people were aware that he had taken silk at an early age, had done exceptionally well in India, and had deserted the bar for the bench, becoming a Judge of the Indian High Courts when still in his ' forties.'

Gossip and innuendo soon scented an old romance in the fact that he was defending Bethel Treveryan, and, although their late engagement was not alluded to by the papers, there were plenty who said, ' I believe I remember hearing——'? and by word of mouth the public were soon *au fait* with the story of ' an old friendship.'

Goddard-Kendall was appearing for the Crown, and the first two days of the case had been taken up by the prosecution. He was a hard, thin, unlikeable man, without much imagination, and was known to be a woman hater. The case, as he put it, looked bad for Bethel. He drew her as an utterly selfish and spoilt woman whose every whim and fancy had been pandered to by the dead man; a warped and unnatural woman—a statement which had drawn a sharp protest from Martineau—whose jealousy had been roused to fiendish and criminal pitch when she found her place in the old home being taken by a young wife, ' of an age tender enough to be her own daughter.'

Lucy, in deep widow's mourning, had gone into the box, and in hushed, broken voice, had spoken of the ghastly quarrels of brother and sister, and had told of the way Bethel had been sent from Treveryan. In heartbroken tones she spoke of the loss of her baby and her own ill-health, and the next day there were large photos of her leaving the court at Bodmin, with captions such as " Delicate Bride-Mother Breaks Down in Witness Box." She was the last and most important of Goddard-Kendall's witnesses.

Martineau then rose to cross examine.

" You have told the court that the accused was on very bad terms with your late husband and yourself. Is it not a fact that the quarrels of which you spoke grew in intensity after you had told the accused you were expecting a child? "

" Yes," Lucy replied.

" Is it true that the accused said to you, ' You must get rid of the child,' or words very similar? "

" Yes. She was continually saying so."

" Is it not a fact that the accused told you that you must have no children by her brother because of the insanity which has run in the family for generations? "

" Yes," whispered Lucy.

A ripple of surprised horror and amazement ran round the court. Before the court adjourned, Martineau put to Lucy a number of letters from Veryan to Bethel and suggested that these letters were inconsistent with the evidence she had given in the box. Lucy, however, whilst admitting her husband's handwriting, refused to modify her statements.

Feverish excitement was now rampant amongst the crowd; friends of the Treveryans looked at each other in aghast bewilderment and shocked surprise, whilst those who only knew of the family from hearsay nudged each other and licked their lips in expectation.

' What are we going to hear? ' was in everybody's mind and heart.

The next day everyone's eyes were riveted on Bethel, who sat in the dock in the same dazed manner as she had done the previous day. Was she mad, too? everyone was asking himself. Was that going to be Martineau's plea?

She looked older than she had done in London, Oswald realized. The misery and horror of the past few months had told on her. He had decided against putting her in the box, for although the new law allowed the prisoner to give evidence he knew only too well that Bethel's own sane answers might prove her undoing in the plea of insanity which he was bringing. As he watched her his heart contracted, and he realized the almost impossible task he had set himself, the task of seeing and thinking of her in an impersonal way, as Bethel Treveryan, his client, impeached for murder. Bethel, his beloved. The case for the defence was opened. After dealing with the preliminaries, and proving the authenticity of certain documents, Oswald Martineau called his principal witness—Lerryn.

There was a stir in court as she took her place in the witness box. She, too, looked older, as though she had bade farewell to youth and its pleasures for ever. Her face was grave and very pale, and as she looked at her sister it was obvious to all that great emotion was near to overcoming her. One or two women sniffed loudly and blew into their handkerchiefs, and suddenly Martineau felt the tempo of the court change, and he prayed as he had rarely done before that the sympathy which had yesterday been Lucy's would shift to Lerryn and subsequently to the unfortunate Bethel herself.

Lerryn took the oath in a low but clear voice. She kept her eyes fixed on Martineau as if she dreaded looking elsewhere.

" Miss Treveryan, you are the youngest of the three children of Simon and Anna Treveryan, is that not so? "

" Yes."

" Your father died when you were a young child and your mother when you were still in the schoolroom. Will you tell the court what you remember of your father's death ? "

" I remember he was taken ill one afternoon and we were sent away two days later to our grandmother without being told what was the matter with him. He died later and we returned, but were never told of what he died."

" Can you remember the occasion of your brother's coming-of-age ? "

" Yes."

" Will you tell the court about the various festivities that occurred and what happened subsequently ? "

" My brother had his twenty-first birthday some months after my mother died. There was a dinner party. At it my sister's engagement was announced."

Loud whispers and murmurings filled the air, and after a stern rebuke from the bench, Lerryn continued:

"A few days afterwards something happened about which I was not told the truth for many years. But, in fact, my sister's engagement was broken off because my brother was told by our doctor that there was insanity in our family and none of us should marry."

"Will you tell the court how much you know of this insanity?"

" My father died quite insane."

Here there was more commotion, and once again Mr. Justice Croften was forced to speak sharply to the public.

" He tried to strangle my mother before he was taken very ill. There were other cases of hopeless insanity in his family, and our doctor, now dead, told Veryan that the madness was hereditary."

" Miss Treveryan, could you bear to tell, in your own words, all you know of the influence this ghastly heritage had on your sister and your brother? Also how you came to hear of it ? "

Oswald loathed having to order Lerryn to bare her own pitiful soul to the world, but both he and Lerryn had realized that it might have great repercussions.

" I was much younger than Veryan and my sister, Bethel.

When I grew up I had become used to the extremely quiet life
we led. It never struck me to wonder why I had no friends
of my own age, nor ever met new people. I had one girl
friend, that was all. I never met or knew any men. But
gradually I became dissatisfied and restless. I grumbled
frequently to my brother and told him I blamed my sister.
I thought her own broken engagement had embittered her,
and that she was jealous of me. I was terribly wrong."
Lerryn faltered. She felt stripped in front of the eyes of all
Cornwall and wondered if she really could go on. Suddenly
she glanced up and saw Bethel looking at her. She knew
then that she must.

"My brother said I was never on any account to talk to
my sister about her past unhappiness, nor was I to grumble.
He went to Africa, to the war; Bethel and I remained alone
at Treveryan. She did everything for the place, and Veryan
relied on her implicitly. It often irritated me that she seemed
so completely wrapped up in my brother and our home.
When my brother returned from the war we were all very
happy, but he became restless and, after a time, went abroad."

There was a pause.

"While he was away, I . . . . I fell in love with somebody."

Now you could have heard a pin drop in court. All necks
and heads craned forward. This was better than any play,
most of the onlookers were thinking, quite forgetful by now
of the woman in the dock. Lerryn was in the pillory now,
as it were, and they leaned forward greedily, excitedly, in order
not to lose a word. What dark horses these Treveryan girls
were, to be sure !

"I kept my—romance—secret from my sister. I felt she
would not approve. After about a year she discovered about
it, and then I said I wanted to marry the man I loved. She said I
could not. Then she told me everything. About the insanity,
and how none of us must ever marry. And about the pact."

"The pact? What was that?" Oswald was feeling
happier. He could see Lerryn had made an excellent impression,
and she was a far better witness than he had ever dared hope for.

"After my sister's engagement had been broken off she and
Veryan had made a pact that they would devote their entire
lives to each other and to me and to Treveryan."

" Would you say they were friends in those days? "

" They adored each other. I cannot believe that any brother and sister could have cared more than they did."

" Why had you never been told of the pact? "

" Because my sister hoped to spare me from hearing the truth. She thought that by never letting me know people I should never fall in love with anyone."

" Was your sister happy? "

"As happy, I imagine, as it was possible for her to be without—the man she had loved so dearly."

Oswald was aware that with one movement the entire crowd of people turned and now gazed at Bethel, who, pale and distrait again, seemed oblivious of their interest.

" Please go on," the judge leant forward and spoke gently.

" Her whole life was centred in our home—Treveryan—and in my brother."

" Was the accused given to what are generally described as ' good works,' I believe? "

" Yes. She did a very great deal in and for the village and helped our vicar's wife considerably."

" When did your brother return, and how? Would you tell the court? "

" We heard he was coming back just after the Coronation. He told us little of his plans, but sent a wire from the boat and also a short letter."

" What was the manner of his homecoming? "

"He arrived with Lucy. I mean with his wife, Mrs. Treveryan."

" You knew of his marriage? "

" No. The first thing we knew about it was when we met her downstairs. It was a terrible shock."

" Why? "

" Because of the promise we had all made not to marry. My sister had a very great horror of any more Treveryans being born with such a taint as ours in their blood. For myself, I was afraid of becoming mad, perhaps, myself. My father was a homicidal maniac, you see."

A woman at the back of the court screamed and was hurried out.

"What were your own feelings to your brother's wife?"

"We have always been perfectly friendly."

"Would you say that your sister had any reason to be more than usually upset by the marriage? Apart, that is, from the pact she and her brother had made?"

"I think so. You see my brother's attitude to Bethel altered a great deal. He became off-hand and irritable, and although I tried to explain that it was natural, she did resent it. Then gradually the things that my sister looked upon as her province were taken away from her and given over to Lucy, my sister-in-law, I mean. Finally, she had very little to do at Treveryan."

"And she had made Treveryan her life work and was tremendously proud of it?"

"Indeed, yes. She worshipped the place and was very proud of being a Treveryan."

"Was there any reason why your sister should have to stay at Treveryan when the terms she was on with your brother became worse?"

"She loved the place, and would have hated to live anywhere else. But, apart from that, she and I have always been entirely dependent on an allowance my brother made us, which certainly would not have kept us."

"Miss Treveryan, why did your sister eventually leave your house?"

"My brother turned her out after a terrible quarrel they had."

Again the sea of faces leant forward.

"Explain, if you can, what you know of the quarrel."

"Lucy told her she was expecting a baby. It was then she told my sister-in-law about the insanity. They had rather a dreadful scene."

"How do you know?"

"I found my sister-in-law in a fainting condition and she begged me to tell her the truth after she had come to. I had to tell her Bethel was right. When Veryan came home—he had been away—he found Lucy very hysterical indeed, and he had a frightful quarrel with Bethel and told her to tell his wife that what she had told her were lies, or at least greatly exaggerated versions of the truth.   She couldn't, of course, and, in the next row they had, Lucy was so frightened that she ran away.

" What happened? "

" Everyone hunted for her throughout the night and she was found in a ditch the next morning very ill, with a broken leg and concussion.   She was ill for a long time, and my brother blamed Bethel for the accident and the running away, and never forgave her.   And he turned her out of the house the very next day."

" Did he tell her where she might go, or make any provision for her? "

" No, he made no provision at all, and said he did not mind where she went as long as she left Treveryan and he never saw her again."

" Where, in point of fact, did your sister go? "

" There was a small cottage in some woods, about two miles from our house.   No one knew about it except myself.   It had been our grandfather's picnic house when he had shot over those particular woods.   It had furniture.   Bethel, at my suggestion, went to live there."

" Who looked after her? "

" No one but herself.   I went and visited her most days and took her anything she needed."

" Were you not worried about your sister?   The conditions in which she lived, her solitary confinement, for that is what it amounted to surely? "

" Yes, I was terribly worried.   The cottage was dark and rather damp.   It was in the middle of a wood which has been deserted for years."

" How long was your sister there?   That is to say, how long had she been living there before the tragedy took place? "

" About five months."

" Had she ever spent a day alone in her life before? "

" Never."

" What did you think your sister's mental condition was like during these months? "

" I began to get worried.   She grew so queer and quiet and, I thought, nervy."

" Was she nervous? "

" She said she wasn't, but I thought she was when she started complaining of rats and noises."

" Did she ask you to help her? "

" Yes, she wanted me to bring her something to destroy the rats. I took her some traps, also my brother's revolver."

" Had you any reason at all, Miss Treveryan, to imagine your sister had any intention against your brother's life? "

" No, no," she cried.

" What was the next thing that happened? "

" My sister-in-law's baby was born dead."

" What did the accused say when you told her of this? "

" She only seemed surprised."

" Had she spoken much of your brother and his wife during the preceding months? "

" Very little."

" And what was your brother's reaction to the death of his child? "

" At first he would not believe it. Then once more he became up in arms about Bethel, and cursed and swore and said she was a murderess."

" Did he seem to you more than usually vehement in his anger? "

" I think I should say, if I were not who I am, that he was insanely furious. But I realize that from one of my family such an utterance takes on a different meaning."

Here several people applauded, and Martineau knew that Lerryn was the heroine of the whole case.

" Did he know of your sister's whereabouts? "

" No, not then."

" What exactly do you mean by those words, Miss Treveryan? " the judge leant down and asked.

" I mean, my lord, that then my brother did not know of the cottage. I'm certain he didn't by the way he raged and stormed. Afterwards he discovered it, for it was in the cottage that my sister shot him."

" What do you know of the tragedy itself, Miss Treveryan," Oswald asked.

" Very little. I had been down to the cottage as usual and had come home again. Quite a bit later I saw, to my utter amazement, Bethel coming to the house. I ran outside and said, ' what on earth are you doing? ' and she said she'd shot him. I didn't know who she meant, and she said ' V.'—that was my brother—' V. followed you, Lerryn. I've shot him. He's dead.' She wouldn't say any more and I could see she was spent and not herself. Yet later she said we must tell the police. I didn't know what to do, and I asked her why she didn't run away if she'd killed Veryan as nobody knew where she was, but she said nothing mattered any more and that the police must know."

" There's only one more question I want to ask you, Miss Treveryan. Did you ever in your life hear your brother threaten your sister? "

" In a way—yes."

" What do you mean exactly by that? "

" I never heard him say, ' I'll kill you,' but I have heard him in one of his bursts of rage say, ' My God, I could kill her.' "

" Thank you, Miss Treveryan."

Martineau sat down.

Frankly he was astonished by the ease with which Lerryn had come through her ordeal. She had been well coached by him, it was true, but one could never be sure how people would ultimately react when finally in the witness box, and he had fully expected the girl, wretched and highly strung as he considered her to be, to let him down by nervousness and hesitation when faced with the sea of faces and legal procedure of the court. Of course she had yet to go through Goddard-Kendall's questioning, but by now she seemed really used to the atmosphere; he was reminded of a young actress for the first time entrusted with a big part, and coming through the nervous ordeal of the *première* with flying colours.

Goddard-Kendall did his best to confuse the young witness, but Lerryn replied coolly and with perfect composure always.

A babel of voices filled the air outside the court and in the streets after the adjournment had been announced for lunch.

Lerryn's name was on all lips, and it almost seemed as if she was a greater source of interest and surprise than Bethel herself. Whatever the opinions on Veryan, Lucy, and Bethel, Lerryn certainly came in for the lion's share of sympathy. But the whole case absorbed everybody, and in Bodmin that day it is unlikely that there was any other topic of conversation.

" She doesn't look like a murderess."

" It's going to be difficult, proving her innocent."

" Personally, I think the whole insanity story very fishy indeed."

" Of course jealousy was at the root of the whole thing, if you ask me. Don't tell me that woman's mad, even if her father was ! "

There was a rush and scrimmage back to the court, and excitement became tense when it was realized that Sir Oswald was making his speech for the defence right away.

All eyes were turned to the distinguished elderly man, as he rose to his feet. Only Bethel sat with her face averted, gazing, it seemed, into space.

He drew a remarkable portrait of the young family growing up, of the deceased and his elder sister enjoying a friendship greater than that which existed in most families, thrown together as they had been by being taught together under the same tutor, playing together as children, seeing little of their parents—the father especially leading a hermit's existence. He spoke of the queer manner of the late Simon Treveryan's death, and the way in which it had been hushed up in the county. He then spoke of the years which Veryan enjoyed at the university, when he and Bethel had written almost daily to each other. Here again were produced letters written by the dead man to his sister. He picked several out at random and read them. All were couched in terms of deep affection. Then Oswald passed to the days of the Golden Jubilee, telling the court of the accused's secret engagement, and of the adamantine refusal by the late Mrs. Treveryan to allow any such marriage.

" You may ask," he said, " why this woman refused to consider the idea of any engagement. The fact was that only she knew the disastrous truth about the death of her children's

father.   Her soul revolted at the idea of telling them the truth.
The accused was hurried back to her home in the country, but
immediately on their return her mother was stricken by typhoid
fever and never recovered. Her children, therefore, never learnt
from her the truth of the insanity which ran in the family."

He went on to speak of the friendship enjoyed by Veryan,
his sister, and the man who loved her, " who will be alluded
to as Mr. X, if necessary," said Martineau.

There were a few people who looked at each other knowingly at this announcement.   Letters were here again read,
letters from the brother siding with his sister on the matter of
an engagement.   ' There was never the slightest reason for
Mama's attitude towards your and X's love for each other.
When I come of age at Christmas we will have a joint party,
darling, to celebrate my birthday and your engagement.'

" Do any of the letters that I have read, read as anything but
letters of deep affection? " asked Martineau.

He then went on to speak of the party itself, of Bethel's engagement, of her illness following the breaking-off of the engagement after the truth was made known about the family insanity.

" Perhaps there are amongst you people who disbelieve the
story of the accused's betrothal, since, to my knowledge, it was
never made public.   I have here a letter written to Veryan
Treveryan, dated 31st January, 1888.   It is signed by Jeremiah
Pearce.   He was the doctor to the family for many years.
This is what it says : ' My dear Veryan, I think we may
consider that your sister is now out of danger.   It has been a
touch and go business, and we must thank Almighty God for
what I hope will be a complete recovery.   As an old friend
the whole business has been very painful to me, yet I firmly
believe I was right when I sent for you, before the announcement was made public of your sister's engagement, to tell you
that there is a very grave streak of insanity in your family, and
that I felt it my duty to warn you that I consider marriage
undertaken by any children of Simon Treveryan to be not
only a disastrous step for a future generation, but a criminal
one.   My dear boy, I think that interview with you was the
most obnoxious I have ever had to take part in.   The tragic
illness of your sister, following the news you had to impart,
might well have proved fatal, but thank God her physical

strength is gaining ground and I have every belief that, with you beside her, she will in time get over the shock—not only of the brutal news I had to give you, but the shattered romance of her own life. I have great hopes of the visit to Torquay, and know you will keep me informed. Yours affectionately, Jeremiah Pearce.' "

Martineau stopped and looked round the court-room. There was not a sound.

" That letter from the old doctor is a better witness for my client than any person living, I think. It shows without any doubt whatsoever his own feelings in the matter regarding the appalling heritage which these young people had only recently discovered to be theirs. It is the letter of a reliable doctor once known to many of you here, I know. It is the letter of an old friend also, an old friend anxious for the future and welfare of young people he had known from early childhood. Do you imagine for one moment that a man in his position would have *dared* to voice an opinion as to any marriage the Treveryans might wish to make, writing with such authority as he did on the subject of hereditary insanity, if he had not been absolutely certain that what he counselled was right? Not only right, but the proper thing to do? "

Then Sir Oswald spoke of the years that followed. He touched on statements made by witnesses called by the prosecution, of how for years no one had ever been near Treveryan, nor been asked; of the surprise Veryan Treveryan's marriage had caused. He pictured the long, empty years, ' empty for most people,' he said, in which this strange family lived entirely dependent upon each other's company, a family still young in years, a young man and a young woman who could never forget that possibly the day would dawn when the dread disease would strike. It was a wonder, he said, that melancholia had not sent them insane long ago. He talked of Bethel's fondness for the people on the estate and in the village, talked of the veritable worship she had for Treveryan. Then the one great companion of her life, her brother, went away, Martineau said. To fight. His own witness had admitted that she was a good deal younger than her sister, and so one must see now that this woman was going to lead a lonelier life than ever. Would it not be quite probable to guess that

there were moments when morbid depression must have seized
hold of her? But later her brother returned, and Miss Lerryn
Treveryan admitted a change in him, he had become restless.
It was not for himself, Sir Oswald said, to go into the matter
of the deceased's life. He had been a brave man, had been
decorated for conspicuous gallantry in the field, and it was
natural that at last the secluded life he had hitherto led at
home should begin to pall, especially after the freedom he
had enjoyed abroad. So he had gone abroad again, leaving
the estate in the capable hands of his sister. Here, again,
more letters were read, in which Veryan's trust in Bethel was
proved without any doubt, letters in which not only was
responsibility shelved, but advice on estate matters asked, and
still couched in terms of deep affection.

"And then what happened?" Sir Oswald paused dramatic-
ally. "He returned with a wife. This man, who for nearly
twenty years had lived for his sister, and with her had shared
in full the horror of possible insanity overtaking them, and
who had, as we have been told, gone to the length of making
a pact renouncing the world and marriage because of this
ghastly and dread disease—I beg you not to forget that his
own father had died utterly insane, after an attempt to throttle
his own wife—this man, I say, calmly returns to his home, the
home he shared with his sisters, married. He never so much
as warned them that he had met the lady who was his wife.
I put it to you, gentlemen of the jury, that such an act was not
only thoughtless but thoroughly callous, that it was an act to
bring shock to any sister in the circumstances, but that to one
who lived from day to day and year to year in fear of one day
losing her reason, it was an act of betrayal and wrong-doing,
which in fact caused the very thing to happen which they had
dreaded. Gentlemen of the jury, I submit that from that
moment the accused's mind became unhinged. She saw the
deed, the marriage, not only as a betrayal to herself and her
beloved Treveryan, but as a criminal act towards posterity.
Had not the old doctor written these very words: ' I consider
marriage undertaken by any children of Simon Treveryan
to be not only a disastrous step for a future generation, but a
criminal one.' *A criminal one*, gentlemen of the jury. These
words had been seen by the accused, can be seen by any of

you in black and white. The writer was a well-known
physician, a man extremely unlikely to make statements of
that nature unless they were true. You have heard how the
deceased altered in his attitude to his sister, that during the
months that followed they frequently quarrelled. If the
accused had feelings of jealousy in her heart, is there a single
man or woman in this court to-day who can fail to understand,
who can fail to sympathize? Gentlemen, the accused is in the
dock on trial for her life, on trial for murder. She is a woman
who has lost everything. All she loved has been wrenched
from her by the evil fate which gave her the mad blood of
the Treveryans in her veins. I have beside me, not only the
late Doctor Pearce's letter to the deceased, but papers of his
father which prove conclusively that other members of the
family died insane. I maintain that before many months had
passed the accused was definitely suffering from an unbalanced
state of mind. Her earlier life and the love that should have
been hers had been destroyed, and with a courage not possible
for all of us, I venture to suggest, she made a new life. A life
with Treveryan and her brother—and younger sister—as the
prime factors, nay, the *only* factors. Her brother's marriage
soon proved that all she had built was crumbling into dust.
Her brother's affections waning, her sister-in-law unwilling to
co-operate in any way, and worst of all perhaps, the very
home she had worked for taken from her and given over to
the new mistress. Is it a wonder that quarrels grew in
strength and number? And always, at the bottom of her
heart and soul, this woman had the knowledge that her
brother had committed a crime. You heard how he refused
to discuss his marriage. Does not that in itself prove the
guilt he felt for his act? Does not the fact that he kept his
wife in complete ignorance of his family's tragic history prove
that only too well? Did he realize the irreparable harm he
had done to not only his sister, but to his wife as well? And
what happened when the accused told her sister-in-law the
truth, as I think she was entitled to do? After another
appalling quarrel the dead man turned his sister out of the
house. I ask you to consider now the mental state of the
accused, already at her wits' end at the loss of her home and
her brother's affection, and the realization that a child was to

be born. This woman, brought up in the lap of luxury, who had never to fend for herself, above all a woman a prey to that ghastly fear which must be for ever present within her? Now turned out of the only home she had known since she was born, without provision, without any thought of her future at all. She was forced to live in a small cottage, miles from her own house, buried deep in the woods and never a soul to see but the faithful sister who did her best to visit her as often as it was possible. Is it a wonder she gradually succumbed to these haunting, nervous fears? It it surprising that at last she became mentally deranged? For five months she lived alone in this isolated condition, without any one to talk to, having to look after herself, cook for herself, sweep for herself. She didn't take sufficient exercise for her health in case it reached her brother's ears that she was still in Treveryan. She could not go away and live on the allowance made by her brother, for it was not adequate, and he made no suggestion of enlarging it. I contend that during those months my client lost her reason and her mind. I contend that when she killed her brother, as she frankly admits she did, she did so, not in a moment of madness, but in complete and inherited madness. Her sister has told you how unhinged the accused became by the very fact that her sister-in-law was to have a child. Yet, when Miss Lerryn Treveryan told the accused of the baby's death she seemed unaffected by the news. I contend that she had by this time lost her reason, and only saw in her brother a breeder of diseased Treveryans. She killed him and she came and gave herself up. That in itself is not the act of a sane woman, not the act of a person guilty of premeditated murder, as my learned friend would have you think. It was the act of a woman with insane blood in her own veins, who, with enough knowledge to realize what she was doing, yet felt it her duty to prevent the birth of further tainted lives into the family of which she was a member. If she fully realized the birth *and death* of the child that had been born, then I contend that the shooting of her brother shows in an even greater degree the pitiful and insane state into which the accused had fallen. There was every opportunity for her to make her get-away after the crime had been committed. Not a soul knew of her whereabouts except her sister. There was not the slightest reason on earth why, if she were a woman guilty of murder, she could not have hidden her brother's body, and probably the crime would never have been detected. I say there was not the slightest reason, *if she had been sane.* But Bethel Treveryan is not sane. And after the story which I have told you—and, gentlemen, in the secret places of your hearts you must agree it is not the story of a mere jealous, spoilt woman as you have been asked to believe, but the pitiful and miserable story of a woman wholly diseased with the ghastly blood of hereditary MADNESS running in her veins—I demand that you spare the life of the accused."

PART
FOUR
2

AT TREVERYAN LERRYN sat alone in the library. She was all alone now, for Lucy had escaped from the 'Mad House,' as she called it as soon as she had recovered sufficiently from the shock of Veryan's death and that of her baby. She had gone to London, determined never to set foot in Cornwall again. Here the law had intervened, making it imperative that she return for Bethel's trial. She was now staying with the Tremaynes, but after everything was over she had plans made to return to Canada, and she told all who knew her that she had no wish to come back.

Lerryn had been glad when she departed, as the situation was an intolerable one for both women, and, in spite of the fact that there had been no animosity between the two, Lucy frankly admitted that the sooner she saw the last of her young sister-in-law and the house in which so much misery and tragedy had been enacted, the better she would be pleased. She had nothing personal against Lerryn, who had gone out of her way to show as much gentleness and tact as she could after the shock of Veryan's death, but Lucy could never forget that she was Bethel's sister, and an affectionate and loyal sister at that; moreover, the Treveryan blood ran in their veins. She loathed the very memory of Bethel, but no longer doubted the story of their madness, and deep in her heart she was not only thankful that her baby had died, but was relieved that she was no longer tied to Veryan. For much as she had loved him, and great as his physical attraction had been for her, she realized that sooner or later something would have occurred which would have terrified her and begun anew her fears of him. She told herself that Bethel's jealous hatred had been the result of the great love she had originally known for her brother; she remembered with horror the quarrel in which they had fought like insane animals, and if, she argued, Bethel could have come to the state whereby she had killed her beloved Veryan in a combination of love and hate, who knew but that one day in the distant future he might not have killed her?

So Lerryn remained in the big empty house alone. Brigit Selworthy had come to stay with her for a fortnight, but had been unable to leave her children for any length of time, and when Lerryn had begged her to bring them with her she had made further excuses that she could not be away from her husband, and Lerryn realized suddenly that Brigit did not wish to bring the young children to the now unhappy atmosphere of Treveryan.

After Brigit left she went for a while to Exeter to visit her old music mistress, and it was then that she remembered the convent where she had been so happy for a week in the past. She returned there for a while and once again found peace.

But now, on this late summer evening, following the afternoon on which Martineau had fought so gallantly for Bethel's life, she was alone. She had hurried home immediately the afternoon's proceedings were over. She expected Oswald that evening, after he had talked with Bethel. She felt tired yet restless, and could not get her sister's image from her mind. Whatever to-morrow's verdict, she knew that Bethel's life was over. She knew that she would never be free again. She realized suddenly that Bethel would never again see Treveryan. She looked around and shivered. How still and silent everything was. Bereft of all voices . . . even Lucy's nasal drawl would have comforted her. This evening the place seemed haunted, already the ghosts of Veryan and even Bethel herself seemed to accompany her as she wandered aimlessly from room to room. The pictures of her ancestors looked down on her; never had their faces seemed so unreal to her. Her footsteps made an echoing sound as she wearily climbed the stone staircase. Presently she thought she heard someone's step.

" Is anyone there? " she called, but no answer came. She wandered into the large double room which had originally been her mother's, and which latterly Veryan and Lucy had used. It smelt of camphor, and she saw that Prudence had already covered the massive four-poster bed with dust-sheets, and that newspapers were spread on the wash-hand stand and odd tables and chairs were balancing upon each other in the strange fashion that is theirs when an efficient housemaid has ' put away ' the room. It looked unused, unlived in and unloved, she thought. Strange, the human dramas that must have taken place within its four walls, she mused. In that bed Lucy's poor baby had been conceived and born. In that bed had she, too, and Veryan and Bethel, first seen the light of day. She sat down in the window-seat, trying to recapture early memories of the room, but everything seemed veiled in a mist. She could remember playing with toys on the white bear rug in front of the fire at a very early age, but that was all. She got up and went out of the room, and noticed that the door was ajar which led into the little boudoir in which her mother had spent so much of her time. This, too, smelt musty and reeked of camphor, as it had done for years. No one had used it since her mother's death, and Lucy had taken an instant dislike to it. It was a dark room and small. Lucy had called it ' poky.' It was full of ugly, Victorian furniture, and the hangings were old-fashioned and unattractive. Lerryn wondered why her mother, who had had such good taste and who always looked so beautiful, should have cared for this strange little room, which had nothing to justify such affection, even its one and only window facing the sunless north. The girl began to look round the room; it was still very much as her mother had left it. She wondered why Bethel, with her love of orderliness, had not thought fit to put away some of the ornaments and knick-knacks which could only harbour dust. Yet as she rubbed her finger along the tops of the books and writing desk, she realized that everything was scrupulously clean, and she supposed that the servants had orders to keep

it so. Queer that for years she had not ever visited the room.
She picked up some of her mother's books. They were most
of them first editions of Thackeray and Dickens; she supposed
they were valuable. She sat down by Anna's writing desk;
it was a huge, cumbersome piece of furniture. She remembered suddenly how, as a small child playing in the room, her
mother would sit for hours writing at this desk. What
engrossed her so violently always, to whom did she write such
lengthy epistles? She looked inside the desk which lay open.
It was completely bare, the big blotter had only a few ancient
pieces of paper which smelt mouldy, and the pigeon-holes
were empty. There was a tiny door in the centre of the desk;
Lerryn opened it, but that, too, was empty. How pretty were
the little carved Doric pillars each side of the little door, she
thought. For no apparent reason she fingered one, and to
her astonishment is came out. She gave a little gasp, for not
only was revealed a secret drawer, but there were letters hidden.
She took them out, a small bundle of them tied together with
faded ribbon. She supposed they must be old love letters
from her father, and started to read them, feeling a little guilty
as she did so. Suddenly she started as the truth dawned on
her. These were love letters, passionate love letters, but they
had not been written by her father. She looked again at the
envelopes and saw that nearly all were addressed to ' Mrs.
Simon Treveryan,' and that some had no envelopes at all.
They were signed with a X. The writer, whoever he had
been, wrote from abroad, but again there was no clue, as the
stamps had been torn from the envelopes and the address was
never anything but the name of a house with a foreign-
sounding name, Casa-something—she could not decipher the
word. The letters had been spread over a number of years,
and it was obvious to Lerryn that they had been answered by
Anna Treveryan from topics mentioned in the letters; the
phrase, ' in your last letter,' occurred frequently. She looked
again at the dates of the letters. They had all been written a
very long time ago, during the early years of her mother's
marriage, and this surprised her almost more than anything,
for she had always supposed her parents' marriage to have
been an exemplary and extremely happy one, and Bethel and
Veryan and old family friends had gone out of the way to

remark on the love Simon Treveryan had borne his wife. Even at Bethel's trial the subject had been gone into, to prove beyond doubt that the man had been mad when found in the act of strangling the woman everyone knew he adored. Nevertheless, as Lerryn continued to read through the correspondence, she realized that without any doubt her mother had had a lover. She had not finished reading when a puff of wind from the window which she had opened suddenly blew the letters from the desk on which they were lying to the floor. By the time she had picked up the scattered pages she saw that the few remaining ones, hitherto unread, were no longer in dated order, so she was obliged to read them at random. Gradually it dawned on her that this romance of her mother's had begun *before* she had married; there were sentences such as ' I swear I shall in time have made enough to give you a home, heart's belovèd, and whatever your mother and the rest of the family have to say, I'm determined to bring you here as my bride '; and ' When you tell me that you love no one but me and never will, and are equally determined to be my wife, it fires me with continued hope, dearest Anna.' What had happened, Lerryn wondered, to prevent her mother and this unknown writer from being granted their heart's desire? Here was another which must allude to some sudden and unexpected parting. ' Belovèd,' it ran, ' I cannot find words to express either the misery in my heart at leaving you suddenly like this, nor the indignation I feel for A.F. at his insistence at my taking this boat. The last few hours of you are utterly precious in my memory, and I cannot believe we have been torn asunder from each other so cruelly by fate. You are the world and everything in it for me, as you well know; if you were anyone else I would damn the family to blazes, but have too much respect and feeling for your ears to hear what I would say, and eyes to read what I would write. I beg you to write me as often as you can. Somehow or other I shall arrange matters in such a way that I can return soon, or else borrow the fare for your journey to me, and we will be married on your arrival. Be brave, sweetheart, and do not grieve. If the latter course seems the only way, I beg you to take it even if it does mean deceiving your mother and the rest ! '

Poor Mama! It was pitiable to realize that she and this unknown lover of hers had been beaten by fate, Lerryn thought as she lit the lamp and picked up yet another letter. Theirs must have been a very great love indeed, she considered, to have continued so strongly throughout the years that followed. Ah! What was this? 'I am utterly distraught by your letter and cannot *believe* what you tell me. Who is this fellow, and how in heaven's name have you allowed yourself to be browbeaten into such a marriage? The hideous haste with which the whole thing has been concluded astounds, sickens, and completely dumbfounds me. Had you so little patience, so little trust in me, Anna? You who have been wholly, utterly and entirely mine, how could you give yourself to another with such abandoned haste? I am heartbroken and beside myself with misery and have lost faith in everything and everyone.' Poor young man! It certainly struck Anna's daughter that such heartlessness needed explaining away. She turned to the next, a short note. 'Oh, God! That I could have done this thing to you! Was there no way by which you could have let me know the truth before your mother discovered it? What can I say, what can I do, now? All I know is that I shall be paying full penalty for the rest of my life. Till the end of time I suppose I shall see you another man's wife, and worse—for the knowledge that in ignorance he will be fathering our child will drive me mad with jealousy, hate and mortification. I try to see and understand it all from your point of view; I do understand that you were in an appalling position without me to protect your name and your own adorable self. I see your mother's frantic panic to avert scandal, and I daresay other mothers would have done the same thing in the same circumstances. Knowing how utterly opposed she and the family have always been to *us*, however, I am fully prepared to believe that she hurried on this marriage with as much haste as she could in order to secure Treveryan as her son-in-law, before being absolutely certain that you really are to have a child. Treveryan—God! I could kill the fellow. How dare any man have you but me! One thing I shall always know, and that is, whatever he may have in the future, I have your heart, and I have your first child. Oh, Anna, Anna, Anna . . .

Why did I never think of such a tragic climax to our love, selfish fool that I was.'

The letter fell to the ground.

What did it mean? What child had Mama had that had not been Papa's? It couldn't mean, it COULDN'T MEAN . . . feverishly she searched for more pages; the next three letters were written at a far later date, and were full of accounts of the writer's life in some tropical country. Wait! Here was one in the same faded brown ink and the same thin-lined paper. ' How I long to see you both! You have no idea what it is to feel that you are a father, and as such may never claim your child—my daughter! You say she is a cross between your own mother and myself. Dear heart, whatever anxiety you may feel as to this, I cannot help but rejoice that little Bethel bears some resemblance to her own father. I want to hear so much more about you. I'm jealous of Treveryan, fiendishly so. Both of the man and of the place. Of the man for obvious reasons, of the place because I can see you love it, and alas! I know no home that I could ever have given you would have compared to it. Thank God Simon " looks after you " and is a " thoughtful husband," but I detest him and all he stands for.'

Lerryn forced herself to grip the side of the chair as a sudden feeling of faintness seized hold of her. For a few moments her mind was a blank, and then, like a flash, she realized the stark and naked truth. *Bethel was not a Treveryan.* Bethel, who to-morrow might be convicted of murder, but whose life would in all likelihood be spared for the very reason of her tainted blood, had, in fact, blood as pure as any in the land. Bethel was not insane, Bethel was not a Treveryan. Bethel was a murderess pure and simple.

Lerryn's brain reeled.

Slowly she rose to her feet and then gathered the letters together. She blew out the candles and taking the papers with her descended to the library. Her mind still felt dazed by the news which she had so carelessly stumbled upon and she scarcely heeded Paul, who was putting a match to the fire and had brought in the sherry.

" The post is on the small table, Miss," he said as he left the room.

More letters! She glanced idly at the few which were

awaiting her attention. She suddenly saw one in Sally's writing, but even news from her old friend would mean little to her this evening, and she read through the pages with scant attention. The girl, who had just heard about Veryan's tragedy, wrote to her from Italy where she and her husband lived permanently. There was no mention of Ted, and Lerryn threw it aside casually and went over to the window to look out for Oswald Martineau whom she was expecting to arrive any minute. She would have to tell him of her discovery because, for all she knew, it might alter the whole sequence of Bethel's trial. Her heart felt heavy with sorrow and frustrated anger as she realized that, if these letters had been discovered before, the tragedy would in all likelihood have never occurred. Whatever shock Bethel would have felt on learning she was no Treveryan, would soon have been quashed on the realization that freedom would have been hers, and as likely as not, once married to Oswald, all would have been well. For Lerryn was ignorant of his marriage; Bethel had told her nothing of it the night she had poured out her heart to her after Veryan's decision to turn her from the house. What years of misery she would have been spared, how altered the whole trend of their lives. But why had their mother been so unyielding in her refusal to allow Bethel's marriage? Veryan had always led her to believe that he had imagined Anna's prejudice to have been one similar to old Doctor Pearce's, that she would have put her foot down on any marriage knowing the truth of Simon's disease and the hereditary taint. Yet, knowing Bethel was no child of Simon's, surely her mother had realized the girl was immune to any such disease? Surely no woman living would sacrifice her daughter's happiness against the loss of her own reputation? Besides, no one need ever have known the true story of Anna Treveryan's romantic past outside these four walls; so argued the girl in her heart. She wished desperately that she knew who the writer had been. It was so tantalizing not to know the name of Bethel's father. Presently she heard the sound of a car and a few minutes later Oswald came into the room.

" Oh, Oswald ! " She went quickly across the room to greet him. " I'm so glad you've come. I have so much to tell you."

Martineau immediately noticed the expression in both her

face and voice, and guessed that something had occurred.

" But first tell me how she was? Oswald, you were magnificent to-day ! "

She thought how tired he looked and was struck by the fact that he had aged considerably in these last few months. She knew how much he adored Bethel and was worried as to what his reactions would be after she had told him of her discovery.

" She was all right—better than I expected. Poor darling, I think she's completely dazed by the whole business by now. A thing of this kind is enough to drive any sane person mad, let alone one in her state."

" Yet you must be so used to ' this sort of thing,' as you call it, Oswald."

" My dear, I've never before had to fight for the life of the woman I love. It's infinitely worse than operating. No wonder doctors can't operate on their own wives and families."

"I've never been to a trial before and, please God, I shall never have to go to another, but I'm sure you would have defended any client with as great feeling and courage as you did her."

" I don't know. I suppose so. I tried to rid my heart of the knowledge it was Bethel. I tried to look at it dispassionately, as just another case. It's a long time since I've done anything of this sort you know, Lerryn."

" Don't you come into contact with murders and killings in India ? "

" Not for some years."

They went in to dinner and Lerryn told Paul not to wait on them, but only to bring in the fresh courses when she rang.

" There's too much for us to discuss," she said to Martineau, " you don't mind if we wait on ourselves, I'm sure."

" What's happened to the old man ? "

" Hockin? Poor old fellow, Veryan's death was a great shock to him. He's retired. Luckily we had been meaning to pension him off for some time, and everything was more or less easily settled."

" Lerryn, what are you going to do ? "

" I don't know," she said after a pause. " Originally this place was left to Bethel and myself for the remainder of our lives. When he first married Lucy he added a codicil to the same effect; but after his frightful quarrel he meant to make a new will, I know, because I happened to overhear something he said to Lucy. It was when the baby was expected. He fully intended to alter it, but I rather think he was waiting until after the child's birth. But it never materialized, and now I suppose it will still be ours."

"Do you want to go on living here? You see, my dear——" he hesitated. "Bethel won't be with you."

There was a long pause.

"Oswald, there's something I've got to tell you. Something so extraordinary that you'll probably not believe me. I only discovered about it this evening. Oswald, Bethel isn't Papa's daughter."

Martineau looked at her in silence.

"I was in Mama's little sitting-room this evening and I suddenly found some letters. I started reading them and soon realized they were love letters. Oswald, Mama had some lover before she married Papa, and Bethel's their child."

He looked at her in blank amazement.

"I don't believe it," he said at last.

"Come back into the library and I'll show you the letters."

For half an hour he pored over Anna's correspondence in dead silence, and Lerryn never took her eyes off his face.

"Good God!" he said slowly, when he folded the last sheet of paper and handed the packet to her.

"What are you going to do? Will it make any difference? You see it means she's no more mad than you are!"

Martineau paced the room.

"It's fantastic! Fantastic!" he muttered.

The hideous nightmare that life had become these last few months now took on an even more grotesque form. He was the first to realize the full truth of what this new situation implied. Certainly the letters proved beyond any shadow of doubt that Bethel had no more Treveryan blood in her veins than he had himself. Therefore it was an obvious fact that she must be, to all intents and purposes, sane. In which case no blame for her crime could be attached to any hereditary weakness. He was still ready to believe that she had killed Veryan *imagining herself* to be mad, that much she had let him understand when together they had worked on her defence. Suddenly he realized one thing above all else; he knew he thanked God from the bottom of his heart that Lerryn had not made her discovery before to-day. Had he known the real state of affairs he would never have been able to plead with the same conviction. There was nothing to be done now but to wait. To-morrow Croften was to sum up, to-morrow they would know the verdict, and he felt pretty certain what it would be. But how ghastly to realize that if Bethel was convicted but detained during His Majesty's pleasure she would have to spend the rest of her life in a criminal asylum. Was it fair to her? Should he after all . . . Again, however, Bethel's face rose in his mind, her face as he had seen it only a few hours before. She had been so calm, so grateful for the battle he was fighting for her life. She knew, had known from the first, what to expect if her life was spared. It was they, he and Lerryn, alone, who knew the truth. Poor darling Bethel believed that she had shot Veryan because at last she was succumbing to the fate of her forefathers. If she were convinced of that and ready to bear the ghastly brunt of the future, then, as far as he was concerned, she should. To all intents and purposes she was mad, for all he knew her mind had become unhinged by now. She had certainly been through enough to turn her insane.

" Well? " Lerryn's voice broke his reverie.

He turned and faced her.

" Must you tell them the truth? "

" I shall do nothing of the sort. The case for the defence is over."

" What shall we tell Beth? " she asked later.

" Tell her? Tell her nothing. I believe if she knew the truth it would kill her. Or worse, I believe it might send her really mad."

" Perhaps you're right. It would bring all the wasted years of her life back to her so vividly and to no end. I see that. And yet—oh, Oswald! It's such a ghastly business. Imagine her in that place from now on. Day in, day out. Beth, who has loved Treveryan beyond everything else, who knows every flower and tree in the place, who——"

" My dear, you're forgetting the alternative, which is not her freedom."

" Oh! " Lerryn shuddered violently. " Surely they

could never—*hang* her?" she said with anguish.

"She would probably get a life sentence. No, my dear, it's best that we leave things to God's mercy."

"I shan't come to-morrow," she said, as she bade him good-night later. "I don't know how I shall get through the day, but I do know I couldn't face to-morrow. Can you come yourself when it's all over and tell me the verdict?"

"I promise you I will. Poor Lerryn, it's been hell for you. You've been so splendid. If they spare her life it will be very largely due to you."

When he had gone she took the letters with her, and read them slowly again, one by one, far into the night.

PART
FOUR

3

ALL DAY LERRYN waited for him until the suspense became well nigh unbearable. It was not until late in the evening that she heard a car draw up outside the front door and a man's voice ask for her. She ran down the stairs not daring to put the question.

"It's all right," he said.

"Thank God," she murmured, and a moment later was sobbing her heart out in Martineau's arms. He said nothing until at last she grew quieter and seemed sufficiently recovered to take in all he had to tell her.

"What happened?" she whispered.

"They found her guilty, of course, but insane. It was the verdict Croften more or less instructed them to bring in. He was very fair, couldn't have spoken better. They, the jury, were out for about an hour."

"What did she do? What did she look like?"

"Her face never changed a muscle. I don't think she realizes it's over at last. She was very sweet when I saw her afterwards, but seemed dazed. It's natural."

"Were people beastly?"

"Oh, no. No, I think she made a very profound impression on most. I'm told a good few people have been staggered at what, I suppose, must be termed dirty linen, but that by the end everyone hoped she'd get off. I doubt even if the truth were known they'd change their minds. After all, sane or insane, her life was entirely ruined by the supposition that she was one of you."

" Shall I be allowed to go to her ? "

" I'll see that you do. She's all right."

" Oswald . . . they won't put her with a lot of terrible people, really mad people, I mean, will they ? "

" No," he assured her.

" Lerryn, have you no idea who her father could have been ? "

She shook her head.

" None. You saw that he never signed any of his letters, and his address was so non-committal."

" Have you no recollection of any admirer of your mother's ? "

" No. Besides, as you know, he, whoever he was, lived abroad, so she must have seen him very little."

" But there were gaps in the dates. Every now and then. I noticed particularly. He must have come home sometimes and seen her. I don't believe these letters could have gone on for all those years without their meeting."

" I do remember that Mama used to go away at intervals. She used to go to her relations, but we never went with her."

" Did your father accompany her ? "

" I don't think he did; no, I'm sure he didn't."

" Then, doubtless, that was when she saw him."

" I wish I could remember more, I was so little in those days. I scarcely remember my grandmother with whom we stayed after Papa was taken ill. The man writes of ' the family,' keeps alluding to them, but I don't remember Mama having a family beyond her mother. She was an only child. There was a cousin, a man, that's all I can remember."

As she spoke, faint, very faint, recollections stirred in her memory.

" Wait a minute, Oswald, I'm trying to remember something."

Way back, and she was a small child . . . Bethel's coming-out ball . . . a necklace . . . a strange relation of Mama's coming to stay, a relation from abroad.

" I believe I know who it was," she said slowly. She began to piece the links together as she put into words her theory.

" I remember that time when they went up for the Golden Jubilee, that time you and Beth fell in love with each other,

that he was in London. Can't you remember? Didn't you
meet him? "

" I can't remember anyone."

" I know he was. I remember Beth sending me a postcard
from London and saying that Mama's cousin had turned up
from abroad and they had seen him. She always remembered
him because of the necklace he gave her. Don't you see,
Oswald, it must have been the same? I can't even remember
his name."

" Where has he been all these years? Surely he'd have
shown up, or written, or something after your mother died? "

" I don't know. Perhaps he's dead, too. He could hardly
claim his child. Besides, as I tell you, he lived abroad so
much. Even if he had heard and written to Veryan or Beth,
I should have been too young to know about it. And they
wouldn't have been particularly interested in him."

" Her cousin." Oswald Martineau said the words aloud.

" Yes, he was her cousin."

" What I cannot understand," he said, " is the reason for
your mother's refusal to our marriage. We always supposed
it was because of the madness, and that she could not face
telling her children. I can't forgive her. She it is really who
is to blame for everything." Once again his heart was filled
with the old bitterness he had felt nearly a quarter of a century
ago.

" I don't understand that either. As you say, she must have
known Beth wasn't like the rest of us."

" I wonder if she would have told me the truth if she had
not died," he mused.

" Lerryn," he said a few minutes later, " I believe what
happened may have been this: being cousins, their family
refused any marriage between them. A great many people
consider the marriage of cousins to be exceedingly wrong and
unhealthy. You remember how, in his letters, he keeps
alluding to the family—he means their joint family. And her
mother in particular must obviously have put her foot down.
I suppose they became lovers without anyone's knowledge,
and after he had gone away she knew that she was to have a
child of his and was forced to tell her mother, or else the
mother found out. Anyway, she married your father in great

haste, and one imagined he never discovered the truth. But supposing we have been wrong all these years? Supposing he did eventually discover your mother's secret, and for that reason tried to strangle her. Insanity was in his family, there was never proved any motive to justify his attack on Anna Treveryan, but here in point of fact is a very substantial one."

" Do you think my mother would have denied such a story even if Papa had accused her? "

" We don't know that he did, for no scandal ever touched her name."

" If Dr. Pearce had any inkling of the truth, could he have prevented Bethel's marriage? "

" Dr. Pearce had no idea of it I am sure; moreover, I have read his reports on your father's case: he was completely insane and very violent. But it is not impossible that the assault he made on your mother gave rise to the violence from which he never recovered."

" But surely Mama would have eventually sacrificed herself —her name, honour—call it what you will—rather than commit Bethel to the unnatural hell of such a heritage as ours? "

Oswald sighed bitterly.

" What her ultimate decision about Bethel would have been had she lived we shall never know."

" It seems incredible that any woman should be so callous where her own daughter's happiness was at stake. I hope with all my heart you're wrong about my mother, Oswald."

" How else explain it all? "

"As you say, we shall never know. But I think you're wrong. I think Mama was most likely sincerely terrified of the insanity in our family, and that you were nearer the truth when you remarked on the aversion many people have for the marriage between cousins. She knew, must have done, that Papa's insanity could be traced back to Tregony, who married her cousin. Old Dr. Pearce would have told her everything, he owed that to her. I think the realization that Bethel was also the child of two cousins preyed on her mind, after she knew the horrible secrets of our family, and that once again she became haunted by the idea that even Beth might not escape the same fate. If Mama had not died things might have been different. Who knows, you might have persuaded her into telling you the truth; she might have relented."

Unconvinced, Oswald got up from his chair.

"I must go now. You look tired out, Lerryn. Promise you'll take some rest. And be quite certain that I'll let you know when you can see Bethel."

"Oswald." She hesitated.

"Yes?"

"I want to ask you something which I have no right to ask, but—has this made any difference? I mean, has the truth shocked you very much? Knowing that Beth is as sane as you are, and that she killed Veryan without being mad?"

He shook his head.

"Nothing could alter my love for Beth, my dear, and even if she deliberately killed him she did so imagining she was insane and thinking it to be for the best."

"Oh, Oswald," tears came into her eyes, "if only we had known about these letters before our whole lives would have been different. If she had been able to marry you, even a few years ago, I don't believe this tragedy would have happened. Why, of course, it couldn't have! For she would have become healed of the spectre of insanity which haunts the rest of us, and could never have shot V. in cold blood whatever she felt."

"Did she tell you of our meeting in London, Lerryn?"

"Yes."

"Didn't she tell you that I married many years ago?"

Lerryn looked at him. For a moment she was speechless.

"No!" she said aghast.

"We parted many years ago. It was not a happy marriage. But my wife was a Catholic and we could never be divorced. So you see, Bethel could never have come to me." His weary voice was tinged with bitterness.

"She never told me," she said.

For a long time that night Lerryn could not sleep. Her mind was distressed, and she tried to push away ugly thoughts which kept returning to her brain. She remembered now, as if it had happened yesterday, the bitterness and seeming misery of Bethel's manner on her return from London, she remembered the words 'something prevents one from making an end to it all,' words which Lerryn had imagined to have meant Bethel's end. Had her sister meant to make an end of Veryan

all the time? 'I'll not kill myself' . . . she remembered Beth
using these words, too. Had her sister become so crazy with
hate and jealousy on finding Oswald again and discovering he
was no longer free, that her very jealousy had tempted her to
put into vile practice the crime which she did commit? 'I
want that rifle,' 'I'd much rather have that little rifle,' 'I must
have ammunition' . . .

As the girl gradually sank into slumber she knew that for the
rest of her life she would be uncertain of one thing. She would
never know whether Bethel had shot Veryan in mad despair,
or whether for months she had deliberately planned his murder.

PART   ONE AFTERNOON ABOUT eighteen months later,
FOUR   Brigit Selworthy was waiting for her friend Lerryn
         Treveryan. It was already past the hour which
4   Lerryn had appointed, and Mrs. Selworthy began
         to feel anxious lest something should have occurred
to prevent her from arriving. It had been a long time since
she had seen her and since the tragedy in her family the girl's
letters had become less frequent; there was so much that she
wanted to know, for in spite of the fact that Mrs. Penrose,
Brigit's mother, lived so close to the family, her letters rarely
contained much news of the Treveryans, her excuses being
always that once again the family had stepped back into
obscurity, and, with Bethel shut away from the world, she
now heard less than nothing.

There had been rumours for months past that Treveryan
was to be put on the market, but this had never been sub-
stantiated, and although Brigit realized what a life of loneliness
Lerryn must lead, she felt desperately sad at the prospect of
the estate passing out of the hands of the family which had
owned it for nearly four hundred years. She hoped that there
was no truth in the rumour, yet it was true that for some time
past Lerryn herself had taken to spending long periods away
from her home. This much she knew, not only from her
mother, but from Lerryn herself, whose now short and infrequent letters were more often than not written from
Devonshire.

Brigit had almost given her up when the door bell rang and Lerryn was shown into the drawing-room.

For the first time in their lives, Brigit Selworthy found herself feeling constrained with Lerryn. Perhaps it was that time had separated them for too long, perhaps it was the knowledge of all that Lerryn had been through, but Brigit certainly felt shy, and for some time they spoke of everyday matters and other banalities which held little interest for either of them. It was when Lerryn began to speak of the future, for Kenneth Selworthy had been given a living and was to be the first vicar of a parish in a new garden suburb, that Brigit felt the ice start to thaw as it were, and she fell into the old ease which had always made her friendship with Lerryn such a pleasant one.

"And you, Lerryn," she said at last, "what are you going to do? You never tell one much in letters, you know. And mother doesn't know your plans, it seems, although she did say there was a rumour that you were selling Treveryan. Surely that's not true?"

"Yes," Lerryn said with a sigh, "it's quite true."

"Oh, my dear!" Brigit could think of nothing to say. She knew how, as a family, they had adored the place, although Lerryn perhaps had not given the same love to it that Veryan and Bethel had done.

"Was it necessary? Did you have to?" she asked a few minutes later.

"I couldn't have gone on living there by myself. It would have driven—there are too many ghosts for me."

"Does Bethel know?"

"Oh, yes. She was quite reasonable, saw it was the only thing to do."

"How is she? I mean, does she know you when you go to see her?"

"Good heavens, yes!" said Lerryn, and longed to add that her sister was as sane as she was. "Of course I'm not allowed to see her often."

"Has anyone made an offer for Treveryan yet?" asked Brigit.

"Yes. I don't know who it is, but they seem very anxious and I've decided that I shall agree."

"Oh, Lerryn . . ." and after another pause she continued:
"What will you do? Things are going to be so sad for

you. I don't want to seem inquisitive, but knowing what I
do now about you all, my heart aches for you."

Lerryn looked up and smiled.

" I think I'm going to be happy at last."

" Lerryn! You don't mean . . .? " she faltered.

Could it be that after all Lerryn was to follow Veryan's
example and marry?

" I'm going to become a nun," she replied.

Brigit looked thunderstruck.

" I can't believe it! " she said after she had recovered from
the shock.

" Why not? I often thought it would be a very wonderful
life, you know. It's true that sometimes I ask myself if I'm
not a very unworthy person, but I believe God won't reject
me. Mine hasn't been an easy life, and I've sinned very much
in the past, but I honestly believe that the peace which the
cloister can give me is not the only reason and excuse for my
decision. It's true that my life has become empty and, if
circumstances had not been as they were, I might have been a
very different person, but I shall not be the first person to take
the veil because I've been unhappy, and I don't feel a hypocrite
about it. I have a very sincere love for the Church, and I
think that a miracle has led me to realize it is the life for which
I am suited."

Brigit could only stare at her friend. Why did the words
Lerryn used embarrass her? Why did they seem as so much
jargon? She felt irritated and depressed by Lerryn's attitude
which seemed to her so utterly foreign to her nature.

" How do you know you are suited to lead that life, Lerryn?
I can't believe you are. You're impulsive, my dear, and
people get hold of you. When I remember how in love you
were——" perhaps that was tactless of her—" I mean—well,
my dear, I know how you love the world and worldly affairs.
I remember when you used to grumble like anything because
you were forced to live at Treveryan without ever seeing a
soul. How you've enjoyed your visits to us up here, too!
Oh, Lerryn darling, I do beseech you to think things over
before you decide to do this awful thing."

" You oughtn't to speak so, as Ken's wife! " Lerryn said
with a smile.

" He would be as horrified as I am," Brigit retorted. " What decided you to do it ? " she then asked.

" You know I left home once and went to a Retreat with Miss Garth? It was then that I first found myself drawn towards the life."

" You're impulsive and emotional, Lerryn. Your love affair came after that, and I swear the Church and nuns and all the rest of it played second fiddle with a vengeance whilst that was going on."

" Yes, I'm afraid you're right. But do you condemn me for ever because I'm impulsive and emotional, as you call it? To some people life is colourless and pointless without something to be emotional about. After Veryan died and Bethel had to go, I admit I went to the Convent in the hope of finding a solution for myself. I don't think you have the right either to reproach or condemn me because I have found that solution. I have lived with the Sisters for many months on end, I know what to expect. I fully realize the life of privation that I shall have to lead. But I know, too, that I shall find love and peace such as I have never known before."

And, unconvinced as she was, Brigit confessed later to her husband that there had been a new light in Lerryn's eyes, a light that made her wonder if perhaps she had been wrong in doubting Lerryn's judgment as to where her future happiness lay.

. . . . .

Lerryn sat in the train which was to take her back to Treveryan for the last time. The property had been sold and she was still ignorant of the identity of its new owner. The sale had been conducted through a famous London agent, and she had been relieved when he had informed her that the prospective buyer wished to buy Treveryan lock, stock and barrel.

She looked forward with as much eagerness as she was capable of to her new life, and no longer dreaded the thought of leaving Treveryan. As she had told Brigit Selworthy, the place held nothing but tragic ghosts and unhappy memories, and now that the long months of indecision were over she could scarcely bear to wait for the day when she should say farewell to her home for ever. She thanked God that it had never been to her what it had to Bethel and Veryan—poor Bethel, how desperately she would have minded having no claim to Treveryan Lerryn could not help thinking. She thought of the last time she had seen her sister. How different had Bethel's reaction been compared with Brigit's, when she had told her of her desire to become a nun. But then Beth was altogether different these days. Her beauty had startled the younger girl, and she could not help feeling amazed at the serenity in her sister's expression. It was as if she had been released from all care, all worry, all unhappiness. Could anyone be a murderess and look like Beth? Lerryn asked herself. Sometimes she was almost assured that her sister's brain had been affected after all, and that she had no more escaped insanity than the Treveryans themselves had. The meetings which she had had with Bethel, infrequent as they were, had been very painful to the younger girl, and she was relieved that they were over. She would probably see Beth again before she took her final vows but there was no longer the usual visit at stated intervals to which she had tried to accustom herself, and which had invariably filled her with dread. That grim building, the massive gates which told their tale only too fearfully, the men and women in uniform whom Lerryn could never look on without shuddering—to her they were warders and not nurses—all filled her with depression and misery. Yet Bethel seemed calm and contented. Sometimes Lerryn wondered if her presence disturbed her, brought back to her memory the life she was hoping to forget. It struck her after the third visit how silent and uncommunicative Bethel was, and both had been obviously relieved when the interview was over. The atmosphere was generally strained, sometimes tense, and Lerryn would feel unnatural and ill at ease.

But in spite of the relief in her heart and the urge she felt to get away as soon as possible, when the day came for Lerryn to leave Treveryan she hardly knew how she was to bear it. She knew she was doing the right thing by giving up her home and she knew that once the wrench was over and done with, all would be well. As she came towards the house from the lake she noticed a car standing by the front door. Her heart contracted as she realized it must be the new owner of Treveryan come to look around, unaware that she was still here. She tried to hide, but as she was about to creep into the old ruined tower she saw a man's figure come out of the house and recognized Oswald Martineau. She ran out and hailed him with a cry of pleasure.

" Oh, my dear ! "   He seemed awkward and embarrassed.

" Oswald, how terribly nice to see you !   Have you come to say good-bye to me?   That was indeed dear of you."

" Why, yes," he said, " I wasn't sure if I should see you."

" I thought you were Treveryan's new owner," she said, " and although I have no regrets about the sale, I cannot bear the thought of . . . Isn't it strange, I still don't know the people's name ! "

They walked across the terrace in silence.

" Lerryn," he said presently, " I have a confession to make."

She looked startled.

" You were right just now.   Right in what you had supposed about Treveryan's new owner being here."

" Oh, Oswald ! "   She looked round hurriedly, " please let me get away before he comes.   I don't want to meet him. I'm sorry if he's a friend of yours, but——"

"Lerryn !" He stopped. "It's I who have bought your home."

" Oswald ! "   And then again a minute later, " Oh, Oswald," she said.

" I couldn't bear to think of Treveryan going to anyone," he began, " and I was afraid that if I told you I wanted to buy it you might have misguidedly thought I was buying your home for some other motive—pity, perhaps—and that you would have refused to sell."

" But, Oswald, how funny you are.   Heavens !   How wrong men can sometimes be.   I couldn't be happier.   Do you know it will make all the difference in the future to think of your being here, you who have known it and once loved it.   You will try to love it again, won't you? " she ended, with an urgent note in her voice.

" My dear, I do love it.   You see, I was here in the happy days, the happiest days of my life were spent here.   And if there are ghosts, why, they are blessed ghosts for me.   I see Bethel as she was at her first ball, I see her again seven years later when she gave me her love.   My youth, our youth, the only happiness we ever had together, was spent at this beloved place.   How could I let it pass to other hands? "

She pressed his hand.

" Does Bethel know? "

" I've not told her. I was afraid it might upset her."

" It wouldn't. If I know anything of Beth at all I feel sure it would make her very happy. Oh, Oswald, I know she would be glad."

" And you, my dear, you're really certain that you're taking the right step? Believe me, I'm not criticizing. I only want you to be certain of yourself."

" I am," she said.

" Because if you're not," he went on, " if you're not I want you to promise that you will still look on Treveryan as your home. In time your own ghosts, the ghosts you told me once you feared, will cease to haunt you. And then if you want to return, you will find it ready. You are Bethel's sister, if she had been my wife I should have looked upon you as my sister."

Lerryn could not speak. Her eyes were full of tears and her heart ached.

" God bless you," she said presently.

PART   ONE AFTERNOON SOME years later a man and a
FOUR   woman sat next each other on one of the green
       iron seats in the gardens of Broadmoor.
5   Oswald Martineau had come to bid farewell to
       Bethel.

After her trial was over he had decided to finish with law for ever and to spend the rest of his days leading the life of a country gentleman in as secluded a manner as possible. With this end in view he bought Treveryan, hoping to find peace in the home of the woman he loved so well. But this was not to be. For many years now he had done his best to live in the place which not only attracted him but had in the past brought him happiness, but he soon discovered that Lerryn had been right when she had spoken of ghosts. It was all so different from what he had expected. Somehow he had imagined that he would recapture the days of his youth, when Bethel had been a girl, his heart's beloved, and young Veryan had been his friend. Instead, he was haunted by the thought of years of suffering, and the unhappy lives of these people, culminating in one of the greatest tragedies he had ever known. Yet something forced him to remain, what it was, he could never say. Perhaps one of the greatest reasons was the pleasure it had given Bethel to know he had bought the place.

" You don't know what it will mean to me, knowing that Treveryan is yours," she had said when he first told her. " Whenever I close my eyes I shall be able to see the two things dearest to my heart, together. You and Treveryan. I have been wretched imagining new people there, people who would neither love nor understand my home. Who would see it as just some rather magnificent house and probably alter it beyond recognition. I was terrified lest some rich man should buy it, a man with vulgar taste and a philistine mentality. Treveryan is alive, as alive as Veryan and I were—once." Oswald had been struck by the natural way in which she mentioned Veryan. How strange and how infinitely pathetic it was, to see how subconsciously she clung to the past after all, allying herself with the man she had killed, so blissfully unaware that she had no rights in the home she adored. She rarely mentioned Lerryn.

" And now, when I think of you Oswald, I shall be able to visualize you there. Wandering down by the lake, perhaps— that was where we first told each other of our love. Do you remember? "

And so for years he had contrived to live in the big house, with few friends to visit him, for invariably if guests arrived they would plague him with tactless questions about the family and the tragedy. He visited Bethel as often as he was allowed, and this, too, was a great strain, for his love did not lessen with the passing of years and he was tortured by every meeting. He knew that she lived for his visits, as indeed he did himself, in spite of the agony which they brought him. There was nothing he did not know of her heart now, for gradually she had confessed everything to him, and pity and understanding had only made him love her more.

" I knew I could prove madness in my blood, and perhaps during those last months I was a little mad," she had told him. " I don't regret it. They're kind here. No one, not even you, dear love, can know what I went through." And through her eyes he saw the frustrated, tortured and embittered life of the woman he loved. And now he was turned sixty and had been offered a fine appointment in the shape of a special mission to India, under the India Office. He knew that it would be madness to refuse the job, but his heart was torn in two. It would solve so many problems for them both if he were to go. Bethel listened in silence until he had finished telling her of the offer.

" Why do you tell me about it? " she asked finally.

" I'm asking you what I must do," he answered.

" Why ask me? A lunatic!" She tried to keep her voice calm.

" Don't say things like that," he cried.

" Do you want to accept it? "

" Frankly, I don't know."

" If it were not for me, would you? "

" Again, I don't know."

" Oswald, tell me the truth. Are you thinking of it as a means of escape? "

He took her hand.

" I never can escape wholly from you. I never wish to, but——"

" But these meetings, this place, the years that drag by till one or other of us is dead—oh, my darling! I know how you feel. Go. Go if you think you can be happier."

" I can never be happy without you. You know that. But I'll admit I find these visits a torturing business. I know you're as sane as I am and I love you. I'm becoming an old man, but all my youth is in you and you're still the woman I love and want. Sometimes I wonder if we're being fair to each other? I don't know, my dearest, I don't suppose it's the same for you. Should we have less pain to bear if I went to India? "

For a long time she did not answer.

" If I thought I was never going to see you again I don't think I could bear it," she said at last. " I would rather they had hanged me. One has so much time here just to sit alone and—think. Oswald, do you imagine I could ever be given my freedom? "

" I don't know. I fear it's very unlikely."

"I suppose when I'm old and white-haired and useless to you."

" There's no reason that I can see why, after twenty years you shouldn't come out. A lifer in prison gets his freedom after that. This, of course, is a little different."

" Twenty years. I should be over sixty, you would be over seventy. Oh, dear God ! " She paused, and then continued :

" Perhaps if I haven't become quite mad by then, His Majesty's pleasure for me will be through. A little late for romance." She laughed bitterly.

" Romance is deathless where you and I are concerned. ' Tenderly—be not impatient,

> ' Strong is your hold O mortal flesh,
> Strong is your hold O love.' "

" ' Be not impatient ' ! Must we wait till we're old and deaf and senile before we can be together? "

> " ' At the last, tenderly,
> From the walls of the powerful fortressed house
> From the clasp of the knitted locks, from the keep of the
>   well-closed doors,
> Let me be wafted.

> " ' Let me glide noiselessly forth
> With the key of softness unlock the locks—with a whisper
> Let ope the doors O soul.

> " ' Tenderly—be not impatient,
> (Strong is your hold O mortal flesh,
> Strong is your hold O love).' "

Oswald spoke Whitman's lines in little more than a whisper. Bethel laid her arm on his.

" Go to India my beloved and take my heart in your keeping," she said quietly.

༄༅

EPILOGUE

I HAVE BEEN TO Treveryan. I have seen with my own eyes the home of Bethel and Veryan and Lerryn. The home which was the centre of so much love and so much hate. The first time I saw it, O.M. was with me. He had recovered

sufficiently to go away and we went to Falmouth together, and
one day he asked me if I should like to see the original of the
picture in his bedroom. He had by that time already told
me a little of his story, and foolishly, and I feated tactlessly,
I had said, 'What a good book that would make.' Like the
grand person he was he neither jumped on me nor appeared
to mind, and for the time being I said no more about the
matter. I suppose it was only natural that the atmosphere of
the place and all its surroundings should bring the family back
to him so vividly, and we had not been in the park long before
he began once more to speak of them.

" Who does it belong to now," I asked, for I hate trespassing
and was afraid lest at any moment someone would appear and
tell us sharply to ' get out.'

" It still belongs to me," was his astonishing reply.

" Why in heaven's name don't you live here then? " I asked
in amazement. It seemed an incredible folly to own such a
glorious place and to ignore it completely. It was then that
he told me the end of the story.

Bethel, it seems, had been promised her release after twenty
years on the understanding that she lived henceforth with some
reliable person. She and Oswald were to be married at last.
His own wife had died some years before and he had retired
from India after his mission there was ended. With the knowledge that in all likelihood Bethel would eventually be granted
her freedom, he had gone back to live at Treveryan and found
to his joy that it no longer depressed him, nor did unhappy
memories from the past haunt him as they had done. He set
to work to improve the house putting in bathrooms and
ridding it of some of the heavy Victorian furniture which he
thought spoilt it. He looked forward as eagerly as a boy to
the day when Bethel would finally be released and join him.

He saw her a few weeks before the end, and thought her as
beautiful as ever. She seemed so well that he never gave
much thought to a letter in which she spoke of a bad cold soon
afterwards. The next thing he knew was a summons from
the authorities telling him she was desperately ill with pneu-
monia. He left immediately, and was with her till she died.

O.M. was so deeply affected by the memory of her death
that he could scarcely bring himself to talk about it. That is

why I have not attempted to record it in the rest of the book
in which I have tried to tell of the story of the unhappy
Treveryans.

Apparently he never lived there after Bethel's death, and
yet some queer feeling, whether of sentiment, whether of
loyalty to her—I could never fathom—kept him from selling
the place.

I could see that he was visibly moved by our visit, and
though I longed to ask him more details of their story and his
own part in it, I did not then like to, and it was not till he had
returned to Hove and was once again taken ill, that he told
me with as much detail as he could, the whole tragedy.

Of Lerryn's life he knew very little, and it was not until
after his own death last year, when I went down to Treveryan
again, that I found, hidden away in the room which must have
been hers, Lerryn's old diaries. Once more I was struck with
the same fancy as of old : to write a book about this family
whose lives were so brimful of drama. I have tried to piece
together the jigsaw of their lives, helped by what I have been
able to glean from O.M.'s private papers, Lerryn Treveryan's
diaries and from O.M. himself. I find it difficult to believe,
now that I have finished, that these people—to me so vivid
and alive—are dead, and, except perhaps for Oswald Martineau,
forgotten. I find it almost more difficult to realize that were
they alive, Bethel would be over seventy and the others nearly
as old. I cannot conceive Veryan as anything but the portrait
I have seen of him hanging in the dining-room in Cornwall;
it must have been painted when he was about thirty; he is
dark, perhaps a little thick-set, with an attractive smile and
flashing eyes. Impossible for me to picture Lerryn as anything but a golden haired girl like her miniature which sits in a
glass-topped table in the drawing-room. I never saw any
painting of Bethel, the shabby little photo, sepia-coloured with
a hard back, which O.M. kept beside his bed, was the nearest
approach. I could not see the beauty about which he was so
vehement, but it was a handsome face, a striking face, and her
eyes were certainly very lovely.

That little photograph had fascinated me from the time I
first remarked it. There was something about Bethel Treveryan. . . . When I first decided to write about the family

I was worried lest such an act might possibly offend Lerryn
who, so O.M. had told me, was still alive. I wrote to the
Mother Superior of her Convent, but the reply I had greatly
saddened me. Lerryn's mind had become affected. I went
down to see if I could perhaps do anything but there was
nothing to be done. She is greatly beloved, I am happy to
say, and is well looked after, and I was told that there was no
fear of her becoming violent. She remembers nothing but is
quite happy in her little cell, and she is allowed to go to chapel
with the rest of the nuns. - Apparently the music from the
organ has a very soothing effect on her.

      •   •   •

I have just returned from Treveryan. I heard last week it
had been sold. How right they were, Bethel and Lerryn and
Oswald, to fear the glosts of that unhappy house.
No one saw me climb the broken fence which led into the
park and I wandered unchallenged and alone. The gardens
and paths were overgrown with weeds, broken boughs and
fallen trees lay scattered in the woods and in the park. I saw
no living thing, neither cattle nor sheep grazed in the meadows
or the park, even the birds seemed asleep. I walked up to
the house and tried to peer inside, but the shutters were
fastened, and when I tried to pull one aside it started to
crumble and a large wood louse appeared. Moss and lichen
had been allowed to riot at will and from where the ivy grew
on one side of the house, a rat suddenly crept. I looked for
the magnolia tree which I remembered noticing in O.M.'s
picture of it, but it must have died or been torn down, for it
no longer adorned the walls. I wandered down to the lake,
the lake beside which Bethel had spent so many happy hours
in her childhood, beside which she and Oswald had told their
love. I fancied I could see them, she with her shawl thrown
carelessly over her shoulders, he young, handsome, head-over-
heels in love. I fancied I saw them down by the rushes,
watching the swans go by. Where were the wild swans now?
I climbed to the top of the hill and looked down on to the farm
where Lerryn used to meet Ted Truscott. I thought I saw
them too, a fair-haired girl in a blue Cornish sun-bonnet and a
handsome young fellow by her side. Where was Ted now,
I wondered? Did he ever think of the girl he had loved

nearly forty years ago? What would he have said had he known she was a poor old nun, bereft of her wits? For some reason or other Veryan's ghost eluded me, neither could I feel Lucy about the place. But then, she had been a stranger, bringing hate and discontent with her, why should her spirit linger? I searched for hours for the cottage in the woods, but never a trace could I find, and at last the sun went down and I felt that I must go. I passed by the house once again, and down by the lake I saw a man's figure. For a moment my own heart stopped beating. Was it Veryan? Could it be Oswald? And then the figure turned and I saw an old man come towards me. He said he was from the farm and had come up for his evening stroll. He walked beside me and chattered as I made my way back to the car which I had left at the bottom of the avenue. When I reached it I turned once again to look my last on Treveryan. It was bathed in the glow of the sun's aftermath and even the lake looked as if it were afire. It made me think of the final stages of Götterdämmerung—the twilight of the Treveryans had indeed passed.

The old man saw me look towards the lake, and maybe he read my mind, for—

" Used to be wild swans in the old days," he said, " but they don't come no more."

It was true then.

" Wasn't there a superstition that the wild swans would cease to come when Treveryans no longer lived here? "

" Aye," he said, " that's right," and walked in front of me to open the gate.

Then I saw the notice board for the first time. It was a monstrous, brutal thing to see hanging on Treveryan's wrought-iron gates, and I wondered how I could have missed it when I had left the car some hours ago. The old man saw me looking at it.

" I didn't see that before," I told him.

" 'Tweren't there. Only put up this afternoon," he answered.

I looked at the huge black board with the agent's jargon written across it in large letters, and saw ' SOLD ' in even larger lettering below. It was not my house, and I had never lived there, but I felt desolated and quite miserable, and from behind my eyes that tell-tale pricking feeling began.

" I hope someone nice is coming," I mumbled.

" I don't know if it's true," the old man said, " but they say as how a big syndicate have bought'n up."

" A syndicate? "

" Aye. They're going to make Treveryan into a hotel or a country club or something of the like. And they talk of cutting down a lot of the trees, specially in the wood, and building."

" Building? "

" Aye. Bungalows."

We stood together in silence.

" Seems a sin to pull the trees down," he said presently.

I started up the car and went a little way down the road. Something made me turn after I had been about a mile and in less than ten minutes I was back by the gates once more. I was crying properly now, but I could not help it. I felt I must see Treveryan once again. I felt that I must let it know that at least one person remained who knew it for what it had been in days gone by. I walked back down the avenue, but when I got to the far end I stopped suddenly. On a seat outside the house, under the dead magnolia, the old man sat. He never heard me come nor looked up at my approach. He had a pipe in his mouth and was reading a slip of paper. Presently he crumpled the paper into a ball and threw it to the ground with an angry curse. From my hiding-place I watched him get up from his seat and move away. There were tears rolling down his face, and I imagined he had just received bad news. I waited for him to go and watched him look back at Treveryan before he departed from my sight in the distance. I went forward and shamelessly picked up the paper which appeared to have depressed him so greatly. It was the Bill of Sale of Treveryan. I stepped on to the terrace, now over-grown with weeds and long grass and looked at this house about which only an old labourer and myself were in tears. I thought of Bethel, Veryan and Lerryn, I tried to visualize Anna and her mad Simon. Dead Treveryans, centuries old, now seemed to march past me in one long ghost-like pro-cession. Sane Treveryans and mad Treveryans, Tregony who had brought the dread disease which was ultimately to put an end to her family for all time. James Treveryan of Armada days. I remembered that monks had once lived here, it was they who had made the lake. Monks . . . Now, suddenly, with a flash, I found myself visualizing the future. A hotel. A bungalow town—a country club. A club and noisy girls in ' beach wear '—young men in shorts and bathing trunks— I could see the lake with a noisy crowd of cocktail drinking girls and ' cherio-boys ' swimming and splashing where once the wild swans had gracefully glided past.

" Farewell, beautiful and noble Treveryan," I whispered as I fled down the avenue for the last time. I was determined that I would not look back this time, and in spite of my tears and the sickness which was in my heart, I got quickly into the car and drove away.

About a mile away a large car hailed me. I noticed it was a smart-looking Bentley and a middle-aged man, wearing brand new tweeds and smoking a cigar, was at the wheel. A woman with palpably dyed hair sat beside him.

" Can you direct me to Treverion? " he asked, in a low, common voice.

" I never heard of it," I said rather rudely, despising his inability to pronounce the name.

" You must be a stranger," said the woman in equally unpleasing and aggressive accents, " it's ever such a well-known estate. We've just bought it. Part of the Fun-for-All Syndicate. Surprised you've never heard of it."

" I'm sorry. I'm afraid I can't help you," was all I could find to say then.

Treveryan. Treveryan. Perhaps you will be spared the fate of Fun-for-All. Perhaps a kindly Nazi bomb will put an end to that speculation. Somehow I cannot believe that four centuries have left you unscathed in order that you may become a centre for the noisy, vulgar riff-raff of to-day.

Treveryan. I like to think of you stately and once so loved, at the end of the avenue of beeches; where once a yew tree stood; where a lake was in which swam wild swans.

Torosay,
I. of Mull.